Dylan
Kings of New York

BLUE SAFFIRE

Perceptive Illusions Publishing
Bayshore, New York

Blue Saffire/Perceptive Illusions Publishing Inc.
PO BOX 5253
Bayshore, NY 11706
www.BlueSaffire.com

Publisher's Note: This is a work of fiction. Names, characters, places, and incidents are a product of the author's imagination. Locales and public names are sometimes used for atmospheric purposes. Any resemblance to actual people, living or dead, or to businesses, companies, events, institutions, or locales is completely coincidental.

Ordering Information:
Quantity sales. Special discounts are available on quantity purchases by corporations, associations, and others. For details, contact the "Special Sales Department" at the address above.

Dylan: Kings of New York Series/ Blue Saffire. -- 1st ed.
ISBN 978-1-941924-35-8

If we listen closely, we can hear the voices of love and innocence.

Our Turn

Ronan

I sit with Danny standing between my legs as she blow-dries my hair while finger combing it. I have my hands on her waist as I smile to myself. Knowing she's carrying our child has me on a high.

"What are you smiling at?" She smiles down at me.

"I've missed ya. Can't yer husband be happy to see ya?"

She leans in and pecks my lips. "You've been driving everyone crazy. You think I haven't heard about you?"

I grin back at her. "What have ya heard?"

"Anika moved because you were at her door nearly every day."

"Ach, if ya think I be the reason she took off, I don't think yer the full shilling at all, so it is. We need to have yer noddle checked, we do."

She bursts out laughing at me. Her face brightens with the gesture. My heart fills with so much love as the sound rings out.

"God, I've missed your voice. Okay, you're right. I've heard about what's been going on with her.

"Still, Lyric has been seconds off getting a restraining order against you. You've been at his office at least once a week. Thank God, Logan and LaSalle put a stop to that before you ruined his campaign.

"You've even been to Ireland to harass your mother, thinking she was hiding me out. I've heard a lot," she says with a rueful smile on her lips.

"Ya think I don't know that she was at some point?" I lift a knowing brow.

Ma and Da did have her there with them during the first week or two. That's where I lost track of her. The way Ma laid into me told me my wife had been there.

Danny sighs. "She's going to kill me when she sees me."

"I doubt that. Yer her favorite."

She snorts. "The only thing that might save me is the baby. I had to leave without a word. I knew she was trying to keep me there until you arrived."

I roar with laughter. "Okay, ya might be right. Although she wouldn't rat ya out once ya were gone. So ya might still have her favor."

"We'll see."

I run my hands up her sides and then back down again. She bites her lip as I move my hands to palm her full ass then squeeze. Lifting from my seat, I look her in the eyes as I lean in to take her lips.

She moans as I groan and kiss her deeply while now hovering over her. The slacks to the suit I've changed into begin to become tight. I want my wife again. Her pregnant pussy feels too grand to ignore.

"Ro, baby. We're going to miss the entire wedding."

I groan and place my forehead to hers. "I can name at least two more weddings that will be here, not including ours." A smile comes to my lips as I think of the vow renewal we were planning before she took off. "After all his planning and fussing, Ryan won't know we're missing."

"Ronan, the baby and I do need to eat. Besides, whoever the DJ is has this place rocking."

She's right, we should be down at the wedding, but we both needed a shower after our session in the bathroom downstairs. I held nothing back after we settled the tension between us.

We had to sneak up to the room I've been staying in for the wedding weekend. I haven't had proper sleep in months. I've been replaying our last conversation over and over at night while in bed alone.

We'd been fighting, yes, but I thought it was about our keeping secrets and my overprotectiveness. When she disappeared four months ago, I didn't think it was because she was pregnant. I know for a fact I'm not the only male around here who has become more watchful over his other half.

What happened with the Alliance has made us all extra watchful. I don't think any of our hearts could take anything like that again. The only reason I didn't completely lose my shit while she was MIA was because Danika ensured I knew she was safe.

"Ach, yer right. I do want to feed ya and the babe. Do ya know what it is yet?"

"Not officially. I wanted to wait to see if you want to come with me to find out."

I kiss her hard. "Of course, I want to be there," I say against her lips.

"I love you."

"Aye, I love ya too. So ya haven't told Ma about the wee 'un yet?"

Danny snickers. "Do you think she would have kept it to herself if I did? We can tell her together."

"In that case, I'll keep it in my pants for now. Let's go tell me oul wan she's going to have another grand."

"I love how you say that with so much pride. I'm sorry I read into things so wrong."

"It's not yer fault, love. This one is on me."

"No, I should've shown more patience."

I laugh. "I hope this babe teaches us both the meaning of the word. Let's not argue over who's to blame. Yer here now and we have the rest of our lives to make it up to each other."

She smiles and begins to bob her head. "Oh my God, "Microphone Fiend." This wedding sounds lit. Come on, baby. I want you to dance with me."

"As ya wish, love. Let's go."

I take her hand and turn her in a circle in front of me. She looks great in the thin black dress she has on. I drop my gaze to her ass and grin like a loon.

Wrapping my arms around her from behind, I then lean into her ear and whisper. "I love the hair, and ya look good enough to eat."

Dean

We get down to the ballroom where the reception is being held and the music feels like it's booming through the floors and walls. Eric B. & Rakim's "Microphone Fiend" is still playing.

I throw my arms in the air and bob my head to the beat. A smile comes to my face as we walk onto the dance floor and find our family and friends showing out. Tasha and Noah are going back and forth doing The Whoop. Paige and Bobby aren't that far away and Bobby is giving it his best.

I'm not mad at him. It's Cass and Laoise who have me laughing so hard I'm doubled over. Neither plans to be left out of the fun, but Lord, they both need to sit down before someone calls an ambulance from thinking they're having a seizure.

"What are ya laughing at?" Ronan says in my ear as he wraps me in his arms.

"I've seen you dance, but your mom and sister … wow. I don't get it." I laugh some more.

Ronan rumbles with laughter as he starts to sway to the music, proving my point. I stop trying to make sense of it. The two little women are too cute as they give it their all.

Let them have fun. Ronan gives me a squeeze and kisses my neck. I can feel his happiness rolling off him.

DJ, Val, and Tasha have been trying to tell me this would all work out. If I had known about Sasha and their baby, I wouldn't have stayed away for so long.

It took about two weeks for me to realize I not only missed my husband, but I also wanted this baby. Yes, I, Danika McGowan, want to have my own crumb snitcher. As long as it's with this man, I'm willing to do just about anything.

The only reason I didn't run back home to Ronan was because I didn't know if this was something he wanted. Between his age and the role he holds in the Alliance and with the families, I didn't think he would be so happy about the news.

"I love you. I'm so happy we're having this baby," Ronan croons in my ear as we sway to the music.

"I love you too. Surprisingly, I'm excited about the baby." I'm smiling so hard my face hurts. As I look around at all the other smiling faces, I know this is going to be all right.

The bride, Carmen, looks like she's having the time of her life dancing with Joe Black, her father-in-law. Ryan grabs his grandmother and tries to help her out a bit as Ciara walks over to Cass and begins to dance with her. A face-splitting smile comes to my lips.

That girl holds a special place in my heart. I took to Ciara from the first time I crossed paths with the little thing. She's full of fire and reminds me so much of myself at her age.

She and her cousin have grown on me and are two I consider friends. I've gained a lot of those over the last few years, along with family. Don't get me wrong, there're still levels to this, but the people in this ballroom have proven they would give their lives to have my back.

If not for Ciara and Dylan, I wouldn't have been able to pull off my disappearing act. Not with my husband. This isn't my first trip to Scotland.

I came here after going to Ireland to my in-laws in the beginning. It didn't take long to realize my mother-in-law was going to sell me out. I only went to Ibiza because I didn't want to drag everyone into my mess.

Logan didn't like the idea of them hiding me out while pregnant with Ronan's baby. Seeing how pissed he was, I took off on my own. I might not have been under his roof, but don't shit move here without Logan O'Brien knowing and having a say.

I learned that fast. Once I was gone, I wouldn't tell anyone where I was so that if Ronan asked, they wouldn't have to lie. I'm grateful to everyone for not trying to stick their noses in my business for as long as they did.

Logan looks over at me as sweat drips down his face while he dances behind his woman on the dance floor. He gives me a smug smile and winks. I shake my head, laugh, and wink back.

"There ya are. It's good to see ya. It's even better to see ye together," Laoise says with a huge smile on her face.

She quickly pulls me into a hug. I squeeze her back as if I hadn't seen her three months ago. We both rock from side to side.

"Don't give him too much hell, love. He be missing ya."

"You don't have to worry. I'm going home with him after the wedding. We need to see a doctor to find out if we're having a boy or a girl," I whisper back.

She releases me and begins to scream. The joy on her face makes my heart ache. She looks between me and Ronan with tears in her eyes.

"Ya will come to spend time with yer oul grand at least twice a year, ya will. I'll spoil ya rotten and send ya back home," she coos to my stomach.

I can't help but laugh as she palms my still flat belly as she talks to it. Her excitement is infectious. Ronan cups my chin as he stands behind me and tilts my head back so he can kiss my lips. I smile up at him as he breaks the kiss.

Laoise clears her throat. Then she looks up at me and narrows her eyes. I bite my lip and wait for what's going to come out of her mouth next. I know it's going to be something only Laoise McGowan can get away with.

"Ya better not be lying to me, lass. I'll batter ya and that melter grinning at ya like a fool." Her face lights up again. "Ya did it, ya big overgrown brat. Ya knocked her up. Jesus, Mary, Joseph, I didn't damage your wee prick when I used to batter yer wee arse.

"The way ya and Cass used to jump around and run from me strap, I thought I might have peeled ya. Four damn years. Took ya long enough.

"Ach, I knew ya were the one. I knew it. Never seen me boy so happy in his life. They won't have to carve *Failed Mum* on me gravestone, they won't.

"Me boy's having a babe of his own. They're going to be a cute little thing too, they will. So it is," my mother-in-law sings out for everyone to hear.

Dylan

The excitement is starting to die down after Uncle Ronan and Aunt Danny's announcement. I couldn't be happier for them.

My heart swells as my gaze lands on Uncle Ronan dancing with his wife. I'm happy to see them together. Uncle Ronan deserves to be happy.

The grand ballroom has been transformed into a majestic backdrop for Ryan's wedding. This has been a beautiful reception. Ryan outdid himself.

I remember this castle from when I was a little boy. We would come here to spend time with Grandda Black. He's the one who taught us what a real grandda should be.

Oland O'Brien sure as shit never showed us an ounce of love. The old bastard tried to crush us one by one. As I look around at the smiling faces of my family, I'm grateful to Brooklyn for making sure the old bastard couldn't hurt us ever again.

"Uncle Dylan," Dae-Dae sings as he and his little brother run over to me.

Landon keeps up as best he can on his little legs. I bend to scoop little Landon up. Felix couldn't deny this little guy if he tried.

He has a bit of his mother here and there, but this one is definitely a Black through and through. I ruffle his curly hair and give him a smile.

"What are you two up to?" I ask.

"I wanted to come check to see if we're still on for this summer. Landon will be coming this time. It's going to be so much fun," Dae-Dae says excitedly.

"As far as I know, we're all good. I can't wait for you guys to get in. I have a few brand-new video games I plan to kick your butt in."

Dae-Dae's eyes light up and he laughs. "We'll see about that. I can't wait, Uncle Dylan. I'll be counting down the days."

"I will too, little buddy."

Someone calls Dae-Dae's name, causing him to turn and look across the room. I smile when I see Jordan, Brodie, and Shauna waving their cousin over. My niece has gotten so big.

I remember the first time I held Shauna in my arms. I was so angry with my grandfather for trying to take her life, along with her mother's. As I place Landon on his feet and he runs over to Felix, I smile at how much my family has grown.

I tune into the music playing and my smile grows. For the last thirty minutes, it's like they've been playing a soundtrack for my life. This time, Ed Sheeran's "Dive" plays as couples sway on the dance floor.

This one hits home. I glance around until I find the little woman who owns my heart. I find her dancing with my da, a broad smile on her face.

She's as beautiful as ever. I can't help imagining what our wedding day would be like. I would have this ballroom customized to her dream wedding just as Ryan has done for Carmen.

A super big *fuck you* to my piece-of-shit grandda. I smirk at the thought of him rolling in his grave. All he did to keep us apart and we'd stand right here in a Scottish castle—me married to my little Black Irish girl.

I can't wait until that day comes. I'm a lucky man to have found her. I don't know if I would change a thing. All we've been through has made us stronger.

I would fight to the death for that woman. There isn't anything I wouldn't do for her. I have proven that more than once.

"Look at ya. Looking like a puppy in love," Brooklyn croons as he walks up beside me and pats me on the back.

I snort. "You would know exactly what that looks like."

"Aye, ya say that like it's a bad thing," Logan says from my other side.

I shrug at my brothers. We've all fought too hard for our happiness to deny it. That's why I was torn when I helped Uncle Ronan's wife take off on him.

I hope he'll forgive me. If it weren't for him and his wife, I don't know where I would be. I owe her as much as I owe him.

"Stop worrying. He's going to forgive us. We've all told a lie or two to get where we are," Logan says.

I glance around the room. With all we've been through, it's a miracle to have all these smiling faces in a room together. The truth has been bent and twisted for the greater good.

We may not all be family by blood, but we've earned our bond and it's thicker than any blood connection could ever be. To be honest, I didn't think the three of us would be as close as we are now. The truth nearly tore us all apart.

"Aye, he will. Ya need to be focused on what ya plan to do next," Cole says, pulling me from my thoughts.

"I don't know if it's the right time."

"We've done all this for ya to be able to do as ya please. It's our turn. We all deserve happiness," Cole replies.

"Answer me this. Is she truly the one?" Logan asks.

"The one and only."

"Ach, then ya should go through with yer plan. We get one life and each second is precious."

I turn to look Logan in his eyes. The words hit harder coming from him. I know all he's been through. He had to earn his happiness through a world of pain.

Right as his words begin to ring in my head, "Dive" ends and Sam Smith's "Fire on Fire" begins to play. My girl turns in a circle looking for me.

This song is another one of ours. I can still remember the first time it took on real meaning for us both. Our eyes lock and I know she remembers too.

My brothers are forgotten as I move to the dance floor and pull her into my arms, where she belongs. She places her head against me and melts right into me. As I wrap my arms around her, I know my brothers are right.

This is what it was all for. This is what we risked our lives for. I won't wait any longer.

It's our turn.

CHAPTER ONE

Stolen Dreams

Dylan

"*Kss, kss,*" I hiss out a breath as I throw a combination and dance back out of reach.

Both punches connect with enough force to ring out through the air as my fists barrel into this unlucky bastard's ribs. He stumbles back and winces as sweat drips down his face. A grin comes to my face.

This is too easy. I'm leaving with the bag tonight. This is my third match and not one of these assholes has made me work for it.

I wouldn't even have broken a sweat if not for this hot-ass underground lot and the mask I'm wearing.

I wear the mask so no one knows I'm here. If my brothers found out, I'd be toast. If they figured out what I'm doing this all for, I'd be worse off.

Nah, I need to keep this my secret and earn this money on my own. The sooner, the better. I'll figure out how to avoid my grandfather once I have the money I need.

"Come on. Is that all you've got?" I taunt as the guy throws a lazy kick at me.

He tries to spin out and come in from the other direction. I block that one too. However, this time I take advantage and slam him to the ground by his leg.

Another victory. The crowd goes wild and my chest swells with the knowledge that I'm one step closer to my goal. I still have a ways to go, but I'm getting there.

A few more underground fights and I'll be on my way. I'm not even tired. I could go another three fighters and be fine. As long as I walk with the money, that's all that matters. When I have enough, I won't have to do this anymore.

"Adam, the boss wants to see you," the ref says in my ear after I'm announced as the winner.

I close my eyes and groan. I knew there was a chance this could happen. While this fight isn't in one of the lairs, it's still run by Ronan and his crew. Their fights bring in the best purses.

I could fight in other fight clubs, but the money isn't as good. I need a lot of money to pull my plan off. Not just for a flight.

I need money for a place to stay and to live in Ireland for as long as it takes to find her again. It's taking longer because I can't fight in the underground circuits as much as I would like, because my older brothers would kick my ass if they found out. Da warned me that I couldn't and shouldn't return to Ireland.

He actually forbade it. That's why it has to be my own money. I won't have the O'Brien support when I go back.

We were banished. My grandfather doesn't want us in Ireland, so he sent my entire family away. If I go back, I'm risking his wrath. However, Ciara is worth it.

I have savings, but it's still not enough. I figured I could get to the real bag here. I thought the fake name, mask and temporary hair dye would work.

However, there's one problem with that. My uncle, through marriage, you would think I were one of Ronan's sister's or brothers' sons.

He has been there like an uncle for as long as I can remember. That's the reason I'm not making the type of money I should around here. No matter what I do, Uncle Ronan knows how I move. He and his right hand, Oisín, spot me every time I show up. His other lieutenant, Tadhg, has started to spot me lately as well.

"Ya have one fucking hard head, ya do. I told ya to stay out of these clubs, didn't I?" Uncle Ronan snarls as I enter the back area where the money is being held and counted.

They keep this area heavily armed, as the money collected at the door and the bets are all brought back here. I remember when shit like this used to faze me. I once was afraid of Uncle Ronan as he was three times my size.

Now, I'm just as tall as he is and probably just as strong. I lift my chin and hold my head high. I know what he has told me, but nothing is going to stop me from finding my way back home.

I made a promise, and I have to keep it. I'm willing to face anything if it means I'll find my way back to her. I will never give up.

"No one but you knows who I am. I come to fight and make money. Nothing else. I'm not trying to start or get into any trouble," I reply.

"No, yer just here to cause me trouble. If Joe or Cass finds out I knew ya were here and allowed it, I'll have to batter ya for the trouble ya'd have me in. Go home, Dylan and don't show up in another one of my clubs or these underground fights."

"I'm not leaving without my money."

Ronan snorts and grabs the bag Tadhg hands him. He then tosses the bag at me. I catch the duffel and hold it close to my chest. There should be close to fifty grand in this one.

"Thanks," I murmur.

"And Dylan?"

"Yeah?"

"Wash that shit out of yer hair. Ya look like an eejit."

I snort and turn to leave. For now, I'll take a break. I probably should have checked to see if Uncle Ronan was in town. I'll do better next time.

CHAPTER TWO

I'm Done

Ciara

I hobble forward with one shoe on as I hold the other in my hand while holding up the front of my torn dress. I run my forearm under my nose and wince when I see the streak of blood across my skin. Rage courses through my system.

I think I'm still in shock. With each step, it sinks in what just almost happened to me. I've reached my breaking point.

"Cee-Cee, stop overreacting. Get back here," Sean calls from behind me.

I nearly trip over my own feet as his voice reaches me and causes my blood to run ice cold. I pull to a stop and turn on him with all my fury.

"I'm overreacting? *Me*? I'm overreacting? Yer friends are twice my size and the three of them just tried to rape me.

"If I were anyone else, they would have succeeded. What the fuck do ya mean I'm overreacting?" I scream at my stepbrother as I look at him like he's lost his damn mind.

"Come on. I promised them a good time. Be a good girl and go back in there and give them what I promised.

"After all we do for you and your little brat brother, this is the least you can do. You wouldn't have been able to fight them off like that if we hadn't taught you everything you know," Sean says smugly.

"Fuck you. Ya can go to hell."

"What are you going to do? Go home and tell my dad? He's already tired of your shit. He's doing you a favor by allowing you to stay with us.

"Don't fuck yourself over trying to act like some prude. If you want to stay in Ciarán's life, you better keep your mouth shut. One word to my father and I'll make sure you lose everything.

"You can say goodbye to your college tuition, your precious little brother, and your shot at the championship. Actually, you better turn your ass around and head back inside before I have Dad finally put your ass out.

"I know Lily would be more than happy to have you out of her way. We own you, Cee-Cee. Do as I say, or you'll never see Ciarán again."

I stand frozen. My little brother is my world. Theo Young and his spoiled brats have made my life a living hell.

I've worked for them, cleaned for them, cooked for them. I've done everything asked of me with one exception. The one thing that makes Sean a spitting mad psycho. However, I never thought he would take things this far.

My little brother, Ciarán, is the only reason I have stuck around for as long as I have. MMA has become a part of who I am. I've been around the ring for as long as I can remember. I love being a part of the team run by Theo, but I'm not selling my soul to be able to fight.

Theo is technically Ciarán's legal guardian. My stepfather has claimed that my mother left us with nothing. I call bullshit, but I've never had proof.

When I turned eighteen, Theo convinced me that I wouldn't get custody of Ciarán without a job or college degree. Back then I thought I'd be better off allowing Theo to pay for me to go to college.

He claimed he wanted to help. Now, I believe he didn't want me to take off and leave them without my free labor. I had a plan.

Once I earned my degree, I planned to take my brother as far away from the Youngs as I could get. However, I'm a year behind in my program because of this asshole.

He made sure I didn't pass and complete my courses to finish my program on time. In this moment, I don't care about a degree or fighting on Theo's team. I'll walk away from it all.

Sean and Lily have always treated me like trash, while Theo has looked the other way. Theo at least pretends to care for Ciarán. I know he tolerates me because I bring in wins for him.

I'm one of his best fighters and trainers at the gym. I also keep Ciarán out of his hair. Theo has little patience for raising a kid.

"Do whatever ya feel ya need to do, Sean. This was the final straw. I'm tired of ya and yer family.

"I want to see how ye all do without me. I'm done with this shit. I'm done with yer family. Stay the fuck away from me," I seethe.

"You're going to regret this," he bellows after me as I turn and walk away.

I fight back tears because I know this isn't how my life was before my mother's death. I can't remember anything from before that day, but I know this wasn't my life. I feel it in my bones.

***

"Just the person I wanted to see," Theo croons, causing me to nearly jump out of my skin.

I clench my towel and toiletries to my chest. I decided to shower before packing and waking Ciarán. I'm not waiting. We're leaving here tonight.

My plan is to get as far away from here as possible. If I never see Seattle again, I'm cool with that. My head hurts as images of a brightly lit city keep flashing in my head.

Vegas comes to mind. There will be plenty of fighting opportunities there. I begin planning to head there, but I quickly change my mind. This nagging feeling tells me that's not the bright city I need to head to. I shake my head as Theo's voice pulls me from my musing.

"I'm sorry, what was that?"

"I want you to come down to the gym with me in the morning. I have a new fighter I want you to spar with. You know those underground tournaments are coming."

"I told you I don't want to enter any more illegal fights. I think I have a shot at the real championship.

"I'm the best on the team and you know it. Why should I keep risking it with those underground fights? Those rings stink of desperation. Fighters only participate in those because they have no other choice."

"We can make a killing."

"We could make even more through sponsorships and the grand prize from the legit tournament, and I won't put my career and eligibility at risk."

He sighs and tightens his grip on the beer in his hand. I already know what's coming next. It's the reason I won't bother to feel bad once I'm gone.

"Listen, kid. I know how much you want to do the tournament with the team. You see how it is down at the gym. Things are tight.

"The finals are in New York. If we make it that far, I don't think I'll have the cash for all five of us to go. I can't leave Ciarán behind; I have no one to watch him.

"We need the underground fights to pay for the official shit, or else none of it matters. I'm going broke raising the four of you as a single dad. I'm not in my prime anymore.

"I'm begging you to do this for me. Just a couple of fights. That's it. I promise."

First of all, those two need to get a fucking job. They do nothing but spend his money. They're not kids anymore, far from it. Why should I jeopardize everything for them—for anyone in this family?

"No, get someone else to do it. I'm the only one on the team who you ask to do this. I'm the only one with everything to lose."

"What about what I have lost? I've burned through every fucking thing. There's nothing left ..." He pauses and takes a calming breath.

"Listen, Cee-Cee. I'm sorry. I've been under a lot of pressure. I didn't mean to say that. You go on and head to bed. We can talk more in the morning."

I nod my head in agreement because I don't plan to be here in the morning. I'm over it all. He pulls me into a hug and kisses my forehead.

His breath reeks of alcohol. Nothing new there. I'm used to the Jekyll and Hyde routine with him. He'll be passed out in less than an hour.

"See you in the morning," I murmur.

We part ways and I rush into my room. I waste no time tossing things into my duffel bag. As I gather my essentials, my mind goes to where to go.

The finals will be in New York that's the ultimate goal. If I'm already there, I won't have to find my way there. I'll just need a team to join that's already heading to the tournament finals.

My mind made up, I grab my phone off the nightstand and begin to look for flights to New York. I become frustrated when I can't find a flight going to New York anytime soon.

I don't want to risk sitting around in an airport. I change plans and begin to look for flights leaving as soon as possible. San Diego seems to be where we're headed. Theo once got into some shit there or something with some guys he tries to avoid.

He never goes to tournaments there. I can go there and fly under the radar for a bit. He's certainly not coming there after me.

From what I can tell, he's scared shitless of whoever is there. In fact, he stays away from California, period. This family has always had red flags. Once the flight is booked, I gently shake Ciarán awake.

"Cee-Cee?" he says sleepily.

"Hey, buddy, I need you to do me a favor. As quiet as you can, grab your bag and pack as much as you can. Take anything you need. We're not coming back," I whisper.

His eyes light up and he nods. I watch as he rushes from his bed and begins to pack. I sigh in relief.

He wants out of here as bad as I do. I look at the time. Theo should be passed out drunk by now. However, I do need to handle one more thing before Sean comes in for the night.

"Keep packing. I have something I need to get. You have five minutes," I say and rush from the room.

We're finally going to be free. This was never our home.

***

"Mommy, where are we going?" I say as I sit in the back of the car.

Ciarán is in his car seat, crying. I try to get him to quiet down for Mommy, but he won't settle. I think he senses something is wrong too.

"We have to leave. I need to get you to—"

"Mommy, look out," I scream and unfasten my seat belt quickly.

As fast as I can, I fling my body over Ciarán's in his car seat.

I pop up from my sleep with my heart pounding. I'm drenched in sweat like always. It's the same thing almost every night.

For years, I've been having the same dream. However, as the cool air of the air conditioning blows down on my wet skin and soaked shirt, I remember I'm not in the small room I shared with my little brother.

Not that there aren't enough rooms in the house for me and Ciarán to have our own. The room I was told used to be mine before my mother's death, Lily uses as a closet. Even after she moved out, I wasn't allowed to have that room or her old one.

Ciarán is ten and I'm nineteen. My little brother shouldn't have to share a room with me. I've done my best to divide the tight space for us both to have some privacy.

Not that we'll have to worry about that any longer. I meant what I said. I'm done with that fucked-up family.

I lift the hood on my hoodie over my head and tighten the drawstrings. I need to change my shirt, but I didn't have time to pack a lot. I don't want to waste an outfit.

My chest feels heavy as I begin to wake and the reality of that dream sets in. There's a deep ache in my heart. I know I lost so much more than my mother, but I can't remember what all that was.

My head hurts as I try to remember anything from before that accident. The doctors said I was lucky to survive. My mother wasn't as lucky.

Ciarán and I lost her in that accident. My little brother was only a baby when we lost our mother. My brain begins to clear, and I look over to my little brother as he sits in the seat next to me.

He's sound asleep. At ten, he shouldn't have a care in the world. I wouldn't have ripped him from the security of Theo's home if that were the case.

My shoulders sag and I frown. This all seemed like such a good idea a few hours ago as I told him to pack a bag after I booked our plane tickets. I had to dip into my savings to get us both on this flight.

Now, I don't know what I've gotten us into. We're headed to San Diego and have no place to stay. I have no job lined up and if I'm honest with myself, I don't have a plan either.

If I can find the underground rings around San Diego, then I can at least make money in those. Yup, I've become one of the desperate. I'm small, but once in the ring, I leave no doubt that I belong.

People underestimate me; that's why Theo loved having me as a fighter. Bets are made before I step in the ring. At first glance, those who don't know better bet against me.

Those who do know say nothing because the odds fall in their favor. In the end, I walked away with my portion of the purse and Theo walked with his betting earnings and part of the purse.

Lily never used to bring in as much as I could. Not in wins or earnings. She used to be Theo's meal ticket before I was old enough to do it. I'm so happy to be away from all of them. However, I don't know what to do now.

"What the fuck, Cee-Cee?" I huff to myself.

I reach into my bag and pull out my sketch pad. I flip through and stare at the image I've drawn over and over again. It's of a boy.

I can't remember who he is. He's about ten or so. I know he's not Ciarán. My brother looks like me, with his green-gray eyes and golden-brown skin.

Besides, I've been drawing this boy since before Ciarán was around his age. I've seen his face a million times in my dreams. He feels like he's important to me, but I don't know why or who he could be.

In my dreams, he has bright blue eyes with golden specks in them and thick blond hair. There's always a mischievous smile on his lips. I run my fingertips over his face and try to remember something.

"Who are you?" I murmur, wishing the page would answer me back.

Nothing comes and frustration builds. I don't have time for this. I need to come up with a plan.

Sighing, I place the sketch pad back into my bag and pull out the envelope with our documents inside. I snuck into Theo's office to retrieve them. I'll need to find Ciarán a new school.

My frown deepens as I read Ciarán's birth certificate. His name is listed as Ciarán Walsh. I take out mine and read the name printed on it. Ciara Walsh is on mine.

I'm taken aback. Although Ciara feels familiar, I've always been called Cee-Cee. As far as I've been told, my last name is Young. Theo has always filled out paperwork for us and placed his last name as ours.

I glance at the names listed for my parents. Iesha Rogers is listed on both documents for our mom. However, I knit my brows as I see our father's name.

Donald Walsh.

My brain tickles a little more. I grab a notepad and scribble the name down. I also copy his date of birth as well. My mouth falls open as I read both my father's and my birthplace.

Ireland.

The accent. It's not as strong as when I was younger. It mostly comes out when I'm angry, but Theo could never explain it. He always brushed me off when I asked and corrected me when it happened.

Quickly, I check what's listed on Ciarán's. My eyes bug out as I see New York as my brother's birthplace. I have so many questions.

Theo was my mother's husband when she died. I've never asked about or thought about my real father. Not that Theo was open about information when it came to my past or anything about my mom.

Sometimes I wonder if he knew her at all. His refusal to give me little tiny details about her has always made me so angry. If he loved her, how could he block out everything about her?

My chest grows tight. What does this mean? I was already nervous about taking my brother with me.

Theo could have me arrested and I'd lose my brother to the system or worse. He'd be stuck with the Youngs, but there was no way I was going to leave him behind.

This is why I'm headed to California. We don't know anyone there, but Theo isn't coming there for us. This will give me time to figure things out.

Hopefully, Theo will forget about us. However, as I look down at our birth certificates, I get this sinking feeling in my gut that this isn't over. My goal is to protect my brother. I will do anything to make that happen.

"Cee, is everything okay?" Ciarán says sleepily.

I look up into his eyes. I hate the concern I see there. He deserves so much better.

"Yeah. Everything is fine."

"Are we almost there yet?"

I look at the screen on the back of the seat in front of us. The map shows we're still thirty minutes out from our destination. It isn't a long flight, but I think we're both exhausted.

I think we both passed out before the plane took off. My heart races as the magnitude of it all comes down on me. When we land, this will all get real.

"Yeah, buddy. We'll be there soon."

"Am I getting a new phone?"

I made sure he left his phone behind before leaving the house. I'll have to get him a new one when we land. For now, I blocked anyone I don't want to be in contact with from my phone. I begin to make a mental note of all the things I need to do.

"Yeah. We'll get you a new phone, and we'll get something to eat. I'm starving. Sound good?"

"Sounds awesome. I'm hungry too," he says with that big, handsome smile.

God, I love this kid. He's my entire world. As long as he's safe and happy, I'm good.

Dylan

I wake in a cold sweat. I've been having the same dream since we moved away from Ireland. However, lately it's been insistent.

For some reason, old memories have resurfaced. I haven't been able to push them back into their box. For years, I have wondered what happened to my friend.

I don't think I will ever be able to forget her. I never really tried to. My life's mission has been to find my way back to her. We were the same, well, not really, but in a way.

We were both different from everyone else. I was the only one out of six brats with blond hair and ice-blue eyes with subtle flecks of golden brown. All three of my brothers and my two sisters have dark-brown hair and green eyes.

I was also the tiniest of the six. My siblings teased me all the time that I was mail-ordered by my parents. I guess all that teasing is why I was painful shy to begin with.

It was only around her that I ever felt like I could be me, like I belonged. It was okay to be different around her because, like me, she was different with her deep, dark-honey-colored, golden-brown skin and those big, bright, green-gray eyes.

They were the brightest eyes I have ever seen. Those long dark curls framed her heart-shaped face and spilled down her back, making her look like the perfect doll. It was amazing to have someone around who was actually smaller than me.

Granted, I was about two years older than she was, but that should tell you just how much of a runt I happened to be. I was never a runt to her though. I was her best friend, her buddy, her hero.

I never thought that day would be the last time our families would live on that same little road together. My family lived in that same home since before I was born and her da's family had owned that big old farm for generations.

Ciara.

Just hearing her name brings back the anticipation I used to have waiting for her to return. Ciara's da was a fighter. He met her ma in the States when he first went there to start his boxing career.

Once he married her ma and she got pregnant with Ciara, they started to make the trips to Ireland to stay on the farm during training seasons. Whenever a big fight came up in the States, Ciara's whole family would go to support her da.

I would miss her terribly every time, as they would be gone for months at a time. However, they always came back. It was that time again.

She was only supposed to be gone for two months. Yet that last day, I felt a sickness I had never felt before. I wanted her to know how much she meant to me before she left. Even at the age of ten, I knew she was taking my heart along with her.

"Dyl," she gasped in a little whisper.

Ciara had enough of an Irish lilt to her tiny voice to think she'd spent more time in Ireland than in the States. "Yer going to get in so much trouble."

Her eyes were wide as she looked at the half a dozen pink roses I cut from my ma's garden. I shrugged my small shoulders and looked at her shyly. Her small, full lips turned into a bright smile.

In that moment, whatever beating I took for butchering the roses would be worth it. Ciara had always said she loved the pink roses in my ma's garden the most. I had to take them, knowing they were her favorite.

My sister will be after me too. I took a roll of her ribbon she uses for baskets to wrap the stems of the roses with. It was the prettiest roll she had, purple with sparkles.

"I don't care. I want ya to think of me when yer in America."

Standing up from her perch on the rock in front of the farm's fence, Ciara's face lit up more as she threw her arms around my neck. "Thank ya, Dyl. I always miss ya when I'm gone."

She squeezed me tightly before stepping back and taking the bouquet from me. I missed her warmth from the time she released me. I don't know what I was thinking, but I pressed my lips to her full little mouth, counting to ten in my head. My eyes were squeezed tight.

I refused to breathe for fear this wouldn't be real. Nine ... ten. I opened my eyes and pulled away.

Ciara's cheeks were heated with a pretty blush beneath her brown skin. Her lips formed a surprised O shape as her green-gray eyes stared back at me, looking like giant saucers.

"I'm going to marry ya someday, Ciara," I murmured and blushed myself.

"Ya'll have to fight my da, and he'll beat ya to a pulp, but if ya survive, I promise, I'll marry ya, Dylan O'Brien," she replied with a small, shy smile of her own.

I puffed out my scrawny little chest and smiled. "I'm going to hold ya to that promise, Ciara Walsh. I'll fight the world if I have to. Nothing can keep us apart. I promise ya that."

I haven't forgotten that day. It's been seared in my brain, embedded in my dreams, just like the day that would crush my world forever. Two months passed and still the Walsh family hadn't returned.

At first, I thought nothing of it. It wouldn't have been the first time Ciara's da won a fight and they had to stay in the States a little longer. I thought that was the case until two more months went by, and they still weren't back.

Ciara hadn't even sent a postcard, since a month and a half after they left. She always sent postcards at least once a week when in the States. I knew she would be back.

I knew in my heart that last day on her farm couldn't be our last day together. All I had to do was wait, be patient, and ignore the sinking feeling in my gut. Then that day came when everything turned on its head.

"Will ye all settle down?" my ma called across the dining room table.

My ma was the voice in our home, but our da was the enforcer. Everyone knew if Ma said be quiet, we were quiet unless we wanted the wrath of my da.

With our lot, it had to be this way. If all six of us were together, we could make a ruckus. However, with Logan, Cole, and Connie all in the States, Kate, Jamie, and I were still a handful.

"Yer da has some big news he needs to tell ye."

My mom is beautiful with her fair skin and dark hair. I took after her, mostly unlike the rest of my siblings. Their green eyes came from Da, although they have Ma's dark hair.

Most I got from Da was his tanned skin and blond hair. Ma swears I have his temper too. She says I'm too sweet at heart to let it get the best of me.

"I think it's best ya tell them, hon," my da murmured, once again proving my ma is the voice.

"Yer father's company is giving him a promotion," Ma started, giving Da a small smile. Bullshit. Da works for my grandda. I learned a long time ago he doesn't work for some company, as my ma tries to play it. "They're sending him to the States to manage one of the offices there."

"Wow, Da, that's great," Kate, the youngest of my two sisters, said.

Da grunted and nodded his head. I sat with my stomach churning. If he was going to the States, what did that mean for us?

I felt all the blood rush out of my face and could hear my heart in my ears so loudly I almost didn't hear what my ma said next.

"We'll all be together again. Your brothers and sister are waiting for us to arrive. We'll start packing this weekend. We'll all be moving with yer da in two weeks," she chirped proudly. "This is big for yer da and we're going to support him however we can."

My dinner turned sour in my mouth. What if Ciara doesn't get back in time? How will she find me?

I couldn't leave and not tell her where I was going. She was the only real friend I ever had.

I pushed from the table, knocking my chair over and ran for the front door. My ma called for me, but I refused to stop. I had to get away. I couldn't leave, not without knowing what happened to Ciara and letting her know what was happening with me.

I pushed my legs as fast as they could go until I passed the Walshes' fence and stood on the front porch of the old, massive house. The house was dark. It was clear no one was home.

There was an eerie feeling as if they would never return. I racked my brain for all the reasons Ciara wasn't back yet.

She made me a promise, and I made her one too. My da taught me and all my brothers that a man should be a keeper of his word. I vowed right there on the porch of the Walsh manor I would keep my promise someday, no matter what.

I haven't forgotten my promise or the girl I made it to. For eleven years, I've been wondering what happened, waiting for the chance to return home.

If I can go home, she'll return to me. The problem is my grandda. The old bastard is a miserable piece of shit. The old bigot hates for me and my siblings to make friends or connections with anyone who isn't pure Irish.

It's sick and fucking stupid. We shouldn't have to hide our friends and relationships from him, but that's exactly what we've learned to do to keep our friends safe. What was once a punishment for my da worked out in all our favor.

Moving so far away from Oland O'Brien was a godsend. This is New York, for Christ's sake. The melting pot. I have friends from all over.

However, we all know firsthand that our grandda has eyes on us from Ireland. We've become smarter. We know better, which has taught me I have to be smart when I find my way back home.

CHAPTER THREE

Gone?

Sean

"What have you done, you idiot?" Lily growls as she storms her way into my room.

"What the fuck are you going on about?" I grumble as I scroll through the group chat with my boys.

They're still pissed off about last night. Grant and Tim ended up at the hospital. Devin needed to go too, if you ask me, but his pride wouldn't allow him to.

He'll have to suck that shit up from the looks of it. I think Cee-Cee broke his jaw. She did break Grant's collarbone and nose. Tim will be nursing his balls, a broken leg, shattered ribs and wrist for the next few months.

For a tiny thing, she hits hard. Always has. She's also strong as fuck. I thought getting Amy to spray that shit on her would have worked.

The only thing I can come up with is that Amy didn't do it right; her stupid ass fucked it up somehow. Cee-Cee didn't look like she was fazed at all. From the job she did on my boys, I'm sure Amy fucked that shit up.

"I'm talking about Cee-Cee. Dad just asked me to come up and see why she and Ciarán aren't down at breakfast yet. Guess why, asshat?" Lily says, lowering her voice.

"How the fuck should I know? What? The shower doesn't have any more hot water left?"

"No, fuckface. I heard about last night. What were you thinking? Do you even understand why she's so important around here?"

"No."

Lily groans and rolls her eyes. "You and I have the best of everything because of those two brats."

"So. What's the problem?"

"They're gone. I went to their room and all their shit is gone," she hisses.

"She's just a little cunt. I thought you'd be happy to get her out of the way."

"Don't try to put this one on me, you scumbag. This was all you. You've been trying to fuck her for years.

"Which is crazy. You have a girlfriend. Amy is too good for you."

I stand and storm across the room. I glare at my sister as she narrows her eyes at me. I'm still letting her words sink in. Cee-Cee is gone?

"If she's gone, it has nothing to do with me. Keep Amy out of this."

"Are you mental? You put her in the middle of this. How do you think I know about last night? She called me in a panic because she knew you were trying to drug Cee-Cee.

"If she tells anyone about this, your ass will be behind bars, you idiot. You only ever think about yourself. You're gonna get Dad killed and your junkie ass couldn't care less."

"I'm not a junkie."

"The fuck you aren't. You push more roids than Big Pham. You're one test away from being banned from fighting.

"My brother, the brother I know wouldn't have gone off the deep end because his stepsister finally agreed to a date with someone else. You were going to have her raped, Sean. Does that sound right to you?"

"I wasn't trying to have her raped. I wanted them to slow her down for you, so you could win the tournament. You're not getting any younger, you know. I was thinking of you."

"That's bullshit and you know it. I work hard for my spot. Cee-Cee or not, I earn my way, you pig.

"You went too far this time, Sean. You have no idea what this could cost us. You better pray she doesn't turn up anywhere she isn't meant to be. Oh, and hope to God Dad doesn't lose his shit on you for this."

"Fuck. Whatever. I'll find the brats and fix this."

"Something tells me you're already too late. You took sibling rivalry to the extreme. I'm going to the gym."

"Really? You're going to leave me holding my dick on this shit?"

"You made your bed. Besides, looks like I'm going to have to lead us to the championship and the purse. You just fucked us all over. In more ways than one," she snaps at me.

A Friend

A groan leaves my lips as I sit up and look around. My phone is ringing, that's what has woken me from my nap. I'm getting old.

Naps are welcome when they find me. These old bones have been telling a tale lately. If I could turn back time …

I snort and shake my thoughts off as I answer the call. "I'm listening."

"She's gone. She took the kid and ran."

"What do you mean?"

"That asshole tried to drug her and have her raped. I guess she's fed up."

"Can you still track her?"

"Yes, she seems to still have the AirTag on her."

"Good."

"What should I do next? I don't think I should go after her; I could be followed, or I could blow my cover. If I do, you won't be able to use me anymore."

"Send me the serial number of the tracker. I will handle it. For now, stay with your assignment."

I hang up and dial in to give an update on what's going on. The feeling in my gut tells me things are about to change in a big way.

"Hello," the man on the other end of the call answers.

"The hidden package is on the move," I say into the phone.

"Fuck, you have to be kidding me. There's too much shit going on right now," he replies and sighs.

Moving away from the phone, he says something to someone in the background in Italian. I catch only pieces of what is said. I'm already in motion to pack my things to be on the move if necessary.

"What do you need from me?" I ask.

"No package, no deal. She's the only thing bridging this gap right now. We need them at the table. All three are important to them, but she's the key."

"Fuck, Logan would want to keep them all safe. Make sure your guys stay on top of this, but all of you need to remain hidden. It is imperative your connection isn't revealed.

"They can't know we've been watching or how far our reach goes. Not yet. Keep me posted if anything else changes."

I nod as if he can see me. I'm much older than this young man, but the two titans of the underground world have my respect and attention. When my best friend's life was taken, I vowed to do everything in my power to help them and their cause.

"My niece is going to stay on top of the canary. I'll handle the treasure."

"I might have something else for you. Be ready to head back to Ireland if I call."

"I'm always ready. *A hui hou*, my young friend."

"*A hui hou*, old friend. *Ci rivedremo*," he replies before repeating the words in Italian.

CHAPTER FOUR

I Need Ya

Dylan

Four months later …

I stand in my gym, lost in thought as I have my arms folded over my chest. I'm up in the office, looking out of the viewing window down onto the floor below. I was so grateful to Da for allowing me to run this place.

Logan and Cole run some of our more complicated businesses. While I step in when needed, I don't think I have the temperament for what they do. At least not on a daily basis.

This gym suits me. My gaze lands on one of my closest friends and a smile comes to my face. I remember how hard things were for me in the beginning.

Taegan changed all of that around. I never had the chance to see Ciara before my family moved to America and New York became our home for good. I went from painfully shy to being a complete introvert.

I even stopped talking to my brothers and sisters, making them all extremely protective of me. My parents were the only ones who could get me to talk. My ma because no one got away with not answering her, and Da because he didn't ask for much in the way of conversation, just a simple response.

America was no better than Ireland. Instead of being teased for being the smallest kid in school, I was teased for my heavy accent and for being scrawny. Well, that was until I stopped talking in school as well.

Then I shot up like a tree in the tenth grade. It turned out I wasn't going to be the smallest in my family forever. By fifteen, I was almost as tall as my older brothers and gaining on them fast.

By the eleventh grade, I was picked on for being tall, lanky, and awkward. The giant Irish mute. I spoke only when needed and I never felt a need to.

I felt like I lost something vital. A piece of me left that island when Ciara left, and it never returned. I didn't care about much once we got here.

I had no friends. Instead, I focused on learning to hone my skills in the ring and counting down the days until I was old enough to return to Ireland on my own. I didn't understand a lot of things back then.

My jaw clenches as I think of all I know now. So much has changed since the day Taegan and I met. I smile just a little as memories of that day fill my thoughts.

"Come on, O'Brien, just give us your money and we'll make this easy today," Roger, the school bully, taunted with a smug grin on his face.

I hated this kid. My dad worked hard for the money he gave me, but this kid and his crew were there to collect every day. Especially since none of my older siblings were around to protect me. Sure, it pissed me off, but it was better to give over the money and be done with it.

I hated it in America and in two more years, I'd be on my way back home, where I could find Ciara and keep my promise. I reached into my pocket and pulled out the money my da gave me that morning. I learned to keep what I wanted tucked away in my sock.

I never let them take it all. When I lifted my head and my hand to hand over the money, that's when I saw her. The little spitfire with the fiery red hair.

Benny Jones snatched the money and pocketed it, but I barely noticed because my eyes were fixed on the bouncing red curls heading my way. I looked at her face to see her brows furrowed and her lips set in a tight grim line.

"What's the matter with ya, O'Brien?" she snapped with her sharp Irish accent. "Ya make us all ashamed to claim ya. Yer the tallest kid in your grade, and I know for a fact yer brothers haven't left ya to be a wuss. Find yer balls and make yer countrymen proud. For Christ's sake, make yerself proud and put an end to this."

Her big green eyes burned into mine as her chest heaved with anger. I don't know what it was, but there was something about her eyes that reminded me of Ciara.

Not the color, but the look that said she believed in me, and I could do anything. Something snapped on the inside. I suddenly didn't want to let them pick on me.

I wanted to fight back. It wasn't like I didn't know how. I'd been boxing since before we came here to the States. Ciara's dad would teach us both and sparred with me when I hung out in the barn with Ciara to watch him train. I continued training when we moved here.

I figured when I found Ciara, I would need to keep up my part of the bargain, and if her dad wanted to kick my ass, I wasn't going to make it easy. However, I never thought to fight back when I needed to. I never took what I learned in the ring outside.

In that moment, my temper became unhinged, and I had a feeling it wasn't going to allow me to lock it back away. I straightened my shoulders and turned to Roger.

"Tell 'em to give me my money back," I hissed.

"Don't let your little girlfriend here get your ass kicked, O'Brien." Roger chuckled.

Before I could think, I smashed my fist into the side of Roger's face. I turned to Benny, who threw his fists up, but he was too slow. Two body shots and he doubled over, groaning.

Let's not forget to mention he wet his pants. I turned for the other three who were with them, but they were running out of the schoolyard, not bothering to look back.

"*I knew ya had it in ya,*" my new little conscience chirped with a wide smile. *She went to lift my money from Benny's pocket as he groaned on the ground next to Roger.* "*No one will be pushing ya around now. Come on, I'll let ya buy me a slice.*"

"*I'm Dylan,*" I murmured as I rubbed the back of my neck with the arm she didn't have her arm linked through.

"*I know who ya are, silly. I dated your brother for six months.*" *She giggled.* "*That's how I knew ya could actually kick all their asses. I don't understand ya, O'Brien.*"

"*Not much to understand.*" *I sighed.*

"*I think there is, and I intend to figure it out.*" *She looked up at me and beamed. She had to look up at me with her petite frame and it made me wonder if Ciara would be so much smaller than me.* "*Ya can call me Taegan.*"

"*Thanks, Taegan.*" *I genuinely smiled for the first time in a long, long time.*

"*Don't mention it, O'Brien. From now on, I'll be the only one allowed to kick yer ass,*" *Taegan laughed.*

She was right. From that day on, she's been the only one I allowed to give me any kind of shit. Ma had been right. I do have my da's temper. Once it was unlocked, I had a hard time locking it back away.

I went from boxing to MMA, needing an outlet for all the rage that had built up inside. Now I'm fighting to earn my way back home.

A smile comes to my lips as I think of Ciara in the ring. I wish I had her talent around here. I shake my head as I focus back on the fighters below. I blow out a heavy breath.

"Fuck, we need some real female fighters. This bullshit isn't going to fly."

I turn and look at the flyer on my desk. I need this gym to win that tournament. When we pull off the championship win, I'll finally have enough to go back home.

It's taking me long enough. Not being able to fight in the underground fights really set me back. Uncle Ronan made sure to banned me from all his fights and clubs, but I'm almost there.

"I'm coming to you, Ciara. I'll be home and you can find me."

"For fuck's sake, now yer up here talking to yerself. I knew I needed to get my ass up here to check on ya," Taegan says from behind me, bringing a laugh to my lips.

I turn and look at her standing in the doorway of my office. She's still the tiny spitfire I met in high school. She gets on Jamie's nerves all the time. I still can't believe the two ever dated.

"What's the problem? You can't find anyone else to bother?"

She sighs and places her hands on her hips. I know that look, I groan and pray for her to turn around and disappear. I want to get my workout in and head home once I shut this place down for the night.

"Don't ya give me that look. Ya promised ya'd hang out with me tonight. What happened to never breaking promises?"

"I'm second-guessing that rule. Every time I hang out with you, I end up in the middle of some shit. You're like a magnet for trouble. Nothing is ever peaceful," I grumble.

"Ya can suck it. I don't bring ya any trouble yer not willing to handle."

I scoff. "Sure ya don't."

"Oops, would ya look at that, I think I went and pissed ya off."

I shake my head at her and go to sit behind my desk so I can get some paperwork done before it's time for me to go down and train. I need to make sure all the paperwork is done for the tournament and check my emails.

"You haven't pissed me off. I'll do whatever it is you have planned. I will keep my word like I always do."

"Grand. I know how much ya need a new stock of fighters. I have someone I want ya to see."

I groan. I guess I'm not the only one who noticed that shit downstairs. I have a bigger problem than I'm willing to admit.

"Is it that obvious?"

"Listen, Cadhla might be my cousin, but she's a shit fighter. Ya and I know she's here because of ya. Ya don't have to spare her feelings on account of me.

"Boot her ass from the gym once and for all. She's a fucking bitch. I come here to chill and kick back, get me work done, and live me good life. She fucks that up all the time," she says as she frowns.

"A year ago, I would have tossed her out on her ass if you said those words. Right now, I can't afford to lose one of the only female fighters I have on the roster. This could be my year."

"Ugh, ya know she's from me psycho part of the family. I wouldn't even claim her if it wouldn't make me look like a liar. I loathe the day she learned we were friends."

I snort. "I'll cut her as soon as I find a replacement."

"Exactly why we're hitting the fights tonight. I heard—"

I hold my hand up as my phone rings. Seeing it's Cole, I give Taegan a nod to let her know I'll talk to her later then answer the call. She shrugs and turns to leave.

"What's up, Cole?" I answer the device.

"I want ya to take a trip with me. Jamie needs to handle some business, so he can't come, but I need family for this one. There's something we need to do for our brother," he says.

"For Logan?"

"Aye, this is all my fault. I think I fucked up and set this shit in motion. He wouldn't be in some prison lost in the system if it wasn't for me.

"I need to make sure everything he left behind is taken care of. It's been four months. This needs to happen now."

"What about Connie and Kate?"

"Connie is where I need her. Kate is with me; I need her too. This needs to happen now and ya need to be with me."

"Okay, come pick me up from the gym. I'll be ready. Do you need anything else from me?"

"Be armed. I don't know what we're walking into."

"Ach, what's going on, Cole? What aren't you telling me?"

"I should have left her hidden. *Fuck*," he roars. "I'll tell ya when I see ya. For now, be ready when I get to ya."

CHAPTER FIVE

Changes Everything

Dylan

"Wait a minute. You've met this girl?" I ask as my chest fills with worry.

"Aye, I've met her a time or two. Logan is in love with her. I should have checked in on her a long time ago.

"I just don't have a good feeling about this. I thought it best to stay away at first."

"I could have looked after her," Kate speaks up from the back seat.

She's been back there fuming. I think she's as pissed as I am that Cole is just speaking up about this. We wouldn't be rushing into this if he had told us.

"Aye, but I didn't want to put ya in the middle. Fuck, I didn't know this would spread. Logan keeps her hidden away nicely, but something came up and I know I need to lay eyes on her."

"What came up?"

Cole falls silent for a moment, and I don't think he's going to answer me at first. I turn in the passenger seat to watch his profile as he drives. Brooklyn has had to take on more responsibility since Logan has been missing.

I'm glad we finally know where to begin looking for my oldest brother, but even I know this isn't good. Cole hasn't told me what all is going on or why Logan ended up in prison, but I know nothing good is behind it all.

When I found out my grandda summoned Logan to Ireland in the first place, I had a ton of questions. I know in the pit of my stomach he's behind this somehow. Cole pulls a hand down his face and blows out a breath.

"I made a mistake. We were so close to the Alliance coming together once and for all, so I did something stupid."

"What did you do, Cole?"

"I asked Felix to find Deja and Ciara."

"Eejit," Kate hisses.

"You what? What were you thinking?"

"I was thinking that I knew ya were up to something. I thought I could cut it off at the pass."

"Fuck."

"They were our friends. We did nothing wrong and neither did they. We were kids."

"He doesn't care."

"I figured if we knew where they were, we could protect them. Things are different. At least they were supposed to be."

"I wish you would have asked me first. What has this changed?"

"I know where Deja is."

"Are you kidding?" Kate gasps.

"Ach, now I wish I were. Once I found her, I started to understand a lot more."

"Like what?" I ask.

"I understand why the oul bastard didn't want us connected to them. It's about more than their skin color or their mixed heritage. The Walsh brothers' mother is Adline McDougal."

"As in the McDougal clan?"

I know the name well. When Logan disappeared, their clan was the one business partnership Da insisted he would handle instead of allowing Cole to step in. He was adamant about it.

From the little I know, the McDougal clan happens to be one of Da's biggest and oldest connections. I've learned more about them since we've all had to step up to help cover for Logan, who previously was the only one privy to this information.

"One and the same. Our friendships and relationships have always threatened Oland with the promise of the Alliance happening. He couldn't afford for us to be near the Walshs or anyone connected to them."

"Okay, fine, but what happened to Ciara and where is she?"

"I don't know that yet. Deja doesn't have a clue, and Felix has been running into dead ends."

"*Brooklyn*," I drag out as his words from earlier come back to me. "How long? What have you done? What happened? Is Ciara in danger?"

He punches the steering wheel. My heart begins to race. My brother never loses his cool. This shit is serious.

"I don't know. I want to tell ya she's safe, but I don't know. I'm doing everything I can to find her before he does.

"I asked Felix to find them about four, maybe five months ago. Right before I took off. Just before Logan left.

"Right now, I'm dealing with one problem at a time. We need to get to Raven and get her somewhere safe until I have a handle on what's really going on. I'm going to fix this, I swear to ya."

"Let's keep our heads cool. We're checking on her now," Kate says.

I clench my jaw and stare out of the window at all the traffic heading into Long Island, where Cole says Logan has a place. Apparently, that's where he and this Raven have been living together. I never knew anything about this woman or this residence we're headed to, but if Logan loves her, I can understand why Cole is so concerned for her.

I would want him to protect Ciara the same. Bringing Kate along is so Raven isn't intimidated by two men she doesn't know. Telling myself this will be fine, I try to believe Cole has done all the right things.

"If anything happens to Ciara, I'm going to kill that old motherfucker," I bite out.

"Not before I do. Ya have no idea how much he owes us in blood. I'm going to see him real soon."

Brooklyn

My stomach is in my ass as we pull up to Logan's house in Long Island. I know something isn't right as I place the car in park. I gesture for Dylan to pull his piece and follow me.

Kate does the same, but I flag for her to move between me and Dylan, so she's covered. Bile rises in my throat as we find the front door open. We move inside swiftly.

Rage fills me as we find Raven slowly dragging herself on the floor. It looks like she's trying to drag her way to the phone or something. I rush over to her as I notice one other thing.

She's pregnant. I didn't know this and I'm not sure Logan does either. Kate snaps into action and calls for help.

"Hey, hey, I'm here, love. Hang on for me. We're going to get you some help," I say as I rush to her side.

She looks up at me with fear in her eyes. Her hand is covered in blood and pressed to her chest. Her wrist is bloody and raw, as if something had been wrapped around it or torn from it.

I look her over and panic sets in. There's blood everywhere. Her dress is soaked. I should have come sooner.

She coughs up blood and gasps. Tears stain her cheeks as she searches my face. Recognition hits her gaze, and she reaches out to me with her hand she had been using to drag herself forward.

Pulling my hand to her belly, she looks me in the eyes. "Brooklyn, God heard my prayers," she says through trembling lips. "Please save his little girl. Keep his daughter safe.

"Go ... the closet. I placed her in the closet for safekeeping. Promise me."

"Wait, what?"

"They attacked me, but I fought back as best I could. Then they shot me. I kept fighting and I got to my gun. I hit one and they took off. I went into labor.

"I pushed her out and placed her in the closet while I tried to get help. Please save her and keep her safe. Tell Logan I'm sorry. I tried to protect her."

Dylan returns from clearing the house and springs into action. He retrieves the small, whimpering bundle from the closet. Kate's face has turned as white as a sheet. I scoop Raven up gingerly and try to apply pressure to the wound in her shoulder.

"Ya hold on for me, yer going to tell him yerself," I demand.

"I called for an ambulance. They're on the way, love. Ya hold on," Kate says as she shakes the shock off.

"There's no one else here. They must have gotten away," Dylan says.

"I'm not going to make it. Make sure she survives. Please. Save my baby. Tell Logan I love him."

"*No*," I roar as she dies in my arms.

I look up at my sister and brother. "He can never know this is how she died. I failed them both, but this shit will kill him. It's not how we'll tell him she died."

Kate nods. "Right. It was me. I found her and called for help, but by the time they arrived, they could only save the babe."

CHAPTER SIX

Crash-Out Sean

Sean

A month later ...

"Have you found anything yet?" I snarl into the phone as I hold the back of this chick's head still while she chokes down my cock.

She's pushing at my thighs, but I refuse to let go. She wanted to have a good time. I'm showing her one. Slut knows I have a girl, and she still sat on my lap with no panties on at the club me and my boys were kicking it at.

"No. I haven't found anything. It's like she and the kid vanished."

"What the fuck?" I growl.

Frustrated as fuck, I release this squirming chick so she can breathe. She falls back on her ass and leans against the back of the couch, gasping for air as her eyes water. She pouts at me but doesn't look too put out.

Ignoring her, I reach for the mirror on the back of the couch that has my coke on it and snort a few lines, then run a hand under my nose.

"Keep on it. I need to get them back here," I snarl.

"Dude, I'm not doing this for free. I need that payment before any work is continued."

"Motherfucker, you haven't done shit for me to pay you for. Are you forgetting the shit I have on you? Find what I need, or I'm going to fuck your entire life up."

"Whatever," he scoffs and hangs up.

"Fuck," I scream and toss my phone across the room. "Everything is shit."

"Are you okay, baby?"

I blink at the bitch sitting on the floor. I almost forgot she was here. I run a hand through my hair as I start to sweat and overheat. My heart is pounding.

I shake my head to clear it. When that doesn't work, I stumble over to my drink on the table. I down the glass and turn to lean against the table.

"Come finish," I say to the slut staring at me.

She's pretty, but not my type. I only brought her home because Amy is a prude. She's still holding out on me. I've been fucking around since we've been together.

I grunt and look up at the ceiling as my shit goes soft. I try to picture Cee-Cee and those amazing tits. If I don't get her back here for nothing else, I want her back here so I can fuck her.

"Fuck," I hiss as not even thoughts of her will get me hard again.

It's not like this slut isn't trying her best. I have too much shit on my mind. I fucked up bad. I fucked up real bad.

Lily wasn't bluffing. Some real bad shit started happening after Cee-Cee and the brat left. The gym is in bad shape and Dad is broke as fuck.

Like, I know he's always been shit with money. Forgetting to pay bills or just not paying them because he doesn't feel like it. Going out to party first before making sure we were fed. Not saving anything in case we needed something for school or got sick.

Shit, Lily and I used to take money right out of his wallet, and he wouldn't even notice. He would think he gambled or drank it away, but there was always cash coming in from somewhere other than the gym that kept things afloat. The gym and the money Cee-Cee brought in from the underground fights served as the cash we all blew through.

Now, everything has stopped. No Cee-Cee, no gym or fight money and wherever that other influx of cash was coming from seems to have dried up.

Dad was so pissed at me about Cee-Cee taking off I had to move in with Amy. Good thing I have her wrapped around my finger.

Amy might be older than me—closer to Lily's age—but she isn't too fucking bright. Cee-Cee has been gone for seven months, and I haven't been able to find her. I'm trying to fix this shit, but in the meantime, I've been living with Amy and using her money for all my needs and habits.

Dad lost his shit on me. Things have been falling apart around here. I've watched my father go from panicked to almost terrified to relieved. However, today at the gym, he looked like he saw a ghost.

I've been trying to make sense of that look all day. I've been wondering if it had something to do with the group I ran into when I entered the gym. They were all blond and stood out.

The one with the big rack and blue eyes caught my attention, but there was something about them all that stopped me from trying to get her number.

I shake the thought off. I overheard Dad and Lily in the office arguing. Dad said something about doing what he needed to do to not lose the house and the gym. I couldn't make out everything during their conversation, but the bits and pieces I got make me feel like this is all my fault.

I roar with anger and push this bitch on her ass. I then begin to toss the place. This is all so fucked. Everything is turning to shit and it's all because of that bitch.

"Get out," I bellow. "Get the fuck out."

I drop to my knees and put my head in my hands. My heart is racing again. The door slams shut, and I grab at my chest and groan.

"Where the fuck are you? I'm going to make you pay for this when I get my hands on you," I snarl.

I don't know how long I've been sitting here on my knees. It is only as Amy enters the apartment, and her words break through the fog, that I realize I've fucked up again.

"What the fuck happened to my place?" she says angrily.

Only, I can't focus on that as my heart feels like it's going to explode. I'm only twenty. I can't be having a heart attack.

"I'll fix it. I think I need to go to the hospital."

CHAPTER SEVEN

This Again?

Lily

Two months later …

I blink back the tears stinging my eyes, only for the tears to cling to my lashes as they slip free. I feel like that helpless sixteen-year-old all over again. Taking a deep breath, I pull myself together.

I sit in this hotel suite staring into the gray eyes of a man I never thought I would have to deal with in my life again. However, I've stepped into danger again. Just like ten years ago, I can't stand by and do nothing.

"I know you don't like me and you didn't want to help me last time. I get it. You owe me nothing. I just ask that you hear me out," I breathe shakily.

He only inclines his head for me to continue. I lick my dry lips and swallow hard. I have to do this. I'm grateful he agreed to come meet with me.

"Ten years ago, I came to you guys because I was a scared sixteen-year-old. I had three younger siblings to think about. You didn't trust me then and you have no reason to trust me now."

It's the truth. I was so excited when I got a little sister. I was just as excited about Ciarán, but I fell in love with Cee-Cee right away. She was so cute with her little accent.

I would dress her up and play with her like my very own little doll. I felt like I bonded with her as I had lost my mother too. However, the poor thing had lost both her parents and ended up in our shit home.

I only wanted to protect her and Ciarán like I did Sean. It didn't take long for me to figure out something was wrong. My father shut down after we lost my mom.

I was left to take care of a six-year-old on my own. It wasn't a secret that my dad had fallen into a shady crowd. That's where it all started.

I clear my throat and continue. "I had to be careful as I tried to find the truth and when I did. You and your partner's names came up and I took a chance.

"I'm taking that same chance. This time, not because I have three kids counting on me to cover for my fuckup of a dad, but because I know in my gut something bad is coming.

"I now have a junkie brother and alcoholic father, which I'm trying to save from themselves before they get us all killed. We're already losing everything.

"As you know, my father and I have lost our benefactors. I haven't been able to get in touch with your partner and my father slipped up and told me about the mess he's gotten himself into," I say.

"You're right about many things. I don't trust you. Never have. I'm not sure what you think I will do for you now. As far as I'm concerned, you've lost your value." He tilts his head to the side. "Have you not?"

"No, I haven't. She's not safe. They're forcing him to continue the job, or they will kill us all. He is desperate, my brother is as well. Desperate people do crazy things."

"Who are we talking about? My problem is six feet in the ground," he says sharply.

"He isn't your only problem. If you help me, I will help you. I'll tell you who they are, and I will keep my pains in the ass on a leash and away from all your interests."

He sits back in his seat and glares at me. This is it. This is the moment I die.

Neither of the men I met ten years ago gave off the impression that they would hesitate to kill me. However, this one made me believe he planned to someday. It was only a matter of time.

"You're brave. I'll give you that, but we do nothing that doesn't benefit us." He pauses and snaps his fingers, then makes a come-hither motion. The dark-haired, blue-eyed guy with him steps forward with a case and opens it. "I heard of your troubles. This should cover the payments that haven't been coming in on our end.

"I also know your father had visitors. I don't need you to tell me anything. I already know who believes I don't have eyes. If you take this money, your gym is now mine.

"Someone will be in touch to handle the paperwork and deed transfer. You will take over and handle your father's bad business habits. This will be the final bailout.

"I don't invest in losses. Hire someone close to you whom you can trust, allow them to help you keep things running. If you fail, your next visit won't be with me or my partner. It will be with death. Do I make myself clear?"

I nod my head vigorously. "Yes, yes, thank you. I know just the person. I won't fail."

CHAPTER EIGHT

Am I Dreaming?

Dylan

Five months later ...

"I love this place. I'm thinking about making some changes to a few of our bars and lounges. I can see a few things here that are inspiring so many ideas," Connie muses as she looks around the bar.

"Really?" I take a glance around and nod.

I can see her point. There's a nice vibe here. Nicer since the DJs have changed. I didn't like the last set that was played.

We like to keep our clubs more lively. If the floor is dead, our DJs know to change the vibe. The last guy didn't seem to know how to make that happen. The movement has been stale since we arrived an hour ago.

If not for the service and ambience, I would have been ready to go twenty minutes in. Connie is in charge of entertainment and hiring at our locations back in New York. It's her job to be in tune with shit like this.

"Yeah, I want to make the changes now before Logan gets back. Jamie is too focused on his new extra duties to worry about my spending," she says with a rueful smile.

I laugh and shake my head. Jamie usually handles all the finances. He's supersmart with numbers. However, he's been doing more enforcing and negotiating since Logan's disappearance.

"What? Ya know he's a tightwad with the money. Ya couldn't squeeze a shilling out of his ass if ya feed him a dozen."

"Listen, I was thinking the same thing about making upgrades at the gym. I don't blame you."

"Ya know I'm going to need to lean on ya to spend more time at the lounges. Is that going to mess with yer training?"

I take a sip of my beer. "No. I've got your back. You take care of what Brooklyn needs from you."

"Yer the best little brother there is. Ya know I love ya, right?"

"I love you too."

I smile at my sister and return to observing the bar. Being that I help out with our family's bars and lounges, I can't help but keep a watchful eye and note a ton of things about the place.

I bob my head to the music and get lost in my thoughts. I can't help thinking about how things turned out for Felix tonight. Connie and I came to the West Coast thinking we would see our cousin and his girl get engaged.

I've seen this proposal coming since Felix first brought Kaye to us for safekeeping. She and Dae-Dae have become family. The little guy is like a nephew to us all. Connie and Kate are very protective of Kaye.

I'm sure Kate would have been here if Brooklyn didn't have her watching over our little princess. We've all fallen in love with Shauna. I was the first to hold her, so Brooklyn was the one to name her.

That little girl will always have a special place in my heart. She's a fighter, just like her mother. I didn't get to know Raven, but I'm proud of her and how she fought to give Shauna life.

My brother will be devastated when he finds out about Raven's death, but he has something special to return to. For now, Brooklyn has been hiding her away between Ireland and Scotland.

My grandfather might be out of the picture, but there are still plenty of people who would like to see my brother broken and unable to complete the Alliance.

That's not going to happen on our watch. We failed him once; never again. My da made sure my sisters were built as tough as us guys. You don't want to fuck with an O'Brien, period.

Kate and Connie have been on baby duty because my grandda has never paid them as much attention as he has me and my brothers. If he does have a successor we don't know about then most likely they're ignoring my sisters as well.

Not that they don't use discretion when it comes to taking care of Shauna. I meant what I said to Felix tonight. I'm grateful that he tried to find Ciara.

Things may not have gone the way Brooklyn had hoped, but the thought and effort mean a lot to me. I don't know how I feel now that I know Donald Walsh is dead.

I've been preparing all my life to fight him for a chance to win his daughter's hand. Now everything has changed. I wish I knew where Ciara was and how she's doing.

Losing her ma and da must have been hard for her. She would be about twenty now. I have so many questions.

I didn't know her ma was pregnant before they left. However, she must have been, or she became pregnant soon after, to be survived by Ciara and a son. I've run over and over the details Brooklyn has shared with me.

"Okay, now this is what I'm talking about. This DJ is much better than the last guy," Connie sings and stands from her seat.

I smile as my sister sways her hips to the music. Both Kate and Connie have been dancers for as long as I can remember.

They went from river dancing when we lived in Ireland to hip-hop, jazz, and ballet once they came to America. Connie introduced Kate to the dance studio she attended before we all got here. I think that's why Logan put Connie in charge of entertainment for the businesses.

Glancing around, I take notice of the guys whose attention Connie's swaying has grabbed. My sisters are gorgeous women. Gorgeous and dangerous.

"Come on, love. Come dance with yer sister. This is what I came out for.

"I want to cut loose and have fun. Everything is so … ugh. Come on," she coos and reaches for my hand.

I shrug my shoulders and follow her to the dance floor that's starting to fill. "Past Lives" by Sapientdream and Slushii is playing as we grab a spot to move around. I frown wondering why the DJ would play this and kill the vibe he just got going. Then it blends into the remix dance pop version.

I pull a face and nod. I'm not mad at all. I grab Connie and move her out of the way as two small women go to dance by. The one in front with the long dark hair looks drunk and has her eyes closed as she pulls the other one behind her.

I scowl at the two and shake my head. However, I come to a dead stop as the face of the second one comes into view. She's gorgeous.

In the dim lighting on the dance floor, I have to squint to get a better look at her face. Her brown skin has a glow to it even under the low lights. Her dark hair is pulled up in a mass of thick curls. She's small, maybe five two. Damn, she has a nice, slim, toned build.

I'd bet money she does some powerlifting. Those thighs are giving it away in those tight jeans. Allowing my gaze to pass back up to her face, I swear hard.

I don't know if it's the music, the beer, or just my longing to find Ciara, but this girl looks so much like her. I can't stop myself from moving closer to her. I need a closer look at her face.

Am I dreaming?

Ciara

"New York will be so much better for us. You'll see. I promise," Daliah slurs.

I laugh and smile at her. Daliah has been like my guardian angel since we arrived in San Diego. I met her in the diner where Ciarán and I stopped in to find something to eat after we landed. She was our waitress.

She was so kind to us and after talking a little, she told me she had just lost her tenant and could offer us a place to stay. I was skeptical at first, but Ciarán looked like he was worried and tired, so I took her up on her offer.

It worked out as she lived in a duplex home with her mother. Her mother has also been a godsend. They helped me find a waitress job and get Ciarán into school.

"I hope you're right. I need to find something more stable, with better pay. I wish I had more time to do things with Ciarán."

"Well, honey, we can throw him the best birthday party ever in New York. You're sure to have time and money there."

I bite my lip and think about our plans. Daliah has wanted to leave San Diego since I met her. I, on the other hand, hadn't planned on leaving.

I haven't found a gym with a team interested in the tournaments; those who are don't have a team that could actually make it. I still work out and train, but I've all but given up on my dream.

For now, Ciarán has been my main focus. He's beginning to need more things that require more money. Something I don't have much of.

When Ciarán showed me a TikTok of a gym in New York, I became curious. They were training for this year's tournaments. I checked out their website and found out they're looking for a few female fighters.

They have talent. Their male fighters are top tier. It looks like they have a real shot.

Not to mention, I'd already be in New York for the finals and wouldn't have to come up with the money to travel there. If I can land a spot on their team, there's at least hope to fight in a real match again.

I scoff. "I don't know about time *and* money. I'll most likely have to settle for one or the other."

"Don't think like that. I have this great feeling about New York. I told you my cousin knows about that gym Ciarán told you about. If you want to fight, my cousin is the one to know.

"She says that gym has like one good female fighter, but she's retired or something. You could probably kick her ass in your sleep. Besides, Vega has connections.

"My stepuncle is a big deal and Vega lives the life. We'll have new jobs in no time. She'll get you the access you need to the underground scene there. It won't be like here.

"You already have an in. She's giving us a place to stay, and the schools are nice in the area. With Ciarán's grades, this is going to be a dream come true for us all."

I roll my eyes. "Those schools cost money. I'll need to make two grand a month just for his tuition. Then there's food and clothing."

She rolls her eyes and pouts. "You sound like you're going to change your mind. The gigs she has lined up for us pay well. We're going to be fine."

I had still been on the fence until I started looking into more information on Donald Walsh. His last mentioned fight was in New York around the time I was eight. I was so mad when the internet connection dropped right as I had been about to find more information on him.

I couldn't get back to the initial site I found when I got my next opportunity to do some more digging. It's all been so frustrating. I know nothing more than I did a year ago, other than the fact that my father was a boxer.

It's weird how hard it is to find information on him. However, once I'm in New York and make my way into a gym, I'm likely to find more. At least that's what I've been telling myself.

"Pull your lip back in. I'm going. Ciarán would kill me if I pulled out now. He's so excited to be going to the Big Apple."

I just hope I'm doing the right thing. Chasing ghosts could come back to bite me. I haven't heard a peep out of Theo or his asshole kids.

What if I'm jumping out of my safe zone by making this move? I honestly need more financial stability and Daliah's cousin is offering a shot at that.

"I've got your back, Ariel. Trust me, it's going to be great. If not, we can always come back here with Mom."

Ariel.

It's been a year, and I'm still not used to answering to that name. I didn't want to go by Cee-Cee in case Theo decided to come after me. I was too afraid to use Ciara Walsh, as I still don't fully understand why Theo never allowed me to use that name. I've been going by Ariel Norwood and Ciarán goes by Chris Norwood.

Daliah knows Ariel isn't my real name. After all, she has been very instrumental in helping me stay under the radar. She's aware that I'm running from something, but she's willing to help anyway she can. She's become a real friend.

"I hope you're right," I murmur.

"I am. Now drink up. I didn't bring you out to this bar to sit around and look sad.

"I want to dance and say our farewells with a bang. This time next week we'll be living the life," she sings.

I look around the bar. The music is a vibe. I think the DJ has changed since we arrived because this place was sort of lame when we first got here.

I didn't complain because Dahila can be Dahila sometimes. Her taste in music will leave you with no doubts that she's a white girl, no matter how cool and down to earth she can be.

I'm so over Taylor Swift. We're going to have to come to some type of agreement when we get to New York because the way this chick will run a record in the ground on full blast is enough to drive anyone crazy and make you hate an entire genre of music. She almost ruined Ed Sheeran for me.

She would have if Ciarán hadn't used his drone to somehow disconnect her Bluetooth. I swear she was driving us both crazy.

"Oh, I love this song." Daliah jumps up from her seat and grabs my hand.

I'm still trying to down my drink as she pulls me out onto the dance floor. This is the first time I've gotten to hang out like this. Alice, Daliah's mother, demanded I go out and allow her to watch Ciarán for me.

Ciarán nearly pushed me out the door. The promise of Alice's homemade cookies was enough for him to forget all about me. The thought of my brother being safe and happy makes me relax a little.

I fall into the music and begin to dance. I close my eyes and lift my arms over my head. This is the most relaxed I've been in ... I can't name a time that I remember.

Suddenly, my back is engulfed in heat. Strong hands land on my hips, and I'm hit with a mouthwatering scent. I open my eyes and look up.

I'm met with intense blue eyes. I knit my brows as they look so familiar. The expression on the guy's face is one of awe ... surprise ... disbelief. I have a hard time placing the look.

"Do I know you?" I ask.

He opens his mouth to say something, but a loud commotion breaks out. People begin to shove and scream. The guy laces his fingers with mine to pull me with him, but Daliah grabs my other hand and tugs me in the opposite direction.

I release his hand because I don't know him. Daliah and I race out of the bar as fast as we can through the side door. We don't stop moving until we're a few blocks away from the bar.

"Ugh, I was just starting to have some real fun," Daliah says.

"Want to head to another bar?"

She pouts. "No, I broke my shoe."

I look down and burst into laughter. This would only happen to us. I guess it's for the best.

My mind goes to the blue-eyed guy at the bar. It was dark, so I couldn't really take him in fully, but there was something about his eyes. I brush it off.

We're leaving in a few days. Besides, I never have time for guys. My last date was supposed to be right before I left Seattle.

Because of that asshole Sean, that never happened. Austin had asked me out for about six months before I said yes. I've never been focused on guys.

I've always had too much going on in my life to date. In seven years, when Ciarán is eighteen and I'm twenty-seven, then I can think about myself and a love life.

CHAPTER NINE

Go To Bed

Dylan

"Are you okay?" I say to Connie as we make our way back to our car.

"Yeah, I'm fine. Just cheesed that the bar I decided to go to broke out in a brawl. This day has been shit."

I look back toward the entrance of the bar and stare. I have to be dreaming. That girl looked just like Ciara. An older, sexy-as-fuck version, but she could be her doppelgänger.

When I first saw her, I thought I was seeing things. It was like a magnet drew me to her. Once I got my hands on her and she looked up into my eyes, I was blown away.

I tried to pull her with me, but she let go. What are the chances I would run into her here at some bar?

"Are ya all right? Ya look like ya saw a ghost. What was that about?"

I shake my head clear and look away from the entrance as it seems people have stopped coming through it. It couldn't have been her.

"Nothing. Let's get back to the hotel. This night is a bust."

"Ya can say that again. I feel sorry for Felix. I know how much he wanted to propose tonight."

"It will work out. Kaye is crazy about him. When this all blows over, it will be fine."

"I hope yer right. I'll get ya back home and then I'm off to help with our wee love," Connie says with a smile.

"I don't need you to babysit me. I can get back to New York on my own."

"Aye, I'm sure ya can, but no little brother of mine will be traveling all about without me."

"You do know I'm twenty-two, right?"

"And?"

I shake my head and snort, throwing my arm around her shoulders as I lead the way back to the car we came in. My mind goes back to that girl. I have to tell myself again there's no way.

***

We get back to our hotel room and I jump into the shower. The hot water goes a long way to burn through my jumbled thoughts. I can't shake that girl from my head.

Normally, Aunt Cass and Uncle Joe would let us stay with them. However, we knew the drive would be long and we didn't want to be a bother.

When I can't stand under the spray any longer, I wrap a towel around my waist and walk into the bedroom. As exhaustion sets in, my mind continues to race. I sit on the edge of the bed, my thoughts going right back to that girl.

I don't know if I'm going to be able to sleep tonight. Those eyes keep flashing in my mind. What if she was real and that was really Ciara?

I could be walking away from the girl I've devoted my life to finding? I run a hand through my damp locks. Frustration fills me as I'm too tired to make sense of any of it.

Do I know you?

Her words have been ringing in my ears on repeat. If that fight hadn't broken out, I would have told her I believe she does. Her lips, they were the same heart shape I remember.

I wanted to press mine to hers and savor the feeling I've been dreaming of for the last twelve years. I groan as I realize how crazy my thoughts sound.

That couldn't have been her. When I find Ciara, I will know right away it's her. I'm sure of it.

"Go to bed, Dylan. You have a ton of shit to do when you get back home. You'll find her soon." I sigh and go to climb between the sheets to try to get some sleep.

Ciara

"Ugh, my stomach hurts," Ciarán groans.

"I bet it does. Alice said she made enough cookies for the both of us. A dozen each. Where are my cookies, bro?"

"They were so good and we're leaving. When am I going to get a chance to have them again?"

"Really, Ciarán?"

He gives me that adorable smile. This kid has me wrapped around his finger. Thankfully, Alice said she knew he would eat mine, so she made me another batch.

"I'm all packed. Can I help you with anything?"

"No, I'm all good. I'll make you some warm water and lemon so you can go poop those cookies out."

"You're the best. I have ninjas in my stomach. I'm never eating that many cookies in one sitting again."

He stands up from the couch and comes to kiss my cheek. I pull him into a hug and kiss the top of his head. My little brother is going to be much taller than me.

I'm only five two. He's already about three inches taller than I am. I haven't forced him to continue training as Theo had.

Ciarán is a good boxer, but he's not in love with the sport like I am. He'd rather tinker with building things and playing games on his computer. I think it would be different if he started the sport under someone else. Theo tried to force it on him.

"I love you, kiddo."

"I love you too, Cee."

I watch as he disappears in the direction of his room. With a smile on my lips, I get up and go into the kitchen to heat up some water for him. My sketch pad on the counter catches my attention.

I place the kettle on the burner and turn it on then go over and open the sketchbook. It opens right to one of the pages of the boy from my dreams. It's one I used colored pencils to draw.

My mouth falls open as I look into his eyes. The guy from the bar comes to mind. His eyes were a pretty intense blue as well.

I shake my head to clear it as the whistle of the teakettle pulls me back from my musing. I swallow hard and close the book. Some random in a bar has nothing to do with the boy in my dreams.

"You need to go to bed, Cee-Cee. It's time to start fresh. Ciarán deserves better," I murmur and turn to fix my brother's lemon water.

CHAPTER TEN

New York

Ciara

"Oh, look over there, there she is," Daliah says excitedly.

I look in the direction she's pointing and furrow my brows. I'm looking for another white girl, but what I see is a girl with deep chocolate-brown skin and a pretty face. Her hair is brushed back into a full curly puff, and she has neat baby hairs around her edges.

When she smiles, it lights up her pretty face. Daliah rushes over to her and the two huge men surrounding her and pulls her into a tight hug. I'm five two even, this chick has to be about five five. She's taller than me for sure.

One of the first things I note is her sharp eyes and her build. She looks as much like a fighter as I do. It's just something I know when I see it. Although there's something else about her. I can't put my finger on it, but there's something else in her eyes.

"Ariel, this is my cousin Vega. Vega, this is Ariel and her brother Chris," Daliah says.

"Nice to meet you guys," Vega says with a thick New York accent.

She then nods at the two men for them to grab our bags. As they take our things to the SUV and load them, Daliah gushes and rambles on. Ciarán looks around with a twinkle in his eyes.

"You all right?" I say to him as I wrap my arm around his shoulders.

"Yeah, I'm excited, but I thought her cousin would be white," he whispers. "I also thought we'd get to go back to our real names here."

I give his shoulder a squeeze and give him a pointed look. I assumed the same thing about Vega, but this isn't the time to express that. I purse my lips and turn my attention back to Daliah and Vega.

"I had time today. I decided to come get you guys myself. Come on, these cops be on one.

"They'll try to give us a ticket in a heartbeat. Dimitri can be impatient. Let's go.

"Climb in and we'll get something to eat and talk about what you guys need. Welcome to my city. You'll want for nothing here."

"*Yes*, food," Ciarán croons.

I laugh and shake my head. This kid is always ready to eat. We follow Vega and the other two men to climb into the SUV. I can feel the excitement coming off Ciarán as he stares out of the window as we ride through the city.

"You guys have a taste for anything in particular?'

"Yeah, I want to try a chop cheese," Ciarán says before I can stop him.

Vega chuckles. "Sure, shortie. I got you. Harlem is the home of the real chop cheese. You're in good hands with me."

"Cool, are we in Harlem now?"

"Nah, we're in midtown, but the good news is you guys will live right next to the original spot. I own the new developments around there."

"Wow. This is so cool."

"Thanks. I appreciate everything you're doing for us," I speak up.

"True story, you're good. I'm happy I can help, especially with your situation.

"You're with family now. Daliah has been one of the best things to come from my father's marriage. If you're a friend of hers, you're a friend of mine," Vega says.

I swallow hard as I realize Daliah has shared more about me than I thought. My heart races and I wonder once again if coming here was the right thing to do. Daliah reaches to squeeze my hand from the seat next to me in the third row.

I turn to her and give her a weak smile. She knows how much my little brother means to me. I know she wouldn't tell anyone my truth, knowing I could lose him if we're found.

I give her a nod and relax. We're here, we're in New York and I'm going to get on a team and win that tournament.

Breathe, Cee. Breathe.

I sit silently as Ciarán excitedly asks a million and one questions. Vega answers him good-naturedly. I tune in to the conversation when Ciarán begins to ask her about the gyms here.

"Ah, yes, Daliah said your big sister is looking to join a gym. The fight scene here is huge. There's something for everyone.

"Underground or the legit stuff. We have it all. I'd love to see what you've got, Ariel. I'll be able to point you in the right direction once I see you in action," Vega says.

"But what about the Irish gym? Are we far from there? I have a good feeling about them," Ciarán says.

"Ciarán, be polite. I'll be lucky to find a gym to take me in. Vega knows the scene. Be patient."

Vega snickers. "Nah, he's cool, ma. Shortie has good taste. He's talking about the O'Brien's gym.

"Roaring Irish gym is fire. If you're going to go big, they're neck and neck with what I have to offer. You better be able to fight though.

"Other than that one chick who has to be fucking someone or related to them or something, all their fighters are A1. There have been some changes around their operation, but the gym and its team are still solid. Excuse my language, kid," she says.

"They're Irish?" I ask as my thoughts go to my dad.

"As Irish as it gets. Fine as fuck too. I never mind when I have to deal with the O'Briens. We're actually on good terms. I coordinate events with their uncle's underground fights."

"Underground fights?" I lick my lips as I think of my options here.

Vega turns in her seat to look back at me. She gives a laugh. "Yeah, I thought so. I know that look. We'll talk more when there are fewer ears," she says, looking pointedly at Ciarán.

Yes, I've become desperate enough to fight underground. However, more than anything, I want to fight. I think I should shake the rust off before I head to Roaring Irish.

"Hey, handsome. Let's get you that chop cheese," Vega sings as the SUV comes to a stop.

Ciarán nearly climbs right over me to get out. I shake my head and allow him to get out first. Daliah hangs back and places a hand on my arm as I try to follow the others out. I note the driver remains in the car.

I'm assuming he's Dimitri. I heard Vega call the other two Nashawn and Ross. All three look scary and like they could snap someone in two.

I look to Daliah. "I told her the truth because of who my family here is. I couldn't tell you much before we left San Diego. You are safe here.

"My stepuncle is a wealthy man, but his brother ... Vega's uncle and mentor, he's something else. No one is going to fuck with us—at least they're not going to live to talk about it. You have a ton of options here.

"I knew if I got you here, I could get you and Ciarán everything you need. I would never put either of you in danger. You're my family now," she says with a smile on her lips.

I tug her into a hug. She has no idea how much I needed those words or her friendship. She's the closest thing to family I can remember ever having.

"Thank you."

"Don't you dare. You don't have to thank me. I'm right here with you. We're going to raise our little guy and find our happy while we're at it."

"What did I do to deserve you?"

"I don't know, but you've got me for life."

Dylan

"Hey, Dylan. I was thinking we could spar and run some drills. I want to show ya what I've been working on," Cadhla says as she runs up on me.

Cadhla is a redhead like Taegan, but she's much taller. She's five eight to Taegan's five one. Where Taegan is short and curvy, Cadhla is tall and lean. However, where Taegan brings her own light with her, Cadhla leaves you annoyed when she walks away, making you dread the next time she enters your presence.

"I'm actually heading up to the office to do some paperwork. Maybe some other time."

What I don't tell her is that I plan to find her replacement soon. I don't need to see what she's learned because I'm going to have a new female fighter, even if it kills me.

Cadhla doesn't have the speed or technique needed to move through the competition in the tournaments. Granted, we can make up for her lack of scoring, but if I had a stronger fighter in her category, we could easily take it all.

She's the weakest link and I can't afford that this time around. Instead of getting into a conversation that will go nowhere, I keep moving upstairs, ignoring Cadhla's spattering as she tries to get my attention.

Once upstairs, I enter my office to find Taegan at my desk. I close the door behind me and go to flop down on the couch. My thoughts go to Logan and Brooklyn. This is where they usually sit when they stop by to check on me.

It feels like it's been forever since Logan has been here. So much has changed in the last year. I can't help but feel like this is only the beginning.

"What's on yer mind, Irish?" Taegan asks as I sit lost in my thoughts.

I smile at the nickname she uses for me. I once asked why and she told me it's so I remember who I am, so I never allow what happened all those years ago to happen again.

"Nothing. What's going on with you? What are you doing up here?"

Taegan has not only become my closest friend, but she's also become like a part of the family—another big sister. When I took over this place, she became my personal assistant. She has stepped in a lot with Logan gone.

We all trust her. However, she understands Kate and Connie wouldn't hesitate to make her disappear if she ever crossed us—my best friend or not.

"I finished the spreadsheets and sent them over to Jamie. Connie called looking for ya. She mentioned ya helping with the clubs. I offered to help out where I could. I'm on party-girl duty," she says and wiggles her brows.

I groan. Connie took off this morning to join Kate. I'll be stepping in to help cover for her and give my brothers a hand where they need me. I'm grateful for any help I can get. Once again, Taegan is a lifesaver.

"Grand. I hate doing that shit."

Taegan laughs. She already knows how much I hate it when I'm asked to handle the task. It's annoying.

Connie and Brooklyn like to hire fresh-faced girls to attend the clubs. Not the bottle-service girls, but girls who party with the patrons and keep them all happy and partying.

"I don't know why ya hate it so much. Maybe ya'll find a nice girl yer willing to date. Then ya won't be so grumpy."

"You're my best friend, not my matchmaker. Mind your business."

"Ya don't have to be mean. I worry about ya. What are ya going to do if ya go back home and she's not there? All this time ya've been wasting—"

"Don't." I cut her off. "I'm going to find her. That's the only option."

She sighs. "Fine. Yer love life is none of my business. How was Cali?"

I furrow my brows as the girl from that bar comes to mind. I haven't been able to shake her from my mind. A part of me wishes I had followed her out or tried harder to find her after the fight.

Scrubbing my hand over my face, I then blow out a long breath. That wasn't Ciara and I would have only been disappointed. My focus needs to be on the tournaments so I can head home, where she can find me.

"It didn't work out for Felix like he wanted," I reply.

"She said no?" Taegan asks with a look of confusion on her face.

She knows Kaye. We all saw how much she's in love with Felix. If she had said no, that would have been a shock to us all.

"No, it's a long story. He never got to ask."

"Oh, I'm sorry to hear that. How was our little buddy?"

"Dae-Dae is good."

A knock comes at the office door and Taegan groans and rolls her eyes. We both already know who it is. I should have known Cadhla wasn't going to catch a hint.

"Just toss the bitch already," Taegan mutters under her breath.

"I'll be focused on making that happen soon."

"Grand. I don't do stupid well and she's a fucking melter if I ever saw one. Pure eejit."

I stifle a laugh and shake my head. "You want to order us some lunch? It's my treat."

"Ya know the answer to that. When do I turn down food? Especially when I don't have to pay."

CHAPTER ELEVEN

Please Reschedule

Ciara

A year and two months later ...

Vega has done so much for us in the last year. The apartment she set us up in is so over the top. I had a hard time accepting everything at first. It was all too much.

I thought we were going to have a normal three-bedroom apartment in a normal building. Not a luxury apartment in a high-rise building with a doorman, amenities, and all. I truly wake up each morning feeling like I've been dropped in the middle of a fairy tale.

It was only after we became friends that it became easier to be okay with everything. After having Theo offer me so much only to make me and Ciarán feel like we owed our existence to him, I refuse to be in debt to anyone like that ever again. It was hard to accept all of Daliah's help when we arrived in San Diego.

If not for having my little brother with me, I wouldn't have accepted so much. I didn't want to push my luck to believe I've yet again run into a fairy godfamily who would turn everything into roses and diamonds.

However, Vega has been just that. She's a boss in her own right and takes care of those she calls family. I didn't know she would be so involved, but she hangs out at the apartment all the time. I do believe Ciarán has a crush on her.

I've been working at a club as a bottle girl for the last fourteen months. It's good money and I get paid under the table, but the place was shut down last week. The owner hasn't said if or when they're going to open back up.

I have Ciarán's tuition, and his birthday is coming. He's going to be twelve this year and the kid has big wishes. Wishes that my jobless ass needs some money coming in to make come true.

I refuse to go to Vega again. I will find something on my own. I already have her to thank for getting me documents in the name Ariel Norwood. She was also able to get Ciarán legit-looking documents for school too.

I didn't need them for my old job, but I'm grateful to have them now. That has led me here for this job interview. I'm nervous as hell.

I need to get this job to pay this month's tuition. I could enroll him in public school, but he won't have the same opportunities. The whole point was to bring him here to give him better. He already loves his new school and the classes they offer.

He did so well last year. I was proud of him for making new friends so fast. I can't fail him now. I take a deep breath to calm my nerves.

I can do this. It's for Ciarán.

"Ariel Norwood?"

I look up at the receptionist who just called my name. She's looking at me expectantly. Right as I stand from my seat, my phone rings.

I can't ignore it. It could be about my little brother. As I look down at my phone, I find a number I don't know. I hold up a hand to the receptionist, causing her to roll her eyes at me.

I bite my lip and move quickly to the corner to answer the call. This couldn't be worse timing. I feel like I've already lost the job.

"Hello?"

"Hi. I have a young lad here who says yer his sister. He came in with a group of kids, but they left him, and it seems they took his money, and he doesn't know how to get back home," a woman with an Irish accent says.

"Oh my God. Where are you? Where is he?"

"We're in Brooklyn. I'm calling from the Roaring Irish gym. My name is Taegan. I'll keep the lad with me until ya arrive to collect him."

"Can I speak to him?"

"Hey, love. Yer sister wants to talk to ya."

"Hello," Ciarán nearly whispers.

"What the hell, Ciarán. What's going on?"

"I wanted to check this place out. A few of the guys from school said they knew how to get here. We had a substitute during third period.

"So we cut and came to Brooklyn to the gym. Troy said he was hungry. I was watching one of the matches and didn't want to leave. The guys told me to give them money, and they would bring me something to eat.

"I wasn't paying attention. I told him to get the money from my backpack. When they didn't come back for me, I found my wallet empty. I have no idea how to get back home. I'm so sorry, Cee. Please come get me," he says, sounding so scared.

"I'm on my way. Don't leave, Ciarán. I'm coming for you."

I hang up and rush over to the receptionist. My heart sinks because I'm about to blow the job completely. However, I still say something just in case.

"Hi. I'm so sorry. I have a family emergency, and I'll need to reschedule this interview."

She paints on a smile, although I can feel the annoyance coming off her. "I will make a note in your file and someone will be in contact with you if the position isn't filled."

"Thank you."

Without another word, I turn and rush from the office. As I make my way from the building, I pull up the address for the Roaring Irish gym. I'm going to kill Ciarán.

I told him I didn't want to rush things. Yes, I missed the tournaments once again. I couldn't make it happen last year with all the changes and moving here to New York.

I had planned to go to the gym to check it out in person when I was ready. I didn't take Vega up on the offer to check out the underground scene.

For now, I'm trying to avoid that route. I've been training, but I haven't set my mind to finding a gym to compete with. Vega has told me to let her know when I want to step into her underground ring if I change my mind.

"Grr."

Dylan

"You're awesome, bro. My sister is one of the best fighters I've ever seen. You kind of remind me of her. She's as good a boxer as she is an MMA fighter."

I look up from untaping my hands to find Taegan with a young kid by her side. He has a look of awe on his face. Right away, something about him seems familiar to me.

It has to be the brown face and green-gray eyes. I shake my thoughts off quickly. Every brown face with green-gray eyes shouldn't trigger thoughts of her. It's not common, but it's not something I've never seen before outside of her.

"Oh yeah? What makes you say that?" I ask with a smile.

He shrugs. "Most who try to maintain the two sports have tells, like getting too low when boxing or not having a strong enough stance. They take time to adjust between the styles. You remind me of Cee … um, Ariel."

"Sounds like you know a thing or two. Do you fight?"

A blush comes to his cheeks, and he reaches for the back of his neck. "Nah. Not anymore. It's just you were able to step right into the ring for the bout you were in.

"I haven't seen that in many other fighters and I've been around a gym since I was a baby. If I had a trainer like you, I think I would still fight," he says.

I pull a face and nod my head. He's right. I do tend to switch between the sports with ease. When I thought I would someday have to box Ciara's dad, I made sure not to lose my skills as a boxer, although I love MMA.

I've formed the habit of separating the two, so I don't show weakness in either. Today I worked with Carter. He's a boxer.

I'm getting him ready for a bout that's coming up next month. Before that, I had been working with David to clean up his groundwork.

"Are you here to train? We're always looking for young new talent."

"Actually, I came to check out your female fighters. I was hoping to see what my sister would be up against and if this gym would be a fit for her," he says.

"Aye, the kid came in with a few lads, but they ditched him and took his money. He's pretty new to the city, seems they took him for a wee bit of a ride as a welcome. Says he lives uptown but doesn't know how to get back. His sister is on the way," Taegan says.

"Not entirely new. It's been over a year, but this is my first time in Brooklyn," the kid whispers as he hangs his head.

My blood begins to boil. I hate bullies. Especially bullies who like to take others' money. I stand and round the desk.

"How about you show me what you've got while we wait for your sister. Boxer or MMA?"

"That sounds cool. I was a boxer."

"Were you any good?"

"Cee … Um, Ariel. That's my sister. She says I'm pretty good. I just need dedication and consistency.

"My trainer was my stepdad. He was an asshole. He made me hate training. My sister hasn't made me train since we … um, left."

I knit my brows, hearing this kid say a whole lot that hasn't left his lips. He actually looks sad about not training anymore. I grab my gloves and nod for him to follow me downstairs.

Taegan moves to take my seat behind the desk, no doubt going to finish up the work I didn't get done earlier before I started my workouts downstairs. I keep my eyes on the kid.

He's pretty tall. His hair is cut in low brown curls. If I'm honest, he looks like he could be Ciara's brother. It's the nose and the lips.

"Hey, kid. How old are you?" I ask as we move down the steps.

"I turn twelve next week."

I nod my head as I do the math in my head. Cadlha heads right for me as we get down to the gym, breaking right into my thoughts. I hold a hand up and take a step back as she tries to step into my space.

"Dylan, I was hoping to see ya today. I thought ya might be gone by now. Do ya want to get a bite to eat tonight with me?" she sings as she bats her lashes at me.

I had planned to leave. I was on my way out when Taegan and the kid walked into my office. I try to be gone before Cadlha comes in on Thursdays and Fridays. That or I remain out of sight until I know she's gone.

"I love you guys' accents around here," the kid says with a huge smile on his lips.

"You don't know anyone with an Irish accent?" I ask, thinking of Ciara's heavy accent when we were little.

If this kid were her brother, he would surely have been around one all the time. Damn, I think I'm losing my mind.

"Nope. Miss Taegan is the first person I've ever met with one."

I chuckle. "Don't let her hear you call her that."

"Who's this?" Cadlha asks.

"A friend. I'm busy. I'll talk to you later. Come on, I have a pair of gloves for you over here," I turn to say to the kid.

Ignoring Cadlha, we grab the gloves, and I tape his hands then mine before we climb into the ring. I'm immediately impressed.

He's good. He reminds me of myself in the beginning. I had been good when Ciara's dad started me out. I got better after coming to America.

"Keep your hands up. That's it. We could work on your stamina, but you have the basics. Great footwork, kid," I coach as we've been sparring for a while.

"You would be willing to work with me?" he says with wide eyes.

"I'll need to meet your guardian, and you'd have to join the gym, but sure. I have an opening." I shrug.

"Cool, you can meet my sister when she arrives. I'll ask her if it's okay."

A glance at the clock tells me an hour has gone by. Suddenly, the air is sucked right out of the gym. I turn to look toward the door and nearly stumble back.

In walks the most gorgeous girl I've ever seen. She's dressed in a pink pencil skirt and a white, silky-looking sleeveless blouse. Her dark hair is curled into deep waves that are layered, causing it to flow and bounce around her pretty face.

She looks around the gym frantically until her gaze lands on the kid in the ring with me. Relief comes over her face. My heart is hammering so fast I think it may give out on me.

"Ciarán," she breathes as she rushes to the side of the ring.

The kid whips around, causing me to knit my brows. He told me his name was Chris. Although he did stutter when saying it, as if he was going to say something else.

My mouth falls open as I look down at the gorgeous girl who must be his sister. She's a tiny little thing; the black patent leather heels on her feet only help her a little in the height department, even though they look to be pretty high.

However, her height isn't the reason I'm standing here in shock. It's her. It has to be. Ciara has just walked right into my gym.

CHAPTER TWELVE

Nagging Feeling

Ciara

I could kill my little brother in this moment. The Uber to get here cost me almost two hundred bucks. I didn't want to risk getting lost on the subway. Besides, these heels weren't meant for any of that.

So not only did I miss out on an interview to get a really good-paying job. I'm out two hundred bucks, which I could definitely use at this point. However, what pisses me off is the fact that I've walked in here and he's dancing around in the ring with a smile on his face like he hasn't a care in the world. The little stinker.

"Ciarán," I breathe as I rush to the side of the ring.

He turns to look at me and his smile grows. My heart pangs. I never thought I would see him look so happy with a pair of gloves on while standing in a ring.

The guy he's been sparring with seems to stumble forward, placing a gloved hand on Ciarán's shoulder as if he's using my brother to help keep himself upright. He's one tall guy.

He's towering well over Ciarán. He's nicely built as well. His hair is damp, causing it to look a lot darker than I think it truly is. He's a blond.

A smile comes to his face as he looks down at me and I'm thrown back in time. I plant my hands against the mat of the ring to keep myself on my feet. Ciarán is talking excitedly, but I can't hear a word of what he's saying.

"Come on, Ciara. Me ma promised us ice cream after school. We need to get there before everyone else eats it all. We'll take the shortcut over the hill and get there first."

"Ach, Dylan, me wee legs are too small to carry me over that hill. We'll be sure to miss out on the ice cream if we go that way, we will."

He smiles at me and hands me his backpack, gesturing for me to put it on. The sunlight dances in his golden locks as his blue eyes twinkle back at me.

"Aye, that's why yer going to get on me back. I'll carry ya over."

"Don't drop me," I whisper.

"Never, I'll always protect ya. Promise."

"Cee, Cee, are you okay?" Ciarán's worried voice pulls me back to the present.

"Is she all right?" The big dude asks as he looks at me with panic in his eyes.

I reach to hold my aching head. I'm so confused. Was that a memory from before the accident? The boy … that was the boy from the dreams and the sketches.

"She gets headaches sometimes when she has memories from before the accident." I hear Ciarán say.

"Accident?"

"Yeah, when I was a baby, she jumped out of her seat to cover me with her body to keep me safe. We survived, but our mom didn't. However, Cee lost her memory."

Anger fills me as my little brother says too much, causing my head to throb violently. I still can't speak. I pinch my eyes closed, trying to breathe and not pass out.

"Is she going to be okay? Should I call for help?"

"No, no. It usually passes."

The next thing I know, I'm scooped off my feet into strong, warm arms. I melt into the safest feeling I've ever had. He presses a kiss to my temple, causing me to sag further into his warmth.

"I've got you," he murmurs.

His words and voice shoot straight to my core. My head hurts so bad, I can only wrap my arms around his neck and hold on as he moves with me in his embrace.

I feel more than see that we're moving up a flight of stairs. He tightens his arms around me possessively. His warm breath continues to fan my skin.

"Oh my God, is she okay? Should I call EMS?"

I recognize the voice as the woman from the phone, Taegan. I can't open my eyes to see what she looks like, but that accent is as thick as it was over the phone, if not more so. I'm trying my best to will the pain away.

"No. Her brother says it will pass," the guy carrying me says.

He lowers into a seat and places me in his lap. My skin tingles as he brushes my hair from my face and palms my cheek. Slowly, I open my eyes.

I gasp as I look into the same eyes I've drawn hundreds of times. He smiles at me and places his forehead to mine as he holds my face between his warm, tape-covered palms.

"*Is tusa atá ann. Fuair mé thú faoi dheireadh, mo chroí, mo ghrá. Táim anseo. Coinneoidh mé slán thú, tabharfaidh mé aire duit. Ní chaillfidh mé thú arís choíche,*" he breathes.

He's not speaking English, but in the back of my mind, I know I should understand him. A gasp fills the room, causing me to turn. My gaze lands on a tiny redhead who's watching us.

"Shut the fuck up. Ya have to be fucking kidding me. It's her? Jesus, Mary, Joseph, what are the chances she's walked right into yer gym?" she says in awe.

"What's going on? Cee, should I call Miss Vega or Miss Daliah?"

"Ciarán, no. I'm fine. Please stop talking. Um, thank you," I say as I stand from this guy's lap.

"Ciara, wait," he says, freezing me in my tracks.

I haven't told anyone about that name. I close my eyes and try to latch onto what my mind is telling me he said.

It's you. I've finally found you, my heart, my love. I'm here. I'll keep you safe, I will take care of you. I'm never going to lose you again.

"Gaelic. You're speaking Gaelic. I know Gaelic?"

I shake my head as if to clear it. In that memory, I had an accent like he did. Where did my accent come from?

Why did Theo make sure I lost mine? He could never tell me how I got it. He only corrected it until it was all but gone.

He stands and towers over me, placing his hand on my hip to draw me closer to him. I tilt my head back and look up into his familiar blue eyes. I place my palms against his abs and bite my lip.

"Yes, you know Gaelic. You don't remember? You don't remember me?"

"I don't know," I whisper. "I'm sorry. Thank you for looking after my brother and for your help. I need to go."

I grab Ciarán by the arm and drag him with me as I race from the office we're standing in. My head is still throbbing a bit, but I can at least see where I'm going.

"Hey. Hey, love. Wait. Ach, please, hold on."

I freeze as we get to the bottom of the stairs, but I don't turn around to face her. I don't know this girl or that guy back there who seems to know me. She places her hand on my arm, causing me to turn slightly.

"I'm Taegan. We spoke earlier."

I nod. She licks her lips and her brows furrow on her pretty face. She and I are probably the same height without my heels on.

"Listen, ya owe me nothing and ya don't know me from a can of paint, but that big lad back there has been my best friend since high school and there's only two things in this world more important to him than me and this gym. That's his family and you.

"Yer the Ciara Walsh he's been trying to get back to Ireland to find since he was a young lad. He's been trying to get back to ya for most of his life." She holds up her hands as I go to cut her off. "Hold on, love. I get it. Something has happened to keep ya from remembering him.

"I want ya to take me card. If ya need anything and I do mean anything. Ya give me a call."

I take the card and read it: Taegan Quinn, Executive Assistant. I look back up at her.

"Why?"

She tilts her head and studies me closely. She's a pretty girl. With me out of the way, she could have him all to herself if she's so important to him.

She scoffs. "Aye, ya think if I get rid of ya, I can have him all to me self. Not so much, love. Irish is mad as a box of frogs for ya."

"Irish?"

"Aye, it's my nickname for him. The only reason he's not chasing after ya now is because he's in shock. I love the big lad, but more like a little brother than anything else.

"I've dated an O'Brien once. It's not for me. I do better as their friend and employee. This is selfish of me to tell the truth.

"He's going to have me track ya down once he snaps out of it. I'm great at my job, so I'm getting ahead of things. Yer young lad says yer newish to the city. Maybe we can help. If not, at least ya know ya have people here.

"Come on, lass," she says as she smiles and rolls her eyes playfully. "I've got yer back. Keep the card. Call me when ya realize ya want to know everything Irish knows about ya," she says in her singsong way of speaking.

I lick my lips and nod. She's an observant one. So much so, I feel like I need to leave before she sees too much.

I'm not processing much properly. I need to get away before this comes back to bite me. They know a name I only learned after stealing my documents to go on the run.

Red flags go off in my head and I decide that for now, I need to run. Shoving the card into my pocket, I grab Ciarán's hand and take off.

"Hope to see ya again, Chris. Yer welcome back anytime," she calls after us.

Another redhead bumps into me as we rush out. My first thought is to put her on her ass, but my throbbing head saves her. I murmur an apology and keep going until we're out of this place.

Dylan

I sit in my apartment staring into space after taking a shower. I left the gym right after Taegan returned to my office to find me standing in the same spot in shock. I had run after Ciara and the kid, but they were gone.

Ciarán.

I like him. He's smart and he'll be a good boxer if he keeps at it. Now that I know for sure who he is, I can see so much of Ciara and her dad in him.

She doesn't remember me? She was in an accident. That's how her mother was killed.

In my world, there are no coincidences. As the shock wears off, my mind begins to spin and my heart races. Chris called her Ariel and she called him Ciarán. Clearly they're hiding from something or someone.

I can't help wondering if they're in danger because of Cole. I snap out of my fog and grab my phone to call my brother and get some answers. I need to know what I'm dealing with here.

"What about ye, little brother?" Cole answers on the second ring.

"I found her. Some shit isn't right though. Do you think whatever you triggered with Deja could be a problem for her?"

"No, I don't think so. Deja's situation is complicated. Tell me where she is and I'll put some guys on her," Brooklyn replies.

"No, I've got her. I'll take care of her."

"Dylan, there's still a lot ya need to know. It's a complicated situation. I'm trying to hold this all off until Logan returns."

"It's already been over two years. How much closer are we to getting him home?"

"I don't have an answer for ya there either. I'm doing the best I can. For now, DJ needs to stay where she is, and we should keep a close eye on Ciara.

"I won't tell them we've found her yet. I'm still trying to figure out who I can really trust."

"Aye, ya need to be sure because when it comes to her, I'm taking heads off first and asking questions later," I bite out.

"Ach, what aren't ya telling me, Dyl? I can hear the missing pieces. Talk to me. I need to know what's going on?"

I run a hand through my hair and start from the beginning. I tell him everything I think I know. I still have a few questions.

"Aye, I don't think yer wrong. With all I've learned, I wouldn't doubt that the accident wasn't an accident at all. Ach, I'll talk to Felix and see what he can dig up. Did the kid mention the stepfather's name at all?"

"No, he never did. She shut him down when she was able to shake the headache or whatever it was. He did mention a Miss Vega."

"Ya said they're staying uptown. Do ya think he was talking about Vega Stratton?"

"Could be. I'd feel a hell of a lot better if he was. Something about all of this doesn't sit right with me. Where has she been all these years and why is she here now?"

"Aye, I'm on it, Dyl. I promise. I'm not losing anyone else, not like Raven. We'll figure this out and keep her safe. Call me if ya learn anything else."

"That's it? Yer not going to tell me anything else?" I seethe.

"In time, Dylan. Everything will happen in time. Keep yer friend safe and stay yer ass out of Ireland."

I frown. I should have known he or Logan would have figured me out. That or my da would. I ball my fists in frustration.

My front door opens and Taegan strolls in. As my assistant, she has a key to all my places. It's not unusual for her to let herself in.

"Listen, I'll talk to you later," I say to Brooklyn.

"I love ya, Dyl. I'm taking care of things. When Logan gets home, it will all make sense."

"I love you too, bro."

Taegan walks over and tosses a file on the coffee table. I narrow my eyes at it then look at her. She turns and heads into the kitchen to grab a couple of tumblers and a bottle of whiskey.

"What's this?" I ask as I pick up the file.

She sighs as she sits down and pours two glasses, handing me one. I don't bother to take a sip as the file in my hand now has my full attention. I flip through the pages, reading the information.

"I figured ya would want that. She's going by Ariel Norwood. The kid goes by Chris Norwood, but I'm sure ya heard her call him Ciarán.

"He's attending one of those uppity private schools uptown. Vega Stratton put the word out over a year ago. Ariel Norwood and a Daliah Gibson are under her protection, but there's something I found I don't think yer going to like," she says cautiously.

"And that is?"

"Vega has set up an exhibition for a week from tonight. Word is, she has a new female fighter she's looking to showcase. Ya saw Ciara. She looks like a shorter version of Jade Cargill without the blonde hair. I'll bet my two front teeth she's the new fighter."

CHAPTER THIRTEEN

Time to Think

Ciara

"What does this all mean?" I murmur to myself as I pace my room.

Now that I have some time and space between me and that gym, everything is crashing down on me. I was able to take a hot shower, and my head feels a hundred percent better. Kind of like a cloud has been lifted, allowing me to think.

Now that I can think clearly, I have so many questions, just as Taegan said I would. However, I don't know if it's safe to get them from her or her boss. I have no idea where I need to start with so much floating through my head.

"This is crazy. Start with the most important stuff first, Cee."

I nod my head at my thoughts. That would be the best thing to do. Maybe I can figure something out from there.

First off, how do I know him? How does he know me? What happened to the accents from my memory?

I lost my memory around nine years old. Why would a boy I knew at eight or nine call me his love, his heart? Who is that guy?

I know Gaelic. I didn't just know his words; I believe I could have replied if I tried. I get the feeling I wasn't just born in Ireland; I once lived there, but when and how did I get to Seattle?

Did I come to America with my dad? I have all these questions and I'm not sure going back to Roaring Irish will answer any of them. I don't even know if that place is safe for me.

"But it's all you've got for now," I sigh.

I pace out of my room and get the card from my purse, where I put it after we got into an Uber once I got us away from the gym. Staring at the card, I try to figure out my next move. My sketchbook catches my attention on the table where my purse is sitting.

I pick it up and flip through it. Stopping on one of the many drawings of the boy from my dreams, I stare down at the page. Those eyes, they're the same. I squint my eyes as if I can see the man from earlier on the page if I stare long enough.

"Hey you," Daliah sings from behind me, causing me to jump and shut the book.

She wasn't home when we arrived. I was sort of grateful for that. I needed time to myself to think.

"Hey. How was work?"

"Awesome. I don't know why you won't allow Vega to help you get a new gig." She shakes her head. "How was the interview?"

"Didn't happen. Ciarán got himself into some trouble and I had to bail to get to him."

"Oh no. Well, I do have some good news. Vega wanted me to tell you to call her. She has something for you."

I pull a face and narrow my eyes at her.

"Don't look at me like that. It's not what you think. Call her."

"Fine, I will."

"I'll order us something for dinner. Chinese good with you?"

"Yeah, sure. Thanks."

Suddenly, I'm starving. First, I go to look for Ciarán. We need to have a talk.

I'm still mad at him. Not only did he cost me that job, but I'm out four hundred dollars in Ubers. His little butt cut school, and he put himself in unnecessary danger.

Not to mention, he said way too much. There's no telling what he might have said before I got there. I curse under my breath as I realize we both called each other by our real names.

I had been in such a panic. A million scenarios filled my head on the ride over to the gym. I questioned all my decisions in the last two and a half years.

"What were you thinking?" I ask as I walk up behind Ciarán as he sits at his desk in his room.

"That gym is so cool. The vibe is everything. They don't treat their fighters like slaves or trash," he says excitedly.

"Ciarán, that's not what I asked you. What in the world were you thinking cutting school?"

He drops his head and looks into his lap. "Ever since I saw their gym online, I had this feeling like that's where you need to be. You said you were thinking about fighting for Miss Vega. She's awesome, but my gut is telling me Roaring Irish is where you should be.

"I just wanted to take a look at the place and see if it had a positive vibe. It does. Dylan and Taegan are so cool. Dylan says he'll train me if I join the gym.

"Look, I've been checking out their membership fees. I added the cost to our spreadsheet. Please, Cee. This is all I want for my birthday. We can forget the new drone.

"Maybe I can get that for Christmas. Dylan didn't yell at me once. He allowed me to fight without making me feel small," he says with pleading eyes.

I scoff. "You think you're getting something for your birthday after what you pulled today?"

The light leaves his eyes and his shoulders sag. I really should put him on punishment, but this is the first time I've seen him so excited to box. Finding out our father was a boxer has made me feel closer to him somehow.

If Ciarán can make that same connection, I don't want to take that from him. I move closer to him and look at his computer screen. Sure enough, he has our shared spreadsheet open.

I chew on my lip as I look at all the things he needs and wants. That four hundred dollars was a huge loss. The drone has already come off the list if I can't find a job.

I sigh and place my hands on his shoulders. "You're grounded until your birthday. We'll talk about you boxing after that. If you ever cut school again, the drone, boxing, and that new computer are all off the table. Am I understood?"

"Yes, I'm sorry."

"Go shower. Daliah ordered Chinese," I say and kiss the top of his head.

"I have a good feeling about the gym. You should go back and see about training there too."

"I've got this. You focus on school and your grades."

I turn and head to get my phone so I can call Vega. Hopefully she has something to say that will put me in a better mood. This day has been insane.

CHAPTER FOURTEEN

Quick Fists

Ciara

"What can I do? What do you need?" Daliah asks nervously.

"You look like you're about to puke. You should probably stop drinking and you probably should have stayed home with Ciarán. A sitter was a waste of money," I chuckle.

She sticks her tongue out at me. I laugh and shake my head as I work on loosening my body up. The music from the arena is thumping through the walls.

From what I've seen, Vega knows how to throw an event. This place is packed and jumping. I can't say I'm surprised.

Ten grand per fight and another twenty when I pull off the win. Vega didn't have to ask me twice. When I made the call to her, she had already set this event up, knowing I needed the money.

I'm slated for two bouts tonight. Vega didn't think I would be up to fighting two men in one night. I told her to bring them on. I'm not scared.

Vega doesn't have many female fighters. She couldn't bring anyone in who wanted a match with me on such short notice. I would have had to wait two months for her to bring in some chick from Miami.

Not to mention, I would have made only half the money. The price is doubled because I'm fighting men. No problem, I do this shit in my sleep.

I'm here to win. I'll have more than enough to stash and take care of Ciarán's birthday gifts and tuition. He's been on his best behavior all week. His birthday is tomorrow.

I still don't know how I feel about the Roaring Irish gym, but I plan to take him there in the morning to join the gym and take my own look around. If I see that guy and get to ask him questions, that's a plus. I've been trying my best not to think about him.

"Ariel, you're up," Dimitri calls into the room.

I roll my shoulders back then move my head from side to side. Bumping my knuckles together, I start out for my first match. Daliah follows nervously behind me. She's never seen me in an actual match.

As we make our way out to the makeshift ring, the song changes to "Simon Says" by Pharoahe Monch. The beat fills my chest, and a smile comes to my lips. I'm getting in the zone.

However, one glance toward the crowd and I stumble a little. As I'm walking to the ring, the big blond from Roaring Irish walks in with the little redhead. This dude has an aura all his own.

It's like his presence takes over the arena. He moves with purpose to a seat in the front row. I now feel like the music is a soundtrack for him.

He moves like he's in step with the thumping beat. People even part to accommodate his movements. Like a king has arrived and they all know this.

I shake off my shock and focus on what I'm here for. The ring isn't so much a ring, but a circle they've made filled with dirt. I can handle this. I've fought in similar settings.

I lock eyes with the guy already waiting in the ring. He's about five seven, give or take. I'd put him at two fifty, two hundred and thirty-five pounds.

He probably doesn't expect my speed or power. I'm sure he's going to come at me with force. Big mistake.

I can see it in his eyes. He looks almost bored and cocksure he's going to take this match. I grin as I mentally list at least ten ways to take him down in the first round.

We're given the rules, and we bump fists. That's when everything else fades. Just as I thought, he rushes me with force, but I'm much faster than he is. Using his momentum, I rock him with a punch combination and move out of his reach before he can react.

While he's dazed a bit, I throw another combination. I rock his head so hard, it snaps to the side and blood flies from his mouth. I don't hesitate.

I take his legs out with a double leg takedown and get him to the ground. He doesn't stand a chance as I place him in an anaconda choke so fast the ref even looks shocked before he calls the match as this guy taps out.

I get to my feet and lock eyes with the blond giant as he stares back at me. I allow myself to take him in this time. He's really handsome. The blond quiff suits him. It lends to the air he has about him.

A smile comes to his lips as he continues to gaze at me, drawing my eyes to his sensual-looking mouth. I'm dressed in a sports bra and shorts, but the way he runs his gaze over me makes me feel like I'm standing here completely naked.

I look away as butterflies fill my belly. I have another fight tonight. I need to keep my head in the game. I release a breath and shake my hands out.

Turning, I head back to the dressing room to await my next match. I feel good. Adrenaline is coursing through my veins and I'm hyped for the next fight.

"That was great," Vega says with a smile on her lips as I go to walk past her, not seeing her there at first.

"Thanks."

"Mitch is a lot bigger than Frank and he's a lot more skilled. Watch your back with him. Take a breath, there are three fights before your next one."

I nod at her and keep moving. Back in Seattle, I've gone from one fight to another. I already know I need to keep moving without tiring myself out.

"Wow, you and Ciarán weren't bullshitting. You were awesome out there," Daliah says as we enter the dressing room.

"You've been one of my biggest cheerleaders. Why do you sound so shocked now?"

"Girl, I'll always be in your corner. If you say you can fart rainbows, I'm going to say that shit is fantastic. I don't need to see it.

"But now that I've seen you in action, I'm going to scream that shit to anyone who will listen. You're fucking badass."

I chuckle and shake my head. It feels good to have her in my corner. Theo would be up my butt about finishing the dude off so fast.

But he's not here and that's already thirty grand you don't have to share.

Dylan

Taegan nailed it. Ciara does look a lot like Jade Cargill. She's built like her and has similar facial features. Although Ciara can't be much more than five feet tall.

I may have had a growth spurt that took me well over six feet, but my childhood friend has remained small. She's small, but she hits hard as hell. I winced every time she hit Frank.

Frank isn't a bad fighter. I've been in the ring with him before. However, he underestimated Ciara, and she kicked his ass. She's fast as fuck.

"I know that look. Cadlha can kiss her ass goodbye. Thank the Lord," Taegan sings from the seat beside me.

"She's good. Really good. I'd be crazy not to be interested."

"Aye, but are ya talking about interested in her as a fighter or interested in getting her beneath ya outside of the ring?"

"*Taegan,*" I drag out.

"Ya think I don't have eyes on me? I saw the way ya were just eye fucking her."

"When does Olly get back?"

"Ach, shut yer gub. Ya know how much I miss him." She pouts.

I place my arm around her shoulders and pull her into me. I kiss the top of her head and give her a squeeze. Olly is a Marine. Taegan fell head over heels for him when he came into the gym looking for a place to work out.

He's good to her. That's all I ask for. My best friend deserves the world.

The next match starts, and we fall silent to watch. I only came to watch Ciara's fights. I'm here to watch her back. It's a known fact that Vega's underground fights can get gritty.

It's not often that females other than Vega fight here. I was livid when Taegan told me Ciara would be fighting tonight. Nine times out of ten, she wouldn't be fighting a female fighter.

When we arrived, I learned she was to fight Frank and Murder Mitch. I wasn't concerned with Funky Frank. One whiff of him and I knew she would make quick work of the fight.

Murder Mitch, on the other hand, is the one I plan to keep an eye on. He's known to always be on some bullshit. Vega is testing Ciara to see if she can handle this.

This is her family's business. I get the precaution and why she's done things this way, but it doesn't mean I like it. I'm here to shut this shit down if things look sideways.

I sit bored through the next three fights. I nearly fall asleep as we wait for them to be over. The arena becomes lively when it's announced Ariel and Mitch will be next up.

Everyone begins to call out bets, still doubting Ciara as they did in the last match. I have faith in my girl. I'll fucking kill Mitch if anything happens to her.

"Jesus, Mary, Joseph, I forgot how big this motherfucker is. Are ya sure ya don't want to step in now?"

"I think she'll be fine. Did you hear how hard she hits? Mitch will fold under a few body shots. She just needs to stay clear of his fists. She's faster than he is."

"Ach, I pray yer right."

The fight starts and my focus is locked in. Just as I said, Ciara is much faster than Mitch. She's weaving around him and his punches like a pro. Her body shots take the wind right out of him, which I'm sure he wasn't expecting.

Mitch allows his anger to get the best of him. Ciara takes advantage of that and runs at him, leaping in the air. She wraps her legs around his neck and uses her body to toss his big ass to the ground. She then begins to punch his head.

I sit forward in my seat. Mitch goes to make a move, but Ciara rolls away just in time. They both get to their feet and Mitch swings, trying to take her head off.

Ciara dips back out of the way, then spins and places a kick right in those ribs she tenderized earlier. Mitch folds into himself, looking like she's knocked the wind right out of him.

"The fuck?" I breathe as I stand to my feet.

Ciara has placed Mitch in an ankle lock so fast I'm still trying to figure out what happened. How did I miss her taking him down to the ground? Fuck, she's fast.

"Yeah," Taegan roars as she stands and throws her fists in the air.

I fold my arms across my chest and smile proudly. Ciara gets to her feet with her chest heaving. She's announced as the winner as the crowd goes crazy.

My smile fades as I see the shit Mitch is about to pull. Ciara has her back to him and he's getting ready to swing for her head. I leap over the little barrier and rush to put him on his ass before the blow can connect.

In my rush, I knock Ciara over. With Mitch knocked out cold, I turn to look down at my girl. She looks confused and a bit dazed.

I squat to help her sit up. "Hey, baby. You okay?" I ask as I cup her face.

"Dylan?" she breathes as she knits her brows.

I smile as I hear my name come from her lips. There's something in the way she says it, as if she remembers me this time. I want to take her pretty lips in a kiss, but I restrain myself and wink.

CHAPTER FIFTEEN

Take You Home

Ciara

"You ready to go?"

I look up from my duffel bag and find Dylan standing in the doorway watching me. I nod my head and lick my lips. I'm still trying to figure out what the fuck happened since winning that last match.

One minute I was fist pumping as I was called as the winner. The next I was careened into the ground. As I hit my head, it was like my memory was jogged. Images of Dylan filled my head on a loop.

A sense of safety filled me. I know for a fact he's someone I can trust. I used to have so much trust and love for him. He was my friend. However, I still don't know what happened to take that all away from me.

"Um, yeah, Daliah went to the bathroom. I'll be ready when she gets back. I have to collect the purse," I reply.

He snorts. "You think I'd let you collect all that money with the vultures in here tonight? Dimitri and Nashawn will meet us at the back door, where my car is waiting."

"Why?"

He tilts his head as he smiles at me. Those stupid butterflies start all over again. I clench my fists at my sides.

"Why am I looking out for you? It's what I do. I've always protected you."

"What happened? How do you know me?"

"Let me get you out of here and I'll answer anything you want. Are you hungry?"

"Yeah, I could eat, but I need to get home. Ciarán is with a sitter. His birthday is tomorrow. I should get home."

"We can order something when we get there."

"Huh?"

"I'm taking you home. This is New York, baby. You should always have security when transporting purses from events like this.

"It's a known fact that Vega pays in cash and all the fighters walk with something. You're a target tonight."

"Thanks, but you don't have to. I'll be fine. I'll see you tomorrow at your gym. Ciarán wants to train there. I'm thinking about signing him up for his birthday."

"Cool, I'll have Taegan take care of both of you. Your membership is on me. I want to talk to you about an opening I have on our team, but tonight I want to fill in those gaps for you," he says.

I squeeze my thighs as his words come off dripping with something raw and dirty sounding. It sounds like he wants to fill more than a few gaps in my memory. I shake my dirty thoughts off and push my feet forward.

As I get to the doorway, he places a hand on the small of my back. I look up into his eyes and my breath is stolen away. God, he's gorgeous. The blond soul patch works for him as it amplifies his sensual bow-shaped lips.

I hadn't noticed it before, but now, as I'm focused and he's this close, I can take in all his handsome features. Dylan is fine as fuck. His lashes are super long and wispy, giving his blue eyes a sexy, dreamy vibe.

"Phew, I'm ready. That restroom line was killer," Daliah says as she appears.

"Taegan is with Dimitri and Nashawn; she'll meet us at the car," Dylan says.

Daliah looks between the two of us and gives me a questioning look then winks. I chew on my lip, but allow Dylan to lead me out to the car waiting for us.

He opens the front passenger door and nods for me to climb in. Taegan appears with Dimitri and Nashawn and passes me a second duffel as I sit with my gym bag between my legs. She then climbs into the back seat with Daliah.

I watch as Dylan climbs his big body behind the wheel, looking like he has all the confidence in the world. Damn, I didn't know I had a type. I have never been into guys.

To be honest, something has always held me back from getting into them. It just didn't feel right. It's like there has always been someone out there for me who would be worth the wait.

I can't help thinking that Dylan may be that someone. My cheeks warm when he reaches to place his hand on my thigh as he maneuvers out onto the street.

"Ya can drop me at me car, love. I have an early morning," Taegan says from the back seat.

"Expect C … Ariel and Chris at the gym in the morning. They'll be joining. I'll take care of their paperwork for membership," Dylan replies.

Looking at his profile, I smile. He's not sure if Daliah knows my real name and he's protecting me and Ciarán. I appreciate that.

I cover his hand and give it a gentle squeeze. He glances at me quickly and returns my smile. I can't help biting my lip and ducking away as my cheeks heat.

"Aye, about time."

Dylan chuckles and I get the feeling I'm missing out on an inside joke. I shrug it off as the comfortable seat and his hand on my thigh bring me a sense of peace. My lids grow heavy, and I snuggle deep into the warmth of the seat.

Dylan

"Chris has been so excited for his birthday. I'm so glad Ariel was able to win so big," Daliah gushes for the millionth time as she perches on the edge of her seat.

After dropping Taegan off at one of our warehouses where she left her car earlier, I'm headed to Harlem, where Ciara lives. Daliah has given me their address as she sits rambling excitedly about Ciara's wins and all she'll be able to do for the kid now for his birthday.

Ciara sits in the passenger seat, fast asleep. While she's knocked out, I've learned money has been tight for her. She's not working at the moment and every dime she does have goes toward her little brother Ciarán.

I admire how she takes care of the kid. My brothers and sisters would have done the same for me if something ever happened to our parents. Knowing how much she loved her da, I feel bad for her.

I want to make up for everything she's lost as much as I can. I glance over at her as I stop at a light. She's so beautiful. It's like looking at a sleeping angel.

My fingers itch to trace her hairline or run over her braids. I wasn't surprised to see her with the cornbraids when I entered the arena, but I was taken aback by how much they changed her appearance. If I didn't know better, I wouldn't have recognized her at first.

She's pretty no matter what, but the braids give her face a sharper look. When she walked into my gym with her hair down, her face had a softer look. There was a sort of innocence I remember from when we were little.

After the ass whippings she handed out this evening, the fiercer look of the braids is fitting. I'm proud of her. Those matches weren't easy, but she made them look like anyone could have won them.

She'd probably be amazing in a regulated fight. I have no doubt she'll be replacing Cadlha on the roster. After the way we lost that tournament because of her last year, there's no way she's representing us this year.

It hits me that I don't need to win the tournament anymore because I've found Ciara. She's sitting right beside me. However, she needs the money.

I plan to win and hand it over to her. She can pay off her brother's tuition and stash money for his college fund. I plan to make sure money isn't something she ever has to worry about again.

"I love the way you look at her. She does so much for her brother, but I would love to see her do something for herself. You know what I mean?" Daliah suddenly says.

I glance up in the rearview mirror to find her watching me. I grin at her, then focus back on the road as the light changes. We're not far from their place now.

"I think I do. This is you guys up here to the left, right?"

"Yup, that's us."

Lucky, I find a parking spot and pull my car in before I climb out and grab my gym bag from the trunk and then move to collect Ciara and her things. As I'm placing my bag across my body, Daliah climbs out of the back seat. I move to open Ciara's door and Daliah reaches in to take the gym bag from between Ciara's legs.

I grab the duffel full of money then lift Ciara into my arms. She's so small in my embrace, but she proved how mighty she is in that ring tonight. My body hardens as her soft one melts into mine.

I try to think of anything but her as we make our way into the building and climb onto the elevator. Lifting my gaze to the ceiling, I begin to count to a hundred. As we ride up, I realize I'm the happiest I've been in years.

Daliah starts to snicker in the other corner of the car. Looking at her, I then lift a brow and give her a questioning look. She smiles back at me.

"We could throw a party once we get to the apartment and she'd probably sleep right through it. She hasn't even so much as stirred," she laughs out.

I shrug my shoulders. "I've waited this long. I'll be here when she wakes."

"I'm dying to know what's going on between you two. Ugh, the suspense is killing me."

I chuckle. "You'll have to wait for her to tell you."

Daliah pouts as the elevator dings and the doors open. She steps out and turns left. I follow her up the hall as she takes her keys out and opens a door in the middle of the hall on the right-hand side.

I take note of the door number as she pushes in and holds the door open for me to follow. Looking around, I take in the apartment and nod. The place is nice.

"You're the babysitter," I say to Ross as he stands from the couch and stretches.

"Vega," we both scoff at the same time.

I give him a nod, letting him know I've got it from here. Ross shrugs and begins to collect his things to leave. He looks at a sleeping Ciara in my arms and gives me a questioning look.

"Did she win?"

"She killed it," Daliah gushes.

"Cool, cool. The kid went to bed thirty minutes ago. He tried to wait up."

"Thanks. I'll walk you out," Daliah says as she bats her lashes at Ross.

Looking down at Ciara, I decide to sit on the couch with her in my arms. I don't know where her bedroom is, and I don't want to violate her by undressing her without her permission.

I get the feeling she's not going to wake anytime soon. Maybe Daliah will help me to change her and get her into bed once she gets back and gets settled in.

"I'll take care of you, gorgeous. Sleep tight," I murmur.

CHAPTER SIXTEEN

For Breakfast

Ciara

Waking from a deep sleep, the scent of bacon and coffee greet me. I stretch and let out a groan as my body fusses at me. As my brain begins to wake, I realize I'm in my bed.

"What the hell?"

I don't remember coming home, forget about how I got into my sleep shorts and tank top and under the covers. Dylan comes to mind and the last thing I remember is riding in his car with his warm hand on my thigh.

Confused and hungry, I climb from the bed and head to the bathroom to brush my teeth and pee. I'm so hungry, I could kiss Daliah for starting breakfast. However, when I get to the kitchen, I find none other than Dylan, shirtless in a pair of sweatpants, cooking bacon and eggs.

"Hey Cee, Dylan's making me breakfast for my birthday," Ciarán sings.

My mouth falls open when Dylan turns to face me. His sweats are hanging low on his hips, and his abs and *V* are on full display. Quickly, I force my mouth closed.

Damn.

Even his belly button is sexy. I'm around built guys all the time in the gym, but this, this is just. Damn.

"Good morning, sleepyhead. Did you have a good sleep?"

"Um … yeah, I think I did. Did you stay the night here?"

"Yup. Had some clothes in my gym bag. I slept on the couch after Daliah helped me to get you changed and in bed," he says with that grin I'm beginning to find irresistible.

"Oh, um. Okay."

"We still need to talk, and I wanted to make my buddy here a birthday breakfast. Not to mention our champ deserves a breakfast of champions too."

I snort. "I'm not the one knocking people out cold."

I shake my head clear and go to hug my brother and wish him a happy birthday. Ciarán's excitement is rolling off him. I sit and tug his head to me to kiss it.

"So you won?"

"Yup, sure did."

"Does that mean you're going to fight for Miss Vega or are you going to try out for Mr. Dylan's gym?"

I give him a look to tell him to shut his lips. I haven't decided if I plan to try out for Dylan's gym. I heard his offer, but I need to know facts first.

Dylan comes to place plates in front of us both. My cheeks heat as he looks down into my eyes the whole time. His pretty eyes drop to my lips, causing me to look away quickly.

He places a hand on my back. Goose bumps begin to rise all over my body and my nipples strain against the thin fabric of my tank top, making me wish I had changed before coming out. I squirm in my seat and try to hunch to cover my breasts.

"Can I get you anything else?" he says close to my ear, sending my pulse racing.

"Um … uh … I mean, n …n … no. Thank you."

He chuckles and moves his hand to the back of my neck, then begins to massage my skin. I make the mistake of turning and looking at his torso. I swallow hard as my mouth runs dry.

He doesn't just have abs. His abs have abs. I bite my lip as I imagine running my hands along his smooth-looking skin.

He reaches beneath my chin with his free hand and lifts my head for me to look into his eyes. There's a sexy grin on his lips as usual.

"Eat up. We'll talk and I'll answer those questions for you,'" he says and winks down at me. He then calls over his shoulder. "Ciarán, I'm going to take you up on that offer to use your bathroom."

"No problem. Take your time, this is so good, bro. Thanks."

I sit frozen as I watch him saunter over to grab his bag and then stroll down the hall to Ciarán's room. I don't think I take a breath until he's out of sight.

"I think you like him," Ciarán whispers.

"Eat your food."

He giggles and continues to devour the bacon, eggs, and hash in front of him. I shake my head clear and tuck into my own breakfast. I moan around the fork.

The eggs are so good. Quickly, I dive into the hash. The potatoes are seasoned and cooked to perfection. I was not expecting this at all.

I tear this plate up. Ciarán belches beside me, causing me to realize I'm eating like a savage. I slow down, but finish it all. Ciarán sits chatting happily as I eat.

"Hey, you should get dressed when he's done in your bathroom. We're going to the gym to sign you up."

"Yes," he croons, and fist pumps the air.

I can't help the smile that comes to my lips. With the money from last night, I'll be able to do more than sign him up for the gym for his birthday.

I can't wait to see his face when his new computer arrives. I plan to order it next week. I know he was just grounded, but he's a good kid, other than this one incident. Besides, he needs it for school.

Dylan appears dressed in jeans and a T-shirt. His hair isn't styled, causing him to look more like the boy from my memories. I shoot Ciarán a look and he jumps up to run to his room to get ready.

Dylan takes the seat Ciarán abandons. I fidget on my stool, wishing I had gone to shower and get ready for the day. I reach up to finger my braids from last night.

"Where would you like to start?" Dylan asks with an open smile on his lips.

The expression allows me to relax. My thoughts are moving so fast, I don't know where to begin. I chew on my lip and take a deep breath.

"You know me. I mean, really know me. You called me by my birth name," I say, searching his eyes, which I haven't seemed to have forgotten.

The one thing I do know is that he used to be important to me. So much so, I still remember his face, although I can't seem to remember anything else from my past.

"We were friends. Your family lived next door to mine. I spent a lot of time on you guys' farm, and you spent a ton of time at my home when you were in Ireland."

I lick my lips and scoot to the edge of my stool. The more I search his face, the more I feel familiar with his presence. Something about his smile tickles my brain.

"Okay, we both lived in Ireland once," I say. "And we were friends."

"We were best friends. We did everything together. We were the smallest kids in our neighborhood. We sort of bonded over that."

I snort and look him over. "I have a hard time believing that."

"Trust me, it's the truth. I'm the youngest of six and thought I'd never grow as big and tall as my siblings. I hit high school and it's like I shot up overnight."

He smiles wider, showing all his white teeth and his eyes sparkle with the gesture. It's like a match is lit against my brain. I see him lined up with five others. However, none of them has his blue eyes and blond hair.

They all have dark hair and green eyes. There are three boys and two girls. I get this warm feeling from being around them. I'm happy with them.

"You remembered something about me, didn't you?"

"I did. You have three brothers and two sisters, right?"

"Yeah, there's Logan, Kate, Cole, Connie, and Jamie," we say the last brother's name in unison.

"Aye, you remember." He gives me a wink that causes my belly to drop.

"Yeah, I do. A little, but I'm confused about a lot. In my memories, you and I have accents. What happened to yours?"

His eyes begin to twinkle. "I've been here in America almost as long as we've been apart. My accent comes out more when I'm around my family or when we're trying to hide what we're saying around others. Other than that, it slips out when I'm angry.

"I think you've been in the States all this time. You guys left for your da's fight and never came back. I'm guessing you've been as Americanized as I have," he explains.

"That makes sense. Wait," I gasp. "You knew my dad?"

"Yeah, he's the one who started us boxing. I was so sad to hear he's gone. I'm sorry for your losses," he says and frowns.

"I don't remember him. I found my birth certificate and his name was on it. I tried to find out more about him after that.

"That's also where I learned my real name. I've been going by Cee-Cee since I lost my mom."

"But why Ariel now?" he asks with his brows drawn.

I look him deep in the eyes, wondering if I should truly trust him. He tilts his head to the side and looks me over as well. Then he reaches to place his hand on my arm.

"You can trust me. I'm here to help. You're safe with me."

I release a heavy breath. "When I woke in the hospital, I was told my mother was dead and her husband was there to collect me and Ciarán. My stepfather and his two kids treated me and Ciarán like real-life Cinderellas.

"More so me than him. I wouldn't allow them to treat my brother like shit in front of me. I've spent my life cooking, cleaning, and looking after those assholes."

I pause to reel in my temper. "Theo's son pulled some shit, and I'd had enough. Instead of waiting to get my shit together so I could get custody of my brother, I took him and ran.

"I could be in so much trouble if they find us. I'm not my brother's legal guardian, but I'm not losing him or allowing anyone to take him from me," I say with more venom than I mean to.

"No one will ever get a chance to try. Do you mind if I ask what the son did to make you risk so much?"

I turn to look away from him. The air shifts in the room. When I look back at him, I swear I can see steam coming out of his ears.

He nods tightly. "That's all the answer I need."

"Oh my God, my dad started me boxing? Theo always made it seem like he started me fighting. It's one of the things he always threw in my face. Like without him, I wouldn't be as good as I am."

"That's bullshit. You're two years younger than me, but you've been boxing longer than I have. Your da started you out as soon as you could hold your hands up."

"What was he like?"

"He was the best. I remember him being patient with us but also making sure we took things seriously. You always brought a smile to his face, and he loved your mom like crazy."

"So how did she end up with such an asshole?"

"You know, that's been on my mind too."

"I'm ready. When are we leaving?" Ciarán comes running out dressed and looking excited.

I look to Dylan, and he nods as if to tell me we can talk more later. I want to hug him. I feel like so many things are starting to fit together.

Dylan

I need to get to the gym to hit something. Ciara didn't have to say a word. Her body language said it all. I'm going to kill that son of a bitch if he ever tries to come around her again.

In fact, I've considered going to find him to end his life anyway. Ciara may be counting on me for answers, but I now have a million questions of my own. According to Felix, Ciara's mom died a year after her dad and that was only a few months after they left.

Why didn't she come back to Ireland? What made her marry someone else so quickly? Neither obit gave a cause of death.

Something stinks and I'm starting to think I might know where the stench is coming from. The one thing I know for sure is that I need to cover my girl.

"This car is so cool. I want one like this when I can drive," Ciarán croons from the back seat.

"You want it? In four years, it's yours. Or I'll trade up to the newer model and give you that," I say with a smile.

"Dylan, no. Please don't make promises you can't keep," Ciara gasps.

"I never break a promise. The car is his."

"This is the best birthday ever. Oh my God. I can't wait until I'm sixteen."

Ciara groans and shakes her head. I reach to place a hand on her thigh. She peeks over at me as I glance out the corner of my eye.

"Don't believe me? You can start driving it to keep it safe for him."

"Ugh, please no. It's mine," Ciarán whines.

Ciara bursts out laughing. I love the way it lights up her face. For the millionth time, I want to lean in and take her lips.

"Don't worry. Once I find a job, I plan to get my own car, brat."

"Speaking of which, why not come and work for me or my family? What are you good at other than fighting?"

She sits with a frown on her lips for a moment. I focus back on the road as a driver tries to cut me off. Manhattan traffic is ass.

I hate coming up here, especially this time of day. I wonder if I could get her and Ciarán to come live in Brooklyn with me. If not at my place, I could put them up somewhere just as nice as the place Vega has them in.

"She's an artist. When I was little, she talked about becoming a tattoo artist until Dad talked her out of it. Fighters use their hands to fight, not draw shit on people," Ciarán says in a mocking voice.

"*Ciarán*," Ciara says warningly.

"Sorry, that's just how he said it. I hated when he would put down the things we wanted to do because it wasn't in a ring," he murmurs.

"I remember you always drawing. Your da had your drawings pinned up all over his training gym. Do you still draw?"

"Yeah, but it's been so long since I've thought about becoming an ink artist. Theo made me work at the gym, training for him. I've been training fighters for as long as I can remember."

"Yeah, which is why I never understood why you couldn't train me. You would have been so much better at it than Theo and he knew it," Ciarán mutters from his seat as he slumps down into it.

"Come to think of it ..." I cut my words off and I think of what I'm about to say.

Ciarán has called this Theo guy Dad. I don't know if Ciara has told him that's not his father. She may not want him to know.

However, I can't help thinking about how much he reminds me of his real father in the ring. This guy may have feared Ciarán triggering Ciara's memories while in the ring.

Probably sensing my hesitation, Ciara changes the subject. She brings up a computer system Ciarán clearly wants. I make a note to give Felix and Wyatt a call. Felix will know all the best and newest shit to get, and Wyatt will have the connections to get all the things that haven't hit the market yet.

"God, that took a long time. I'm starving," Ciarán croons as I pull in front of the gym.

"Taegan has menus in the office. Why don't you head in to find her and I'll treat you to whatever you want," I say as I park.

"Cool."

As soon as I have the car in the spot, he jumps out, leaving me and Ciara in the car alone. Ciara turns to me and glares. I unfasten my seat belt and turn to face her.

She sighs. "Dylan, listen. I'm grateful for how you're helping me, but you can't keep spoiling and promising that kid everything he asks for. I don't want him getting used to things that I can't continue to give him."

I reach to cup her face. "If you and your family would have returned to Ireland, this would be his life. I would have been around to look out for him and spoil him just like I would have done you.

"I promised you I'd marry you someday when we grew up. I've been waiting for you since you left and didn't send me one of your postcards to tell me how you were doing in the States. Then my da had to come here for work and I vowed I'd go back and find you.

"Now you're here. I'm not going to allow anything to happen to you and I plan to make sure anything you and that kid want is all yours. I'm not hurting for anything. Neither will you," I say.

"Dylan, I …"

I lean in to kiss her as her words trail off. I'm a breath away when my phone rings. I bite out a curse because it's the family business ringtone. I can't ignore it.

I pull away and let out a long breath. It probably isn't the right time for me to kiss her. I want our first kiss to be special.

"I need to take this. Go on inside, I have a friend who's coming in to meet you. Taegan will get you settled until she arrives," I say.

Disappointment covers her face. I know the feeling. It's the same one I have. She climbs out of the car, and I answer the call.

"Hello, Cole. What's up?"

"I need ya to handle something for me. Head to Hell's Kitchen. Go see our friend over there and find out why they're late with our money," he growls.

"How late?"

"Late enough for him to be considered *the* late. Ya understand me. If ya don't like his answer, ya already know how I feel. Make an example."

"Got it."

He hangs up before I can say another word. I look at the gym, longing to head inside after Ciara. I purse my lips and shoot off a text to Taegan. Then I text Aidan and Booker to let them know to be ready when I get to them.

"Ach, and this is the life of a true O'Brien. We still have a city to run."

CHAPTER SEVENTEEN

Big Mistakes

Dylan

Nothing but tension fills my body as I stand here. My chest is heaving and anger courses through me. There are a million places I'd rather be than here.

We pulled up just in time as Hanson was skipping his happy ass into this apartment building like this is just an ordinary Saturday. He didn't even see us coming. Although I got the sense after we got him in here that he knew we were coming.

Why would a man be so resigned to his fate? Something more is going on here. That's the only reason I haven't killed him already.

My gut is telling me to get the truth before I make a decision. O'Briens always follow their guts. It has saved us a ton of times.

"I hate when people make shit harder than it needs to be. I asked you a question, now answer it." I seethe as I look down at Hanson's battered ass.

I'm going to need to shower and change after this because he couldn't just cough up the answers I came here for. I'm not in the mood to kill anyone today. I'm trying to give him a chance at redemption.

Blood drips from his nose and out of the corner of his mouth, but he's still trying to be defiant. That shit is about to get him killed. I get the feeling he knows this but he's choosing to be a sacrifice for someone.

"I don't have an answer for you."

"That's bullshit," I snap. "Book, get him to his feet."

"No, no. I really don't have an answer. Tell Brooklyn it won't happen again. I'm cracking down on my crew. I'll take care of it."

"You see, the problem is ... I don't think my brother cares anymore. Your fate is now in my hands. I'm not satisfied with your response," I say and punch him in the gut.

The sound of his ribs cracking again fills the air. I look around his place at all our family has afforded him to build. He wouldn't have any of this if it wasn't for my family and yet he thinks he gets to choose when he delivers our return on our investment.

"Oh God," he gasps. His face turns bright red, and he looks like he's about to puke. "My little brother. He ... he's been wanting more responsibility, so I gave him some. He was jumped and they took the money."

"Why the fuck couldn't you tell me that in the first place?" I snarl.

"It was the cops ... they're the ones who jumped him. They're blackmailing me. They want names, but I just needed time to figure out what to do.

"I need ... I need to get him out of this, but I'm not going against you guys. Your father ... he was good to my father and Brooklyn and Logan have always been good to me. This is my mess ... I need to fix it."

I nod to Aidan for him to verify this. He returns the nod as he takes his phone out and gets on it. I saunter over to the couch and have a seat. Pulling my phone to check it, I see the time and scowl. I've wasted my day here.

I'm closer to my parents' house, but it would still be a while before I get back to the gym. I think of my talk with Ciara earlier and I remember something I want to give her. I'm not going to make it back anytime soon, so I decide to text Taegan.

"He's not lying," Aidan says as he returns. "Strong and Vargus are pressing him. The kid stabbed Detective Baker while they jumped him. They're threatening him with attempted murder. He's holding it down, hasn't said anything, but they're using him to squeeze Hanson."

"Shut that shit down. Bring the kid to me when he's released. Get this motherfucker to a medic," I command.

"Dylan, what are you going to do to him?"

"I'm just going to talk to him. You worry about healing up. Next time some shit like this happens, you come to us first."

"Don't make us come to you. If this happens again, I'm cutting out your tongue first and taking two fingers. Am I clear?"

"Yes, yes. This won't happen again, I promise. Please don't hurt my brother," he sobs.

"You were willing to die for him. I'm just going to make sure he was worth it."

I get up and walk out. My work is finished here. Da and Brooklyn will want to know this.

Clearly, someone on payroll isn't paying attention. Maybe it's time their pay was docked. Not my call.

It's time I go back to my corner. I wonder what my girl will think of my place. I can't wait to see her again.

Ciara

I walk over to the bleachers and take a seat, then lift my bottle of water to my lips. I've been working out and sparring with Halley, the fighter who used to be on Dylan's team a few years ago.

I like her. She has a good vibe like Taegan. She's also a good fighter. Smart about the ring. Her MMA IQ is impressive.

"Dylan is right about you. You'd make a great replacement for me. If you want to join the team, I'd be happy to come back on as your trainer," Halley says.

"Do you mind me asking why you left?"

"Got pregnant, had a kid, then got married. My munchkin just turned three and his father travels a lot for work. I miss this place, but I'm getting old and I'm not the fighter I once was.

"I know I'm not in competition shape. Dylan is extremely competitive. He hates to lose. He's not going into the next tournament without fighters who can win. Besides, my husband and I have been talking about baby number two." She shrugs.

"Why did he ask you here to meet me?"

"Dylan wanted me to see you in action because he knows I want to be involved in the gym again somehow, but I'm not training that bitch he already has. That's a waste of my fucking time," she adds and rolls her eyes.

I chew on my lip, wanting to ask what the deal is with that. I overheard someone else mention not liking one of the female fighters who trains here. They only have two. One is injured and the other is this woman no one seems to like.

I don't know that I've met her. Taegan ordered lunch and we stayed up in the office while she filled me in on the membership, which I had planned to pay for despite Dylan saying it was on him. That was until Taegan informed me he had handled all of that.

She then gave me a quick tour. I did see a few other women, but I can't say if any of them are this woman I keep hearing about. I shrug it off and decide not to ask.

"Speaking of the bitch," Halley mutters under her breath.

I look up from tying my shoe as I sit on the bleachers where we've been taking a break. The redhead who bumped me last time I was here makes her way over to where we are with a stink look on her face.

"What are ya doing here?" she snarls at Halley.

"Oh, hell nah. I'm minding my fucking business like you need to be doing. You still don't want this smoke, Cadlha. A baby hasn't changed that much," Halley hisses.

"What are ya doing here again?" Cadlha changes her attention to me.

"Oh, honey. You don't want to go there either. Go find yourself something safe to do," Halley warns.

"Who are ya?"

"Yer replacement," Taegan sings as she walks over with a smile on her face.

"What are ya going on about?" Cadlha scoffs at Taegan.

"Ciara, I want ya to meet and then ignore my cousin, Cadlha. She's irrelevant. I'd disown her if I could."

"Ya don't even fight. Why are ya always here? Dylan would be so much better off if ya got lost."

"Aye, she's talking to herself now. Don't need much more to get ya out of here, but keep talking so I can have Dylan put ya out on yer ass today," Taegan says as she folds her arms over her chest.

"Whatever."

"Ya want to watch out for this one and that big-ass head, she thinks it's a third fist or something since she can't manage to throw and land the other two properly," Taegan taunts, causing Cadlha's face to pinch and turn red.

"The only thing you know how to throw are words."

"Words and bullets. Play with me if ya want. I'll teach ya a lesson or two, with yer oul big-ass water tower head."

"Fuck off, loser. Ya just keep out of my way and stay away from Dylan, he's mine," Cadlha hisses toward me, causing me to whip my head back.

"*Ha.* Does he know this? Ya crazy bat. Go work on trying to land a punch or blocking one from knocking ya on yer ass." Taegan waves this crazy bitch off. "Ciara, Dylan called. He wants us all to meet him for dinner at his place; he's not going to make it back to pick ye guys up.

"Halley, he said for ya to call him. Give me a minute to get Oscar to handle things here and lock up and I'll be ready."

"Yer taking her to Dylan's place? What the fuck?" Cadlha bites out. "Where the fuck did ya come from?"

"Anyone ever tell ya to shut yer fucking gub? I'm not a problem ya want to find out about, so stop fucking around while ya can," I snarl, having enough of her damn tantrum.

"Oh, yer just like Dylan. The Irish comes out with yer ire. Love it," Taegan says as she cackles.

I blink at her. I didn't even notice. Now that I think of it. That has happened in the past. Now that it's been brought to my attention, I can remember Theo correcting my speech when I was younger. In the beginning, he corrected me a lot.

"Are ya mocking me, bitch?" Cadlha snarls.

"No, ya nub. Yer a fucking eejit. She's more Irish than ya are. Everything isn't always about ya, ya twit."

"One."

"What are ya going on about?" Cadlha glares at me.

"Keep going and you'll find out. I promise," I say and wink.

She flips her hair and storms off, pushing Ciarán when she moves by him. I ball my fists at my sides. Remembering this is Dylan's gym and I'm new here, I bite back my anger.

"Two," I call out after her in warning.

She looks back and narrows her eyes at me. I give her a look to let her know that shit doesn't faze me one bit. Taegan and Halley burst into laughter.

"I knew I liked you. About time someone put that bitch in her place. Fucking psycho," Halley says.

"She's a monster of my own making. I allowed her to think she could get away with that shit for too long. Dylan only gives her a pass because of me. I should have told him a long time ago how I truly feel about her ass," Taegan says and rolls her eyes.

"You can tell Dylan thank you, but no thank you. I'll pass on dinner. I'm going to head home."

"Cee, Cee, did you hear? Dylan wants us to come to his place for dinner. He has a gift for my birthday. When are we leaving?"

Taegan shrugs as she gives me a mischievous smile. "The kid was upstairs with me when I got the call."

"Fuck," I mutter under my breath.

CHAPTER EIGHTEEN

Original O'Brien

Dylan

I walk into my father's study as he sits there on a call. The house smells of Mom's cooking, making my stomach growl. If I didn't already have plans, I would stay for dinner.

"Aye, we do need to talk. It's time. I can be in Inverness within the week," he says into the phone.

I lean into the doorjamb and fold my arms over my chest as he listens to the person on the other side before continuing. "No, it's not a problem. Logan and LaSalle haven't changed their minds. This was all a minor setback.

"Things will be back on track soon. I'll just be your point man once again until Logan returns."

My brows shoot up. What could he need to go to Scotland for? What could it have to do with Logan and LaSalle? Cole is now the Lord over the O'Brien clan since our grandda's demise.

Uncle Finlay isn't ready to step down as far as I know, so my curiosity is piqued as I listen to my da's words. It's not lost on me that Brooklyn has been going to Scotland and Ireland a lot. My curiosity is growing.

My da glances at me and gives me a nod as he ends the call. I step fully into the room and round the desk. Placing a hand on his shoulder, I then give it a squeeze and lean down to kiss the top of his head. When I go to pull away, he grabs my forearm with a surprisingly strong grip.

He then turns to look at my knuckles. "Ach, I see Cole had ya go take care of that problem. Get some ice from yer ma. How are ya, lad?"

"Can't complain. What about ye?"

He looks up at me with his green eyes and narrows his gaze as if trying to see if I'm telling a fib. When he finds what he's looking for, a huge smile comes to his face. He stands and pulls me into a hug.

"I don't tell ya how proud I am of ya enough. How's the gym?"

"We're doing good. I might have a new fighter and a new potential coming on," I say with a grin.

My thoughts go to Ciara and Ciarán. While I would put Ciara in a fight today, I have a few things I want to work on with Ciarán. Stamina and strength are what I plan to focus on first.

"It makes me sick what ye boys have gone through because of me da. We're going to make things right. In the end, it will all be right," he says cryptically, pulling me from my thoughts.

"Am I missing something here, Da?"

He pats my cheek. "No, no. Are ya staying for dinner?"

"Ach, no. I'm having dinner with a friend. I'll come by soon to spend some time with you and Ma."

"Aye, next time bring yer friend with ya. Yer ma already gives me shit because I don't force ye boys to come around more. She's even starting in on Con and Kate. For fuck's sake, ye all have lives. Just do yer oul fella a favor and stop in more."

I chuckle. "I've got you, Da, promise."

"That's me big lad."

"I thought I heard ye voice," Mom says, causing me to turn for the study's door.

She's standing there with her hands on her hips, looking like a female version of my Uncle Joe. She's five nine and has the same golden eyes as my uncles and their father. Her dark hair spills down her back to her butt and has a natural wave to it.

Athena Kara Black-O'Brien is one gorgeous woman. I can see why my da fell for her. We used to tease Uncle Joe and tell him he was supposed to be a girl with his pretty face that looked just like Ma's. To be honest, we all take after Ma and her good looks.

I move to tug her into a hug. She wraps her arms around me and holds me tight. I can't help thinking about how Ciara is so much shorter and smaller than me.

"Ye stink of sweat, but yer still handsome as ever. Come let me feed ya."

"I can't. Not today. I need to talk to Da for a bit, then I have to head out."

"He has a date," Da chuckles from behind me.

My cheeks heat. I never said it was a date, but I guess he's right. I do plan to spend some time with Ciara. I'm a bit nervous.

There's still something Ciara should know about me. I've been warring with how or if I should tell her at all. Maybe I shouldn't.

"Well, if that means ye plan to make me grands I can actually spoil, have at it."

My heart pangs. Ma hasn't been happy about not getting to spend time with Shauna. She understands why, but she's still not happy.

Once Logan is out, we'll all be able to move more freely. Ireland will come with less caution. Brooklyn may be the Irish lord, but he has to watch his back for now. Thank God for the McGowans.

They have really stepped up in the wake of Cole's transition to fill my grandda's position. Once this alliance fully forms, a lot will change. I may not be in the know of all the details, but I know enough to know things will be a lot different.

"Hold on, Ma. I did want to ask you for something," I say as I remember why I wanted to see her while I'm here.

"What is it, love?"

"Do you remember those photo albums?" I ask as I look into her eyes.

Recognition fills her eyes, and they soften. "Ye mean the ones we made when we moved here."

"Aye, do you think I can get those?"

She reaches to cup my face. "Aye, I'll go get them while ye chat with yer da. Is everything all right, love?"

"Yeah, everything is great. I'm just looking for something for someone. I think I'll find it in those."

She pats my cheek. "Yer a good lad, ye are. Go on, I'll get them out for ye. Ye will have them before ye go."

"Thanks, Ma. I love you," I say and dip my head to kiss her cheek.

"Love ye more."

CHAPTER NINETEEN

My Place

Ciara

I've been feeling awkward about coming here since my run-in with Cadlha at the gym. I'm not here to get into some drama over a guy I barely know. I would have rather gone home and figured out my next move.

I don't think Roaring Irish gym is for me. I'm going to find another way to get into the tournament. Last night was a one-off.

I can't risk getting hurt or ending up in the middle of a raid if those underground fights get busted. I have Ciarán to think about. While I can make fast money in those fights, they're not the answer or my endgame.

"Stop looking so nervous. Ya can make yerself at home," Taegan says as she lets us all into Dylan's home.

I'm not even going to ask about that one. Ciarán looks around excitedly. This kid is on cloud nine.

Taegan makes her way over to the couch while I continue to stand close to the door. I'm trying to think of something to come up with so Ciarán and I can leave.

It's lame, but I think I finally come up with something. I open my mouth to make our excuses when the thud of footfalls catches my attention. I turn toward the staircase on my left.

Can I express how mind blowing this place is? The apartment is almost as breathtaking as the man jogging barefoot down the suspended glass staircase. Dylan looks like he just stepped out of the shower.

He has on a pair of black slacks and an open white dress shirt. Once again, that *V* and those abs are on display. His hair is still damp and has a curly wave to it.

"Hey, Dylan," Ciarán croons. "This place is sick."

"Thanks. Make yourself at home. Can I get you guys something to drink?"

"I'm cool," I reply as I pull my phone and check it like I have tons of messages waiting for me.

Daliah and Vega are my only friends and Daliah is at work today and Vega is doing Vega. My phone has been dry as shit since we left Seattle. I can't risk calling anyone back there.

Everyone I knew was somehow tied to the Youngs. It's better this way. No contact, no connections.

"Everything okay?"

I look up to find Dylan towering over me. I force a smile and nod. Cupping my face, he searches my eyes for a beat.

"You were never any good at lying to me. What's wrong?"

"I'm tired. I want to go home."

He purses his lips. I can see the frustration that fills his eyes. We're going to need to get a few things straight.

"Listen, Dylan. I'm grateful for your help and all, but I have a lot going on. I don't think I'm in a place to date anyone.

"Especially not someone I'm already getting threats over. I need to stay under the radar. This ... whatever this is. It's complicated. I don't have time for complicated."

"Someone threatened ya?"

The way his face changes as pure rage rolls off him causes me to take a step back. He looks like he's about to murder someone. He has a crazed look in his eyes.

"Cadlha thought she would claim her territory. She blew around a bit of smoke, but yer girl handled herself," Taegan calls out from the couch. "Ain't nobody thinking about that bitch. Ciara, please."

I groan. "This is what I mean. You guys keep calling me by a name I'm not even sure it's safe for me to use. What are we doing here, Dylan? This is my real life."

He cups the back of my neck and pulls me to him. His body heat engulfs me, and his cologne wraps around me like a warm hug. I look up into his eyes and get lost.

"Cadlha doesn't have a death wish. Ya don't have to worry about her or anyone else. No one will ever lay a finger on ya. I've been waiting for ya since I was ten years oul. I'm not about to lose ya again.

"This is yer home as long as yer here. Nothing complicated about it. I'm here, yer here. We belong together."

"Aye, kid. Let's go for a walk. I'll treat ya to some ice cream for yer birthday," Taegan sings to Ciarán as I stand frozen in Dylan's grasp.

"All right," Ciarán croons.

"When ya return, his gift is in the blue room. Ya can take him there," Dylan murmurs to Taegan, not looking away from me.

"Got ya, boss."

Taegan and Ciarán move past us to leave. I knit my brows, trying to figure out what to do next. I'm drawn to him, but my common sense is telling me this could be a colossal fuckup.

"So, people threatening me makes you angry?" I taunt, lifting a brow at him. "Or is it the fact that I'm not interested in dating you?"

Before I can wrap my mind around what's happening, he backs me into the door behind me that his assistant and my brother just left through. I gasp as he lifts me onto his waist and crushes his lips to mine.

I whimper into his mouth and push my hands into his hair. He groans and deepens the kiss. His kiss is hungry and a bit aggressive, but I'm not complaining.

I should push him away, but my brain isn't with that idea. Neither is my body. I shiver against him as he pushes his hand under my shirt and cups my breast.

I'm a decent *C* cup, but his large palm engulfs my entire mound. His big hand is so warm. A moan leaves my lips as he flicks his thumb over my nipple. My entire body awakens to his touch.

"You were saying? You're not interest in what?" he breathes against my lips as he breaks the kiss and presses his forehead to mine.

"Huh?"

He chuckles and places me back on my feet. "Come here, I have something for you."

"Dylan ... I ... I'm not ready for that. I'm still a virgin."

"So am I," he says and winks. "As much as I want you, that's not what I'm talking about. Come with me."

"Wait, are you serious? You're a virgin? But you ooze sex."

He scoffs a laugh and shrugs. "Maybe, but aye, baby, I've been waiting for you."

"What if you never found me?"

"That wasn't an option. I made you a promise. You will be my wife someday. Now, come on," he says, leaving me speechless.

A look crosses his face so quickly, I don't have time to try to place it. He links his fingers with mine and tugs me with him. It's crazy, but in this moment, I think I'm falling for him. My mind is reeling with this new information.

"How old are you?" I blurt out as he leads me to the couch to take a seat.

"I told you I have you by two years, remember? I just turned twenty-three. Don't sound so surprised. All my firsts belong to you. You were my first kiss. I want to give you all the rest too."

I'm stunned. Oh yeah, I'm falling hard. As we sit, he reaches for a tote bag sitting on the coffee table.

Reaching inside, he tugs out two photo albums. I watch with curiosity, while still playing his words in my head on repeat.

All my firsts belong to you. You were my first kiss. I want to give you all the rest too.

"When we left Ireland, I was devastated. Ma thought making these would help. I had planned to give you one. I remember having them and thought you would like to take a look," he says with a blush on his cheeks.

I drop my gaze to his lips, wanting to kiss him again. He's sitting so close his thigh is touching mine. Seeming to read my thoughts, he leans in and pecks my lips.

Pulling away, he places one of the photo albums on my lap. I run my hand over the top and smile at the purple ribbon tying it closed.

I'm hit with another memory and gasp as I palm my head. Dylan scoots closer and runs his hand over my head. The look of concern on his face only draws me in more.

"Are you all right?"

"Yeah, I'm fine."

"Another memory?"

"Yes, our first kiss and the roses you gave me tied in the same purple ribbon," I say as I finger the sparkly fabric.

A smile lights up his entire face. "You were so pretty. I don't know what made me kiss you that day."

"I remember being surprised but happy."

"Let's see if we can spark something else," he says, pointing to the album.

I clear my throat and begin to turn through it. Tears come to my eyes as I find a picture of the little boy and girl from my memories. I run my fingers over the face I've drawn so many times, not knowing it was him. A tear spills free and falls onto the page.

"I don't think I ever truly forgot you. I've been drawing this face for years. I just didn't know who he was. I would dream of your face and wake to draw it, over and over again," I say just above a whisper.

"Nothing could keep us apart forever. You're here now, you're safe and where you belong."

I begin to turn the pages once again. I freeze as I get to a few pictures of a man holding us both in his arms. One on each side.

In one photo, he's looking up at me with a huge smile on his face. I know right away that's my dad. Tears really start to fall as I get choked up.

Nope, I'm not falling. I think I'm officially in love with Dylan. My heart aches as I continue to go through photos of me, my old friend, his family, and my parents. Warmth fills me and I know for a fact I'm safe here with him.

I get to a page with an autographed photograph of my dad in the ring. He has on gloves, and his hands are thrown in the air. I smile as a memory of Dad pops into my head.

"Ye two might be small, but ya have skills. Remember that next time they pick on ya. Dylan, ya keep their focus on ya.

"Ciara, ya hit the hell out of them. Then ye both pounce. The way ye two have each other's backs will always work in yer favor. Ye have more of something none of them have."

"What's that, Da?" I asked.

"Heart, love. Ye both have tons of heart. That's something no one can take from ya. They'll try, but I know it in me gut. They'll never take that away. Dylan, ya asked how ya can protect her?"

He paused to pat Dylan on his little scrawny chest. "Use what's in here. Ya will always have the heart to win when it comes to protecting our girl. Ya use that and ya will never fail."

My lips tremble as I swipe at my tears. Suddenly, I remember that day so clearly. Dylan and I were being picked on in school. One of the kids pushed me to the ground and Dylan got into a fight with them.

When we got home, my da was furious. He made us train for hours before he sat us down for that talk. Then he took us out to ride our bikes to get ice cream.

I go to ask Dylan if he remembers that day, but the picture on the next page catches my attention. It's of my dad surrounded by three other men. I lean in closer and gasp.

"I know him, not from my memories, but from Seattle. He used to come around the gym," I say as I point to the man.

Dylan reaches for the album and pulls it into his lap. He then pulls back the protective film and lifts the picture out. He squints at the picture then points to the man I mentioned.

"Him?"

"Yeah." I lick my lips. "Do you know who he is?"

"I believe his name was Laki. He was a part of your da's corner crew. I remember them being close; his whole team was. He's like Polynesian or something; he would carve us these little figurines. I think I still have a few back at my parents' place."

"But why did he never say anything? I mean, he was always there in the shadows. When I would fight in those underground fights for Theo, he was there.

"He's a big guy, like you. He would cling to the back of the crowd, but I always spotted him. He seemed harmless, like he was only watching, not a threat."

"I doubt he would have threatened you. Your da's entire team was protective of you. They treated you like their own daughter. Can I ask you something?"

"Yeah."

"Do you remember or know anything about what happened to your father?"

"No. To be honest, I didn't know I had a dad before I decided to run and found his name on my birth certificate. Theo wouldn't talk to me much about my mom. I'm positive he wouldn't have given me much information about my dad."

A pensive look comes to his face. "Do you mind if I try to find him? Laki, I mean. My family happens to be in the business of tracking people. I want to see if we can find him and maybe get some answers."

"No. I don't mind. I now have more questions I want answered."

"Cool. Don't worry about it. I'll have my cousin look into him and we'll see if we can get you those answers. If he can't get us answers … I'll go to one of my uncles. He'll definitely be able to track him."

"Thank you, Dylan. All of this means so much to me," I choke out.

"Do you remember him now? Your da?"

"A little. Bits and pieces are starting to come."

"Good. You can have this one," he says, handing the album back.

"Thanks."

"Anytime. Are you hungry? We can head up to the rooftop."

"What about Taegan and Ciarán? Shouldn't we wait for them?"

"Taegan will take care of him. She's giving us some time. I sort of set up our first date."

I bite my lip as I search his face with my eyes. It's been thirteen years, and he's waited that long for me. Suddenly, I realize my heart and mind have been waiting for him too. I'm just catching up.

Placing the album on the table, I then reach to cup his handsome face and lean in to kiss him again. He takes over the kiss almost instantly. I laugh when he pulls me into his lap so he can devour me more thoroughly.

"Too much?" he pants as he pulls back and looks into my eyes.

"No, you're a really good kisser."

My stomach growls before he can reply. I glance at him sheepishly. He chuckles and shakes his head.

"Come on, I'll feed you."

Dylan

"You never did tell me what you want to do for work," I say as I look over my glass at Ciara.

I'm dying to kiss her again, but I don't want to come off as thirsty. The date is going well so far. I'm not going to lie and say there isn't a ton of sexual tension flowing around us.

I smile as I think of her words from earlier. My girl hasn't allowed anyone to take what's mine. I wasn't sure I was going to tell her that I'm a virgin, but when she said it, I sort of blurted it without thinking.

I'm not ashamed of it. I'm not even worried about when the time comes or my performance. I haven't had sex, but I know a thing or two.

You don't grow up in the O'Brien family and not learn about sex and passion. Heck, my oldest brother is a silent partner of Club Desire. That place is a classroom of its own.

"You know, I've been thinking about that a lot since you asked," she says, pulling me from my musings. "Ciarán was right, I once wanted to get into ink. I wouldn't mind working at a tat shop. You know, as an apprentice for a while or something.

"Maybe even a receptionist to get me in the door. Then I can move into slinging ink later."

"Do you have any ink of your own?"

"That you will have to find out for yourself," she says with a little smile. "You?"

I bite my lip and look her face over as my mind goes to peeling her out of her clothes to find any ink that might be on her skin and then spending hours tracing it with my tongue.

"I guess we'll both have to wait until we can play a game of ink and seek."

She laughs and shakes her head. I grin back at her, loving that musical laugh. I want to keep that smile on her face forever.

"Corny?"

"A little."

I shrug and change the subject. "I think I might be able to help you out."

"Enough of you trying to fix my life. Tell me more about you," she says with a bright smile.

"Not much to tell. I run a gym and fight."

"This place says otherwise. Come on, I practically ran a gym for years, I know that's not bringing in this kind of money. What else do you have going on?"

"That gym must have been ass. I earn pretty damn well with mine."

"Come on. Even if you do earn well, look at this place. The rooftop space is out of a magazine.

"The floor-to-ceiling windows downstairs are breathtaking and the view. Really? Dylan, you have to have some other source of income for all this."

I laugh and give her a smile. I'm not about to go into any of that. In time, she's bound to learn my family is into a whole lot of shit, but I don't want to send her running tonight.

"Yes, I do have other sources of income, but the gym isn't hurting for anything."

"Would one of those sources have anything to do with your busted knuckles? They aren't like that from knocking that dude out last night."

I snort and shrug. "Maybe."

"Okay, so you have secrets. Fair enough. You've only just met me."

"I've known you most of my life. This is just a topic ... You know what, you're not the only one to fight in those matches. I used to spend a lot of time in those rings."

"Ugh, I would love to get a place like this for me and Ciarán, but that's not the answer for me. The more I fight underground, the more I'm risking my future in the real ring as a pro."

"This place isn't as far out of your reach as you think," I say.

She tilts her head and studies me. "What's that supposed to mean?"

I wink at her and stand. Then I hold out my hand for hers. She places her small hand in mine, and I lift her from her seat.

Walking us to the putting green in the center of the roof, I pull my phone and turn on the sound system. "Dive" by Ed Sheeran begins to float through the speakers. Ciara smiles brightly at me as I tug her into my embrace and begin to sway with her in my arms.

"You didn't answer my question, Dyl."

I close my eyes as she calls me by the nickname she used when we were little. I still can't believe she's here. I have her in my arms, finally.

When I open my eyes, her green ones are locked on me. I cup her face in my palm and run my thumb across her full lower lip. She was a pretty little girl, but she's grown into a gorgeous woman.

"Everything I have is yours from my heart to all the land and property in my name. There isn't a thing I have that doesn't belong to you.

"I know you're still figuring things out for yourself, but you can move in whenever you're ready. You don't have to want for something that's already yours," I finally answer.

"What if I'm not what you expect? What if I've become someone you don't like?"

"I doubt that," I say and take her lips.

Sparks fly and my skin hums from her nearness. I devour her mouth and hold her close. Her mouth tastes of the sauce from dinner. It's sweet and salty.

I groan and dive deeper into her mouth. She lifts onto her toes to get closer to me. I wrap both arms around her and lift her from her feet without breaking the kiss.

"Shit," I bite out as my phone goes off.

I place her back on her feet. Taking my phone out, I find a text from Taegan. I've been so wrapped up in Ciara, I almost forgot about them.

Taegan: *Ciarán has eaten and opened his gift. I need to go. Call you later.*

"We should get downstairs. Taegan is leaving."

"Oh my God. What was I thinking? It's Ciarán's birthday. I should be with him."

"Relax, we'll spend the rest of the night with him."

She palms her forehead. "This is crazy."

"Ciara, stop freaking out, baby. It's going to be fine."

She huffs and turns to rush downstairs. I push my hands into my hair and tug. I don't think Ciarán has thought about us at all.

Taegan has my credit card, and she used it to get the kid anything he wanted. She's been texting to let me know how much fun Ciarán has been having the whole time we've been up here.

I sigh and shut everything down before I head downstairs after Ciara. This is going to be harder than I thought.

CHAPTER TWENTY

Birthday Wish

Ciara

"Ciarán, Ciarán," I call as I get downstairs.

The sound of a TV blaring leads me to a room up the glass stairs on the second floor. I get to the room to find my little brother lying on a bed with his shoes off and PJs on as he watches the huge TV mounted on the wall.

"What are you doing? Where are your clothes?"

"I was fading. Taegan told me this is my room. I took a shower and got ready for bed." He gives me a huge, sleepy smile. "I had so much fun. This was the best birthday ever.

"The arcade was so cool, and I got a ton of clothes at the mall. I even got that tablet I was looking at. Where's Dylan? I want to thank him for the boxing gloves and all the other cool stuff."

My head is reeling. I thought Taegan was taking him for ice cream. The arcade? The mall?

"He's um ... I don't know. You should get dressed so we can go home."

"Aw, man. Come on, this bed is so comfortable. Come sit, see for yourself. I don't want to leave," he whines.

"Ciarán, we can't stay here," I huff, but walk over to the bed to sit on the edge.

I roll my eyes because the mattress is comfortable. Ciarán gives me a smile as if to say *I told you so*. I reach to pinch him.

"Is he your boyfriend?" he whispers, glancing at the doorway.

"Would that make you mad?"

"Absolutely not. You take such good care of me. You always have, but you don't do things other sisters do.

"I want to see you happy. I want to see you go on dates and get pretty to go hang with friends. Sometimes, I feel like you're not living the way you should and it's all my fault.

"I appreciate everything you do for me, but you're an adult. You should do normal adult things. Please, Cee. My birthday wish is for you to be happy.

"Dylan seems to really like you. It's okay to let him be your boyfriend. Look at all he's done for me for my birthday. I think he'll be good to you. And if he's not, I'll kick his butt," he says and gives me that smile I love so much.

"Oh my God, Ciarán. Nothing is your fault. All I do is for you and I wouldn't change a thing."

He yawns. "Okay, so we can stay? This bed is calling my name."

Grr. I look around. There are a ton of bags in the corner. This man has given my brother his own room.

I shake my head and turn to tell Ciarán maybe next time. However, he's fast asleep when I look back at him. I snicker to myself and bite my lip.

"Good night. Glad you had a great birthday, kid," I say and run my head over his hair as I lean in to kiss his forehead.

I kick my shoes off and get ready to climb into the bed next to him. Movement by the door catches my attention. I turn to find Dylan standing there watching me.

He crooks his finger to beckon me to him. I glance at Ciarán then back at him. With a sigh, I pad to the door.

"There are three other guest rooms for you to choose from, or you can spend the night in my room."

I bite my lip and look up at him through my lashes. The heated look in his eyes tells me to go find one of those guestrooms, but something in the back of my mind screams for something else entirely.

"I don't have anything to sleep in. I should sleep in my own room."

"You're welcome to wear anything of mine. Besides, I thought we could talk some more. You say I might not like who you've become.

"Let's get to know each other. I know how this ends, Ciara. Allow me to get you there with me."

I think of Ciarán. I never thought he felt like I don't have a life because of him. It breaks my heart because I've never thought twice about taking care of him. His words ring in my ears.

Please, Cee. My birthday wish is for you to be happy.

"Okay, Dylan. Okay," I say and place my hand in his.

He squeezes my fingers. Then we walk nearly across the apartment, leaving me to wonder how big this place really is. We walk through a set of double doors, and the huge king-size bed comes into view.

My heart rate picks up. Everything is moving so fast. What if we hate each other?

"Stop overthinking. The bathroom is over there. I'll get you one of my shirts. We're not going to do anything you don't want."

"Um, okay. Right."

The problem is, I can't say this isn't something I want. There's this energy surrounding us. I couldn't deny it if I wanted to.

Before I change my mind, I rush off to the bathroom to hop in the shower. Once behind the closed door, I start to freak out. This is the first time I've ever considered losing my virginity.

I glance at the time on my phone. It's almost midnight. I can stay in here freaking out, or I can shower and grow a pair.

"Ciarán is right. I'm an adult, I'm an adult, I'm an adult," I repeat to myself as I try to calm down. "Well, fuck, if you're an adult then act like it."

Looking in the mirror, I chide myself. I frown as I look at my braids. They're already fuzzy from Dylan and Daliah not knowing to cover them when they put me in bed last night.

Leaving them for now, I undress and climb into the shower. Reaching for his bodywash, I then sniff it. That's part of his amazing scent. I smile like a goofball as reality sets in.

Excitedly, I make quick work of my shower and hop out to dry off and take my braids down. When my hair is free, I run my hands through it. I can't help wondering what Dylan will think.

Shaking my thoughts off, I then grab a towel to wrap myself in. I have nothing else to help me stall. I shrug and gather my things to hold to my chest as I exit the bathroom.

I step out to find Dylan in a pair of sleep pants as he stands by a chest of drawers. Music is flowing softly through the room and candles are lit. I begin to chew on my lip as I shift from foot to foot.

He turns to face me, holding out a T-shirt. "I thought I had some old shirts that shrank in the wash. I can't seem to find any of them. Here, you can have this one. I'll take all of that."

I move to take the shirt from him. A blush comes to my cheeks as I drop my gaze to below his waist. My mouth falls open as I see the bulge and print his dick makes beneath the thin fabric.

I quickly lift my gaze and grab the shirt he's holding out as my face heats. He grins as he takes my things from my grasp and turns to place them in the accent chair in the corner. I bite my lip as I check out his tight ass.

When he turns back to me, he catches my eyes on him. I feel like such a creep. I made a fuss about spending the night, but he's just busted me ogling him not once but twice in the last two minutes.

Seeing I haven't placed the shirt on yet, he turns his back again and allows me to slip it on. Then I drop the towel I have beneath. I clear my throat after picking up the towel and go over to tap him on the shoulder. He turns to me with a heated look in his eyes.

Tossing the towel over my shoulder, I cross my legs at my ankles and clasp my hands in front of me. Dylan closes the small distance between us and lifts a lock of my hair in his hand. A smile comes to his lips as his gaze searches my face.

"What?"

"Now you look more like my little buddy," he murmurs.

"Is that a good thing?"

"You're gorgeous either way. I was a little taken aback to see it in those loose waves when you first came to the gym, but I knew it was you."

"I had it cut before we left San Diego. I wanted to keep up with the maintenance for my job interview, so I went for a trim and had it blown out and put in waves," I ramble.

His brows knit. "You were in San Diego?"

"Yeah, we lived there for a year. That's where I ran to. Theo seems to be scared of someone who lives there. I thought it would be the safest place to be."

"It was you. You were the girl in the bar. I thought I was dreaming or making shit up in my head. That was you and Daliah."

I gasp. "The guy before the fight broke out."

He nods. I look down at my feet as I try to process this. As my mind pieces it all together, he tugs me into him and holds me close. I wrap my arms around him and hold on tight.

This feels like where I belong. I can't deny the fact that it seems like fate has been pulling us together. Running my hands up his smooth back, I pull away and look into his eyes.

"Come, let's get into bed so you can tell me who you are now. We can play twenty-one questions." He gives a little smirk.

Dylan

"Wow, I can't believe you remember so much about me. I mean, some of that stuff I didn't remember until you said it," Ciara says from where she's lying on her back.

We've been up talking for hours. It's been so easy and effortless to fall back into our friendship. I've been lost in the sound of her voice a few times.

Like now, I'm sitting with my head back as I lean against the headboard with my eyes closed and my arms folded across my chest, her voice bringing a sense of peace to the room. Her words cause me to laugh and open my eyes to turn and look down at her. She has her eyes closed with a smile on her face.

"I remember more than you know. You were my best friend," I say.

"I wish I could remember everything. Like, did I change after the accident, or am I still me? Do you know what I mean?"

I can't imagine what this must be like for her. I'm happy I can trigger so many memories for her, but the really important stuff isn't coming back as easily, like what happened to her father.

While that's frustrating me, I'm happy to hear the hopeful sound in her voice. She's the most relaxed I've seen her since she walked into my gym.

"Yeah, I do. Let me see something," I say and move to find the spot I know she's most ticklish in.

I find it right away and she begins to squeal and laugh just as I remember. It's music to my ears. I begin to laugh with her.

"Dylan, oh my God, please stop," she gasps as I tickle her.

"That squeal is priceless. You haven't changed as much as you think," I breathe into her ear through my laughter.

She pushes a hand into the front of my hair as I let up and settle beside her. I look her over and my breath catches. My T-shirt is swallowing her. One shoulder has slipped down her arm, exposing her smooth-looking skin. Her hair is wild and splayed all over my pillow.

"You take my breath away. I've missed you so much."

She runs her hand through my hair and then back down over my neck to my shoulder. Locking eyes with me, she begins a path down to my bicep. I reach for her bent knee and begin to trail my hand up her thigh.

She swallows hard as her hand begins to shake. "You *have* changed a lot. Your voice, your body, you're all man now."

"Aye, and you're all woman. Ciara?"

"Yes?"

"We don't have to. I'll wait as long as you want me to."

"Now I know I've been waiting all this time for you. We've waited long enough. I'm yours, Dylan. Remember, nothing can keep us ap—"

I capture her lips before she can complete the words I said to her the last time we saw each other, when we were kids back in Ireland. Devouring her mouth, I reach for her weeping core. I groan as I find her soaking wet. She whimpers into my mouth as I find her nub and begin to rub it as I slip a finger inside her.

"Dylan," she cries out as I work my finger in and out, then add another.

The feel of her snug walls has me so hard. The sound of her wetness fills the room, causing me to groan. I can't get enough of her sexy mouth as I find a rhythm that makes her juices flow more for me.

Lifting up, she then reaches for the hem of my shirt and pulls it over her head. Her full breasts come into view, and I groan. I'm instantly painfully hard.

"You're so fucking sexy, baby. Do you like that?"

"Yes, please. I need ... Dylan, please."

With a grin on my lips, I start to kiss my way down her body. Pausing at her breasts, I pull a nipple into my mouth and suck on it before I swirl my tongue around the tight peak. My baby gets loud as she plants her feet, lifts her hips, and begins to ride my fingers.

Her body starts to quake with her first orgasm. I want to beat my chest. I did that.

I pull my hand from her pussy and lick my fingers clean. She tastes so good on my fingers; I need a direct taste. Slowly, I start back down her body until I'm flat on my belly like a sniper.

I look up her body as I move to take my first lick. We moan together as I begin to eat her pussy. She pushes her fingers into my hair and takes a tight grip.

I take my time, watching her body's reactions and testing to see what brings her pleasure—pulling on all the things I've learned to make this amazing for her. When she tries to run from me, I take my fingers out of the equation and lighten the pressure of my tongue.

"No, no. Don't stop," she pants.

I hum into her wet pussy and dive in deeper, adding my fingers once again. Her stomach caves and her thighs begin to shake. It takes no time for her juices to fill my mouth.

I lap them up, then begin to climb up her body to get to her sweet lips. I take her mouth as I palm one of her breasts and pinch her nipple. Her breast fits in my hand perfectly. I love it.

She smooths her hands down my back and shoves them into the back of my sleep pants to palm my ass and tug me toward her. I'm trying to hold my weight up off her. Ciara moans as she sucks my tongue into her mouth.

"I want you," she moans as I kiss my way down her neck.

I'm trying my best to take my time and not rush this. Right now, I know I need to slow down. However, she's driving me crazy with the sounds she's making and the way she has her hands all over me.

She glides her hand from my ass to my front, where she palms my length. I hiss and reach for her wrist. I swallow hard and take a deep breath.

"Hold on, baby, or this will be over before we get started," I say tightly.

"Okay." She nods. "I just want to bring you pleasure too."

"Believe me, you are."

I capture her lips again. My head clears a bit as I shove my pants down. I break the kiss and reach for my nightstand.

Reaching for the box of condoms I bought after I left my parents' house, I then tear it open. Ciara reaches for my arm.

I turn to look at her. She has a brow lifted as she looks at the box. I crack a sheepish smile.

"I thought—"

"I bought them today, just in case. I promise you, you're my first. That was my first date earlier. That was the first time I've eaten pussy. You can trust me."

"Okay." She nods.

I bite into the foil packet and roll the condom on. Quickly, I run my forearm across my forehead. I'm sweating like a motherfucker all of a sudden.

I settle between her legs and crush my lips to hers once again. She wraps her arms around my neck and kisses me back with so much passion. Reaching for her thighs, I pull her legs to wrap around me.

When I keep slipping through her slick lips, I break the kiss and pull back to see what I'm doing. Reaching for my shaft, I then push the tip into her. Lifting my gaze to hers, I look into her eyes as I push in more. Her mouth falls open in an *O* shape.

I reach for her waist and begin to rock in and out. My eyes roll back on the fourth pass when I thrust a little harder to get by her barrier. I still my hips when I break through and she whimpers deeply.

"Are you okay?"

She nods her head and whimpers. "Mm-hum."

I kiss all over her face before I take her lips. I moan from deep in my chest as she wiggles her hips beneath me. I take her cue and begin to move again. She cups my face and kisses me passionately.

I'm pumping into her slow and easy, trying not to go too deep so I don't hurt her. That is, until she locks her legs over the backs of mine and grabs ahold of my shoulders.

I forget all about the things I'm trying to keep my mind on, so I don't fuck this up. I growl and start to plow into her pussy hard and fast. My heart races and my balls tingle.

"Dylan, yes. Oh shit, yes. That feels so fucking good."

"Fuck, baby. I'm trying to take it easy. This pussy feels so fucking good. Holy shit," I bite out as her pussy ripples around me.

Latching my lips onto her neck, I suck as I continue to pound into her. She's so wet and tight. I pull my shit together and slow the fuck down before I come.

Reaching for her palms, I link our fingers together and lift our joined hands above her head. She throws her head back into the pillow and cries out my name. I drop my eyes to her breasts to watch them bounce as our bodies move together.

"Fuck," I growl out as I feel myself losing this battle once again. "Fuck, baby. This feels so fucking insane."

"You feel so good, Dylan. I can take more. You didn't need to back off."

"I did if this is going to last," I chuckle, breathlessly.

"Come, we can do it again. I want you to do what feels right to you."

I groan. "You're so fucking perfect. This was worth the wait. I want you to come first," I say and release her hand to reach between us for her clit.

She begins to shake. I grit my teeth and start to switch between deep strokes and shallow ones. I bite my lip, knowing I'm not going to last. I should pull out to hold off, but it might be best to get this one out of the way and try again once I recover.

"Fuck, baby. You're killing me," I moan when she lifts her head to latch her lips onto my neck as her pussy continues to ripple around me and suck me in deeper.

I come with a roar, thrusting a few more times as my scalp tingles. That was amazing. I felt the connection between us.

I love you.

I don't say the words out loud as I'm not sure she's ready for that, but it's the truth. I love her. I always have. I'm never losing her again.

CHAPTER TWENTY-ONE

Waking Up His

Ciara

I wake and go to stretch like a cat. I wince when my body screams from places I've never known could ache so much. That's when I register the welcoming scent engulfing me.

A smile comes to my face as I remember where I am and what happened last night. Or I should say this morning. A glance to my right tells me that I've slept in for most of the morning. I'm a little disappointed not to find Dylan in the bed with me.

He did say he's an early riser. We got to talk a lot more after our hours of passionate lovemaking, after round after round of hot sex. We soaked in his huge tub before we called it a night.

That was enough to make sure I slept like a baby. Well, that and being wrapped in Dylan's big, strong arms. I've never slept better.

A goofy grin comes to my lips. I sit up and look around the room in the light of day. This place is super nice. I smile at the black-and-white framed photo on the wall of Dylan in the ring, looking at the camera with such intensity in his eyes and sweat dripping down his face. There's a single bead on the tip of his nose.

Damn. That's my man.

Laughing at my thoughts, I fall back against the bed. I allow myself a moment before the reason I woke up reminds me that I need to get up. I stand on shaky legs and double over as soreness in my belly tells me I need to move a little more gingerly.

"But why do I still feel him? It's like he's still inside me," I mutter to myself as I hobble to the bathroom.

I empty my bladder that's screaming at me and then go to take a shower. Once I'm done, I find a robe on the back of the bathroom door and wrap it around me.

I can't help but laugh as it swallows me. I could probably wrap it around me twice. I have to hold the hem up so I don't trip over it.

If I can get to my gym bag, I can put on my workout gear at least. My stomach growls and I decide to go in search of Dylan and my bag. I should probably check on Ciarán while I'm at it.

When I pass by the room Ciarán was in last night, I find it empty. All his things are spread out as if he went through his haul this morning, but he's nowhere to be found.

I head for the stairs to go down to check the kitchen. On my way down the steps, I begin to hear voices. The delicious rumble of Dylan's voice sends goose bumps up my arms and across the back of my neck.

I bite my lip as I remember him speaking against the back of my neck while he thrust into me from behind in the wee hours of the morning. I will never be able to say my first night wasn't one to remember. It may have been his first time, but he treated my body like someone who knew exactly what to do with it.

I freeze just out of sight as Ciarán's words float to me. My heart squeezes as I listen to what he's saying to Dylan. He's taken to him so quickly.

"I think we've been lucky. I don't think Theo and Sean will stay away forever. Lily had her moments. She wasn't all bad all the time.

"However, she didn't want to see Cee go either. She always got this look when Cee would say we were going to be gone one day. Cee did everything for them.

"If it wasn't for her, there never would have been food in the house, and the place would have been dirty. She kept the gym going too. They never deserved to have her in their lives.

"They didn't appreciate her and always demanded more without thanking her for a thing. Sure, they made me clean up and if I was around, it was like their legs and hands didn't work.

"Ciarán, get me something to drink. Ciarán, where's the remote? Ciarán, I'm hungry. Get me a sandwich.

"Ciarán, get my shoes. Ugh, I hated it there, but Cee always had it worse. She could have left when she turned eighteen, but she stuck around for me.

"They're not going to let go. I know they're not. I need to be ready to protect her when they come. That's why I want to fight now. You make it fun and don't make me feel stupid if I mess up, so that's the reason I asked to train at your gym," Ciarán says.

"I want ya to fight because ya want to. Not because ya fear some assholes from yer past. They are yer past, Ciarán.

"I'm here now. Ya and Ciara are safe with me and my family around," Dylan says, his accent coming through thick.

Ciarán giggles. "That is so cool how you sound like a New Yorker one minute and then you sound like Taegan the next."

Ciarán doesn't seem to realize yet that Dylan's accent slips when he's angry. I'm sure he's pissed off from hearing how we were treated. Ciarán actually gave a mild version of it all.

"Ciara and I will have to take ya home, so ya can learn more about Ireland. Taegan and her family are from a town not far from where Ciara and I used to live."

"Why do you keep calling Cee that?"

"I used to know your sister when I was a little boy. When we were friends, her name was Ciara Walsh."

"Oh. I wasn't even one when Mom was killed. I don't know anything about before then. I wish I was older to help Cee remember more."

"I've got her there too, buddy. Finish your food and get back into that tape. That's a good site to learn from. Mondo is a good buddy of mine. His fighters have great technique."

"Your videos online are great too. You should start your own channel like Mondo's for MMA fighters and boxers. That way, he doesn't feel like you're copying or stepping on his toes," Ciarán says.

"You're a smart kid, you know that? I'll think about that one. It's not a bad idea. The editing and stuff will take up a lot of time I don't think I have."

"I could help with that. We could even use one of my drones to record footage. Bro, I have so many ideas."

"Slow down, killer," Dylan chuckles. "I have a lot on my plate, but I'll let you know when I'm ready."

"Cool, cool. Did you see that combo? Wow, this guy is good."

I take a deep breath and push forward so they know I'm there. I have to cover my mouth to stifle my laugh when Ciarán comes into view. The pajama shirt he had on last night is gone. He's sitting shirtless in his sleep pants just like Dylan is.

However, my brother doesn't have the muscles and chiseled body my man has. Ciarán may have shot up in height, but he's sitting with his little bird chest out, eating a sandwich and what looks to be chips while his tablet sits on the countertop between him and Dylan.

I walk over to see what they're looking at on the tablet. I kiss the top of Ciarán's head. He looks at me with a huge smile on his face. Dylan wraps an arm around my waist and tugs me between his legs as he kisses the back of my neck.

"Taegan dropped off a bag of clothes and toiletries for you. The bag is in the chair with your other things in our room," he says into my ear.

"Our room?" I crane my head and lift a brow.

"Cee, Dylan said we could all hang out today. Can we go to the beach? Please," Ciarán pleads, pulling my attention back to him.

"It can be our second date. I have time today and I know the perfect beach," Dylan breathes, sending a shiver through me as his breath fans the skin of my ear and neck.

I turn in his embrace to look up at him. His eyes are sparkling as he looks down at me. Placing his forehead to mine, he inhales deeply and tightens his hold around me.

"I thought I asked you to stop promising him things," I say.

"Come on, Cee. I did my homework Friday night. We've never been to the beach. Please," Ciarán pleads.

I only cave because I feel bad about spending so much time with Dylan yesterday during Ciarán's birthday. Before I can say a word, Dylan crushes my lips with his. Then breaks the kiss to place his chin on my shoulder.

"Why don't you go get ready while I feed your sister."

"Yes, I know just the fit. Taegan helped me pick it out. I love New York," Ciarán sings and rushes off.

Dylan buries his face in my neck and groans. The too-big robe falls open and he slides his hands inside to glide over my bare skin. My nipples tighten and my pussy begins to pulse.

"You're driving me crazy. I want you so bad, but I know we shouldn't again," he breathes into my neck.

"Why not?" I moan.

"You soaked after, but I'm sure you're still sore. Your body needs to recover."

"Okay, I have questions about your knowledge of sex and your level of experience."

He cups my neck and tilts my head back with his thumb. Then he ghosts his nose across my lips, my cheeks, and then the bridge of my nose.

"Before you get your license to drive a car, what do you do?"

"Take driving lessons," I reply breathlessly.

He nips my lower lip and tugs. "I've been waiting and preparing for you. You don't have to have sex to learn how to please a woman."

Sliding his hand up to my breast, he pinches my nipple. I gasp right before he shoves his tongue into my mouth and kisses me deeply. I lock my arms around his neck and lift onto my toes to get closer to him.

I drop my head back as he takes the same hand and slides it down between my legs. I suck my lip into my mouth as he tests my seam, rubs my clit, and then pushes his fingers in and out of me. Dylan gives my neck a gentle squeeze with the hand he still has wrapped around it.

Like last night, his simple touches make me instantly wet. I crave his touch and being near him more than I would like to admit. The sound of my juices validates the claim he has on my body.

"Don't worry, baby. I plan to share all I know with you and I'm going to enjoy every minute of it," he whispers into my ear.

"Oh my God, I'm gonna come."

"I know. That shit is so sexy. Come for me, baby."

"Fuck," I moan.

"That's my girl," he murmurs against my temple as I fall into him, shaking with my release.

My legs buckle and he has to hold me up. He releases my neck and begins to rub my back. I can't believe we just did that.

Ciarán could have walked in on us at any second. I look up at Dylan as the sound of his hum catches my attention. He's licking his fingers clean like he has honey all over them or something.

"I should probably go get dressed. Once my legs are working," I laugh.

He stands and scoops me up. "I'll have something for you to eat when you're done. Take your time," he says as he carries me back to his room.

Dylan

I hum to myself as I bob my head to the music playing in the background while I make Ciara a sandwich and my signature homemade potato chips.

I'm feeling good. Last night and this morning was amazing. Watching my girl come in my kitchen was such a turn-on. If I didn't know I fucked her more times than I should have last night and that Ciarán could return any minute, I would have bent her over and taken her again right then and there.

Her response to my touch is amazing. A smile comes to my lips as she walks up behind me and wraps her arms around me and presses a kiss on my back. Grabbing a chip, I half turn and hold it to her mouth.

She takes it and her eyes light up. I can't help dipping to peck her lips. Giving her a wink, I then turn to plate her food.

"Tell me more about this beach," she says as we move to the island for her to sit and eat.

"I've been thinking. Ciarán would probably like Coney Island. There are rides and a beach. However, Far Rockaway Beach is a vibe. We could skate and eat and chill."

"You skate?" She turns to look me up and down.

"Come on. Do I skate? You and I used to skate all the time."

"Yeah, but you're like what? Six-six, six-seven or something. I can't imagine you skating now."

"I'm six feet, six and a half inches. Two forty-five. I'm not scared of a pair of skates, I know what to do with my body."

"Yeah, I can't say you're lying there."

I snort and lean over to peck her lips as she chews on her food. She's so adorable. She has her hair piled on top of her head, showing off her ears and neck.

I reach to rub at the passion mark I left between her neck and shoulder blade as if I can wipe it away. She shrugs against my hand, trapping it in place. I can't help smiling. She's ticklish there too.

"Well, to be honest with you, he would love to skate more than he would like the rides. But we don't have skates," she says.

"Far Rockaway it is. We'll get you guys skates." I wink.

CHAPTER TWENTY-TWO

My Protector

Ciara

I have a face-splitting smile on my face as Ciarán downs his hot pretzel then turns and skates off. We've been having so much fun. For once, I feel like I'm getting to watch my brother enjoy being a kid.

I'm actually having fun and allowing myself to relax as well. Dylan has been so attentive. He took me and Ciarán to get our own rollerblades. However, Ciarán opted for a new skateboard.

Dylan had his own blades but purchased a board once Ciarán had to have one. The two have been showing off since we got to the boardwalk. It's so nice here.

I've had frozen drinks with plenty of alcohol to mellow me out and some of the most amazing tacos ever. Things have been so chill, with the exception of when I took off my top to reveal the bikini top beneath.

Dylan wasn't a fan. Taegan left me a cute tank top and a pair of cute shorts that Dylan eyed as if he was going to protest.

Instead, he said nothing but has been right on top of me wherever we have gone. I bought the purple swimsuit for myself when we stopped for the skates and boards.

I've been skating in the bikini top and shorts. Dylan has been eyeing me with a mix of lust and something else. Possessiveness and something I haven't pinned down.

I can't say I don't understand the feelings. I've caught women ogling him all day. Those well-fitting jeans show off his firm ass and thick thighs.

His black T-shirt is tight enough to leave nothing to the imagination. Every muscle, every ab screams, *Look at me.* They have all been looking while drooling.

"Yo, yo, shortie, hold on," a guy calls out as I go to skate after my little brother.

"Nah, you good," Dylan booms as he moves up behind me and places his hands on my waist.

"Oh, that's you, fam. My bad. She's a baddie though, you might want to keep that close."

I snort. "Excuse me?"

"No disrespect. You're fine as fuck. If he don't have no hands and he not toting that thing, he better keep you close for when his ass has to run for it," the guy says and all his friends laugh around him.

"Bro, find something safe to do," Dylan says.

"Like you gonna cause me problems? Please," the guy scoffs.

"You're looking at two sets of registered hands. We got plenty of problems to hand you," I hiss.

"Son, look at her. I don't think she's capping," one of the others says.

"What about me tells you I'm not holding? Don't let these gentrified folks get your head blown off," Dylan bites out. "I wouldn't even waste my time knocking you the fuck out."

"Y'all be acting like y'all ain't never been outside. I told y'all fucking with the white boys out here ain't it. Ace, you better shut your stupid ass up and let's go," one of the others says.

Another in the group speaks up. "I'm not getting caught out here after dark. The next train is coming. Let's get to the station before we miss it."

"Whatever, white boy don't know what to do with none of that. Your loss, ma."

I roll my eyes. We've been having way too much fun to allow this guy to get under our skin. I turn my face up to look at Dylan.

He still has his eyes on the guy and his friends as he holds me close to his front. His skateboard is between my legs as he has one foot on it. Without taking his eyes off them, he dips in and pecks my lips.

"Y'all get on back to Brooklyn safe. See you around." Dylan winks at them.

"Yo, how you know—"

"You never know who you're talking to. I'm safe anywhere I go in my city. Can you say the same?"

"Fuck, I told you to leave them alone. I knew he looked familiar. You one of them O'Briens ain't you. The one that fights and shit," one of the others who's been silent says with wide eyes.

"Tell your brother Dyl says what's up. I'll be by to collect my disrespect fee during the week."

"Aw, man. This ain't even my fault. Shit. I hate you, Darius. My brother is going to fuck me up," the kid whines.

"Come on, man. I need to get home. I'm not looking for no smoke," one of the others says, tugging at the one who tried to give his friend the warning.

They take off. Dylan finally turns his attention fully to me. I give him a smile, but his expression remains tight.

Moving to turn so I can face him, I place my hands under his black T-shirt and run them up his back. A gasp leaves my lips as I graze what feels like a gun.

I look up at him with wide eyes. I thought he was bluffing. I had no idea he had a gun on him. Dylan palms my ass and rolls me closer to him.

"I told you, you're always safe with me." He searches my face with his eyes. "Does that scare you?"

"No, I'm just surprised."

He pecks my lips. "There is a lot you're going to learn about me and my family. Your comfort level with being around guns should be pretty high. Do you think that's something you can handle?"

I smirk. "Depends. Do I get one of my own?"

He laughs and relief passes over his face. "We'll get right on that. You can't be the only female in the family without one."

It's good to see the ease and smile return to his face. Man, he has a temper. His anger had been pulsing in the air.

Kissing his chest, I then place my cheek against it. He wraps me in his arms and kisses the top of my head.

"Time to continue our date," I say.

He grunts and pulls a sour face. "Come on, let's catch up with Ciarán. Time to get out of here and it's time for you to cover up. That's going to happen more the later it gets."

Dylan

"I had so much fun. Thanks," Ciara says as she looks up at me.

She is lying with her head in my lap as we sit on the couch at her place. The TV is on, but it's muted. We've been more interested in each other and our conversation.

I brought her and Ciarán back to their place in Harlem. Finding parking was a bitch. I almost told them to pack a bag so we could head back to my place. I'm not ready to let my girl out of my sight.

"I'm glad you enjoyed yourself. Ciarán seems like he had fun."

"I think he did too. Tired him out for sure. I heard him snoring when I went to the bathroom earlier. That kid never goes to bed this early willingly." She snickers.

I had a great time with them too. If not for those little assholes, it would have been the perfect date. I'm already thinking of other dates we can go on.

I know I have to plan them around Ciarán. He's a big part of her life I can't ignore. Honestly, I don't want to.

I really like the kid. He's grown on me. As the youngest, I've never known what it's like to have a little brother.

Ciara is more than his big sister. She's his guardian. I smile at what that makes me. Finding her again has been more than I expected in a good way.

"What are you planning to do with your day tomorrow? Ciarán has school, what will you be up to?"

"Ugh, *no*," she drags out. "I had so much fun today. I don't want to think about adulting."

I chuckle and run my hand through her hair. That was a bad move. The semi hard-on I've had for the last two hours comes to full life.

"I only want to know what we're doing with our day," I say.

"We?" she says and lifts a brow.

"Yeah, unless you have something you need to do. I thought we could drop the kid off at school and spend the day together."

"Don't you have a gym to run and training of your own?"

"I do, but you're more important to me. I want to make up for all the time we lost."

"Honestly, I would love that, but I need to find a job. I'll blow right through that money from the other night. If Ciarán brings home one more trip slip, I'm going to scream.

"That place is expensive enough. Why are the field trips so bougie and expensive? He's always so excited about them. I don't have the heart to tell him no.

"He's a good kid. It's not his fault I lost my job."

I shrug. "He can bring those to me from now on. I'll give him the money. All you need to do is sign for permission."

She pouts and rolls her eyes. "No, Dylan. I need to find a job to take care of my brother myself."

"What were you doing at the job you lost?"

"I was a bottle girl."

I try to stifle the frown that comes to my face, but I fail epically. I hate the idea of her working in a nightclub or bar. That's not happening again.

"Oh my God, look at your face. You have a jealous streak. You can chill. I don't want to do that again anyway," she laughs.

"Come work at the gym. You said you ran the one you grew up in."

"That would be a no. Too much drama. I'm not even sure I want to train there."

I work my jaw as I think of the reason for that. Cadlha will be gone soon. She doesn't have to worry about that.

"I want you to reconsider. I've been stretching Taegan pretty thin as my assistant due to the need to step in for some family business. I could use you at the gym to take a load off her.

"Try it out. See if you like it. Once I make some necessary changes, there won't be any more drama. However, in the meantime, we can brainstorm something else."

"Like what?"

"How about the tatting? Let me see some of your artwork. I'll tell you if you're trash and need to find something else. We may need to put your ass in trade school or college."

She gasps and glares at me. I laugh. She gives me a smile as she sits up and punches me in the arm.

"Ow," I say as I rub my arm.

The shit really does sting. Damn, she hits hard and I don't think she put much behind that. She sticks her tongue out at me.

"If I remember correctly, you could only make sad little stick figures when we were younger. I'm already ahead of you."

I wink at her. "I'll be the judge of that. My stick figures were the shit. I always made sure you were cute."

She bursts into laughter that lights up her beautiful face. Shaking her head, she then gets up to head for her drawings. I watch her walk away and bite my lip as my eyes land on her ass in those little shorts.

I'm glad she can take a joke. She'll have to have thick skin around my family. We're always teasing and taunting each other and anyone else who enters the line of fire. No one is safe.

I can't wait for everyone to know I've found her. I know Mom will be ecstatic. My heart swells with pride.

My girl is gorgeous and smart. My family already loved her when she was little. I know they will be proud of the woman she's become too.

She returns and sits down, placing a sketchbook in my lap. I look into her eyes and feign nervousness. She pokes me in my side and leans in to kiss my lips.

I don't allow her to pull away, grasping the back of her neck and taking over the kiss. She wraps her arms around my neck. I deepen the kiss and groan.

She pulls away, breathless with a smile on her lips. I run one hand over the side of her face, then palm it as I stare into her eyes. The dreamy look on her face echoes how I feel.

She clears her throat. "Don't judge me too hard," she says and bites her lip.

I shake my head and release her face to open the sketchbook and flip through. The first page I open to has a drawing of half a young boy's face. I keep turning and find other images then more of the boy. Each image of him gets more detailed.

My mouth falls open when I realize it's me. It's almost as if I'm watching how she remembers me more and more, drawing by drawing.

"Well?" she says a little above a whisper.

"You're amazing. I'm speechless. These are so far from our little artwork when we were little. Damn, baby, you're good."

"Thanks, but I don't know if that will translate into tatting."

"Let me ask you something."

"Okay," she says, looking up at me with those big, pretty eyes.

"Is it something you would want to try?"

"Yeah, I think it is."

"Okay. That's all I need to know. Forget looking for a job. Give me a bit of time and I'll have something for you."

"*Dylan*," she drags out.

I shove my hand into her hair and tilt her head back. She looks back at me, searching my eyes. I do have something.

"Trust me."

Before she can say a word, I take her lips and kiss her passionately. She pushes the sketchbook from my lap and climbs into its place. I get lost in the moment as I palm her heavy breast.

Someone clears their throat, causing us to break apart. Well, Ciara tries to break the kiss, but I follow her lips as she tries to back away. I grunt as Daliah begins to speak.

"Damn, you two are fire together. I hate to interrupt, but I just wanted to check to see if I should order something for you guys to eat too," she says.

I stand and take Ciara's hand. "Nah, sweetheart. We're good. We're calling it a night," I say and walk us toward Ciara's bedroom.

"Wait, you're staying the night?" Ciara looks up at me and asks.

I shove my hand down the back of her shorts and start to finger her from behind as I bite my lip and lift a brow. Lust fills her eyes as she pulls her lower lip into her mouth.

"Okay. I'll take that as a yes."

CHAPTER TWENTY-THREE

Always This Way

Ciara

"Look at ye. Ye've grown up so much and yer so pretty. I remember when ye were this high," Dylan's mother says as she holds her hand up to demonstrate.

"It's so good to see you again."

"Come, come. I want to know all about ye. I've been baking and cooking since Dylan called to say he'd be bringing ye by. I can't believe it's ye," she gushes.

She looks so happy as she looks between the two of us. Her eyes are twinkling, and she has a huge smile on her face. She has hugged me at least a dozen times since we walked through the door.

"Ma, you're going to scare her away," Dylan groans teasingly.

The smile on his face says he isn't bothered at all. It's crazy, but the scent of her home brings back so many memories of her. I can remember her and my mom talking in the kitchen while Dylan and I played together.

The scent of freshly baked cookies makes my mouth water. Ciarán would love her cookies. She makes these apple butter cookies with white chocolate that I remember loving.

"I have apple butter white chocolate chip cookies for ye," she says as if reading my mind. "I wish Dougie were here to see ye."

We enter the kitchen, and Dylan takes a seat at the nook, then pulls me into his lap. The last week has been amazing. Dylan's life is insanely busy, but he always makes time for me.

He has spent every night at my place and drops Ciarán off at school for me every morning. I've hesitantly started to work with Taegan, allowing her to train me as Dylan's second assistant.

All has gone well as Cadlha has been away on vacation or something. I'm not really worried about her. Taegan and Dylan have said she'll be dismissed from the team when she returns.

Amara, the other female fighter on the team, is sweet as can be. I've worked out with her a few times. I will officially take Cadlha's spot in two weeks when Halley comes on board as my trainer. I'm sort of excited about that.

"So, love. Tell me about yerself. How have ye been?"

"There really isn't much to tell. It's me and my brother. I spend most of my time taking care of him."

"Oh yes, Iesha was pregnant before ye all left. I remember her being so excited for baby number two. She and Donald planned to tell everyone once …" She cuts off and her cheeks turn pink.

Dylan clears his throat and changes the subject. My heart swells as he tries to protect both our feelings at the same time without making it painfully obvious.

I have a great time as we spend the morning with his mom. The cookies are as delicious as they were when we were little. We play cards and have easy banter before Athena or Kara—as she insists I call her, since I'm family—serves us lunch.

I'm a little sad when we have to leave. Kara seems to be too. I promise to come by again and bring Ciarán along next time. I leave feeling like I've learned another side of Dylan.

A side I'm falling for. He's such a loving son. It's clear to see how much he adores his mom and how much she loves him.

"I loved seeing you with your mom."

"She was on her best behavior," Dylan says.

I laugh. "She's sweet. She didn't have to send Ciarán cookies and the rest of lunch."

"You're family. She will always take care of the both of you. Watch out."

He grabs my arm and pulls me into him right before I step into dog poop as we walk to the car from his family's home. I look at the pile and frown. There's another dried spot a few steps away.

"Ugh, does anyone around here scoop up after their dogs?"

"Nope, not at all," he chuckles.

Lacing our fingers together, he then maneuvers me toward the car. I laugh to myself as he opens the door for me, and I realize he doesn't drive the car he promised to Ciarán anymore.

"What's that look about?" he asks as I climb into the car.

"If I said I liked this car, would you give it to me?" I tease.

He shrugs. "Do you want it?"

"No."

He winks at me and closes the door to round the car and climb in behind the wheel. I watch him closely as I take in his every move. Dylan is so comfortable in his skin. He moves like a well-trained fighter in and out of the ring.

I love how his T-shirt clings to his skin. I lower my gaze to his thighs and my mind goes to his naked body and the tattoo on his right outer thigh.

It's two pairs of boxing gloves. A smaller pair on top of larger ones. It seems like they're hanging from strings. The artwork is mind blowing. They're 3D and so realistic.

"I can feel your eyes on me," he murmurs as he pulls to a stop at a stop sign.

He turns to glance at me. That smile does it to me every time. I reach to brush my finger over his lips. He pulls my thumb into his mouth and sucks on it, then twirls his tongue around it.

"You're hard not to stare at," I say breathlessly.

"You're hard not to taste. Ciarán has strength training today. Booker picked him up and took him to the gym. You want to do a little shopping or go see a movie or something?"

"You have a five-thirty meeting. We should head into the gym, but I'll take you up on the movie some other time."

"Cool, I'll have Book drop another car off for me tonight. This one is yours."

I gasp. "Dylan, it was a joke. I don't want your car."

He shrugs. "It's already yours."

Dylan

A smile comes to my face as Ciarán comes running into the kitchen at my place. We just got in and I'm washing my hands to start dinner. Ciara is sitting at the island as she texts on her phone.

I think she's talking to Taegan. The two are becoming close and work well together. My life has never run more smoothly.

"Cee, holy freaking cow. You have to see my room. It's not like it was last time.

"I have a new computer with a sick setup. There's a brand-new laptop. Transformer bedding, a drone, and the closet is full of clothes.

"It's like I live here or something. It's so me, like it was taken out of my brain. You have to come look."

I turn to look at Ciara and she's looking at me as if she has a ton to say. I wink at her. The only reason I spent the entire week at their place is because Taegan was working on remodeling the room and Ciarán had school.

We'll have to wake up early to get him to school on time tomorrow, but his room was ready, and I wanted to surprise him with it.

"Have you booted up the computer? I had my cousins customize it for you. They know their shit. You have things that haven't hit the market yet," I say.

"Yo, bro, thank you so much. This is ... oh my God, you're so cool. Come on, Cee."

Ciara shakes her head and gets up to follow him as he takes off. I go to follow, but my phone rings. Instead, I fall back and pull the device to answer.

It's Aidan. I groan. I'm not in the mood for this tonight. I wanted to stay in and have a quiet night with my girl and her brother.

I was going to make dinner and suggest a game night before Ciarán needs to get to bed. I know nothing good is on the other end of this call. I'll be out the door in the next ten minutes.

"What's up?" I say as I pick up the call.

"Need you down at The Clover. Some douchebags came in and tore up one of the VIP rooms," Aidan says.

"Okay, why is this something I need to come handle? You know what to do."

"Yeah, I thought the same thing until one of them dropped a calling card from the Scorpions. This is above my pay grade."

"The fuck. I'll be there. Don't let them out of your sight."

I frown and hang up. The Scorpions run under the cartel. They're one step below the big guys. I have no fucking clue why they would step foot in one of my family's establishments to trash the place, let alone drop a calling card.

That's not something any of us would take lightly. The disrespect is understood and received. Now I'm going to set an example of why we're not to be fucked with.

***

"You don't want to do this, man. You do this, you're starting a war," one of the four guys who trashed the VIP at the club says as I douse him and his three buddies with gasoline.

"Shut his gub," I sneer.

Booker moves to rip the sleeve from one of the other's shirt and stuffs it into this guy's mouth. They had their turn to speak and I didn't like shit they had to say.

I kick him in the chest, causing him to fall back into the building puddle of gasoline. He tries to wiggle around to sit up as his hands are bound behind his back. I snort.

I said I don't want to do this shit all the time, not that I don't enjoy it when I get to blow off some steam. They're lucky I was in a good mood today. I'm actually showing some mercy.

"Yer first mistake was thinking ya could walk into a business my sister runs and threaten her or my family. Ya weren't expecting to come face to face with me, were ya?" I sneer.

He's trying to scream something through his gagged mouth. I couldn't care less what. Logan's absence and Brooklyn's diverted attention have given some people balls.

As if Jamie and I aren't here to hold shit down. To be honest, if Kate and Connie were here instead of me, this probably would have ended worse for the sorry bastards. Trying to extort the O'Briens, they must have bumped their fucking heads.

"When ya get to hell, tell them yer plus-one is on the way. Yer boss will be coming to join ya. I didn't start this war."

"Ya did when ya walked into our club, but I promise ya, I'm the one who will finish it. That's enough, boys, let's go," I say to Booker and Aidan.

I let the rest of the gasoline from my canister spill out as I go. As we get to the exit, I pull out the lighter I took off the leader of this little crew and set fire to the calling card that called for my attention.

"The audacity," I grunt then toss the burning card over my shoulder.

I grin at the hiss the flames make as they come to life. I don't even bother to look back. There will probably be consequences for this. So be it.

"What do you think this all means?" Aidan asks as we stand across the street watching the Scorpion's headquarters burn.

I go to answer him when an SUV speeds up and stops before us. I put my hand on my piece at my back until the front passenger side door opens and Czar hops out. I can't help wondering what he's doing here.

He gives me a nod and moves to open the back door. I sigh and signal for Booker and Aidan to put their pieces away. They do as told.

"You guys take off. Make sure the cameras in the area are taken care of," I say as I move for the SUV.

I climb in and sigh. I don't know why I thought I was going to head straight home to shower and relax. However, my curiosity is piqued as I look at the man waiting in the back of the vehicle for me.

"What's up, LaSalle? What can I do for you?"

"Nice work," he says and nods at the burning building as the SUV pulls off. "Your brother wasn't sure you would take the initiative."

"They threatened my sister. I'm sure Brooklyn will understand."

"I'm not talking about Brooklyn. Logan thinks it's time you understood the Alliance a little clearer," he replies.

"Logan? You've been in touch with him? When is he coming home?"

"We're doing all we can to get him out, but the red tape we have to cut through is thick. That little situation has been brewing because murmurs are getting out that we're working to bring him home.

"I like that you didn't call Brooklyn for permission to settle the problem. You handled it your way. What Logan and I intend to do will take many hands.

"There's no place for egos, jealousy, or greed. We need to know we have people we can trust to keep everyone in line. We'll have enough enemies out there.

"We don't need them within the camp as well. New York is huge. There will need to be more than one captain here. You have proved you're ready.

"I've been hearing about you and how you've stepped up since Logan's been gone. He's proud of you and wants to give you a crown among the ranks."

"Even if I just started a war?"

He chuckles. "You haven't started anything we didn't want. Don't worry about it. It's all a part of the plan."

I sit in silence for a moment, allowing his words to sink in. I had no idea Logan had plans for me. I hadn't planned to be here.

I thought I would be in Ireland waiting for Ciara to return to me, but she's here and my grandda is gone. So much has changed.

"What if I don't want it?"

"You're already in deeper than you know. This didn't start with me and Logan. Heck, it didn't start with Dougie. Sure, your dad has played his hand, but your grandpa Ian saw something no one else did and he placed us all on the board one by one.

"Make no mistake, you were a rook from the day you were born. Your place on the board was cemented a long time ago. As roles are being assigned and reassigned, you have been given a purpose.

"The rules have gone out the window, kid. Forward is the only motion you have, Dylan. You will rise to be a king among kings in New York.

"Your grandfather Oland knew what he was stacked up against. It's why he tried so hard to stop it. Trust me, when the time comes and you understand it all, you won't want to trade places."

***

As I drag my exhausted ass into my apartment, LaSalle's words are still ringing in my head. I spent another two hours in the back of that SUV as he explained to me how the Alliance will work and what my role will be.

My head is still spinning with it all. God, if they can pull this off … nothing will be the same. The kind of power they're talking about is … I have no words for it.

However, if there's anyone who can do it, it's Logan and LaSalle. There was something LaSalle said when he dropped me off at the train station to get home that stuck with me. I'm not sure what he meant by it. I guess that's why it's rattling around in my head.

"Nothing has been done without a purpose. Every dot makes a connection. Your grandfathers set us up.

"One set us up to fail, the other set us up to take over. Don't take anything for granted. Everything is a gift," he said as I went to step out of the vehicle.

I shake my thoughts clear as I walk by Ciarán's room and hear him and Ciara talking inside. A smile comes to my face. As long as I have them safe in my home, I can handle anything.

Not wanting them to catch the scent of gasoline on me, I head for my bedroom for a shower instead of letting them know I'm back. Once in my bedroom, I strip from my clothes and bag them for the fire.

I'm on my third scrub down and rinse when small arms wrap around my waist. I push my wet hair out of my face and turn around in her embrace. Ciara's eyes are filled with concern.

"Is everything okay?"

"Yeah, I handled the situation."

"Did you eat? We saved you some of the pizza we ordered. Although I had to fight to make sure you had more than one slice when you returned."

I laugh. That kid can eat. He's a growing boy and those workouts are making sure he needs more fuel than usual.

"I'm good. I might get hungry later, but I'm straight for now."

She runs her hands up my chest as I reach to palm the globes of her ass. I'm hungry, but it's not for pizza. Seeming to get that, she lifts on her toes and reaches to tug my head down to her.

I close the distance and seal our lips together. I groan into her mouth as she reaches between us and palms my length. The restraint I've been showing for the last week breaks.

I spin and lift her into my arms to slam her against the shower wall. As I devour her mouth, I thrust into her tight heat. I growl and my eyes roll back.

"When are you moving in? I need you here with me. Our lives should always be this way. You and me together," I breathe against her mouth as I move in and out of her tight body.

"Dylan, please," she pants as she tightens around me.

"Are you begging me to make you mine or to make this your home?"

"Both, I want both."

"Say no more," I grunt as I thrust harder and pin her to the wall.

CHAPTER TWENTY-FOUR

Are You Crazy?

Ciara

This is my third week working at the gym. Dylan and I have fallen into a routine that includes work, training, and taking care of Ciarán. We're like a happy little family.

Dylan has continued to take Ciarán to school in the mornings even though he has to wake earlier to get Ciarán uptown in time for class. He has Booker or Aidan pick Ciarán up after school and bring him to the gym.

I was hesitant about that at first, but Taegan promised my brother would always be safe with the two and Dylan would take their heads off if anything ever happened to my brother. In her words, they are willing to die for Dylan and anyone important to him.

It's so clear to see how important Ciarán has become to Dylan. He treats him like his own little brother. Ciarán has been so happy since we moved in with Dylan. Daliah was sad to see us go, but we text every day.

I'm excited because she's coming by the gym today. I've been going through the inventory list Dylan needs while I wait for her. This time of the day tends to be quiet on a Friday. Dylan stepped out to FaceTime with his brother Cole about an hour ago.

Taegan isn't in yet. She had to take care of some of Dylan's other business. I smile as I think of her and look across at the little desk Dylan brought in. It was meant for me, but Taegan took it over and insisted I take Dylan's desk.

He doesn't need to be up here as much now that he has the two of us. He spends more time down in the gym or on the couch in here while we use the desks.

My stomach growls loudly, breaking into my thoughts. A glance at the clock tells me it's time for my lunch break. Deciding to go out for lunch to stretch my legs, I finish what I'm working on and log out.

The portal the O'Briens have set up for all their businesses is so cool. It has a POS system, chats for everyone to communicate through and so much more I don't even have access to.

I'm enjoying my new job here. I grab my purse and look at my heels, debating whether or not I should change back into them. Dylan's eyes were filled with so much lust this morning when he saw me in my tight light blue jeans, black sleeveless satin halter and black six-inch heels. Remembering that look, I toe off my sneakers and slip my heels back on.

I'm humming to myself as I jog down to the main floor. I get halfway to the front door when a red-faced Cadlha appears. Her eyes look crazy as she looks around frantically.

"Ya," she growls. "Ya did this. Everything was fine before ya showed up. Ya and that fucking brat he fawns over.

"I told ya to stay away from him, but no, ya went and got me thrown off the team so ya can try to take him from me. Ya will pay for this."

"Three," I breathe and drop my bag as I come out of my heels lightning fast.

This bitch thought I was playing. I did try to warn her. She's taller than me, so I go for her body first, folding her with a punch to her right side before I lay her out with an uppercut.

"Damn," Taegan calls out, causing me to turn and look at the entrance.

She and Dylan are staring at Cadlha on the floor in a heap as I stand over her, not even breaking a sweat. I nudge her leg with my toe to make sure she's still breathing after the way I rocked her head back.

She groans and releases a whimper, but her ass is down for a nap. I shrug, turning to step back into my heels and grab my bag to go and have lunch.

Dylan grabs my arm when I go to walk by him. I look up at him and frown. He palms my face.

"Ya can relax. I just need lunch and some air," I murmur.

A smile comes to his lips, and he leans in to kiss my forehead. Before I can turn and leave by myself, he tugs me into his side and starts off with me.

"Taegan, get her a medic. Then get her ass out of my gym," he calls over his shoulder.

Dylan

Cadlha deserved what she got. I had stopped her before she entered the gym once I ended my call with Cole. I let her know she was off the team due to her poor performance last tournament.

I didn't banned her from the gym, but she would no longer fight for me. Now her ass can never enter my gym again. I'd been scrolling through texts and looking at flights in case I have to go to Cali, as Cole and I spoke about.

Something is going on with some business interests of his and a friend of Wyatt's. Nicholas Lincoln is considered family. Someone is fucking with family, and I might have to take a trip to step in and help out.

Apparently, it's better if it's one of us, as the problem knows Wyatt and the rest of my cousins. They're all too close to the issue. Cole believes they're closing in on the threat, but he's calling me in just in case.

I'm a little frustrated as Ciarán has school, so I doubt I'll be able to take him and Ciara along with me and I don't know how long I'll be gone.

"What are you still stewing about? I told you I'm fine," Ciara says as she tilts her head and studies me.

I turn my gaze to her and focus. I've been staring off into space. I smile as I think of how well we're able to read each other.

Our connection is growing so strong, so fast. Even without her full memory back, it's like we've known each other forever and no time has passed. She makes everything about my life better.

"Cole needs me to come to Cali. I might be gone as soon as week after next," I reply.

"Oh," she says and looks down with a sad face.

I reach to lift her chin, so our eyes meet again. "I don't know how long I'll be gone, but you guys will have the place to yourselves and Book and Aidan will be around. Taegan will check in daily to make sure you guys are all right," I say.

"We'll be fine. You don't have to bother any of them. I'm just going to miss you."

Leaning in, I take her lips in a searing kiss. I haven't left and I miss her already. This is going to be rough.

"I'll feel better if they're around and I already miss you. I wish you guys could come along with me."

"Wait, week after next? Ciarán has a week off from school. Daliah and Vega planned his birthday surprise vacation for that week." She pauses and bites her lip. "Maybe ... I mean, if you want. Maybe Ciarán will be okay if I go with you for a few days."

I search her face with my gaze. "You must really be falling in love with me."

The brightest smile lights up her face. She reaches to tug at the hair beneath my lower lip, then cups the side of my face. I reach to lace my fingers with her other hand.

"I do love you. I also wasn't invited on the trip with them. Something about giving me time to myself and that was before I had a boyfriend."

I stand to lean across the table and palm the back of her head as I kiss her deeply. I fucking love this girl. Beyond a little ten-year-old's crush.

She's more than I could have ever asked for. I wouldn't change a thing about her. Not even that temper.

"I love you too, baby," I say against her lips as I break the kiss.

Retaking my seat, I pick up my fork and spear one of her shrimp from her plate. I pop it into my mouth and chew as I smile back at her. In my head, I rearrange my plans so I can bring her along to Cali.

A few days are better than nothing. Cole said he needs me there just in case. I can spend a few days with my girl.

Cadlha

"Fucking bitch," I growl as I stomp into my apartment.

My head is still ringing. That bitch snuck up on me. If it were a fair fight, I would have kicked her ass. Don't worry, I'm going to get my fair shot. I'll find a gym and she'll have to face me.

"I'm going to make you both pay," I scream at the print hanging on my wall of Dylan.

It's the black-and-white one Taegan had ordered for his home. I stole the original one that came in and she had to order another, thinking the company screwed up.

I hardly ever invite the bitch to my home, so she'll never find out I took it. Fucking bitch. I'm so done with her.

"I'm her family. She should've had my back. I'll show them all.

"First, I'm going to find a new gym. Then I'm going to find out where the fuck that bitch came from and I'm going to send her right back after I kick her fucking ass.

"I'm going to make ya pay, ya bitch. If it takes the rest of my fucking life, I'm going to make yer life hell. Just ya wait," I yell.

I grab my phone and start making calls to put my plan in motion. I know people. Taegan isn't the only one with resources. The little bitch is from Ireland. Let's see who she belongs to.

CHAPTER TWENTY-FIVE

I've Got You

Ciara

"Dylan," I giggle as I try to get away from him tickling me.

I'm supposed to be packing for our trip. We leave in the morning. I already saw Ciarán off for his trip with Daliah and Vega. He was so excited.

They're taking him to Universal Studios. I wish I could see Dimitri, Nashawn, and Ross in the theme park. I have no doubt my brother will be safe, but I'm sure it will be amusing to see those big guys trailing him and the girls.

I'm so happy Ciarán has so many people who love and care for him. I'm going to miss him this week. Dylan started tickling me because I've been moping as I pack.

"We can take him again on his next break," he breathes into my ear.

"It's not that I'm not going on the trip. It's that I'm not going with him. I'm going to miss his little face."

"How could he be so happy to leave me behind? My heart hurts." I pout.

Dylan stops tickling me and wraps his arms around me as he kisses the top of my head. His warm embrace begins to soothe me as he rocks us from side to side.

"He's twelve, baby. He's going to be homesick within a few days, and he'll be calling you every five seconds. Right now, all that's on his mind is all the fun he plans to have," he says against my neck as he buries his face there and inhales.

I sigh. "I better hurry up. I should have done this by now, but I was too focused on making sure Ciarán had everything he needed."

"Let me help you."

"If that help comes with you keeping your hands off me, then sure."

"Shit, in that case, you better get your ass to packing. You're on your own."

I burst into laughter and toss the shirt in my hand at him as he flops down on the bed. He catches the shirt and brings it to his nose to inhale. I roll my eyes and turn my focus back to packing.

"You and Ciarán's shit always smells like fresh laundry. You have to show me how you do it."

I laugh. "I don't know, I can't show you all my tricks."

"Give me time, I'll figure them all out," he croons.

I pause and let reality hit. It's been four weeks, I've already learned a lot about Dylan. I can't say I've learned anything off-putting.

However, now that Ciarán isn't here. It seems like things have slowed down in this moment and I have to wonder what we're doing and where this is going. I frown and stare down into my suitcase.

Dylan reaches for the front of my shirt and tugs me to him. He then lifts my chin for me to look at him. I search his eyes as my thoughts race with all the things I should be focused on.

"What just happened?"

"Just thinking."

"About what? Talk to me."

"Maybe I shouldn't go. I mean, I might need this time to myself to think."

"Think about what?"

"Us, this, what I'm doing. Yeah, the chemistry between us is insane, but is that enough for this to last? This might be too good to be true. What happens when we disagree?"

"Do you kick me and my brother out? Will you fire me from my job? I think I'm fucking up because you're the most familiar thing in my life.

"You're attached to a past I want desperately to remember and connect with. However, I've given you so much power in my life and I swore I'd never do that again. What if I'm caught up in a fairy tale that ends badly? I have more than just me to worry about."

"Baby, first you need to understand I'm not an asshole. I would never leave you out on the street with nothing. Second, there's nothing you could do that would make me so mad I don't want you.

"If you need time to yourself to think—" He pauses and shrugs. "I want you to come with me, but I'll give you the time you need. I'm going to miss you, but if you want to stay, that's up to you.

"I have always belonged to you and always will. I'm here. I will remain in your life no matter what capacity you decide that will be in."

"Gah, you know you're not helping, right? You're too perfect."

He tugs me to him for a searing kiss. I climb onto the bed to straddle his lap. He palms my ass and deepens the kiss.

My thoughts and emotions settle as I melt into him. My safe place. With Dylan, I always feel like everything will be okay.

I've tried to fight that feeling, but his actions always justify my deeply rooted response to him. I've fallen so hard for him, and it scares me. As if he knows and understands this, he wraps his arms around me and holds me tightly.

"You're the one who's perfect. I love you," he says against my lips.

I sigh. "I love you too. I better get back to packing."

"If you hurry, we can go on a date."

"I thought you would want to stay in. It's the first time we've had the place to ourselves." I wiggle my brows.

"Oh, I've thought of that. Trust me, I have. I have plans for later," he says and winks at me.

Dylan

It started raining, so we opted to stay in for the night. I planned to cook for us, and I have a little surprise for Ciara. While sitting with her as she finished packing, I remembered the moment I knew I would love her for life.

It's been playing in my mind so clearly. I want her to remember that moment, or at least the feeling. We were so young, but the way she looked at me and held on to me told me she felt the same.

I didn't know the feeling as the love I have for her today, but I knew then that I would love her and protect her in any way I knew how. I'm lost in my thoughts as I get everything ready to start prepping dinner.

Right before Ciara finished packing, I drew her a bath to soak in while I came down to the kitchen. A text to Taegan and my plan is already set in motion. When we leave here in the morning, I want Ciara to have no doubts that I'm in this for the long run.

There's a second entrance to the rooftop that doesn't require coming through the apartment. Taegan and whoever she has helping her will be able to come and go without Ciara knowing. Thankfully the rain has slowed and the part of the rooftop I plan to use is covered for nights like this.

The design and attention to detail are what sold me on this place. Since Ciara and Ciarán have been here, it feels more like a home. Music is playing throughout the apartment, and I notice I have a smile on my face. I have everything I ever wanted and more.

The one thing that's been nagging at me is how to fulfill the entirety of my promise. Her dad is gone. How do I fight him for permission to marry her?

I've trained my whole life for that fight. I want to keep my word, but I don't know how to make that happen. I'm going to figure this out.

I'm thinking of ways I can keep my promise as I set the table for a candlelight dinner. There has to be something I can do. My father's words ring in my head.

If ya make a promise, ya keep it.

"I plan to, Da. I plan to," I say to my thoughts.

"Should I be concerned? You're in here talking to yourself."

I turn to find Ciara standing watching me with her arms folded over her chest. She's in a pair of yoga pants and a tank top. I chuckle and shake my head.

My phone buzzes in my pocket, dragging my attention from her. I pull it out to find a text from Taegan. I smile as I read it.

Taegan: *All done. Enjoy the rest of your night and have a safe trip. I'll hold down the fort.*

Me: *Thanks. Buy yourself something on me.*

Taegan: *Don't have to tell me twice. You don't have to buy my loyalty, but it never hurts our friendship. Love you, Irish. This shit is so romantic by the way. Later.*

Me: *Love you more, tiny creature. Get home safe.*

Taegan: *Ha!*

"Tell Taegan I said hi," Ciara says, bringing my attention back to her.

"She's gone for the night," I say and shrug. "Come here."

Opening my arms, I wait for her to come to me. She steps into my embrace and wraps her arms around my waist. I'm filled with so much peace in this moment.

"What are you making? Can I help?"

"Chicken and rice with creamed spinach. Come on, it might be fun to cook together."

"I'll be able to make sure everything is seasoned," she murmurs.

"That happened once, and I told you I got distracted and missed a couple of things. It wasn't that bad."

"Bro, that shit was so bland I wouldn't have fed it to the cat," she snorts.

"We don't have a cat, smart-ass."

"But you would look so adorable holding a kitten."

I reach to shove my hand down the front of her yoga pants and cup her pussy as I turn her into me, her back to my front. A gasp leaves her lips as I lean over her and suck on the back of her neck as I begin to finger her.

"Am I adorable now?" I breathe in her ear.

"Dylan," she whimpers.

I bite my lip, loving the sound of her calling my name while she pants for me. I don't stop until I have her soaked and shaking. Licking my fingers clean once my girl comes, I then get us started on dinner.

With our easy banter, dinner is finished in no time. I've set a romantic dinner for two in the dining room, and we eat and enjoy the night like a couple who's been together forever, not just four weeks.

Ciara sighs and falls back in her seat. "That was so good. Want to watch a movie, or should we go to bed to get up for our flight?"

"Actually, I have something I want to show you."

"Oh really?"

Standing from my seat, I then blow out the candles. I scoop Ciara up into my arms. She wraps her arms around my neck and kisses my cheek.

Holding her tight, I make my way up to the rooftop. I smile as the glow from the lights and candles comes into view. Once outside, I walk over to the tent I had Taegan purchase and set up for me. Then I place Ciara on her feet in front of the opening.

More lights and candles light the inside. There are also two sleeping bags. Ciara steps inside as I wave her in. I then duck in as best I can after her and quickly take a seat on one of the sleeping bags.

"What's all of this?" she asks.

Then her gaze lands on the little ballerina with boxing gloves on. I had Taegan commission the piece two weeks ago, as I remembered her father giving her a similar item. His only played music and spun around on its pedestal. This is a figurine on top of a jewelry box.

It still plays music. "Time After Time," just like her old one played. During our chat tonight, she mentioned liking to dance and how it sometimes helps her in the ring.

Her mother was the dancer, but Ciara took to fighting more than her dance classes. Her ma and mine would take her and Kate to dance. I wasn't sure if the piece was ready, but I'll have to thank Taegan because it's the perfect touch.

Ciara reaches for her head and stumbles to take a seat across from me. Quickly, I crawl over to her and palm her face. I search her eyes as they seem to be a bit distant.

"Your brothers teased me and told me there would be snakes in my sleeping bag. I cried, but you were there, and you hugged me until I calmed down," she says as she looks back into my eyes.

"Yeah, I did. That was the first time I realized I loved you and always would."

"But … why did the ballerina trigger that memory?"

"Your dad gifted you one just like it that same day. I played the music from it while you calmed down and you fell asleep."

"I carried her around with me all day, didn't I?"

"Yeah. How is your head? I'm sorry, I wasn't thinking about the headaches. We can save the champagne and strawberries for another time. If you want to go back inside, we can," I say and kiss her forehead.

"No, no, it's fine. My head is okay. It's already passing.

"This is so romantic and cute. I want to stay. Thanks, Dylan.

"You just reminded me of the day you became my little hero. I think I might have known I loved you that day too."

I crush her lips with mine and kiss her deeply. Everything else is forgotten as I make love to her in the tent on my rooftop. It's one of the most amazing nights of my life.

CHAPTER TWENTY-SIX

Distracted Mind

Dylan

This week has gone by entirely too fast. Ciara has only been here with me for four days and has to head back today, but I don't want her to go. However, I have no choice but to let her.

Cole was right. He did need me here. Lincoln's wife's friend was shot and is in a coma.

I've been tasked with helping my cousin John look after Mark's girlfriend. She was an eyewitness to the shooting and saved the guy's life. I agree that she needs someone to look out for her.

John and I have been taking turns here at the hospital since the shooting. I only got to spend one day and night with Ciara since we've been here.

"Hey, go on. Take your girl to the airport. I've got this," John says as I look down at my phone, frowning.

I look up into his golden eyes and think of my mother and her brother. Uncle Joe was happy to see me when I got in. I could tell by the bear hug he gave me.

I've often wished we all lived closer to one another. However, I now know that wasn't possible because of my scumbag grandfather. From what I know, we're lucky to have the relationship we have. Especially the relationship we had with Grandda Ian before cancer took him from us.

"Nah, you've been with Bailey all day and last night. I've got it," I reply.

"Dylan, she hasn't left Mark's side. You can take your girl to catch her flight, and I'll hold things down here. If you see her to her flight safely, your head will be here and not on that phone. Go on," John says pointedly.

I lick my lips and think about this. I have been more focused on my phone than anything else. I start to feel like shit because my focus should be here with my family and business.

Releasing a long breath, I nod. "All right, I'll be right back as soon as she's on her flight. If you need me, call."

"It will be fine. See you when you get back," John says and pats me on my back.

I jump up, look down at my watch, and take off. I have enough time to pick Ciara up from our hotel room and get her to the airport for her flight. I'll be back before anyone notices I'm gone.

Ciara

"Book will be waiting for you at the airport. Taegan upgraded you to first class. You have the keys I gave you?"

"Yes, Dylan. I know how to take a flight and get home," I giggle.

He's worse than a parent sending their kid to day care for the first time. You would think I were a child the way he's been fussing over me. Reaching for the straps on my carry-on, he fixes them for the millionth time as he leans in to kiss my forehead.

"Call me as soon as you land," he says as he searches my eyes.

I lift onto my toes and cup his face as I peck his lips. Before I can pull away and settle back on my heels, he takes my lips in a scorching-hot kiss. I'm blushing when he releases me.

I bury my face in his chest and inhale him as I give his waist a squeeze. The last couple of days weren't what I thought they would be. I spent most of my time alone in the hotel while he took care of whatever it was his brother needed him to do.

I may have been here in Cali with him, but it's been lonely. I don't think I want to know what life is like without him. I'm not looking forward to getting back to New York and being in that big apartment all by myself.

It will still be two days before Ciarán gets back and there's still no telling when Dylan will be home. This is going to be so hard. I've grown so used to waking with him or going to bed in his arms.

"I should go," I say and release him.

"I love you, baby. I'll be home as soon as we wrap things up here."

"I love you too. See you when you get home."

I start to back away, but he doesn't let go. Instead, he holds on until his long fingers can no longer reach my fingertips as I back away. My stomach drops.

No longer able to watch the wide range of emotions running across his face as he balls his fists and works his jaw, I turn and head for my flight. I keep telling myself everything will be okay. However, I have this feeling, like he shouldn't be here.

CHAPTER TWENTY-SEVEN

Failed Again

Dylan

I stand in the parking lot of the hospital feeling like a small child as my brother intercepts me by my rental car. We've been out here for about ten minutes now as he goes in on me for my mistake.

I already feel like shit, but each word he says feels like tiny blades cutting me over and over again. I fucked up. This one is on me. John should have gone home and I should have stayed put.

"I asked ya to do one thing for me. One. Why would ya bring Ciara here knowing ya would be distracted from yer task?" Brooklyn shouts at me.

I can't call him Cole right now. He's so angry with me, I don't know if he sees me as his brother. Bailey is missing.

If I were here, this wouldn't have happened. I think I understand the hurt and anger in his eyes. This isn't about Bailey.

This is about Raven and Shauna. He's seeing Raven dying in his arms again. I think that knowledge sours my stomach even more.

"I'm sorry. I didn't want to leave her alone back in New York. I thought it best if she were with me. At least until Vega and the others were back," I try.

"Bullshit. That's total bullshit and ya fucking know it. Taegan, Book, Aidan … fuck, any one of our guys back home could have stepped in. Yer not a kid anymore, Dyl. Ya have real responsibilities. Ya can't drop the ball like this."

He gets right up in my face as his nostrils flare. Right now, it doesn't seem like he has to look up at me or that I'm looking down at him; his anger is so palpable and overshadows everything around him.

He lowers his voice to continue. "Do ya understand what's going on around ya? Have ya forgotten who ya are, what we do? Ya can't afford to be slipping, we can't afford it, not with what's coming.

"Not after what I've set in motion. Bailey could have been one of ours. We should have treated her like one of ours.

"Ya were supposed to help John, not leave him with his dick in his hands. Fuck, Dylan. If we can't protect her, how am I supposed to trust bringing them home? I expected so much more from ya."

"I fucked up, Cole. I'm sorry. I'm here now. I'll help find her and get her back. Maybe she just went home for a nap."

Brooklyn spins away from me and walks a few paces away. "Are you fucking kidding me? I told ya, she never made it home. If she's taking a nap, it's the kind that says we failed … again.

"Get the fuck out of my face, Dylan. Take yer ass back to New York where yer head is. I'll let ya know *if* we find her," he growls and storms off.

Ciara

I was exhausted by the time Book got me home to the apartment. He carried my bags upstairs for me and took off once he knew I was inside, safe and sound. I was surprised not to receive a reply from Dylan after I got his voicemail when I called.

He hasn't returned my texts either. I fell asleep waiting for his text after I showered and talked to Ciarán. My brother is having a ball while getting spoiled. Daliah sounds like she's having a great time as well.

I owe her and Vega for this. My brain starts to come awake with that thought. That's when I register the sound of someone else in the apartment. I jump up and go for the gun I know Dylan keeps locked away on his side of the bed.

My fingerprint unlocks the box, and I pull the gun out and hop up out of bed to see who the fuck is in here. I should be the only one in the apartment until Ciarán gets back home in two days.

I move through the hallway as quietly as I can. As the fog clears from my brain, I realize there is music playing low in the gym at the end of the hall. Dylan usually lifts weights in there when he's home.

I wasn't in there before I fell out, so I'm not the one who turned the music on. Maybe Taegan came by? I shake that thought off because she would have let me know first.

Sound from downstairs catches my ear and I head down that way, still moving as soundlessly as possible. When I get downstairs, there's movement in the kitchen. I turn the corner and find Dylan's big ass standing there, dripping in sweat as he downs a glass of water.

"What the fuck?" I breathe as I place the gun on safety.

Dylan looks to me and his eyes go wide. "Shit, did I wake you?"

"Well, duh. What are you doing here?"

A frown comes to his face. "I don't want to talk about it."

I move closer and place the gun on the countertop. Placing my hands on his bare torso, I look up into his eyes. He looks frustrated, angry, and … hurt.

"Babe, talk to me. What's going on? Why are you here? Did something happen?"

Tears begin to swim in his eyes. He looks up at the ceiling to try to hide them from me. I cup the sides of his face.

"Hey, hey, what's going on? Talk to me."

"He's not wrong. I fucked up. I had one job, and I fucked it up," he chokes out.

"Dylan. You're scaring me. Are you all right? Is everything okay? Is Cole okay?"

"He's fine. He's pissed as fuck at me, but he's fine."

"Do you want to talk about it?"

"No, I've had enough time on the flight to think about what I did. I just want to clear my head and think of anything else. You should go back to sleep. I plan to work out some more before I hit the shower and go to bed."

"Dylan, please don't shut me out. I want to help."

"Talking isn't going to help me right now, baby."

"Then what will? I'm here. Tell me what you need."

His eyes darken and he backs me toward the other side of the kitchen, where the wall of cabinets is. When my back hits the hard surface behind me, he reaches around me and grasps ahold of my butt. It dawns on me that I had fallen asleep in my boy short panties and lace bralette.

He looks me deep in the eyes. "I need you. I need to ground myself in the knowledge that you're real and you're here, safe, where I need you," he breathes against my lips before he kisses me.

I moan into his mouth as I run my hands up his sweaty torso. My palms glide over his smooth skin and hard muscles. My head falls back as he starts to kiss his way down my neck and then my body. I whimper as he pulls down the cups of my bralette and sucks my nipple into his mouth before releasing it with a pop.

He continues to move downward with open-mouthed kisses as he peels my panties down my legs. He tosses them aside then spreads my legs and buries his face in my core. Wedging his big shoulders between my thighs, he tosses my legs over his shoulders and stands with me in his hold.

I startle and yelp, trying to find something to hold on to. Dylan grasps my ass in a firm grip and settles me in place without missing a beat as he hums into me. I can do nothing but moan and lock my fingers into his hair.

My eyes roll back and my stomach caves as he continues to devour me. My back hits the cabinets behind me and I try to grab ahold of them, but that's useless. Dylan reaches for one of my breasts as he shoves his tongue in and out of me.

"Fuck, Dylan. Holy shit, baby. Yes, yes, yes. So good. I'm about to come."

He begins to bob his head more vigorously as he inhales deeply, as if breathing me in. I gush all over his face. He laps up my juices and turns his head to suck on my inner thigh.

He then allows my body to slide down his front and places me on my feet. I drop to my knees and peel his sweat shorts down his hips until I get them to his ankles and his heavy erection springs free.

I bite my lip as I stare at his length. Dylan has a dick that's as gorgeous as he is. The sight beckons me in for a taste, causing my mouth to water.

I've only gone down on him once with his patient guidance. I wasn't great at it, but he took his time to tell me what he liked and what he wanted. I promised myself I'd learn and do better next time.

I take a deep breath as I get ready to test that theory. Wrapping my hands around him, I lean forward and take him between my lips. He groans and reaches to scoop my hair into his hands, away from my face.

Looking up through my lashes, I find him watching me with unrestrained lust in his expression. His lip is trapped between his teeth, and his brows are threaded as he clenches his jaw. It's hard not to look at him and be turned on.

I begin to work my hands with my mouth, but he has other plans. Reaching for my hands, he laces our fingers together and pins my arms up above my head against the cabinets behind me. He then begins to pump his hips into my face.

Without control, I have to breathe through my nose and take whatever he's giving. Drool starts to slide from the sides of my mouth and down my chin. He pulls out to allow me to gasp for air.

Saliva drips down onto my breasts as I gulp down as much air as I can. Dylan releases his hold on my hands to place both my wrists in one of his palms. He then takes his dick and guides it back into my mouth.

"Open up and stick your tongue out," he commands.

I do as he says while looking up into his eyes. He taps his tip on my tongue a few times and then shoves his way back into my mouth. He's entering my mouth at an angle that's causing him to hit my cheek with each thrust.

Reaching for my hair with his free hand, he grasps ahold of the back and holds my head in place as he widens his stance and fucks my face. I start to choke and he backs off for a beat before he starts to thrust into my mouth again.

"Shit, baby. That's so fucking good. This is why you're all that's on my mind. You're all I want," he hisses out through his teeth.

I hum around him as my eyes begin to water. I start to bob my head as he releases my hair. He begins to get harder in my mouth. Suddenly, he pulls out and grasps a tight hold of my face before he bends to kiss me hungrily.

Without breaking the kiss, he lifts me to my feet. Once I'm standing, he reaches to squeeze one of my breasts as he begins to turn me to face away from him. Grasping my waist, he moves me to bend over the countertop in front of him.

I cry out as he enters me. We decided weeks ago to stop using condoms. It was my suggestion. I'm on birth control and neither of us has ever slept with anyone else.

I claw at the counter as he rocks into me fast and hard. My eyes roll back in my head. He palms my breasts as he fucks the shit out of me.

"Is that too much, baby? Can you take this?"

"Yes, yes, I'm fine. I can take you, babe. I was made to take you, Dylan."

"Fuck yeah, baby. Tell me who you belong to. Whose pussy is this, Ciara?"

"Yours, Dyl. It's so yours. Fuck me. Fuck me harder. Please."

I whimper when he pulls out. To my surprise, he lifts my leg up and out and thrusts back in. He then unfolds my leg and lifts it until I'm stretched in a split with my leg pinned to his chest.

He begins to rock into me like this, and I lose my fucking mind. Thank God my brother isn't home. I'm crying out so loud it's echoing around the space.

"What are you doing to me?"

"Fucking you like you want me to," he groans.

Dylan

I keep fucking Ciara like I can chase my demons down inside her pussy. As I pin her leg to my body and hold her open in a split, I thrust into her sexy body.

"Fuck, that's my good girl. Take it all, baby," I groan.

I drop my gaze down to her ass and bite my lip to hold in a growl. Her ass looks so good as I hold her spread open for me. She's creaming all over me.

I lick my lips as I watch my cock slip in and out of her. With my free hand, I reach to squeeze her ass cheek as I pound her pussy out. She looks up at me as if she's in awe.

"You feel how hard you make me? I'd protect you with my life. You mean everything to me. Do you know that? Tell me you understand that."

"Yes, Dylan. I know, I understand."

Leaning in, I kiss her hard. I have her on her tiptoes as I tear this juice-ass pussy up. This is exactly what I needed.

Cole wasn't wrong. I should have been there and focused on Bailey. We can't afford not to do our part.

Not now, not ever. If I had failed one of my brothers or cousins, I wouldn't be able to live with that. I've been praying they find Bailey.

I can't imagine how Mark will feel to wake and find out she's gone. I would be destroyed if that were me and this woman in my arms. My heart aches with the thought of losing her.

So much so, I start to fuck her harder. I had come in to find her sleeping. The plan was to allow her to sleep no matter how much I needed her.

Now I'm so happy she woke. I needed this connection. I was so hurt by Cole's words, but they hurt because I know how right they were. I'm not a kid anymore and this world we're in doesn't have time for me to half-ass shit.

I growl at my thoughts and start to chase down my release. It tingles throughout my body. I roar her name as she comes and rips my climax from my body with hers.

"That was exactly what I needed," I pant as I release her leg and pull out.

"Happy to help," she says breathlessly.

I kiss the top of her head and snort. I'll do better. I know I can with Ciara in my life. I have no choice but to.

CHAPTER TWENTY-EIGHT

Return to Family

Dylan

Four months and a week later …

"I miss you too. I wish you were here," I say to Ciara as I pace the grounds of the McGowan property.

I wanted to bring Ciara and Ciarán along, but my father and Cole didn't think it was a good idea. In fact, my father got this look on his face I still don't understand, and he wouldn't elaborate.

Not even when Cole asked about it. I got the feeling Dad knows more than he's letting on. However, he made it clear this wedding wasn't the time for Ciara to appear.

"I wish I were there too, but you said you would be home as soon as the wedding and that business trip with your family are over. Focus on your family. We'll be here when you get back."

"Hey, baby. I love you. I'll call you back after the wedding reception when I get back to my room."

"Love you. Talk to you later."

I hang up as I keep my eyes on my brother standing off to the side, outside the tent where Toby's wedding reception is being held. He's staring down at his phone with his lips pursed in concentration. It's the first time I've been able to get him alone since last night.

I walk over to say the words that have been rattling in my brain since we parted ways. A few things were revealed while we were out drinking with our cousins. I need to say this before it burns a hole in my chest.

"I might have been drunk, but I heard what Carrick said last night," I say to Cole, sounding as hurt as I feel. "DJ is here."

Cole hasn't told me once where DJ has been, but Carrick and the others seemed to know more about her than Cole has ever shared with me. After what happened in Cali, I'll admit the revelation stings.

He looks up from his phone and locks eyes with me. "Aye, I can hear yer thoughts. I've been meaning to apologize to ya. I was too hard on ya over what happened.

"Deja wants to come to the States, but I can't guarantee her safety there yet. I've finally gotten a handle on things here for her to come back to Ireland, but not without a lot of eyes on her and hoops I'm jumping through.

"I was frustrated with the situation and blamed ya for one of my biggest fears. I'd do anything to keep her safe. It's hard to do that when I can't give her the answers she wants.

"I'm still earning her trust, which is hard for reasons ya wouldn't understand. What happened with Bailey wasn't yer fault. This shit is taking a toll on me, on everyone.

"It's been two years. He should be home. Until he is, we still have to be careful. Like I said, I've finally tamed the bullshit here, but that doesn't mean they won't try me. I'm doing what I need to make sure everyone, especially Deja and Shauna, comes out on the other side of this."

I swallow down my hurt and nod. "You're doing a great job. Logan will be proud. I know Da is.

"You don't owe me anything. I was wrong, but it will never happen again."

My brother snorts and pats my cheek. "Aye, it will. You're in love. We become blind when we fall. Fuck, I'm walking into walls left and right." With that, he walks off and joins Wyatt and Noah as they horse around at the entrance of the tent.

Walking into the tent, I spot Granny McGowan sitting with Auntie Cass. The woman has already put away more alcohol than the lot of us combined. Everyone is happy for Toby.

I'll be hitting the gym hard after this trip and all the alcohol I've been consuming. I shake my head at myself and head for the table my cousins have gathered around.

Cadlha

"What do ya have for me?" I say to the asshole across from me.

Arnold has had a crush on me since I joined Roaring Irish. However, I have always had my sights set on Dylan. Although I did keep Arnold close enough to be my pet.

Ten grand and the promise of a date made him not only my pet but my spy. While my cousin back in Ireland works on trying to find me something on that bitch, I'm working my angles from this end.

"Right now, Dylan is away at his cousin's wedding, but he didn't take her or the kid with him."

"That's it?"

"No, no. The kid, he's your in. She's protective of him and would do anything for him. You could totally use him to get her to do anything you want. If you can get him away from Book and Aidan, you can use him against her.

"Tuesdays, that's when you can strike. Booker drops him off at the gym, but there's like a thirty-minute window between when his trainer arrives and the time that she's with Halley.

"Taegan is never around during that time. I don't think they've realized the hole they created during that time since Dylan has been away. Any other time, he's covered by someone at all times. As long as you pull this off before Dylan gets back, you're good," he says, looking around nervously.

He would be nervous. I had him meet me for drinks at one of Dylan's family's bars. I want him to be seen here. If this shit goes south, he's catching the fall for it.

"Do you know how long he'll be gone?"

"Another two or three weeks, from what I overheard Taegan say."

"Good, I'll be ready by Tuesday after next. It will be close, but that's the soonest I can get things in place. Can ya get him to me?"

"Cadlha, I don't know about that. Do you know who Dylan's family is? You're playing with fire.

"I said I would get you information, but taking that kid is something else altogether. If I'm caught, I can kiss fighting goodbye and I might even end up dead," he says with panic in his eyes.

I bite my lip and pull my sunglasses down my nose. Giving Arnold a look of lust, I drag my foot up his leg under the table. His pupils dilate and he drops his gaze to my breasts. I lean in to give him a better look down my shirt.

"If ya help me, I'll give ya another ten grand and I'll make sure that date I promised ya ends with a happy ending."

"Okay, fine. I'll try."

"Good, I'll have a car for you and the address of where to bring him."

Taegan

I narrow my eyes at the screen in the office upstairs in O'Brien's Corner. I'm covering this place for the family since everyone's in Ireland at the wedding. I've been on rotation between three of the bars as Booker and Aidan handle the clubs.

My nights have been pretty busy. Dylan didn't want Ciara in on this task. It would have been easier if she could have stepped in with all the responsibilities I have with him gone. Too bad he's too possessive and overbearing when it comes to her.

"That is ya, ya banjaxed slut. What the fuck are ya up to?" I say to the screen.

I noticed when Cadlha sat at one of the back tables. The sunglasses and Roaring Irish skully gave the eejit away. I swear her breast milk was laced with stupid.

I fold my arms over my chest and watch her and the melter sitting with her. I can't see his face yet, but I plan to wait for him to face one of the cameras so I can see who he is. I don't trust my cousin as far as I can throw her.

"I'm still pissed at the lie ya told to get into Dylan's gym, ya box-headed twerp. Ya always take a wee inch and run for the hills. Ya keep it up, I'm going to make yer da a childless da," I murmur to the camera.

"Hey, you okay in here?" Susan, one of the waitresses, says as she pops her head in the door.

"Aye, I'm fine," I say and wave her off.

"Cool, I wanted to talk to you about picking up a few extra shifts."

"Give me the dates ya need, I'll try to fit you in the schedule where I can."

"You're the best."

I just want her to go so I can focus on the screens. I toss a pen and pad toward her and shoo her off. Just as she walks out, the guy with Cadlha turns toward camera four.

"You have to be fucking kidding me."

CHAPTER TWENTY-NINE

Where is He?

Cadlha

Two months later …

"I have the kid. We're at the spot. What do I do now?" Arnold says on the other end of the phone, sounding like a pussy.

Finally, he got the job done after botching it while Dylan was away. All that planning on my end was a waste. In his defense, that Tuesday his sister picked him up from school and they never went to the gym.

It took another ten grand, but I talked him into sitting on the kid and finding the right time to nab him for me. He enlisted a buddy to help. Something I'm not happy about, but I plan to use to my advantage.

"You and Mike make sure the kid is secured. Then you come meet me at the Fighting Irish in Brooklyn," I reply.

"Are you fucking kidding me? Do you know who owns that place? You're trying to get us killed," he hisses.

"Grow a pair. When she shows up, I'll get what I want, and she'll get the brat back. Ya said yerself, Dylan has been busy with something and isn't around much. Do as I say," I snarl and hang up.

Rumor is Dylan can't enter his uncle's lairs. That's why I chose the Fighting Irish for this. Even if he finds out what's going on, his bitch will be on her own.

"I'm going to teach ya a lesson, ya fucking bitch."

Ciara

"Hey, hey, what's going on?" Taegan asks as she finds me pacing outside the gym.

I tug at my hair as I try Ciarán's phone again. He should be inside with Corey, one of his trainers. Corey steps in whenever Dylan isn't around. My brother has his own team now.

Booker said he dropped him off at the usual time. However, Ciarán wasn't here when Halley and I returned from our run. I thought maybe he went for something to eat.

I went to all his favorite spots looking for him, but no one has seen him today. I have a sick feeling in my stomach, and I don't know what to do. I can't call the cops.

This is just the type of shit that will expose us. I haven't called Dylan because something has been going on with his family. All his cousins from Cali are here in New York. I don't want to take him away from that.

"Ciara, me wee ass is too small for me to be clenching me cheeks this long. What's going on?"

"I can't find Ciarán. He wasn't here when Halley and I arrived," I say as I shake my hands out in front of me.

"Okay, calm down. We'll go inside and see if the cameras show us anything. I'll call Dylan and he'll—"

"No, I can't bother him."

I turn and rush back into the gym to head up to the office, where I can log into the cameras. However, when I step inside, Marty, one of the fighters who trains here, stops me to hand over a note.

I take the note and open it quickly. It's my worst nightmare. I'm looking at a ransom note for my little brother.

> You want the kid back, show up at this address tonight and be ready to fight for him. Come alone or this goes bad.

"What the fuck?" Taegan says beside me.

"Not a word of this to Dylan. I've got this," I say as I turn to her.

"Do ya even know where that address leads?"

"Do you?"

"Yes, somewhere that motherfucker will regret. Ya should call Dylan."

"This isn't his problem."

"But—"

"Taegan," I choke out. "Ciarán is all I have left. If they want me to fight for him, I'm going to fight for him. I can't afford for anything to happen that will jeopardize his safety."

Without another word, I take off for my gym bag so I can head to this address. I'm getting my brother back. No matter what.

Dylan

"Dude, will you come on? I haven't seen Nolan and Crush perform live in years. I want to make this concert. That charity concert was sold out before I could get tickets," Jamie fusses.

I want to take Ciara to the Briggs compound so she can see them perform there too. However, she's not answering my calls or texts. I know she'll be pissed to miss this.

I decide to call Taegan to see if she knows what's up and why Ciara isn't answering my calls. I haven't spoken to my girl since before her session with Halley. They were going out for their run when last we spoke.

"Hello," Taegan answers her phone, sounding nervous, which is weird for my friend.

"What's going on? Why can't I get in touch with Ciara? And don't lie to me. I always know when you're lying."

She releases a heavy sigh and launches into what's going on. My head feels like it's going to explode by the time she's done. I'm already moving out of Jamie's place, heading for my car.

"What are you going to do? You can't go there."

"I'm on my way. I'll deal with Uncle Ronan when the time comes."

"Irish?"

"What?"

"I'll meet you there. I think I might have something else ya might want to hear."

Before I can reply, she hangs up. I'm fuming, so I don't bother to call her back to ask her what she's talking about. I don't think I'd be able to comprehend a word she says at this point anyway.

"Yo, where are ya going?" Jamie calls after me.

"The Fighting Irish. Someone took my girl's little brother and they're forcing her to fight to get him back," I growl.

"What the fuck? Who has lost their fucking mind?" he says as he jumps into the passenger side of my car.

"What are you doing?"

"Making sure ya don't do anything that's going to get yer ass in trouble."

I grunt and pull off like a bat out of hell. I have so many things running through my head as I race across town to get to my girl. I'm going to kill someone if a single hair on her or that kid's head is harmed. Jamie is right. Someone has lost their fucking mind.

CHAPTER THIRTY

Cadlha

"What happened to Arnold?" I say to Mike as he walks up to me.

"He's with the kid. He sent me to meet up with you. What do you need me to do?"

I blow out a breath and roll my eyes. Ugh, good help is so hard to find. Why do I even bother?

"Fine, I need you to make sure this goes into her water bottle before the fight," I say.

"You want me to drug her?" He gives me an incredulous look.

"It's just a little something to slow her down in the second round. I get to kick her ass in the first round and make sure she goes down in the second for a little extra cash. No big deal. I'm only guaranteeing my win on all fronts."

Mike scoffs. "Dude, you have to make it through the first round."

"What's that supposed to mean? I still train. I'll be just fine."

He coughs behind his hand and says something that sounds like *unusual*. I roll my eyes and ignore him.

"Just take it and make sure it gets into her water bottle before the second round," I snap.

He makes that scoffing sound again and takes the powder before he walks off, shaking his head. Ignoring him, I turn to text Arnold to tell him where to drop the kid off after the fight. Then, I get back to getting ready for the fight.

"Get ready, bitch. I'm going to take everything from ya like ya did me."

Dylan

"Oh no ya don't. I was told not to let ya in."

"I promise ya, ya don't want to try me tonight. Move out of the way."

"Yer banned. This is my first night on the door. Don't fuck this up for me, O'Brien."

"Oh, give it a rest, Eoghan," Taegan says as she runs up beside me.

Eoghan rolls his eyes. "Jesus, Mary, Joseph. Why tonight? First, that bag of crazy, that's that cousin of ours, shows her face here, now you two. How's a guy to move up with the lot of ye trying to sabotage me?"

"What's going on? Why are ya banned?" Jamie asks, looking at me suspiciously.

I sigh. "Long story. Uncle Ronan thinks he's protecting me. Move out of my way, Eoghan. Take our money and step aside. I'll deal with my uncle later.

"He doesn't want me here fighting. I'm not here to fight, but if you want me to go through ya, I can change that. Move," I growl.

"If Oisín sees ya, that's my ass," Eoghan groans.

"Then ya better hope he's too busy fucking some broad's brain out," I mumble.

"Aye, go on, but do me a favor. If yer caught in there, tell them Finn was at the door. He's been doing my head in for weeks. Fucking asshole."

"Don't worry, cousin. We got ya," Taegan says and pats him on the chest.

"Bag of crazy? Was he talking about Cadlha?" I ask Taegan as we walk into the building.

This place is louder than usual and there's a different type of energy flowing. The crowd is going crazy over the fight happening in the cage. We haven't reached the point where we can view the cage yet.

"Aye, one and the same. That's what I wanted to tell ya. She was at the bar while ya were away at the wedding. She and Arnold met up there. I have a feeling he's the one who helped her with this," she says.

"Arnold, as in Arnold from the gym?"

"Aye."

I tighten my jaw. That asshole has always had a thing for Cadlha despite her not giving him the time of day. If he is helping her, he can forget ever fighting again. I'm going to break both his arms and legs. He'll be lucky if he can shit straight once I'm done putting my foot up his ass.

"Is this a fucking joke?" I snarl as the cage comes into view, and I see the fighters inside.

Ciara

I crack my neck and cross my arms back and forth to loosen up. I still don't know who has my brother or who has called me here to fight to get him back, but I'm ready to do whatever I have to. Whoever did this will regret that shit when I'm done.

"Yo, yer up next, love."

I turn to find one of the guys who was at the front door peeking his head in the locker room I'm in. I nod and go to follow him out. I glare at his back as I walk behind him.

This place isn't like Vega's. It has a darker vibe to it. Not just the lighting, but the people and the energy of the place are dark.

This is the type of underground scene I'm used to Theo taking me to.

From the armed bouncers at the door, to the hungry gazes of the guys looking to win some money and find some drunk girl looking to help them spend their winnings. I can't say I don't see the money around this place; it's just not the same.

Vega's fights reek of upscale clientele looking to watch a fight and return to their posh lifestyle in the morning. These people here look like they have deals to make in the back rooms and if they go sideways there might not be a morning.

"Hey, what are we calling ya? They need to know?" A tall guy with green eyes asks as he slides up beside me.

"Killer Walsh," I bite out.

The name just comes to me and spills out. It feels right as I move toward the cage in this place. The guy jerks his head back and narrows his eyes at me.

"My da loved that guy. He was tough as nails. Did ya know him?"

I punch at my chest. "He made me."

The guy nods and takes off to give them my name. When I get to the main room and the cage comes fully into view, my blood begins to boil. Cadlha is standing in the middle with a grin on her stupid face.

This is who's behind this? I should have known. A grin comes to my lips as the DJ in this place starts to play "No Limit" by G-Eazy, Cardi B and A$AP Rocky.

As they repeat *it ain't safe*, I know that to be the truth. Fucking with me isn't safe. The guy who asked for my name comes running back over.

"I'm Liam, by the way. You mind if I stand in as your second? I was around fifteen when Killer disappeared.

"If yer who I think yer saying ya are, it would be an honor," he says.

"I'm not really going to need you. This will be over before it starts," I growl.

"Cool, but it's the rules for one of us to step in if a fighter doesn't come with a team."

I shrug and put my mouth guard in as my nostrils flare. Punching my right hand into my left palm, I then roll my shoulders as I move to climb into the cage.

"Okay, ladies, welcome to the Fighting Irish lair. Let's make sure ya understand the rules around here. When ya leave here, we never saw ya and ya never came here. Other than that, one rule, there are none. Am I understood?"

I nod. I have nothing to say. I'm going to beat this bitch ass and get my brother home.

"Hold on, I have a few rules for this fight," Cadlha says as she tries to stare me down and intimidate me. "If ya win, ya get yer brat back. If I win, ya take yer brat and the two of ya disappear. Ya forget about Dylan and never come back around here again."

"No problem," I say around my mouth guard before I allow it to settle back in place.

"We have a special one for ye all tonight. First time to lair for these lasses. In the pink shorts, we have Cobra Cad," the announcer says, causing me to scoff.

This bitch is no more cobra than I'm Andre the Giant. Delusional ass.

"And in the blue shorts, we have Killer Walsh. Let's see if the tiny thing can live up to a name like that one."

The frenzy of betting starts, and we're sent to our corners to wait for them to finish. I'm ready to be done with this. After a few minutes, the crowd settles and they're ready for us to begin.

I grit my teeth as we're signaled to the center and the fight begins. I've never seen a fighter as sloppy as Cadlha. If she didn't fuck with Ciarán, I might feel bad for what I'm about to do. I might.

Yeah, fuck that.

I allow her to throw the first punch. It's as if she doesn't know she's supposed to land the damn thing. I don't move and she still misses completely. I snort and commence whipping her ass.

I work her torso first, making sure she's going to feel me for the next two weeks. She doubles over. The look she gives me could do more damage than she can as a fighter.

I get her to the ground and go for a choke hold. She actually manages to get out of it before I lock her in. I'm cool with that. I climb on top of her and start to beat the shit out of her with my fists.

I black out and keep pounding on her. She tries to block her face at first, but it's no use. The sound of her forearm breaking under the force of my hits fills the air before her screams ring out. I don't let up until strong, familiar arms wrap around me.

"She's not worth it, baby. Besides, we need her to get Ciarán," Dylan says against my ear.

There is a mix of boos and cheers coming from the crowd. The ref tries to get Dylan out of the way, but I feel Dylan stiffen as his growl vibrates through my back. The ref backs off.

Dylan helps me to my feet. I turn to look at him with knitted brows. He looks pissed off.

Taegan appears and grabs Cadlha by her hair as she leans into her ear and says something. Cadhla sobs something to her as she cradles her arm to her chest. Taegan looks to me and Dylan and nods.

"I know where he is," Taegan says.

I squat and look Cadlha in the eyes. "Did ya get what ya wanted? If I were ya, I wouldn't try me again, I wouldn't. Come near me, my brother, or Dylan again and it will be yer life. That I can promise ya," I hiss.

"I fucking hate ya," she sobs.

I shrug. "Feeling is mutual, bitch."

CHAPTER THIRTY-ONE

Let's Go Home

Ciarán

I'm so angry. I thought Arnold was a friend. He's always so nice to me.

I can't believe he's the one who kidnapped me. Well, he and his friend. I had been going to put my things away in my locker at the gym to get ready for training with Corey when my face was covered with a cloth and I passed out.

I woke up here in this apartment with Arnold's friend staring nervously at me. Ciara is going to be so angry. I hope she's okay.

I'm so hungry and tired and my wrists hurt. They have had me in zip ties since I woke up. Arnold has seen me in the ring. He's smart to keep me tied up.

I'd kick his ass and his friend's too, if I could get loose. I wonder where his friend went. If I got away, could I make it far enough before he came back?

I look to see my backpack is by the other sofa. My phone is in there. If I can get to it, I can call for help. Miss Vega or Miss

Taegan would come and get me. Ciara doesn't know the city like they do.

I don't want to risk getting caught trying to wait for her to find where I am. I might just call Dylan. He'll kick Arnold's ass and take me home.

"I can hear you thinking, kid. You're going to get out of here soon. I'll get you back to your sister. I didn't want anything to do with this in the first place. You hungry?"

"No," I lie, not trusting him or anything he'll give me.

"I'll order a pizza anyway."

I ignore him as I look around again, trying to figure out how to escape. I need to get my hands and feet free first. I've been working on my hands, but my wrists are so sore I've taken a break.

"Why did you take me?"

"Your sister pissed someone off and they want to get her back. It's a stupid plan and she's going to get her ass kicked, but I … shit, I don't know what I'm doing anymore," he huffs and runs his hands through his hair.

"You could take me back. I promise I won't say anything."

He goes to say something, but his phone goes off. He reads the text message and the blood drains from his face. Standing up, he begins to pace.

"Fuck, I knew this was going to happen. Shit, fuck," he screams.

"What happened? Can we leave now, and you drop me off at the gym?"

"I don't think I have that type of time. They're coming for you. Crazy bitch got her ass whipped. I'm a dead man after this. I told her this was stupid."

"I don't even know who she is. Can you cut me loose?"

It's a lie. I know he's talking about Cadlha. She was always so mean to me, and I saw the way she looked at my sister.

She was pissed when she found out she was banned from the gym. I was there the day she tried to enter after she was cut from the team. She totally lost it.

I had heard something about her and Ciara getting into it. I don't know why she would want to fight my sister. That's just stupid.

"Fuck, I'm sorry, kid. Please don't tell them it was me. The best thing is for me to run and leave you here. Someone will find you and release you, but if I'm here when they get here, I'm dead."

Tears burn the backs of my eyes. He's going to leave me here tied up in hopes someone finds me. What if Ciara doesn't come?

"Please don't do this. Cut me loose before you run," I plead.

"Kid, you're going to be a monster when you get your power up and hone your skills. I'm not crazy enough to cut you loose. Your hands are too fucking fast. You'll be okay. I promise," he says and takes off, not looking back once.

I start to panic and wiggle in my seat. Tears roll down my cheeks as the zip ties tear at my skin. My heart is racing and my stomach feels sick.

I nearly pee myself as the front door bursts back open. Relief washes over me as Dylan comes through the door, followed by Ciara, Miss Taegan, and some other guy I don't know. However, I can't stop sobbing.

"I've got ya," Dylan says as he cuts my feet loose with a blade he pulls from his boot.

The other tall guy with him frees my hands as my sister wraps me in a hug. When my arms are free, I wrap them around her and hold on tight.

"I was so scared, I didn't know if you could come for me, if you would find me. I want to go home."

"Shh, I'm here. I will always come for you and nothing in this world would be able to keep me from finding you." She pulls away and cups my face to wipe away my tears. "I love you so much, Ciarán. I've always got you. No matter what, I've got you."

Dylan

"What aren't ya telling me?" Jamie says as we sit in my kitchen while Ciara puts Ciarán to bed.

I sigh and rub my eyes. "Do you realize who she is?"

"Who? Your girlfriend? No, but she's hot as fuck. I thought she was going to beat Cadlha to death. Who is she?"

"Ciara Walsh."

"Get the fuck out of here. I thought ya had given up on that and just found some hot bird to shag. That's little Ciara?"

"Fuck me, I sort of thought ya had a type. I didn't think that was her."

"Aye, it is. Cole knows I've found her, but he's not telling me something. There's a lot going on and I'm trying to keep her safe."

"And the kid?"

"Her little brother. He was born before they lost Uncle Don and Aunt Iesha."

"Wait, lost them? What do you mean?"

"I don't know," I say in frustration. "I'm still trying to figure that out. All I know for sure is that they're both dead. First, Uncle Don then Aunt Iesha. She was killed in a car accident that took Ciara's memories of everything before then."

"Fuck, Donald Walsh was the shit. I'm so sorry to hear that. Iesha was such a nice lady. She was Ma's friend."

"Yeah, Ma was hurt for Ciara, but I could tell she was upset about her friend as well."

"Ma knows about her?"

"Aye, Da does too."

"How long have ya been keeping this to yourself?"

"Almost a year. It hasn't been that hard with everyone so distracted and scattered."

Jamie releases a low whistle. I get ready to tell him I'm calling it a night, hoping to avoid the answers he had really asked me for. I see the moment that's not going to fly.

"So what does all of that have to do with ya being banned from the Fighting Irish?"

I groan and pull a hand down my face. Being the youngest sucks ass sometimes. All I want right now is to go upstairs and make sure my girl and the kid are all right.

I've been furious since Ciarán told us how it all happened. The locker rooms don't have cameras. I'm guessing that's one of the reasons they knocked him out in there to take him.

I'm still trying to figure out how no one saw them carrying a kid out of the place. Heads are going to roll. When I find Arnold, he's going to wish he never took his first breath. It was smart of him to run.

Fucking coward.

He was right to be afraid of Ciarán's hands. In the last seven months, the kid has made a ton of progress. His dad would be proud.

"I had been fighting the underground scene to make some money," I mutter.

"Are ya crazy? Ya could have fucked up your career with that shit. We have plenty of money, ya didn't need to be in those fights …" Jamie trails off.

He looks at me like I lost my mind. I turn away, not wanting to read the look on his face. I know what's coming.

"It was because of her. Da forbid ya from going home, but yer hardheaded ass was going to go back anyway, weren't ya?"

"Yeah, I had to find her. I knew she would find her way back to me."

"He would have had ya killed, ya eejit. Dyl, Da, Logan, Con, and Brooklyn don't tell us everything for a reason, but what they do say, ya sure as fuck should listen to. That man was evil.

"I don't trust that his death was the end of him. Just ya wait, his hate is bound to resurface sooner or later," he says, his words ringing in the air with an eerie truth to them.

"Don't worry. I'm listening now. Besides, she's here. That's all I ever wanted."

"Yeah, well, I'm happy ya got the kid back and she's okay. Now I get why ya've been throwing me all the meetings in the lairs. Yer ass can't go in them," he snorts as he rounds the counter to pull me into a hug.

I return the embrace. Jamie only wants to see me safe. It's good to know he has my back no matter what.

"I love ya, kid," he says and kisses my forehead as he releases me.

"I love you too. Now get out so I can go check on my girl."

"Fuck ya. I'm coming over for breakfast. So get yer dick wet tonight and have my pancakes and bacon ready when I get here in the morning."

"Whatever," I scoff.

He tosses me a two-finger salute and saunters out of my apartment. I lock the door from my phone and turn on the alarm system before I head upstairs.

I find Ciara in Ciarán's room, right where I knew she would be. They're curled up together watching TV. Ciarán is wrapped up in the covers like a burrito. He peeks out at me with a small smile on his lips.

"Hey," he says.

"Hey, buddy. How are you?"

"Better. That stuff Miss Taegan put on my wrists helped a lot. Just happy to be home. Sorry you guys missed that concert."

My chest swells to hear him call my place home. Finding him in tears destroyed me. Ciarán is a good kid; he didn't deserve this.

I wave him off and shrug. "True Life is family. If we call in some favors, we can work something out. No big deal. Jamie will get over it."

He yawns. "Cee, I'm really tired. I'm going to go to sleep. You don't have to stay. I'll see you in the morning."

"You sure? I can stay the night if you don't want to be alone."

"No, I'm okay."

"Okay, if you need anything, let me know. No matter what."

"I'll be fine. See you in the morning."

She kisses the top of his head and gets up to come to the door where I'm standing. I step out into the hall and wrap my arm around her shoulders as we walk to our bedroom.

"This isn't over. I'm going to make that bitch pay," she snarls as she leans into me.

"Aye, yer right about that, but for tonight, we're going to forget about all of this and get some rest."

Cadlha

"How am I supposed to go on the run like this?" I huff to myself as I sit in this motel room.

I'm not going down for kidnapping and I know all about the O'Briens. I have family who works for them. Had I won, I was going to call on those connections to smooth things over between me and Dylan.

He wasn't supposed to find out about the kidnapping, so it would have been a lot easier to pull off. Now I'm fucked. The worst part is that I'm out of the twenty grand I bet against her. That was my last twenty grand.

I needed that money, I thought that bet would get me back in solid shape. Now I'm down to nothing and I need to get the fuck out of here before they find me.

Connie and Kate will be a fucking problem. Those bitches are batshit crazy when it comes to protecting their brothers. That was all fine when Dylan was mine.

I knew then that they would stab any bitch who tried to take my man away from me. They never like anyone. I don't know how this bitch is getting a pass.

"Ugh," I growl in frustration as I struggle to open the painkillers I need to take.

My fucking arm is broken in three places and most of the blood vessels are broken up and down my forearm. That bitch is a fucking animal. They said I have a fucking concussion.

My phone rings, bringing me out of my ranting thoughts. I groan, not wanting to talk to anyone while in all this pain. However, I see it's my cousin from Ireland who I asked to get me some information on that man-stealing slut.

"Hello," I say into the phone.

"What about ye?"

"I've been better. Do you have something for me?"

"No. That name isn't ringing any bells around here."

I sigh in frustration, but then something comes to my pain-fogged brain. When we were announced for the fight tonight, that bitch was announced as Killer Walsh. That kid calls her Cee, but I've heard the others call her Ciara, not Ariel.

"Do me a favor. Try the name Ciara Walsh and see what ya come up with," I slur.

"*All right*," he drags out. "But ya owe me big time for this."

"I've got ya."

"Get some rest, ya sound like shit."

"Simon, hold on. I need one more favor."

"What's that?"

I need help getting out of here without coming up on the cops' radar. I'm not going to jail for this. With Simon's help, I know I can make that happen.

"I need to get out of New York fast, and I need a bit of cash."

"*Cadlha,* what have ya gotten yourself into?"

"Nothing. Are ya going to help me or not?"

He sighs. "Give me thirty. I'll get ya out of there."

"Thanks."

CHAPTER THIRTY-TWO

A Gift

Ciara

A month later ...

It's been a month since Ciarán was kidnapped. I still can't bring myself to let him out of my sight when he's not at school. I have rearranged my schedule to be the one who picks him up. On days when I can't, there's always someone I trust waiting for him to arrive at the gym for the handoff.

Booker has started to hang around a bit to make sure Ciarán gets settled in with his trainer before he takes off. Corey is still training Ciarán since Dylan has been spending more time outside of the gym, busy with some project.

I'm surprised he's been around so much today. To be honest, I'm starting to get suspicious. He hasn't stopped smiling and he insisted on taking me and Ciarán out once we arrived from Ciarán's school.

He won't tell us where we're going or what we're going to do. He just told us we were leaving, now we're off to who knows where. Since Dylan has been brooding for the last four weeks up until earlier this week, I'm going to give him a pass.

"You're not even going to give me a hint?" I ask as I look up at him while walking at his side.

"Nope. Besides, we'll be there soon enough. It's not that far away," he croons and glances at me with that gorgeous smile on his face.

"This better be good, O'Brien."

He chuckles and squeezes my waist as he keeps his arm around me. We're about a block and a half away from the gym when he turns into a shop that has the windows covered.

Dylan waves for Ciarán to head inside ahead of us. My brother bounces through the doorway with a huge smile on his face. I walk in next and stop in my tracks.

"Dylan?" I call out as I stumble back and bump into his chest. "What have you done?"

"I told you to trust me and give me time. This is my gift to you."

"A freaking tattoo shop? Are you kidding me?"

"Not kidding at all. This place is all yours. I placed the deed in your name."

I look around with my mouth open. There is a huge sign on the wall that reads C&D Irish Ink. There's black-and-white art on the black and gray walls that have graffiti painted on them.

The reception area is sleek and welcoming, with a cute waiting area off to the right of it. A pretty dark-skinned woman with bright brown eyes steps forward and offers me her hand. I take it and shake it, not knowing what else to do.

"This is Kary. She will run the place for now. You will be her apprentice."

"Congratulations. It's so nice to meet you. I signed on for two years to get this place up and running for you and help out with getting you your hours and license.

"I'll get you through the paperwork and exam. Any questions, I'll be happy to answer them for you. I've managed three shops in the last ten years. One in Chicago, another in LA, and Dylan poached me from right here in Brooklyn," she says.

"I … I …wow." I turn to look at Dylan with my brows knit. "A hole-ass tattoo shop. Really?

"Like, when, how? You did this right under my nose. This is only like two blocks from the gym. How didn't I know about this?"

"Because he threatened us all with bodily harm. Not to mention the man is crazy about ya and worked us all into the ground to get this done for ya," Taegan sings as she and Daliah appear with a cake in their hands that has the shop's name and Congratulations on it. "Congrats, love."

"Congratulations," Daliah gushes as she bounces on her toes.

"Oh my God. Thank you. Kary, I'm so sorry. It's nice to meet you. I didn't mean to be so rude. I'm a bit in shock at the moment."

"Girl, you're fine. I wish I had a man this in love with me. Come on back and I'll show you the suites."

"Suites?"

"This place is so cool, Cee. Wait until you see it all," Ciarán croons.

"Wait a minute, you knew about this?"

His cheeks start to glow, and he looks away, turning his gaze anywhere but toward me. I fold my arms across my chest as I look at everyone around me. They were all in on this.

It hits me what this all means and tears fill my eyes. I love working at the gym now that there's no drama. I feel like it has helped Dylan and me grow closer. However, this.

I used to dream of being a tattoo artist. For Dylan to create a place of my own for me where I can learn and grow means more than he could ever know.

I've been looking into the idea and have found a whole culture and community of ex-fighters who are now tattoo artists. This is something I've been thinking can become a real thing. However, this man has gone above and beyond to ensure it is a real thing without a doubt.

As the shock wears off, I run into his arms and wrap myself around him. He places his hands on my butt as he buries his face in my neck. I don't think I can love him more than I do right now.

"Thank you," I breathe. "Thank you so much. I love you."

"I love you too, baby. Do you like it?"

"I love it. Why C&D Irish Ink?"

He releases a laugh. "Ciarán thought I should name it after you and me. Taegan chimed in and said I should add my nickname since she calls you Tiny Irish behind your back."

"Ciara and Dylan Irish Ink. It's perfect. You're perfect."

"Come on. Let's show you to your suite so I can tell you what I want you to ink for me as your first client."

I look him in his eyes and beam at him. "You're going to allow me to put ink on you?"

"I'm your blank canvas. Do as you want with me. I'll even let you touch up my gloves."

"That piece is amazing. I don't think I'm ready to touch that one."

He pecks my lips. "When you're ready." He winks at me and starts to walk farther into the shop with me still wrapped around him.

I'm in complete awe. By the time we're finished with the tour, I'm stunned into silence all over again. I will never forget this day.

I wish I could put into words how this has made me feel.

Dylan

"Yeah, you can call the guys off. I'm going to use another way to find her. Taegan is sure she skipped town at this point," I say into the phone as I walk out of the bathroom with a towel around my waist and sit on the side of the bed.

"Got it, boss. I'll call you back if I have any updates. Oh, I meant to tell you. Hanson wants to talk."

I grunt. "Set it up. I'm gone," I say and hang up.

Nothing can ruin my mood after today. Not even that crazy bitch Cadlha. I knew four weeks ago that she was going to run for it. Around three weeks ago, I was pretty sure she was already gone.

However, I was banking on her arrogance to bring her back to her place—one more time—where my guys have been sitting. What Cadlha doesn't know is that we're not going to risk reporting her to the cops and putting Ciarán's custody at risk. This is a situation I'm going to deal with directly, so there's nowhere for her to run that I won't find her eventually.

I push all thoughts of that shit aside. I haven't been able to stop smiling all day. Dinner with Ciara and Ciarán was the icing on the cake. I took them to this place Ma and Da used to take us for special events or to celebrate certain occasions.

It felt good to have my little family there with me. It felt right, like they've always belonged in my life. I couldn't have asked for a better reaction from Ciara.

The place came out way better than I had planned. Once I hired Kary, I was able to put on the finishing touches and make it the kind of shop I thought would fit Ciara.

Seeing her so happy made my day. I'm going to miss having her as an assistant. Taegan and Ciara have worked together to make my life flow better than it ever has.

It's become so much easier to stand in when Brooklyn needs me to and also run my own businesses and handle my responsibilities. The two have a way of finishing my thoughts and getting things done before I can ask. If not for Taegan working with Ciara the last few months, I wouldn't have been able to pull off the opening of Ciara's shop.

I never thought about how my best friend and Ciara would get along once I found my girl. However, now that Ciara is here, I know I don't have to worry about that. Taegan loves Ciara and I get the feeling Ciara feels the same way.

"Hey, what's on your mind?"

I come out of my thoughts and look up. Ciara is standing before me naked as she studies me closely. We had been in the shower together when I noticed my phone lighting up on the counter.

I stepped out to see what Aidan wanted. If not for business, I'm sure we would still be in the shower. Ciarán has some new thing he's working on, so I'm sure we're not going to see him for the rest of the night.

"I was thinking about how happy you were when I gave you your gift," I reply.

"You didn't think I would be?"

I reach to glide my hands up her sides. Her skin is always so smooth and soft. It's no wonder that I always want to have my hands on her.

"I wasn't sure, to be honest. I hoped you would."

Cupping my face, she leans in to kiss me. I capture her lips and devour her. As I take the kiss deeper, I pull her to straddle my lap.

She breaks the kiss. "I've been trying all day to put my feelings into words. I want to tell you how your gift made me feel and what it means to me."

She pauses and searches my eyes with her gaze as she runs her fingers through the front of my hair. I give her waist a gentle squeeze of encouragement. She takes in a sharp breath before she continues.

"Dylan, all my life I've wanted to feel safe and loved. To have a loving family. I mean, I've always had this feeling, like once upon a time I had that.

"Then I came here, and I found you and you're proving that I did have all of that. The shop isn't just a gift. It's a gift that says so much.

"I know you see me, and you want me to be happy. I get that this is your love language. You mean it from the heart.

"It's not a carrot you're dangling for my trust to be pulled away the moment I don't do as you want. You asked me to trust you and I do. You've shown me over and over that I can.

"That Ciarán can. I don't just love the shop. I adore you for giving me something I can have as my own and learn to grow in. Since you have been in my life, you haven't just helped me to remember.

"You're helping me to find who I am as a person and restoring the love I have within myself. The love I've buried because Ciarán has been the only one safe to share it with.

"One of the most dangerous things in this life is love. Especially when you want it so much and have so much to give. People take that for a weakness and exploit it.

"However, while dangerous, it's also beautiful to have and share. I have never wanted to share my love with anyone as much as I want to share it with you. You turned the lights back on just before the darkness took over.

"Before the little love I had left was lost forever. Only to be seen by my brother and his kind heart. I was bitter, hurt, and angry without knowing what caused the root of it.

"Now I want to wrap myself in all the love you give and return that love tenfold. It doesn't matter how I got here like this. I want to be here with you for as long as I can be," she says while staring into my eyes with her tear-filled ones.

With my thumbs, I reach to wipe away the tears that begin to fall. If I thought I was happy with myself earlier, her words have brought a new level of satisfaction. All I want is to make her happy and safe. I want to be her family.

"You are loved more than you know. If I can show an inch of the love I have for you in any way, I'm going to do my best to do so, believe me," I say before kissing her soft lips.

She moans into my mouth and wraps her arms around my neck. I wrap my arms around her body and hold her tightly against my chest. As we kiss, I move back into the center of the bed, bringing her with me.

"Make love to me, Dylan."

"That's exactly what I plan to do, baby," I whisper in her ear as I grasp her throat and tilt her head back to kiss my way down her skin.

She cries out my name as I suck her nipple into my mouth. My towel has fallen off, so there's nothing between us. I grasp her ass cheek in one hand to stop the motion of her hips as she grinds her hot pussy against me.

Both of our skills have improved, and so has our knowledge of each other's bodies. I know Ciara like the back of my hand. I've learned how to get her so wet she soaks the sheets.

However, tonight I want to take my time. I don't want to rush this connection I feel. This is different. It's a moment I feel we need to capture.

We reconnect our lips and kiss passionately. Ciara whimpers into my mouth as I roam my hands all over her body. My body buzzes with a hum I can't explain.

I hiss when she takes things into her own hands and seats herself on my erection. She slides down with a sigh and her head rolls back. I bite my lip as a deep groan leaves my throat.

I can't take my eyes off the woman I love. Although my soul calls to hers and I wouldn't have cared what she looked like when I found her, she has turned into an enchanting woman.

That's the only way I know how to describe her because she has put me under her spell. I wake with this woman on my mind and go to bed every night thinking about the time I'll get to spend with her when I wake once again.

"Dylan," she moans as she rocks and swirls her hips.

I cover her chin with my mouth and breathe her in. Then drag my lips against her flesh, tasting her sweet flavor on my tongue. I don't know how or why she always tastes so fucking sweet.

Clawing my fingers down her back, I send shivers through us both. I groan and close my eyes. As if to tell me to stay with her, she cups my face and brushes her lips against mine.

I grasp her waist and start to rock up into her as I plant my heels into the mattress. Our eyes lock as she leaks down my shaft. The love I see in her gaze reaches into me and makes me feel like our souls are connecting. Every stroke ties us deeper together.

"Oh yes," she keens.

I growl as I feel her soak my balls. Her juices run into my ass, and the sound fills the air as she rides me to a pace we can call our own. I grasp her shoulder and bury my face against it as I soak her in.

So turned on, I groan and tighten my grasp as she claws her fingers through my hair. Her panting and moaning are turning me on so much. When she lowers to the base of my cock and grinds against me, my eyes roll back.

I can't help myself from sucking her flesh into my mouth. Her body convulses against mine and her walls squeeze around me. I move my mouth against her ear and growl, knowing what that does to her.

She digs her nails into my shoulders and begins to snake her body against me. The motions are everything in this moment. I'm growing harder by the second.

"Fuck," I breathe.

We keep this sensual pace going for I don't know how long. She comes at least four times before I pull out and shift her to all fours. Her juicy, fat pussy is on full display; her thighs and pussy are soaked in her essence.

I groan as I dance my eyes over her. Climbing behind her, I tap her pussy with my dick. She moans and wiggles her fat ass at me. I give it a hard slap, and she moans my name.

"Dylan, please," she whimpers.

I grab her hips and thrust back in. I'm still hard as fuck, but I'm not ready for this to end. When holding on to her hips isn't enough as I pound into her pussy, I reach for the headboard.

Ciara drops onto her belly as if she's trying to get away from me, but I chase her pussy down and keep plunging deep. Making love has long been forgotten. I'm now fucking the shit out of her tight little pussy.

"You belong with me. I'm always going to love you and show you that I do. Nothing can take me away from you. I was always going to come and find you, baby.

"You are mine. Always have been, always will be. You want a family? I'm going to give you one.

"You're going to carry my babies and I'm going to love you all. Do you hear me, Ciara? You understand me, baby?"

"Yes, yes, yes, fuck yes," she screams.

I sink my teeth into the skin beneath my lip and keep pounding as I watch her ass bounce with each thrust. My climax rushes me, and I know I'm not going to be able to hold back much longer.

"I'm yours forever, Ciara, I promise, and I always keep my promises."

My eyes cross as I groan and come hard. So hard my sinuses begin to burn. God, I love this girl.

CHAPTER THIRTY-THREE

Boss Moves

Dylan

A year later …

I sit staring into a mug of hot chocolate, trying to smile and laugh at Ryan as we sit in the family room in the O'Brien Manor in Dublin. This is one of the perks Brooklyn has gained since taking our grandda's spot. This place has taken on new life after that bastard's death.

"You remember that one time we made Brax cry in here and my mother whipped all our asses. Bro, I swear granddad looked like he licked his lips in joy to see her beating the shit out of y'all," Ryan goes on.

"Then Noah's big ass farted while she whipped him and Mom gagged, so those of us who didn't get our whipping yet got to take off," he says and bursts out laughing.

My cousin Ryan has the type of sense of humor that can drive you crazy or keep you laughing for hours. Usually, I'm one of the ones laughing. However, today, that's hard to do.

Logan is home, but he's pissed at all of us. Lunch was a shit show. Brooklyn never told him about Shauna and made the rest of us promise not to either. I understand where both of them are coming from.

I can't say that I blame Logan for his anger. That scar on his neck alone has brought anger to my blood. My grandda's deception is still revealing itself to run deeper than anyone could imagine.

He tried to have Logan killed while he was trapped away, lost in that prison system. It's hard to laugh when I can't stop thinking about all Logan has lost and been through.

I watched Raven die, and not too long after, my brother was fighting for his own life. I will never understand that man's hatred. I'm sure he died without a single person grieving him.

"Hi."

At the sound of the tiny voice, I look up to find Shauna's big green eyes on me. My mind goes to Ciara and what our little girls will look like. I love that woman more than ever.

It was so much harder to come to Ireland without her this time. In the last year, we've been more than happy. Her shop has been a success, and she's still been helping Taegan out with my shit.

It's like she never left the gym. Ciarán has shot up and looks like he'll be as tall as I am, much like his father. He's become like my real little brother, and I love it. Yeah, I can't wait to start having kids of my own.

"Hey, love. What's up?" I say to Shauna.

"Yer my Uncle Dylan, right?"

"Aye, I am."

A gorgeous smile breaks across her face. She then comes to climb into my lap and wraps her small arms around my neck. I envelop her in my embrace and give her a good squeeze.

"They said my da is here to meet me. I'm a wee bit nervous. Will ya be there to meet him with me?"

"Aye, love. I'll be right here with ya," I say and wink as I run a hand over her thick locks.

"Dylan, ya should be in the meeting. Logan said to come for ya," Jamie says as he appears.

"Ugh, am I the only one not invited?" Ryan groans. "Hey, pretty. You want to come with me to see if we can find your auntie Con or auntie Kate?"

Shauna nods and rushes over to take his hand. I stand and head to follow Jamie. When I enter the room, I look around at all the men inside.

Damn, I don't think there's a nationality that isn't represented in this room. My gaze scans the room as I take everyone in while I remember all the things LaSalle told me about the Alliance. I know for a fact that there are Italians, Scots, Irish, Greeks, Africans, Japanese, Australians, Native Americans, Cubans, Albanians, Persians, Spanish, Dominicans, Russians, Germans, Norse and …

I stop dead in my tracks as I lock eyes with one man in particular. I would know his face anywhere. Laki. Donald Walsh's friend from the photo.

Felix never did find him for me. Uncle Ronan has been in Ireland so much, I didn't bother to ask him. I have so many questions now that he's here in this room.

There are two men on either side of him who look like they might be related to him. If not related, they're from a Polynesian background as well. I notice they all have similar tats on their forearms.

He gives me a nod. I snap out of it and go to take the seat Brooklyn is pointing me to. One other thing that stands out to me is the empty chairs. I can't help wondering who should be in them and why they're not.

There's nothing but power in this room. It's in the air. There's unmistakable energy flowing around everyone. I think it's starting to set in how much things are about to change.

"Now that we're all here, let's get down to business," Logan says after I'm seated.

***

My mind is blown by the time the meeting is over. LaSalle brought his own lawyers to make this real and binding. That Cam woman looked like she was in as much awe as I felt.

Bobby, on the other hand, looked like it was just another day in the office. My brother and LaSalle have acquired parts of every family's business in one way or another. Most of the contracts have placed them on the controlling end of the deal. If the Alliance fails, they will make sure the businesses and the families follow.

With their own wealth securing their livelihood, it won't bother them much to lose any of these interests. The way they have set things up, it would be stupid to go against the Alliance, and few will survive if they try.

Logan and LaSalle have covered everyone's asses, especially their own. As everything in that room unfolded, I couldn't help but think of Grandda Ian. My ma's da was a master chess player. I used to watch him move us kids around to get what he wanted and make us think it was our idea.

Logan spent the most time with grandda and right now, it shows. This shit is fucking genius. The craziest part is, I don't think the others knew the power they were relinquishing when entering the business contracts with Logan and LaSalle.

"Aye, there he is," Logan says to Laki as I walk out of the house and find them and LaSalle in the courtyard.

"You were looking for me?" I ask.

"We were talking about you and the company you keep," Laki replies.

I lift a brow. Logan smiles and pats me on the cheek. My gaze bounces between him, LaSalle, and Laki.

"We need to talk. Yer probably the first one I plan to forgive. I may have been hiding something from ya too. We'll call it even, we will."

Ciara

With Dylan away and Ciarán on an overnight trip with his school, Vega and Daliah asked me to come out with them to one of Vega's establishments. I had no idea they planned to take me to a strip joint.

It's not even a male strip joint and we're all straight as far as I know. Vega said the chef here is the best in the city. Better to look at some titties and ass than eat ass food—her words, not mine.

I have to say, I've been having fun while here. What I wasn't expecting was the pretty friend of Vega's who showed up not that long ago. She's fun, but she has that vibe I always get from Vega.

It's something in their eyes that they try to hide, but it's there if you look long enough. In fact, she's the first person I've seen Vega show respect to as if she's not a badass boss in her own right.

If I didn't know any better, I would think Vega was her subordinate. For the last hour, I've watched and listened. Most of what they've said sounds like it's in code.

"I'm surprised you came in person," Vega says to her friend.

"Until Lyric gets back, the top levels deal with me. Besides, from something revealed to me recently, you and I should remain close."

I take that as my cue to head to the bathroom. I don't need or want to know what they're talking about. "Money, Cash, Hoes," featuring DMX, starts to play as the girls dance on the main stage.

As X growls, my mind goes to Dylan. My nipples tighten and I realize how much I miss him. I love it when he gets into sex and growls into my ear like that.

What I would give to be in his arms and hear that sound right now. He was sad to leave me behind but happy his brother would finally be released from jail.

I bob my head as I check my phone to see if he's sent me any messages. Disappointment hits and I continue to the bathroom to finish my business. The song has changed to "Balance" by Too Short when I exit the bathroom and head for our table.

Vega and her friend are in deep conversation as I make my way back. Daliah is still making it rain by the stage. I laugh and shake my head.

However, I slow down and narrow my eyes as one guy catches my attention. He's staring in Vega and her friend's direction. My hackles go up as he starts to move toward them.

A flash of metal catches my eye, and I pick my pace back up. That's when he pulls the gun and goes to aim it. Lightning fast, I grab his arm with the gun and twist it behind his back.

I then punch him in the back, caving his whole shit in. Then I slam him down against the table in front of Vega and her friend. The guards who arrived with her friend now pull their guns, place them to the guy's head, taking over.

I look up with my chest heaving and lock eyes with the woman. That aura I've been talking about is at full force as she looks back at me.

"What's your name again?" she says.

"Ciara."

"We call her Ariel around here. She's kind of like you."

"Oh yeah, how so?"

"She needs to keep her identity close to the chest," Vega says.

Looking right into my eyes, she says. "Ciara, I'm Danika. You ever need anything, you give me a call. I'll make it happen."

With that, she stands and leaves. Her men take the guy from me and drag his ass out. I stand staring after them.

"Wow, you've just made one powerful friend. I'm not on that level. At least not for now. You need a connection to drop a body or make one disappear, and I'm not around, that's your person," Vega murmurs.

"I'll keep that in mind. Was that meant for her or you?"

"Doesn't matter, he's finished. Thanks, hon. I owe you one."

Dean

"I'm only going to ask you this once more. Who sent you?" I growl.

He glares into my eyes and remains silent. I bitch-slap him across the face with my Glock. His head whips to the side and he spits out blood.

"Bitch, I don't know you. I don't have to say shit," the guy snarls.

A smile comes to my lips. I figured he would say something like that.

I'm already in a bad mood because my husband had to leave for that roundtable in Ireland. I'm not in the mood to play games. I had to check in with Vega.

She's a smart and talented woman. I was there for business, so I hadn't paid her friend too much mind. Not until the little thing single-handedly handed this asshole his ass.

She saw this motherfucker coming before my men did. I'll handle that later, but this asshole needs to be dealt with now. Until just now, I didn't know who his target was.

Now that he's opened his mouth, I know he was after Vega, not me. Knowing this, I decide I'm done here. I lift my gun and aim between his eyes.

I tilt my head to the side. "You don't know me? Good. Night night, motherfucker."

I pull the trigger and turn to leave. My guys can clean up here. I have some shit to do.

CHAPTER THIRTY-FOUR

Love My Life

Ciara

Six months later ...

Today has been such a long day. After training this morning, I had an appointment for a six-hour piece. To say I'm exhausted is an understatement.

I am getting better and faster. The shading on that last piece impressed me and Kary. The client was so happy and gave me a nice tip.

A smile comes to my lips as I clean up my suite. I love my life. The tattoo parlor has become a huge success and we're champions. The team from Dylan's gym took the championship with ease last year.

It looks like we're going to take it again this year. I love watching my man fight. Dylan dominates in the ring. Winning is the only option for him.

"What are you smiling about?" Dylan says as he walks up behind me and wraps his arms around me.

I startle at first, but his hold relaxes me instantly. I know it's him from the feel of his embrace and the scent of his cologne. A glance up into the mirror confirms what I already knew. I sink back into him and crane my neck to look up at his face.

"I was thinking about you and how much I love my life."

His face breaks into a huge smile. Dipping his head, he then takes my lips in a searing kiss. I can't believe how he can still set my body on fire with a simple touch. I thought I'd be immune by now or something.

However, I crave Dylan more and more with each day. It's the love he puts into his touches and how he always finds a way to make me feel special and cared for.

"How about I give you something else to smile about? I brought you dinner. Ciarán is at Jamie's for a sleepover. It's just me and you."

I smile wider. I love how Dylan's family has taken Ciarán in like one of their own. They all spend time with him all the time.

Logan can be a bit intense, but he's growing on me. I feel so bad for him and Shauna. When Dylan told me their story, I was in tears.

I got the feeling it was a lot for Dylan as well. When he got to the end, he tensed up and froze like there was more, but he couldn't bring himself to tell it.

Luckily, Ciarán had needed my attention, and Dylan didn't get to continue. I haven't pressed him to go any deeper into the subject since.

Logan and his adorable little girl have been in America for about five months now. I met Shauna after they all came back from Dylan's cousin Noah's wedding.

I had to miss that one too. I was booked solid at the shop and Ciarán had school. I am also nervous about taking him out of the country with the fake documents we have.

I hate that I had to miss it. From the pictures Dylan showed me, it looks like they all had tons of fun. Dylan had been gone for an entire month before the wedding on family business in Dublin.

That time was so hard, between the time zone difference that kept us from talking as much as we wanted to and the distance itself. I never want to deal with that again.

"Come on, I'll help you finish up and then we can eat," he says, pulling me out of my thoughts.

"Is Kary gone?"

Daliah came out to shop with me this morning and she hung out for a bit. She and Kary made plans to go clubbing tonight. I opted out because I knew I would be too tired and didn't want to bring them down.

"Yeah, I told her we would lock up."

"Thanks. You don't have to help. I'm pretty much done in here. I'll do the inventory tomorrow."

"Did you find a dress yet?"

"Yes, I did. Taegan and Daliah went with me before I had to come in today."

"I can't wait to see you in it."

"I'm looking forward to seeing you in your tux," I say and smile at him.

He pecks my lips. "Come eat. I don't want the food to get cold."

I follow him out of my suite and find candlelight and pink rose petals heading toward the back rooms. My heart fills with so much love for this man. He's always doing something romantic for me.

From carriage rides in the city, to surprise dates for no reason at all, to spa days in the middle of the week because I look like I might be stressed. I can call myself truly spoiled. I've gone from Cinderella to the princess of the ball.

The candlelight leads to one of the empty suites that haven't been rented by an artist yet. When we step inside, I can see the little area he's set up for us to have a candlelit dinner.

There's a little table covered with a tablecloth and a vase of pink roses sitting in the middle. I smile to know he remembers how much I love pink roses. When I realize the tablecloth is purple and sparkly, I can't help but laugh.

"Really, Dyl? Hey, I meant to ask. Did your mom kick your ass over those roses?"

"Aye, she did. So did Kate for taking her ribbon," he chuckles. "But it was worth it. I got to kiss the girl and now she's mine forever."

I'm smiling so hard now my face hurts. I lift on my toes and turn my face up. Dylan steps into me and meets me for a quick kiss.

Sparks fly between us. I grasp the front of his T-shirt to keep him with me. He grins as he leans back in for another kiss.

Once again, he breaks the connection far too soon for my liking. "Food, I know you haven't eaten since breakfast. I promise to feast on you later. You need real food in your belly right now."

I can't argue with that. Besides, it smells delicious in here. My mouth begins to water as I move to take a seat at the table he has set up.

I snicker when he pulls out Chinese food from my favorite spot around here. He plates our food on real plates he must have brought with him then sits across from me. Once I start to eat, he turns on some music to play softly in the background.

We eat in a comfortable silence for a bit, stealing glances at one another. I'm so happy I could float right from my seat. Three years ago, I never would have dreamed this would be my life.

"Tell me more about this event I needed to find a dress for," I say to start a conversation once we finish our food.

He shrugs. "It's nothing much. I need to show my face. I want you on my arm. It might be fun, it might not."

"That doesn't sound promising," I snicker.

"Anywhere we are together is always full of promise," he says and winks at me.

"Um."

"You don't believe me?"

"I don't know," I tease as I side-glance him.

He stands up and holds his hand out to me. "Fine. I'll prove it. Dance with me."

I tune into what's playing. I like this song. As Muni Long sings of praying she doesn't miss the love of her life as "Butterfly Effect" plays, it hits me how this song could apply to our relationship.

I could have missed out on being loved completely, and so deeply, it feels like a dream. I could have been right here in this big city, walking right by opportunity after opportunity to meet the love of my life, and it never happen.

I take his hand and stand, not wanting to miss a single moment of being in his arms. He pulls me into him and places one hand on my hip as he cradles my hand against his chest with his other one.

We begin to sway to the music as he looks into my eyes. I'm so completely in love with Dylan. I don't know what I would do without him. Again, I realize how much I truly love my life.

"I love my life too. I love having you with me and I love every moment I get to spend with you," he says as if he can read my mind.

I place my head against his chest and continue to sway with him. Burying his hand in my hair with one hand, he begins to rub my back with the other. I breathe him in and comfort washes over me.

"I don't ever want this to end. I want you to know how much I love you and that I would never do anything to hurt you or lose you. Everything I do is to protect you and keep you safe," he murmurs, causing me to look up at him.

"There is nothing you could do that would make me leave you," I say, surprising myself with how much I mean the words.

"There's always something. That one last straw."

"You buy the toothpaste. If you want to waste it by forgetting to place the cap back on, that's on you. It's not enough for me to stay pissed past grumbling at you every morning and night."

I shrug as I laugh. "I'm not leaving, Dyl. I love you too much to live this life without you. I know what it's like not to have you in my life and I don't want to go back. I'm staying. You're stuck with me."

"Promise?"

"Cross my he—"

He crushes his lips to mine before I can finish my words and kisses me breathless. When he breaks the kiss, I'm a little confused. I get the feeling there are words not being said.

However, I don't want this moment to end. I want to stay safely in the bubble he's created for us. I want to be here with him, happy.

***

I'm still on cloud nine as I shower once we get home. Dylan didn't join me because he had to take a call. That phone is always ringing.

I'm not stupid and I'm not in denial. I'm dating a guy with some deep connections in the underworld. I know the signs from growing up with Theo.

Theo may have been low level at best, but he had people around all the time who were the real danger. It's another reason I would never leave my brother behind with those assholes. There's no telling how they would have tried to use Ciarán.

When Dylan has to deal with business, I fade into the background and mind my own business. If I'm honest, watching him in action is always sexy. He has a command of his guys that demands respect. In fact, I get the same vibe from his brothers as well.

It's funny. Dylan seems so quiet and reserved outside of business and the ring, but when it comes to business, it's like a switch flips. The shy, quiet guy fades and he becomes someone else completely. It's the same way in the bedroom.

Which leads me to the change that happened earlier this evening. He has been a bit distant since. I don't know what I said wrong.

I try to figure it out as I absentmindedly rub on lotion and put on a pair of shorts and a cutoff T-shirt. Once dressed, I make my way downstairs to where I left Dylan when we came in. I note that music is playing as I move down the steps.

When Dylan comes into view, I stop and stare at him. He's sitting, staring down into his palm, lost in thought himself. He frowns and murmurs something I can't hear.

"Is everything okay?" I ask, causing him to snap his head in my direction.

"Yeah, come here," he says as his gaze roams over me.

I bite my lip and pad across the room to him. When I stop between his legs, he places his hands on my hips and draws me into him to straddle his lap.

He places his head against my chest and holds me in his arms as we sit in silence for a moment. I run my hands through his hair as my thoughts race.

"Did I say something wrong?" I blurt out when I can't hold it in any longer.

He lifts his head and looks me in my eyes. I search his gaze, trying to see what I'm missing. I see frustration and … guilt, but that doesn't seem right.

"What do you mean?"

"You've been distant since I said … when I said I'm never leaving. Something changed. Was that too much?"

He scoffs. "I pray you meant every word. I'm just frustrated with some shit I have going on. It's not you."

"Anything I can help with?"

"No, I've got it. It's already being handled."

"Are you sure? I'm here, Dyl. I know you have things you don't want me to know about, but I'm here if you ever need me to be. You can trust me," I say.

He grasps the back of my neck and crushes my lips in a deep kiss. I moan into his mouth as I return the kiss. I wrap my arms around his neck as he slips his hands up my sides until his large palms settle beneath my breasts, which are bare and peeking out the bottom of my shirt.

As he moves his lips to my neck, I lift my gaze to the ceiling. I shiver as he rubs his thumbs across my nipples. My eyes roll back as he pinches my hardened peaks between his fingers, while he nuzzles and kisses my neck.

"Do you know how perfect you are? You're everything I've ever wanted and more. I do trust you, Ciara. You never have to question that.

"I don't want you to worry about any of my shit. I'm taking care of everything that needs to be taken care of. All you need to concern yourself with is being happy," he whispers into my ear.

"Then fuck me because that makes me happy," I breathe back.

"That's my girl. Stand up and take your shorts off."

Dylan

"Come here," I say once she has pushed her tiny shorts to the floor.

My gaze drops to her bare pussy and then lower to her cute little white-painted toes with the silver sparkles on them. Everything about her is perfect. Here she is telling me I can trust her when I'm the one who can't be trusted.

She comes to me and climbs back into my lap. Cupping my face, she kisses me like the angel she is. I consume and devour her like the bastard I am.

"I love you," she whimpers into my mouth.

I swallow the words from her lips along with the bile that rises. I feel sick to my stomach. So much guilt is eating at me.

For about seven months now, I have known the answers to fill in the gaps for Ciara. I know what happened to her father and what led to her mother's death.

I know things I wish I didn't, but I was asked to promise not to share these things with her. Timing. Everything around us relies on timing.

There is also the fact that I know Logan left something out. Something that wouldn't have allowed me to make that promise to him. My oldest brother knows me well enough, but I know him as well.

There wouldn't have been a promise made if he revealed whatever he's still holding back from me. The alliance is important to him and my family. Sacrifices were made to see it come to life.

For that reason and that reason alone, I didn't press Logan for the full truth. However, now that guilt is riding my ass, I've been holding back what I know and looking my girl in the eyes every single day as if I can't provide her with answers.

"I love you too," I groan as she frees me from my jeans.

We work together to push them down my hips. I need to be inside her. I have to claim what's mine before the walls all close in on me.

Everything is building up. I need to put an end to this shit with those dirty cops and Hanson. I have a job for the brothers. They will play a part that's useful to me and the Alliance.

It's time I use my role in the Alliance for what it is. Those detectives are still trying to press Hanson and his little brother. They've been at it for far too long. It's clear they don't have shit to stand on, but the petty shit is starting to get on my nerves.

They're trying to force me and my brothers into the spotlight where they can nail us on whatever bullshit they're cooking up— if not just to extort us for themselves. However, we're too smart for that and they lost that opportunity the moment Logan stepped out of that prison.

"Dylan, come back to me," Ciara says as she pulls my face to hers.

"I'm here, baby. I'm with you," I groan as I hold up my shaft for her to seat herself.

I drop my head back and stare up at the ceiling. As she begins to move her hips, guilt consumes me. Not only am I bringing her into a life she knows nothing about, but I'm holding the truth from her.

It's selfish of me to want her love so much and not be able to come out and tell her what loving me means. Yet I know I can't let her go. I close my eyes and try to push down the guilt.

I'll be able to tell her the truth someday. I can feel it all coming to a head. My gut tells me I'll have no choice but to be real with her sooner rather than later.

Logan and LaSalle aren't wasting any time. Even with LaSalle's wife's death, things are still moving forward quickly. Ellen's murder seems like it has made things move faster.

I get it, Logan and LaSalle can't show any weakness. I can only hope that I get to tell her the truth before it reveals itself and ruins this for me. "Fire on Fire" by Sam Smith begins to play in the background and I open my eyes and lift my head.

Her green gray eyes are on me with an intense look I can't ignore. It's almost like she's pleading with me to open up to her. I lock eyes with her as she continues to ride me and sets the pace.

Reaching for the hem of my T-shirt, I pull it off over my head, then I reach beneath her top and palm her breasts. As always, our connection deepens as we continue to reach for each other through our passion and love.

"Dylan," she moans.

"Your tight pussy feels so good. Keep bouncing, baby. Keep that pussy bouncing," I groan.

"Yes, yes, Dylan. Yes. You feel so good inside me. This dick is everything."

"This dick is yours. I'm yours. You're my reason, Ciara. You're my reason for all I do."

She looks into my eyes and plants her hands on my shoulders. I grasp her ass and begin to thrust up into her. She cries out and gushes all over me.

"So fucking good," I moan.

Pulling her shirt over her head, she tosses it aside. Wasting no time, I lean in and suck one of her nipples into my mouth. She moans and cups the back of my head to hold me to her.

With a supertight grip, she squeezes around my length. I allow her peak to pop free from my mouth. Her full globe glistens back at me as I watch her big tits bounce in my face.

I tap her leg for her to stand so I can turn her around. She lifts and climbs to her feet. However, her legs give out, and she falls on her ass.

I can't help it, I burst into laughter, and she does too. I lean forward to help her up, but she grabs my arm and tugs me to the floor with her. I go willingly, but turn her onto all fours in front of me.

Ciara sinks down with her arms stretched out before her like she's a cat, then lifts her ass into the air for me. I slide into her warm, wet heat and groan. Unable to hold back, I thrust into her as the sound of our skin slapping fills the air. She moans and whimpers my name.

Reaching for her arms, I then tug them back at her sides and use them to pull her into me as I rock into her tight pussy. Groaning, I throw my head back and look up. My cheeks puff out, and my eyes roll back.

The sound of her pussy becoming so wet it starts to blow kisses at me causes me to drop my head back down. The way her ass bounces against me has me so hard. The sound, the sight, it all has me mesmerized.

I can't take my eyes away. My mind wanders to how much she trusts me and how willing she has been to give herself to me from the beginning. The guilt returns and I try to chase it away through her tight core.

"Dylan, oh shit," she gasps. "Oh, fuck, babe. That feels so good. I'm going to come."

"Come for me. Show me how much you love this. Show me how much you want me. I want to know you know it's yours."

"Don't stop fucking me, Dyl. Harder, baby. Harder," she keens.

I throw my head back, not releasing her arms and pound harder. I'm doing the right thing. We're made for each other. She'll forgive me.

It all has to be okay. I can't live without her. This shit can't come back to burn me.

CHAPTER THIRTY-FIVE

Real Pressure

Detective Strong

"Detective, good to see you."

I nod, not in the mood for this shit, as I stand in the middle of the commissioner's ball, looking around at all these suits who puff their chests out like they're the ones out in the streets keeping our city safe. Fundraising and smiling as if any of the ticket money goes where it belongs. They all make me sick.

Half of them don't know a thing about what we face out there, but their pockets are lined with our blood, sweat, and tears. Meanwhile, even with overtime, most cops are struggling to make ends meet without having to work under the table.

I've watched good guys become the real monsters out there because this shit puts them in a squeeze. Exhaustion, bills piling up, their own neighborhood turning bad or outpricing them. Too worried about home to be able to make sound decisions on the job.

But at the end of the day, I'm a detective and I'm here to smile and dance for these assholes to raise money for our department and whatever other departments they've lied to this year. The right connections will at least get you in the right position to get ahead an inch.

"We need to talk," Baker whispers as he walks by me and takes a drink from the passing tray the waiter is carrying.

I grab a glass too and follow him a few steps away out of the earshot of anyone else. Vargus is already waiting for us with a tense expression on his face.

I do my best to hold on to the tight smile I'm forcing. Shit has been getting weird, and I don't know how much longer these boys will last under the pressure.

We thought we would have a bag coming in from Hanson and his boys a long time ago. However, there is always something that comes up to block our pursuit. At times, it feels like our superiors might be onto us.

Although I doubt it. My boys play things smart, unlike some of the other crews in the PD. We all came up together and know the rules. We've studied how things work on both sides, and we keep our noses clean for the most part.

I know Baker has a problem with the booger sugar, but he's functioning. It's never gotten in the way of work or business. Not until that night that kid got the best of him and stabbed him.

However, in the end, we thought that was going to work to our advantage. It almost did. We were just about to break the kid before someone up top sprung him.

"What the fuck is going on? None of this is a coincidence. We need to find out where this shit is coming from and stop it," Baker bites out.

"Calm down. We don't know that this is coming from anywhere," I snap.

"The fuck we don't. My wife's restaurant got shut down and she lost her liquor license just out of the blue. You know how hard it is to get one of those in the city.

"I don't know if we'll ever get it back. That's the bread and butter of that place. My kid's day care was shut down for a week and when it reopened, Lou was no longer on the roster. Come on, man," Vargus hisses.

"Right, and my fiancée lost her job in the clerk's office without any provocation. Her mother has been getting tickets left and right and I was told the system is down whenever I try to clear them for her, but I watched Jones clear some shit for his niece with no problem.

"You said yourself that fancy school that offered your boy a scholarship suddenly reneged for no fucking reason. Yeah, none of it seemed to connect, but when you look at it all collectively, we have a fucking problem, Strong." Baker seethes.

"For now, let's keep our heads on a swivel. We'll be careful about business for a bit. See if the pressure backs off."

"Motherfucker. Is that …"

I turn to follow Baker's gaze. My mouth falls open as I find what he's glaring at. It all clicks into place.

I think we just found our answer. As the commissioner raises his glass in a toast with these motherfuckers, I know we have. This shit is about to get real.

Son of a bitch.

Dylan

"You boys clean up nice," I say to Hanson and his brother Oliver as I fix Oliver's tie.

"Dude, what are we doing here?" Oliver asks nervously. "This is the police commissioner's ball. We need to get the fuck out of here."

"Relax. We're the commissioner's personal guests. No one can touch you," I reply.

Like I said. It's time I reveal the power I hold in my new position while showing just what the Alliance means. We run this city.

I don't have to make my point the way we used to do things. Our relationships at the top come with no other option than a *yes*, and *how soon*. Those dirty cops have been trying to make life hell for Hanson and Oliver.

Oliver turned out to be a good kid. However, those motherfuckers are trying to push him and Hanson into a corner that's going to make them come out swinging while not caring who gets hit. I can't have that.

Brooklyn and Logan want this shut down as much as I do. That's why I've been fucking with the comfort of Strong, Vargus and Baker's family's livelihood. I want them to feel what it's like to have someone pressing them.

"Wow, on second thought. I don't think I'm ready to leave. Who's that? I didn't think they would have baddies like that here," Oliver says while nearly drooling on himself.

I turn to see what he's talking about, and my breath stops as Ciara comes into view. She and Taegan spent the day at the spa and with a glam squad. I had to be here to meet up with Hanson and Oliver, so the girls came in the limo. Booker dropped me off in my Rolls I keep in a garage for nights like this.

My mouth falls open as my gaze runs over Ciara. She's in a purple satin-looking gown that cuffs around her neck, where stones sparkle in an oval pattern. Then there's a keyhole just below her throat, down to right below her breasts.

The dress molds to her body in a mermaid-like shape that shows off her curvy frame and pools into folds of fabric. Almost like she has on an upside-down tulip. Her hair is down and curled into large waves that frame her face, much like the first time she walked into my gym.

However, it's the confidence she walks in with that blows me away. Her little ass walks in like she's the queen of the city. I'm ready to bow at her feet and worship her. Instead, I drop my hands in front of my crotch and cross them in hopes no one can see the massive erection I'm now sporting because of this woman.

"Hey, you. You look amazing in your tux. Good enough to eat," she sings as she stops in front of me.

I reach to palm her ass and pull her closer to me as I dip in to devour her purple-tinted lips. Reluctantly, I break the kiss and pull away as Taegan clears her throat.

"You take my breath away. How am I supposed to focus on anything else tonight?"

"Damn, that's you?" Oliver says, breaking into the moment.

"Yeah, she's mine," I say with a smile. "Ciara, this is Oliver and Hanson. They work for me and my family."

"Hi, nice to meet you," she says with a smile, but she hasn't taken her eyes off me.

"Well, what am I to ya? Did ya miss that I came in with her?" Taegan teases.

I look to her and smile. She looks nice as well in the green gown she's wearing. It works with her red hair, green eyes and pale skin. Taegan has always been pretty.

"Guys, this is Taegan. I know you've heard of her. Now you know her by face."

"Aye, now yer talking. Good to meet ya boys. Here comes the commissioner."

I turn to see she's right. The commissioner is heading straight for me. Pulling Ciara into my side, I then turn to face the commissioner fully.

"Dylan, I want to thank you and your associates for the generous donation."

He lifts a hand to wave over one of the waiters with a full tray of champagne. I take two glasses, handing them to Ciara and Taegan before I take another for myself, nodding for Hanson and Oliver to take one as well. The commissioner takes one, then lifts it to give a toast.

"I'm looking forward to our endeavors in the future. To new paths and strong allies," he croons as he holds his glass up.

"Speaking of the future. I want you to meet those friends of mine I was talking to you about," I say.

"Yes, yes. I've already launched an investigation into that matter."

"That's good. I'm sure this will be well received."

"Good, good, I'm here to do my part."

"We can see that. This is Hanson and Oliver Adams. They're productive contributors to the community.

"Oliver has just signed up for his first semester of college, but your officers have been harassing him like he's a criminal, asking him to compromise his well-being for them to gain what …" I lift a brow as I stare the commissioner in the eyes.

"I assure you, this is not how I operate. I intend to deal with Detectives Strong, Baker, and Vargus. Hanson here will start his new position in my office next week, as Mr. Locatelli has requested. I will personally vouch for Oliver at the university and put in a word with the fraternity, as Mr. O'Brien suggested. All will be taken care of."

"Good to hear. Now, if you will excuse me, I do want to dance with the gorgeous woman on my arm this evening," I say, dismissing him.

I've done all I came here to do. Those detectives have been trying to place Hanson and Oliver in a room with one of us O'Briens. Now they have and there's nothing they can do about it.

At least, nothing they had been planning for. Game over. All their latest problems have been courtesy of the Alliance. We're not even at full capacity and our reach rings bells.

"Do you mind if I cut in?" I turn to see Detective Baker eye fucking my girl.

Meanwhile, Detective Strong is glaring at me. I look him over and smile. I release Ciara and hold my hand out to for Detective Strong.

"Dylan O'Brien," I say as I give him a cocky grin.

He takes my hand and tries to squeeze it. I'm not even fazed. I stare into his eyes defiantly.

"I know who you are."

"Good," I say and tighten my hold on his hand.

This motherfucker can't keep the wince off his face as I nearly crush his hand. He had planned to intimidate me, but that failed before he started. I grin wider and step into him as I drop my voice.

"Now that's real pressure," I snarl. "But you already know what pressure feels like, don't you? Back off the kid and his brother and I'll think about easing up on your families.

"That's a nice school your kid wants to go to. The restaurant business gets harder each day. A liquor license isn't something a place can survive without. Wrong target, wrong city, wrong motherfucking time," I hiss and shove his hand away.

I look to his friend, who looks like he's about to try to dance with Ciara even though she's looking at him like she's about to knock his ass the fuck out. I should let her.

"I wouldn't do that if I were you. Touch her and I'll release your soul from your body for you and help you ascend to that God you pray to every weekend in Queens."

"What the fuck did you say to me?"

"I don't stutter, and I haven't spoken to you with an accent. You fucking heard me. What? You thought we wouldn't find out everything there is about you," I bite out.

"This isn't over," Strong fumes from beside me.

"Ach, yer wrong. This has been over. Yer just too much of an eejit to realize yer barking up the wrong tree.

"The moment ya try to come after us again, ye all will find out how out of yer league ya are. Cut the bullshit and move on. I'm tired of hearing yer names."

With that, I wrap my arm around Ciara and walk off. Couldn't even enjoy a dance with my girl. At least I made my point.

CHAPTER THIRTY-SIX

Amy

"Hey, Amy, there's some redhead down in the pit looking to talk to someone in charge," Cooper, one of the trainers, says as he pops his head into the office.

"Show him in. It's not like I'm doing anything in here," I say, my words dripping in sarcasm.

I look around at all the paperwork and things I still need to get done before Lily shows up, freaking out. She stresses me out at least once a week about this place.

I can't blame her. Her family is a shit show. I had to help her find a way to hide the profit we actually do make off this place before her father and brother could get their hands on it.

"It's not a him. It's a her," Cooper says.

"Gah, fuck me," I huff. "Where is she? Let's get this over with."

I roll my eyes, wondering what Sean or Theo has done this time. Those two are hell-bent on running this place into the ground. The drugs, the drinking, the gambling, it's a wonder the place hasn't folded under them.

I can't even pretend to want Sean at this point. Shit, he doesn't pretend to want me either. Not since I found him fucking some chick in my place.

I should have let him OD that one time when he trashed my place. After all I did for him, he turned around and fucked some chick right in my bed and fell asleep like the place was his and it was normal for him to have some shank in my bed.

To be honest, I knew in my gut it wasn't the first time. I put his bum ass out and changed my locks. By then, Lily had already hired me to be her second-in-command here at the gym.

I've been running this place since she asked for my help. I've been helping her keep the doors open and covering her reject dad and brother's asses when trouble comes knocking.

Sean's drug problems are his own. His stupid ass will end up dead soon anyway. Between the drugs and gambling like his dad, his days are numbered.

"Oh, hello. I thought I would find Theo or Sean Young. Do ya know when they'll be in?" The redhead asks as she steps into the office.

I sit back in my seat and steeple my fingers in front of my lips. "You asked for someone in charge. That's me. How can I help you?"

"This is Raising Young gym, right?"

"Yes, it is."

"Amy, those checks ready?" Sean walks into my office as if he owns the place.

I roll my eyes. It's not even payday and his ass doesn't do enough to earn the check he gets if you ask me. He barely shows up to train his clients.

"It's Tuesday, not Friday," I grunt.

"Well, I need you to write a check for me today. I have shit to do."

"Whatever," I mumble.

"And who do we have here?" he purrs to the redhead.

The twinkle in her eyes causes me to need to hold back the bile that rises in my throat. I will never understand why women throw themselves at him. Sean was once attractive to me, but he's still an asshole.

You can pretty much figure that out before he opens his mouth. With all the steroids and coke, he looks a fuck fright these days. I narrow my gaze at her as something about her profile nags at my brain.

"I'm Cadlha. And ya are?"

"Oh, love the accent, sweetheart. I'm Sean Young. It's very nice to meet you," he says.

"Oh. Yer just the man I came to see. Is there somewhere we can go and talk? I have some information I think ya might be interested in."

"Is that right?"

"Does the name Ciara Walsh or Cee-Cee Young ring a bell?"

My hackles go up and warning bells ring in my head. Everything clicks into place, and I know exactly where I've seen this chick before.

"Fuck yeah. Do you know where I can find her?"

"I might. That is, if ya can help me. Like I said, we should go somewhere to talk."

"Right this way, gorgeous," he croons. "I'm going to need that check before I leave, Amy."

Asshole.

Cadlha

This locker room stinks of musty balls and armpits, but as long as I can get what I want, I'll grin and bear it. Simon hit pay dirt when he uncovered that bitch's true identity.

It led me right here to Seattle with the family she used to live with. I had a feeling they would want to know where that slut is. I was right.

The way Sean's eyes lit up when I mentioned that slut said it all. The rage that followed promised me the results I came looking for. I'm going to ruin that bitch's life one way or another.

"That bitch has been in New York all this time," Sean growls as his face turns red.

He's been pacing back and forth as I have been relaying all the information Simon shared with me. I'm sitting on this bench, ready to jump for joy. I'm going to get my revenge. I can taste it.

I shrug. "I don't know how long she's been there, but I know when she showed up and fucked my life up and that she's still there."

"My dad has been trying to find her. If he can hand her over, he can get those motherfuckers off our back."

"Hand her over?"

"Yeah, dead or alive. They want her gone before some other assholes get ahold of her or some shit. Dad has to finish the job before the clock runs out. How soon can you get us to her?"

"How soon can ya be ready to go? I've been looking for this opportunity for almost two years now. Two years is too long to be on the run from my city.

"The sooner the better. As long as I'm there to make sure this gets done, we could leave now."

"I like you."

"Play ya cards right, we might be able to do something about that," I say and give him a smile.

CHAPTER THIRTY-SEVEN

From the Shadows

A Friend

"*Nyet*, I not doing this today. I not in the mood. Every time I see his face comes with bullshit. Fuck off," Misha grumbles with his thick Russian accent as he enters the underground room where I'm waiting for him, LaSalle, and Logan.

LaSalle is smart, this room is genius. I entered on the far side of his property. If I didn't know better, I wouldn't even know this was a part of his home.

Misha goes to turn to leave, but LaSalle and Logan each place a hand on his shoulders. I can't say I blame him. I am the bearer of bad news in a lot of ways.

In the Alliance, it's my family's job to have a finger on the pulse of the important things. We're the watchers. I get things back to LaSalle and Logan that they need to know.

The only reason we didn't know what happened to Logan in the beginning is because he and LaSalle didn't want to risk Oland finding out about our connection. The old bastard used to see too much.

That's what got O'Shea and his brothers killed. For all Oland's hate for mixing and working with others outside his race, he jumped into bed with others when it suited him.

"You will want to hear what I have to say. Trust me, the last thing I want to do is come in here with bad news. However, I'm here with what you all need to know. Especially you," I say.

"It's good to see you, Laki," LaSalle says as he takes a seat.

"How are you holding up?"

"He is engaged and moving on with his life," Misha says, his words dripping with something I'm trying to pinpoint.

It's not quite sarcasm. Maybe skepticism. I let it go as LaSalle shoots him a hard glare.

"*Da*, we are all still broken, my friend. How have you come to break us some more?"

Between the death of LaSalle's wife, the murder of Misha's fiancée, and Logan's imprisonment and loss of the young woman he was in love with, you would think I were in a room filled with broken men. However, I see something else.

The strength in this room proves Ian Black knew exactly what he was doing. Never afraid to move one into place to cover for another. These men were handpicked, as was I.

He was such a master at this they have begun to do it themselves. I've watched from the shadows as LaSalle has been Logan and Logan has been LaSalle. Now, Misha Krupin and Uri Donati have become a part of the dance to make a four-headed monster.

Although it seems LaSalle has taken the lead since Logan has been gone. I chuckle to myself. From the outside, one would think that's by mistake. I knew Ian Black enough to know that was indeed by design.

"What has changed to bring ya here?" Logan says as he sits next to LaSalle across from me.

Misha continues to stand and pace like a bear. I'm used to him and his temperament. I'm not intimidated by his crazy.

"Orla Murphy passed," I reply.

"Aye, I know this. Brooklyn was with Deja during the services."

"Yes, but what you don't know is O'Shea Walsh left a black box with his grandmother, and she left that box to me, not Adline or one of the others. I now have my hands on the will and the key to the original Alliance lockbox.

"The other key? All this time it was with her?" Logan says.

"Yes, I have it all. Including O'Shea's and Ian's lost journals."

"This means they can come out of hiding?" LaSalle says.

"Aye, it's time to tell the lasses the truth."

"Good, nothing to do with me," Misha says and goes to walk out.

"Not so fast. You need to hear the rest. Your father wasn't your biggest or only problem," I say.

"What do you mean?" He seethes and turns his glare on me.

"This all started with secrets and has continued on secrets."

"*Da*, your point?"

"There are still secrets being hidden that you don't control."

"I don't have time for this. What do you know?" Misha growls.

I hold my hands up. "I have a question for you all. Have you ever asked yourself why? Why you? Why this?

"Ian sent you boys to me, but have you ever asked yourselves why me? Why not his boys or someone else? Or better yet, why any of this?"

"Aye, I have asked. The oul man promised I would know when the time came."

"I guess that time has come. I have the journals with me. I'll leave them with you."

"Still not explanation," Misha bites out.

"Your family has secrets that are playing a hand in the background. Secrets that are coming for you all, but they're coming through your blood. It's time you ask Fiona what your father hid from you. Then start with Eliam Pérez and your family's interest in him.

"That will unravel what you need to know. But you want to move with caution. If you don't, you may not address the problem. Not every head is meant to be taken; some will show themselves to be in shoes just like yours."

"What are you babbling about?"

"Ach, now ya know how we feel when you pull that shit," Logan chuckles.

"Fuck you. Is that all you have to say?"

"To you. Yes." I shrug.

Misha rolls his eyes then storms out. I shake my head and note to myself to have someone keep an eye on that situation. There's a lot Misha still doesn't know.

"That means ya still have words for us," Logan says once Misha is gone.

"My niece is heading this way."

"Why?" LaSalle asks.

"Theo and Sean Young," I reply.

Dylan

"Good, you're both here," Logan says as he walks into the living area of our parents' house.

The first thing I note is that he's hiding his accent. Out of us all, Logan hasn't lost his accent as much. I think his time in that Irish prison has a lot to do with how thick it has been these days.

His consciously tucking it away catches my ear immediately. Something is up. I look to Brooklyn, who's been in his own world as he's been on the phone most of the time he's been here.

Ma asked us all over for dinner. Cole stopped in, but he doesn't plan to stay. He's headed out for business or something.

"Ach, I'm here, but I'm leaving. I have a plane to catch," Cole says.

"Aye, I know where you're heading. You should hear what I have to say before you go. You both should."

Again, I caught that only Logan's New York accent is present. Cole narrows his eyes as if he's now catching that fact too. However, he still stands as if he's going to leave.

There is still so much tension between these two. To be honest, this is the first time I've heard Logan address Brooklyn directly. While Cole might talk straight to him, Logan has been ignoring him and speaking to anyone else in the room but our brother when he can.

"Sit down, Cole. You need to know this before you walk into what's waiting for you," Logan bites out.

"Now ya want to talk to me? Text it to me. I'm not missing my flight. I need to get to DJ. I'm not losing her because I'm—"

"What? Not there like I wasn't there and lost Raven? Ya fucking selfish prick. Ya're the reason all of this is falling onto our heads. Ya will sit the fuck down and listen to what I have to say," Logan says with his chest heaving.

"What? What the fuck are ya talking about? Are ya blaming—" Brooklyn stumbles back, pain clear on his face.

"No, I'm not blaming ya. I'm stating facts. I have kept ya the closest.

"Ya were my right hand. Did ya think once that ya should have asked me before going to Felix?"

"I was protecting Dylan. I had been watching him plot to do something stupid. I thought I could cut him off at the pass."

"Which is all ya had to say to me. Instead, ya handed that oul bastard the knife to put to me neck. None of this had to be this way. I would have brought them all into the light when it was time."

"*Logan,*" Cole drags out. "What the fuck are ya talking about?"

"All this time, I've had all three of them covered. They were where I could see them."

"Wait, what?" I speak up for the first time.

"It was my job to keep the Walsh cousins safe. I was supposed to keep an eye on them.

"Orla took Deja in. She was safe in Scotland, away from Oland. He couldn't touch her there. I had Raven covered. No one could get to her ..." Logan pauses and swallows hard. "If I had been here, she would have been fine.

"Ciara's situation was fucked up, but as long as Oland thought he was in control of everything around her, she was safe, and I always had someone watching over her and someone watching over them."

"What are you saying?" I growl.

"Walsh cousins? Are you saying Raven was related to DJ and Ciara?" Cole asks, sounding more lost than I feel.

Cole wasn't there for the things Logan shared with me. He was still too angry to speak to him. I can see why he's a bit more confused than I am, although this too is a shock to me.

"Yes and no," Logan replies.

"What's that supposed to mean?" Cole asks.

This is it. The holes Logan left in Ciara's story. I need to know how it all connects. Why did I have to hold back what I know all this time?

"There were three Walsh brothers, not two. However, the third and oldest one was adopted. Adline Murphy-Walsh was, in fact, once Adline Murphy-O'Brien."

"What?" I breathe in confusion.

That's not our grandmother's name. How the hell did Ciara's grandmother have our last name? My stomach begins to turn as I try to think my way through what this all means.

"She was Oland's first wife and the reason the old bastard became such an even bigger fucking bigot. Adline couldn't conceive in the beginning of their marriage, so she begged Oland to adopt," he explains.

My stomach eases and I realize how tight my jaw is set. I wipe a hand across my forehead and breathe in a deep breath. I had no idea our grandfather had been married more than once.

Logan continues as I slide to the edge of my seat. "However, when he agreed and Adline went to the orphanage to pick a child, she fell in love at first sight with O'Shea. A little brown baby whose family had been killed in Ireland, not too long after his birth. Oland lost his shit. He wanted a child who could pass for his.

"The two divorced, but he had loved her and couldn't let go. Sucked for him. Adline met and fell in love with Bram Walsh. Oland wasn't as big an eejit as he portrayed. Adline's real maiden name was McDougal, not Murphy.

"However, her father didn't want her to marry Oland to begin with and stripped Adline of everything until she was divorced, so she went by her mother's maiden name, Murphy, until she and Oland married.

"Her father, Lennox McDougal, favored Bram and his marriage to Adline. Oland wasn't about to go at Bram head-on with this knowledge. Back then, everyone knew you didn't fuck with two families in Scotland.

"The McDougals and the Blacks. Those names are feared to this day. Adline married Bram and Bram took O'Shea in as if he were his own son. Not long after they were married, Adline conceived and gave birth to Angus.

"A few years later, she had Donald. Oland was furious. In his mind, that Black child ruined his life and that evil woman tricked him.

"If he hadn't fallen for a Scottish woman, none of it would have happened. To him, women were inferior and anyone without Irish blood wasn't worth breathing, nor could they be trusted."

"Fucking asshole," I mutter.

"Aye, ya don't tell a fib," Logan snorts. "That's why he found a young Irish bride to give him children and submit to him. Da was born, but Oland's hatred only grew," Logan explains.

"How does Grandda Ian fit into all of this?" I quiz.

"Grandda Ian and Bram were best friends, and O'Shea Walsh became Grandda's godson. When Grandda took O'Shea to America to meet some of his birth family, Oland made his move. O'Shea wasn't killed in the attempt but a few of his family members were and O'Shea came really close to death himself.

"Grandda Ian had already had thoughts of the Alliance in mind, but this cemented things for him. Oland needed to pay. It wasn't good enough to go to war with him.

"Grandda Ian wanted a legacy that would wash Oland and his bullshit away forever. However, it was too soon for Uncle Joe and Uncle Finlay to be groomed for what he had planned. Don Donati's death proved they were all moving too fast.

"None of them were ready—the originals where the concept was birthed—but things started lining up for him to shake up the world as we were born. Grandda started his match when it was time for his children and the others to find brides and start families. The seeds of *what if* were already planted.

"LaSalle and I started to fill in the spaces as Don Alfanzo decided his successor wouldn't be one of his sons, but his nephew, and I fell in as the firstborn grandson. Grandda had Lennox's ear. He was willing to fund the operation as long as it didn't cause a war too big to handle for his Scottish clan.

"Unfortunately, Lennox's oldest son didn't like the idea. He also didn't like the fact that O'Shea was next in line."

"Let me guess. He had O'Shea killed," I grumble.

"Aye, that day would come. O'Shea met and married during one of his visits to America. He brought his wife and daughter back to Scotland with him. Not one of them was Scottish born, but the clan was going to O'Shea.

"O'Shea was killed in a car accident when Raven was nineteen, going on twenty. Raven and her mother returned to America. However, Lennox was pissed and determined to stick it to his sons. The other three hadn't helped Archie, but they hadn't stopped him either.

"Raven wasn't Scottish born or a McDougal by blood, fine. He placed a ton of assets in her name that still served the Alliance in the end. Same for Deja. Angus met and married her mother soon after she was born. Deja's mother was widowed, losing her active-duty husband," Logan says.

"But Ciara is a Walsh through and through. She has McDougal blood in her veins, as does Ciarán," I say as I start putting the pieces together for myself.

"Aye, she is the true heiress. The McDougal clan belongs to her. The will names her as Lennox's successor.

"That was Grandda Ian's big fuck ya to Oland. He may have been dying from cancer, but everything was in place for us. I promised him we would see it through. The Alliance comes to life from Ciara's inheritance and succession."

"Oland had her mother and father killed in hopes he'd get to her too," I breathe in the knowledge as the pieces finally lock in.

"Aye. Theo Young was supposed to kill her and her brother, not raise them as his own. However, once he learned of their inheritance from their mother and father, he kept them and forged documents to steal their money.

"Our dear oul grandda accounted for everything except me. I started the rumor that ya were in the will. Ciara would only gain it all after an arranged marriage to ya. Instead of killing Theo Young for his disobedience, Oland paid him to keep her away from us, especially ya, until he could figure out how to use ya to gain control of the estate.

"That brought us the time we needed to find the true will that somehow disappeared after O'Shea's death. Lennox had placed it in O'Shea's wife's possession right before he died from a heart attack. Queeny handed it over to Orla Murphy for safekeeping once Donald and Angus turned up dead."

"And ya didn't tell me all of this. Ya gave me half of the truth because ya knew I would find and kill that son of a bitch." I seethe.

"Aye, we didn't have the will until today. Theo Young has played a bigger part in all of this for a while. We couldn't wipe him off the board until we were sure he hadn't found the will himself to manipulate the situation.

"We hadn't known the full story of why Oland chose him and allowed him to live for so long. What we did know was that he had already tried to bargain with empty hands. As for Ciara, he hasn't counted his losses yet.

"He believes he still has options. There's been a lot of back-and-forth; the McDougal clan has kept him thinking they don't care for her safety, although they've warned us to keep her safe.

"They wouldn't allow her to take her rightful place without the will or the original Alliance argument. Ciara's surviving uncles aren't against her taking over if the will says so.

"They plan to honor the Alliance as well. They just want proof. Ken has kept things going in her absence. Orla was a fierce woman herself, and she was adamant that they all honor their father's wishes.

"I get the feeling she didn't know what all was hidden in the black box she had in her possession. However, she trusted me to keep Raven, Ciara, and Deja safe from all of this," Logan replies.

"Ya knew, ya fucking knew what they meant to us. Why not tell us?" Cole says, sounding lost.

"The only people who knew were those who needed to know. We didn't want to place them in more danger. Oland had been trying to find a way to get to them and hurt them.

"He needed control of them or their assets. He didn't care if that meant dead or alive. I fucking fell in love with her. He killed Raven because she was the least valuable to him and because I've always defied him and it would fucking gut me."

"Ya motherfucker, ya let me believe this was all my fault," Brooklyn growls.

"It is. Ya fucking hothead," Logan snarls. "She's dead because ya took things into yer own hands."

"Fuck ya." Brooklyn takes a swing at Logan, and all hell breaks loose.

It's like two lions are fighting in the middle of my mother's living room. They tumble onto the coffee table and smash it, glass shattering all around them. My mother comes running into the room, yelling and looking frantic.

That's when I notice Ciara standing there with her arms wrapped around her middle as tears stream down her face. Grunting and growling fill the air as Logan and Cole continue to rumble. However, I can't tear my eyes away from Ciara as she looks back at me with so much pain in her eyes; I feel sick.

"Stop this. Ye stop this right now," Mom shouts.

That seems to break the stare off between us. Ciara turns and runs from the house. How much did she just hear? I'm hot on her heels. I have to catch her and explain.

CHAPTER THIRTY-EIGHT

Breathe

Ciara

"Ciara, Ciara. Baby, wait." I can still hear Dylan calling after me as I ran from his family's home.

However, I moved too fast for him to catch me. I was able to get to his truck and grab the key I know he keeps in the hidden lockbox behind the back plate.

I took off without having a clue where I planned to go. Ciarán is with Taegan today. He won a bet between them, and she owed him lunch and a new game.

She was supposed to drop him off at the house after. I'll have to text her to bring him to me when I figure out what I plan on doing. I heard everything.

I had been right outside the room when Logan arrived. I don't even think he saw me when he walked past. Seeing the look on his face, I took a pause and was ready to turn around and head back to the kitchen with Kate and Kara.

However, curiosity got the best of me. I stood there listening to my history unfold. To be honest, I don't know how to feel about any of it. I'm devastated and confused.

Shauna's mother was my cousin? Logan knew everything. He knew where I was and who had me.

I feel sick to my stomach. My parents … heck, my entire family has been picked off. And for what?

Some inheritance I knew nothing about. Speaking of inheritances. I'm going to fucking kill Theo. He fucking kidnapped us. Then he spent every dime of my and Ciarán's money. That's why he was so desperate right before I left.

My head begins to hurt. I palm my forehead as the memories hit me. It's the day of the accident, but not from the same point I always dream of and remember.

It's earlier. Before Mom rushed us into the car. It all begins to make sense.

"Laki, what do you mean? The police said there was no foul play. He OD'd in that hotel with that woman," Mom nearly sobbed into the phone.

It was on speaker so I could hear the next words of the man she was speaking to. "Iesha, Don loved you and those kids more than he loved life itself. He would never cheat on you, and you know he wouldn't touch that shit.

"Damn it. This wouldn't have happened if I were there."

"This isn't your fault. You had to go home to take care of your family. Don understood that," Mom sobbed.

"Yeah, but you don't find it strange that something came up with all the guys at once, leaving Don all by himself? Those cops are setting him up. It's all bullshit.

"Listen, baby girl, you're not safe there. I need you to get out of America now. Get to Scotland to your mother and grandmother-in-law.

"You'll be safe there until I can get to you guys. This is all bigger than Don. I can't get too much into it right now, but they can help keep you safe once you get there."

"Laki, I'm scared. I need to protect my babies. Don would want me to protect our kids.

"I'm just so confused and hurt. I've been on my own for months, trying to figure things out. I miss him.

"I never thought it was true, but they made me believe it was. Who do I know here to find out the truth?" Mom sobbed into the phone.

"It's going to be all right. I'm here now. Get to Scotland and I'll take care of the rest.

"We'll get justice for Don. I promise. My brother isn't going to die in vain. Call me as soon as you touch down. You can reach me at this number."

"Okay, we'll leave now. I'll pack the kids up and get out of here. Thanks, Laki."

"Anytime. I will protect you all with my life."

I come back to the present as my head throbs. My mother never married that asshole Theo. I was right all along. He didn't even know her.

I blink and realize I'm standing in Dylan's apartment. I didn't even think about coming here. I'm just here.

However, the comfort I used to feel isn't here anymore. I feel so cold inside. Dylan knew the truth and didn't tell me. I get that he didn't know everything, but I could read between the lines that he knew more than I did.

"What do I do now?" I sob as I wipe the back of my hand across my face. "I know one thing. I can't stay here."

I take off jogging up the stairs. When I get to the bedroom we share, I rush straight to the walk-in closet I have called my own. Grabbing a duffel bag, I start to toss things inside.

The tears haven't stopped, but I ignore them and keep packing. Vega has some things of her own going on. I'm not about to call her for help.

Ciarán and I could go back to our old place with Daliah. She hasn't moved, but she was talking about getting roommates because she's been lonely there all by herself. However, I don't want to put her in the middle of all this.

I'm forming a plan in my mind as I toss the things I came here with into my bag. I refuse to take anything Dylan has given me. This is already going to kill me.

"Fuck me," I sob as music starts to float through the house.

I thought I had more time to get out of here. As Benson Boone croons about beautiful things, I can't stop sobbing. My life was beautiful for just a little while. Now I don't know what to think.

I'm losing everything all over again. Too weak to deal, I slide to the carpeted floor of the closet and lie there in a heap. I'm completely heartbroken.

Dylan

Taegan and Ciarán pulled up right after Ciara took off in my truck. I had Taegan drive us home. The tracker I keep on my vehicle led us here. I'm so lost.

I never meant to hurt her. I didn't want her to find out like this. Hearing movement inside our bedroom, I pause and pull out my phone. Connecting to the sound system in the bedroom, I play the first song that comes to mind to block out any arguing we might do.

Taegan and Ciarán went up to the rooftop to give us space. Taking a deep breath, I then walk into the bedroom in search of the woman I love more than anything. As "Beautiful Things" plays and Benson Boone begs for her to stay, for me, I move to the closet where the lights are on. I freeze when I find her lying on the floor.

Panic fills me. Seeing that she's only lying there as she sobs and she's not physically hurt, I drop to my knees and crawl over to her slowly. When I get about a foot away, I reach for her ankle and wrap my fingers around it, needing to touch her.

She jerks away, killing me. I move closer and hover over her small body. My own tears sting the backs of my eyes.

"Baby, come here. Talk to me, let me be here for you," I whisper in her ear.

She curls into a tighter ball. Reaching for her back, I begin to rub it. She turns her head slightly to look at me.

So much hurt fills her gaze. I cup her face and press my forehead to the side of it. Ciara reaches for my shirt and fists her hand in it.

"You lied to me," she says softly.

"Baby, I planned to tell you everything once I had all the details and the okay. Logan said it wasn't safe to tell me everything while we were in Dublin. He asked me for some time," I reply.

"How much did you know?"

"I knew how your parents died and that my grandda had something to do with their deaths. Not what or how. The rest I learned today with you and Cole."

"Can you give me some time? I don't know how to feel right now. I'm hurt, angry, and confused."

"I want to be mad at you, but if not for you, they would have killed me and Ciarán like our parents. Somehow, you're always keeping me safe, whether you know it or not," she scoffs.

"No matter what, I always will. I love you. I'm not going to allow anything to happen to you. I swear, I wasn't going to keep this from you forever."

"But what does it all mean? What's the Alliance? How do I fit into that?"

"It means you've been the key to one of the most powerful movements in the underworld. The Alliance will be the future of the world. The power, the money, the change.

"It means my evil-ass grandfather is rolling in his grave because we're about to turn the world on its fucking head … together." I swallow hard as I say the last word, unsure if she's still with me.

She pushes me away as she turns on her back and looks up at me. I stare down at her, holding my breath. Blinking back tears, she pushes her hand into the front of her curls that are sprawled wildly around her head.

"What exactly am I inheriting?"

"A very old, very powerful Scottish clan. Cole inherited Clan O'Brien in Ireland, and like yours, Clan Black in Scotland has been passed down to Logan. From what I understand, all three clans come with names and power.

"We'll be here for you. We'll help you. It's what our grandfathers wanted. We'll finish this for your ma and da and for Raven. If you'll allow me, I'll be there every step of the way."

"Dyl, I'm open to hearing them out, but first I need to settle the score with the Youngs. They owe me in blood. I won't rest until I collect."

"I hear you, baby. We'll make that happen, I promise."

She sits up and cups the sides of my face as she kisses me. I'm finally able to breathe again. Wrapping my arms around her, I hold her tight.

The more our lips touch, the deeper she seeps into my skin. I would never survive losing her. One way or the other, I'll make this right.

"I need you," I groan against her lips.

"I'm numb and confused. I want to feels safe and sure again. Can you do that for me?"

"Yeah, baby, I can. I told you I'm always working to keep you safe and protected. That's all I've been doing.

"I love you. I've got your back. You can always trust me. I love you so much."

I run my hands down her back and tug her shirt from her jeans. We breathe each other in and begin to peel each other's clothes off. A desperation begins to set into our connection.

Our lips, teeth, and tongues are all involved in the passionate kisses we exchange. I know I need her more than anything. On the way here, thinking I lost her forever burned me deep inside.

"I love you too, Dylan. Never lie to me again."

"I won't, baby. It killed me to have to keep things from you for so long. From here on out, we're in this together."

"Dylan," she cries out as I sink into her tight heat.

I haven't even gotten my jeans down all the way. I've only shoved them down under my ass and freed my cock and balls. That's how much I need her.

"Mm, baby. I need you so much."

I reach for her hands and lift her arms over her head as I move my lips from sucking on her neck to capture her lips. Lacing our fingers together, I thrust deep inside her.

She wraps her legs around my waist and locks her ankles over my ass. It's as if she can't get close enough. I totally understand the feeling.

I want to get deeper. I want to be closer. I want to be wrapped in her until there's no telling us apart. She's getting so wet and I'm so hard for her.

"Dylan," she screams.

The music is still playing, thank God, because between her screams and my groaning and grunting, anyone outside this room could hear us going at it.

"I love you so much. I'll die before I lose you," I groan in her ear.

"Dyl, I can't even pack a bag and leave. It hurt so much to think I'd never see you again," she snicker-moans.

"Don't ever leave me, Ciara. No matter what, I know we can fix it. Even now, take all the time you need to process this, but remember I'm here. I belong to you and always will."

"Ah, yes, okay. Okay, babe. I'm not leaving. I love you too."

We make love on the floor of her closet until we're both breathless and spent. As we lie catching our breath, I look up at the ceiling, wondering the same thing as Ciara.

What does this all mean for her?

CHAPTER THIRTY-NINE

Called Away

Ciarán

"This is it, kid. You sure you should be here? It doesn't look like a place for someone your age. I can wait here," the driver says with concern written on his face as he looks back at me.

At fourteen, I know my way around the city a lot better. I only took this Uber because it's late and I didn't want them to get away before I got here. I vowed I would be ready to protect Cee-Cee when they came for us.

What I've never told my sister is that I have been using one of my devices to track the Youngs. I knew they would come for us someday. They're here.

They are in our city, and I know they are here for me and Cee. We're not going back. I've been stashing money away in the account Dylan opened for me.

I knew I would need it one day. I'm grateful for my allowance, but this requires my own money. *I* need to protect Cee like she's always done for me.

I look at the screen on my tablet and then at the building in front of me as the Uber driver comes to a stop. This is where they are. I ball my fists as I look at the sign above the doorway.

Fighting Irish.

It doesn't look like a gym. In fact, the place doesn't look like it's open. Looking around, I notice the construction equipment and dumpsters. I'm pretty sure this place is under some kind of construction. My heart begins to race.

It would be so messed up if the Youngs were moving here to New York. Maybe this will be their gym and the place used to be Fighting Irish. I don't know what they're doing here in New York, but they need to leave.

This is our home. Dylan and Cee may have been fighting today, but I know they'll make up. Dylan loves us. He wants us to be safe and have nice things.

I haven't been treated like a slave once since we've been here. Miss Vega, Miss Daliah, Miss Taegan, Auntie Con, Auntie Kate, Uncle Book, Uncle Aidan, Uncle Jamie, Uncle Brooklyn, and Uncle Logan, they're our new family. They took us in and helped us.

"No, you can leave. I'll be fine. I can handle myself," I say as I grab my backpack with the Glock in it from the floor.

Dylan will probably be mad at me for taking it, but I have to protect my family. Ciara is all I have. That name is so pretty for her. I'm glad Dylan remembers it.

I don't want people taking anything else from us. Not our names and not our happiness either. It stops here.

"Okay, kid. Suit yourself. Be safe out here."

"I will. Thanks."

I hop out and move to the building to look around and find a way inside. That's when I notice Taegan's car. I frown and try to get a closer look. I don't think there are too many sparkly pink BMWs.

"Well, well, well, look at what we have here. Sean's going to be happy to see you," someone says as they place a gun to the back of my head.

"Don't shoot. I'm harmless. I'm looking for my friend. That's her car right there," I say quickly as I think fast.

"Shut up. You're saving us some time. To think I only came out here to take a piss. Fucking bathrooms are a part of the renovation inside," he says.

I think I know his voice, but I can't put a name to it right now. He grabs my arm and turns me to shove me toward the building. I wonder what Miss Taegan is doing here.

When we get inside, I realize I might be in trouble. I pull my backpack against my chest and cradle it there as I try to gauge when to pull my gun.

I'm grateful that when Dylan taught Ciara how to shoot, he took me along to learn for sport. I don't think he intended for me to be in a situation like this when I would need to use live ammo for the first time.

There are more people here than I was expecting. Sean, Theo, and that redheaded lady are all here. What was her name? Cadlha.

My nostrils flare as Arnold comes into view, standing next to some guy I don't know. The guy who just caught me and brought me in here moves to their side and I can now place the voice and his face. *Devin.* Sean's stupid friend, who used to watch Ciara like she was a piece of meat.

Stay calm, Ciarán. I have to help Miss Taegan.

She's unconscious and they have her tied up. There's another guy sitting next to her and he's tied up and gagged. However, he's awake. Yet his eyes look wrong, like he's been drugged.

"Ciarán, it's good to see you," Theo croons.

"Right, we won't have to work as hard to get Cee-Cee here," Sean says.

"Let's get this over with. Call her and tell her to get her ass here now," that Cadlha lady snarls.

"You guys are going to be sorry." I fight not to allow the tears to fall.

Even if I pull my gun now, there are too many of them and I won't get them all without Miss Taegan getting hurt. Maybe if I wait, Ciara and I can do this together. Dylan is sure to come with her.

Yeah, we'll do this as a family. Dylan and I can protect Ciara together and we'll never have to leave or be scared again.

I'm going to fight for my sister. They're going to leave us alone. This is our home. New York belongs to us.

Dylan

"Keys, keys," I murmur to myself as I pat myself down.

I go to grab the key to the SUV, but remember it's in the clothes I had on earlier and Ciara has the spare. Instead, I grab the key for the Porsche. I note how quiet the place is.

Taegan and Ciarán can't still be up on the rooftop. Maybe they went out to get something to eat or something. I pull my phone to text her as I leave out of the front door.

I'm already annoyed because I had to be called away from Ciara to deal with this shit. I don't like repeating myself. Having to repeat myself after the day I had is even worse.

These fucking dirty cops are barking up the wrong tree. Jumping in the Porsche, I head for the city where these fucks are demanding my attention. Like, who the fuck are they to be summoning me in the first fucking place?

I tried to call Brooklyn, as this all started with some shit on his books. I didn't get an answer, so I'm taking things into my own hands. The only problem I have is that they're luring me out of my territory.

I'll have to think before I do anything in Manhattan. I have a million things on my mind during the drive. As I stop at a light, it dawns on me that Taegan hasn't replied to my text yet.

I look at the time. Maybe Ciarán was in his room and Taegan called it a night. It's not uncommon for her to place her phone on Do Not Disturb so she can read and have time to herself.

I shake the thought off. I'm sure Ciarán is safe in the apartment. In the last two years, I've never had any trouble out of him. Right now, I need to focus. I know these assholes are up to something and I need to head them off at the pass.

"One issue at a time, Dyl," I blow out as I turn onto the block this meeting is on.

Once I get to the end of the street, I realize it's a parking lot by the water. I head in and ride to the row they gave me. Three cruisers are parked across the lanes as if in warning not to come back here to park.

I climb out of the car to find all three of these bastards waiting for me, sitting on the hoods of their cars. I glance around and can see the lights and camera back here seem to be out. Someone smashed the lights and the live light isn't active on the cams.

"Good to know," I murmur to myself.

"What the fuck do the three of you want?" I snap as I move to the front of my vehicle.

"You didn't think we were going to give up so easily, now did you?" Detective Baker speaks up first.

"Especially not with those deep-ass fat pockets you and your family have," Detective Vargus adds.

I shrug. "Your IQ isn't my problem. I'll give you the smart … no, the only option. If you want to play a game of fuck around and find out, be my guest. I have a bunch of stupid prizes to hand out."

"Big talk," Detective Strong says as he tilts his head to the side. "We noticed the girl is a weakness of yours. So we started to look into her and that little ink shop. Funny, her license and the deed to the place say Ciara Walsh, but she's on all the kid's school shit as Ariel Norwood.

"That got my attention, and I decided to do some more digging. Did you know your girlfriend isn't his legal guardian? We could bring her in for kidnapping and I'm thinking about adding trafficking to the list, depending on how well you cooperate."

I clench my jaw so hard I'm surprised my teeth don't break. These stupid motherfuckers are out of their minds if they think I'm going to allow anything to happen to Ciara and Ciarán. They should have spent more time doing homework on me.

Exhortation isn't even on the menu. Now the only option they have left is death. I go to step forward to beat the shit out of all three of them, but my phone rings, holding me back.

Knowing it's a call from Booker, who I left sitting on my building to watch over Ciara, I pull out the phone to pick up. I'm not even concerned with these three.

"What is it?" I bite out.

"Ciara just sped out of the garage like a bat out of hell. I'm on her, but I don't have a good feeling about this. She's alone. The kid isn't with her."

"When was the last time you spoke to Taegan?"

"Just before she took off from your place. She said Eoghan called and wanted her to hang out."

"How long before I left was this?"

"About an hour or two before you let me know you were heading out. She said she was heading to the Fighting Irish for drinks and to watch a match or two. I was going to head there to chill with them before your call."

"Wait, she hasn't been with Ciarán? Fuck, Book. The Fighting Irish is closed for renovations," I rush into the phone as I turn to jump into my car. "Stay on Ciara, something is wrong with the kid."

"We're not fucking done with you," Baker snarls after me.

"But I'm done with you."

I don't bother to look back as I start my car and race back to Brooklyn to my uncle's fight club. I know in my gut something is going on with Ciarán and Ciara is heading for him.

"Fuck," I roar.

How does Taegan fit into this? Why would Eoghan lure her there? They're pretty tight and Eoghan has been trying to work his way up in Uncle Ronan's organization.

This isn't making sense. I start to make calls as I floor it. I try Cole first, but don't get an answer again. So I call Logan next.

"Aye, ya left before I finished talking to ya. Is everything okay with the lass?"

"I don't know. I think she's heading to the Fighting Irish. Something is going on with Ciarán. Bro, I don't have a good feeling about this."

"That's what I was trying to warn ya about. Laki and his niece Amy are here."

"Who the fuck is Amy?"

"My eyes. She's been watching over Lily Young for me to keep her in check, but that can wait. The Youngs know where Ciara is, and Cadlha found them and they're all here to start some shit."

"Fuck, that stupid fucking bitch," I roar.

"I'll meet ya there."

I look into the rearview mirror and see I can't catch a break tonight. The same three cruisers from the lot are following me. If I'm about to walk into some shit that's going to make me drop some bodies, I don't need these fucks on my tail.

"Shit, I have another problem. Where's Brooklyn? I haven't been able to reach him all night. I need him to take care of this shit with those cops. They're literally on my ass."

"His phone broke during our tiff."

I snort. If that was a tiff, I'd hate to see what he thinks a brawl is. I shake the thought off as I try to lose these pricks.

They haven't turned on their lights, which says a lot. They either don't want anyone else to know they're following me, or they're too far away from where they belong. I plan to take advantage of that.

"I gotta go," I say and drop the call.

My next call is a courtesy call because I know what I'm about to do. It's only fair I show some respect. After all, this might get real messy.

"Aye, what about ye?"

"Uncle Ronan, this is a courtesy call. You're going to need a cleanup crew at the Fighting Irish. I don't know how many bodies there will be, but anyone who doesn't belong to me is going to drop."

Ronan

"Did he just hang up on me?" I mutter to myself as I look down at my phone.

I frown and look up at my wife. She's just getting off her own call. We were about to have a good shag before her line rang first.

"What did ya say yer friend's name is?" I ask Danny.

"I didn't," she replies as she gets up and starts to get dressed.

"Love, this isn't the time to play with me. I think yer problem has just become my problem. What's her name and what the fuck is going on?"

"Her name is Ciara. Someone called her and they have her fourteen-year-old brother. Veg—" She cuts off and takes a breath. "The person she would usually call for something like this isn't available, so she's calling in a favor."

"Where is this favor?"

She shrugs then looks down at her phone as it buzzes. "Ah, looks like this is an *our* problem. Isn't this the address of your fight club?"

"Let me guess, we're heading to Brooklyn to the Fighting Irish," I sigh.

"Yup, that's exactly where this is."

"Let's go. I think that's me nephew's bird. The lad is about to tear me place apart."

"Our nephew. Your family is my family. The girl is a friend. I owe her. This is personal."

CHAPTER FORTY

Surprise Guests

Ciara

"I'm on my way."

I hang up with Danika and gun this truck as fast as it will let me push it. I'm not crazy, I know Cadlha has a trap set up for me. I just can't understand what has made her so bold that she would return here and take my brother again.

I feel sick to my stomach. I hadn't known Ciarán wasn't home until that call came in. I had rushed to his room, praying she was lying on the other end of my phone. However, by the time I jumped out of the bathtub and ran into Ciarán's room, I knew for sure she wasn't lying.

I tried Taegan's phone but she's not answering. I couldn't call Dylan. He left on business. He already looked pissed off as he left.

I don't want to distract him. He has enough on his plate. I'm going to go and kick this bitch's ass again then get my brother back.

However, I called Danika because this time, when I'm done with Cadlha, she's not going to be breathing. I furrow my brows as I turn into the fight club lot and I notice Taegan's car. I also note the other three cars. Two with rental plates.

Grabbing the gun I took from the lockbox in our bedroom, I tuck it into the back of my jeans. Then I jump out of the truck to head inside. There's construction plastic all over the place once I enter, as if the place is being renovated.

Nothing at all like what it looked like when I first came here. I keep moving until I get to the large back room where the money counting and betting had been. That's where I find them waiting for me.

"Ah, here she is. My little girl. Good to see you, Cee-Cee.

"Or should I call you Ciara? It seems you've remembered your real name since you've been gone."

All I can see is red. Rage consumes me the moment I see Theo and Sean, but what has me ready to spit nails is the fact that Taegan is tied up and Ciarán is sitting in a chair next to her, clutching his backpack against his chest. I don't know the other guy they have tied and gagged with them.

Taegan begins to groan and her eyes flutter open. She looks around wildly then anger fills her face. Before I can reply to Theo, Taegan begins to growl at them.

"Ya fucking pieces of shit. Simon, yer no better than this stupid cunt. No wonder none of the family will fuck with either of ya. Wait until I get free. I have a bullet for the both of ye," she snarls.

"Oh shut up. We only drugged Eoghan to gain access to this place and to get him to coax ya here. I thought we would need ya to get to the kid and this bitch, but now that we don't need ya," Cadlha says as she pulls a gun and lifts it toward her cousin.

"Put that shit down. Do ya know the shitstorm ya'd start if ya killed her. I didn't come here for that, ya eejit," the dark-haired, lanky guy growls.

"Shut up, Simon. Ya didn't have to come here at all."

"Would all of you shut the fuck up," Sean shouts, spit flying from his mouth.

I narrow my gaze on him. It hasn't slipped my notice that his buddy Devin is here with him. I can't help wondering where Lily is.

"Ya have me here, so what's yer plan?" I hiss.

"Ugh, I thought I crushed that accent out of you. Whatever, I have some friends who have a price on your head. I get you back to them and I get two million," Theo croons.

"You didn't tell me that." Sean pouts like a child.

"If you don't shut the fuck up. Where the fuck did you think all our money came from? Did you miss that we didn't have shit before she arrived and we ain't had shit since she's been gone?

"Fucking idiot. That piece-of-shit gym hasn't ever earned me enough to live a real life. Now your sister is forcing me to take a fucking allowance when the place is turning a fucking profit like never before.

"Why would I tell you anything? So you can fuck it all up for me. Nope, not this time. Although I don't plan to turn her over just yet.

"Rumor has it there's a big fucking payday coming her way. All she has to do is marry that Irish motherfucker she's been here fucking."

"Are ya fucking kidding me? The deal was I would bring ya here to her and ye would get rid of her for me. I knew ye couldn't be trusted," Cadlha screams. "She's not fucking marrying my man."

"Yes the fuck she is. I'm going to take our little Ciarán here and she's going to do whatever the fuck I tell her to if she wants him back. I am his legal guardian after all," Theo seethes while snatching Ciarán out of his seat.

I make eye contact with my brother to let him know I've got him. I'm proud of him as he gives me a small nod to let me know he's okay. I need to keep Theo calm and talking to give Danika time to get here.

I take a deep calming breath. "Relax, you don't need to do this. You're not his guardian either. This could blow up in your face if you take him, but I'm willing to work out a deal with you.

"You said two million. I'll double that. Just—"

Theo releases a maniacal laugh. I freeze and start to inch for my gun. I will blow his head off if he so much as moves wrong toward my brother.

"Two million. Do you think I'm stupid? The McDougal clan is worth billions, and you are set to inherit it all. I don't want a measly two million. Shit, I ran through the twenty million your parents left you within five years. Thank God O'Brien was willing to pay me to keep you away from here.

"I don't want the two million, sweetheart. I want it all. Every single dime. Your boyfriend is loaded. You won't miss a dime," he scoffs.

I reach for my gun. Twenty million dollars? My parents left us twenty million dollars, and we were forced to live like shit.

"I wouldn't do that if I were you." I stiffen at the sound of the voice that comes from behind me.

Devin. I should have made sure he could never walk again. I'll make certain to fix that this time.

Dean

Ronan pulls up to the Fighting Irish right as a Porsche comes flying into the lot. I wouldn't find that strange if three undercover police cruisers didn't arrive just moments behind it. Dylan jumps out of the Porsche and storms into the building, ignoring the cars that are chasing him.

I would know his big, tall, blond ass anywhere. That BDE walk he and his brothers have radiates off him in this moment. My scalp begins to tingle. I don't get the feeling these guys are friendly.

Especially when they don't get out of the cars to follow him inside. Something stinks. From what Ronan told me on the way here, Dylan is in *don't give a fuck mode*. This can't be good.

"Ronan, baby. Get out of the car and head inside to help. I've got this."

"Ach, what are ya thinking? I don't like the look on yer face."

"I'm going to buy Dylan some time."

Ronan reaches for the back of my neck and kisses me hard. I can feel his possessiveness in the kiss. He shouldn't worry so much. I've got this.

"I'll be fine. No record, remember?"

"Aye, but that's my point. There's no trace of ya. This will place ya in the database."

I shrug. "It's for my family. We all sacrifice at some point."

I wink at him as he groans then rushes out of the vehicle. From this angle, we can see the cop cars, but I don't think they can see us. Ronan moves swiftly to head inside through the back entrance.

I chew on my lip. With the renovations, the back of the building is a challenge to go in through, but it's the best option right now. It would take too long at this point to go around to the side entrance and these assholes are sitting out front. I climb across the console into the driver's seat.

Placing on my seat belt, I then put the SUV in gear and fly around the corner to ram right into one of the cruisers. The other two turn on their lights, but not the sirens. I grin and sit waiting for them to come to me. When I see who the officers are, I roll my eyes.

These assholes have a death wish for sure. LaSalle has already had a conversation with me about them. Their photos are on my desk.

"Good evening, Officers," I purr as I roll down my windows. "I'm so sorry about that. A spider startled me, and I lost control. My husband is going to be so angry with me. So much for game night with the family."

"Can you please step out of the vehicle?"

CHAPTER FORTY-ONE

Our Heart

Dylan

"And just where the fuck do ya think I'll be while ya take her money and hold her brother hostage?" I say as I step into the old back room, where the money counting happened.

My voice booms and echoes in the space with its vaulted ceilings and stripped walls. The guy who just took Ciara's gun spins and aims it at me. I don't miss how fast he moves out of Ciara's reach to make sure she's not at his back and he has the gun trained on us both.

"Who the fuck are you?" The guy I'm assuming from the pictures I've seen is Sean Young, bites out.

"I'm none of yer fucking business. Ya should have stayed in Seattle, where I've been allowing ya to breathe."

"Allowing me to … You're not allowing anyone to do shit. Who is this fucking asshole?"

"That's the prick she's going to marry. Devin, bring her over here. I'll let her say goodbye to Ciarán before we leave. One of you check him for guns. Can't have him trying to play the hero."

"You really think I need a gun for any of ye? Yer as good as dead, I can promise ya that and I never break a promise."

"Dad, you fucking moron. Let Ciarán go and stop this foolishness."

"What are you even doing here? Go back home and mind your business," Theo Young growls.

"I'm here to save you and Sean from yourselves. Your plan is stupid. If you cross those Russians, you're going to end up dead. Did you even think about that?"

"With all the cash I'll have, I won't have to worry about them. They're not after the money. They want to put an end to what the money is for."

"Amy? What are you doing here?" Ciara says, causing me to glance out the corner of my eye.

Laki and a pretty young woman are standing there, glaring at Theo and his son. Neither of them has a weapon drawn, but they're both giving off a lethal vibe. However, it looks like we're no longer outnumbered.

Panic begins to fill Theo and Sean's eyes. The dark-haired, lanky guy with Cadlha starts to inch his way toward the door. He's the only one who seems to have any sense. The guy who took my gun off me has moved across the room with Ciara.

They are now standing by Theo. "Take him," Theo barks as he shoves Ciarán.

Arnold's bitch ass steps forward and takes him by the arm, looking like he wishes he weren't here at all. Ciarán looks at me and then looks down at his backpack. However, I'm not sure what he's trying to tell me.

I turn my attention back to Ciara as Sean grabs ahold of her. She begins to struggle and the other guy next to Sean licks his lips and grabs his crotch. I don't know how, but I instantly know this guy had something to do with her making a run for it with Ciarán.

He's definitely going to die by my hands. When Sean hands her off to him and he gropes her breast, I see nothing but red.

Ciara goes to make a move, but Sean pulls a gun and aims at her head.

"Don't you fucking dare," Sean growls. "Dad, you see, I'm not as greedy as you are. I can live with two million. I'd rather that than ever allow this big motherfucker to touch her again."

"What? Are you crazy? Sean, I swear to God. I will end your sorry life myself," Theo snarls.

"The two of you need to let them go. This is over. You had no right to take them the first time.

"I was so happy to have a little sister. I didn't think to ask you where you got them from. They were so cute and little.

"She was everything to me. Then I figured out what you had done. What you were supposed to do.

"The only reason I was ever cruel to either of them was because I wanted to protect them from the two of you. You needed to believe I hated them as much as you two did, so I could help them."

"Help them how?" Theo hisses and narrows his eyes.

"You were always too stupid to see what was happening around you. They were going to kill you back then. You keep bringing shit down on our heads."

This is it. I'm going to make my move. I start to head for Theo. He snaps his attention back to me and pulls his own gun to aim at me.

"Stop right there. I said don't fucking move."

I ignore him and keep walking. I'm done with all this back-and-forth. Theo's hands are shaking as I move in on him.

Words Ciara's father once spoke to us come back to me. I begin to speak them to Ciara. We can end this together.

"I'll keep their focus on me. You hit the hell out of them. Then we both pounce. The way we have each other's backs will always work in our favor. We have more of something none of them have," I say in Gaelic.

"And what's that, Dyl?" she replies, just as she once asked her father.

"Heart, love. We both have tons of heart. That's something no one can take from us. They'll try, but they'll never take that away," I repeat her father's words once again.

"What the fuck are you two talking about? Speak English. I said stop or I'll fucking shoot."

I grin at him as I close in. The war between shooting me and losing the money or allowing me to get near him and rip his head off plays across his face. Preservation wins out.

He pulls the trigger, shooting me in my side. I grunt, but I don't stop moving. Instead, I grin wider and tilt my head at him before I bat the gun down and punch the shit out of him.

"No," Ciara screams.

I feel the sting of a second bullet as it grazes my arm before I register the sound. Theo is on the floor in a heap. He'll be out for a bit.

Ignoring the pain, I turn for Ciara and Ciarán. Sean is doubled over, holding his side. Ciara must have hit him when he pulled the trigger to shoot me.

She begins raining blows down on him that ring out through the room. I wince as his neck makes a cracking sound under the force of one of her punches.

A few paces away, Ciarán has gotten free of Arnold's hold and is beating his ass. I smile. The kid's form is damn near perfect.

Arnold swings, but Ciarán ducks and comes up with a killer uppercut that sends Arnold flying back like a piece of paper in the wind. My chest swells with pride.

It all happens so fast. The guy who had been holding Ciara before gets to his feet and scrambles for the gun on the floor that Sean dropped. Ciarán grabs his pack and pulls what looks like my favorite Glock that I keep in my office.

He then aims at the asshole who's reaching for the gun to aim at his sister and fires a shot at his leg. The dude cries out and reaches for his leg, the gun he didn't have a firm grasp on falling to the floor.

Ciara kicks him in the face, but he grabs her foot and throws her a little off balance. I rush over and place the asshole in a choke hold. He taps my arm frantically as I squeeze the life out of him. My arm and side are burning, but I'm not letting go until he's not breathing and never will breathe again.

"Don't you fucking touch my sister," Ciarán barks out, his voice cracking like it's been doing a lot lately.

I glance up to see Sean has gotten back on his feet. His face is pretty fucked up. Ciara whipped his ass.

"Ciarán, you don't want to do this," Lily Young says.

"I'm tired of him picking on us. I'm tired of you guys trying to take our happiness. This is our home. We're happy here. You're not taking me from my sister and you're not taking her away from me."

"I don't want to take either of you away, honey. I came here to make sure you guys remain safe. But Ciarán, I need you to let the adults handle this. Put the gun down, sweetheart," Lily coos.

Slowly, she's inching toward Ciarán to try to get the gun from him. Ciarán begins to lower the gun, but Sean's stupid ass lunges for Ciara. Ciarán lifts the gun and shoots.

I toss this guy's body to the side and jump to my feet. Lily jumps in front of the bullet meant for her brother and drops to the ground. It all happens so fast.

Ciara ducks out of the way as Sean tries to grab her. She then takes him to the ground and wraps his neck with her legs as she pins his arm. My chest swells with pride as I watch the light go out of his eyes.

His body goes limp, and Ciara gets to her feet. She rushes to pull Ciarán into her arms as Laki goes to wrap around them both. The look of relief that covers his face is evident. Ciarán is shaking as he hugs his sister back.

"We've got you, buddy. Your dad would be proud of you. We're going to take care of everything," Laki chokes out.

"Look at what we found," Uncle Ronan croons as he and Logan drag Cadlha and the lanky dark-haired guy back in.

"We need a medic. She doesn't deserve this. She's not like them," the one Ciara called Amy cries out.

"They're safe. That's all I ever wanted," Lily says as she lies in her arms.

"Lily, don't you do this. Not for that piece of trash. He's not worth your life. You fight. Come on, stay with me," Amy pleads.

"A medic and cleanup crew are en route," Uncle Ronan says.

"Ach, you should go, they put your wife in one of the squad cars and took off," Brooklyn says.

"Aye, she knows what she's doing. She's luring them away."

"That's a problem I need to address. I'll come with ya."

"Ya don't have a working phone. I'll go," Logan says.

Another shot goes off, and I turn to see where it came from. Ciara is standing with a smoking gun. Cadlha is lying at Uncle Ronan's feet with a bullet between her eyes.

"I told her I was going to do it." Ciara shrugs.

"Welcome to the family, love," Uncle Ronan croons.

Ronan

After making sure Dylan got medical attention and giving instructions for the bodies he and his bird collected, I took off to take care of my wife. I had already put in a call to get her representation before I could arrive.

I find Bobby Mairettie is already here as we enter the station. Brooklyn and Logan are on either side of me. While they know I'm married, Brooklyn is the only one who has met my wife.

"McGowan, I didn't know you were in town. You didn't check in," Detective Strong—or Detective Shit Face as I like to call him croons as he saunters over to me.

"And I'm pretty fucking sure I told ya it would be a cold day in hell and every witch on a burning stake there would have frozen tits before the day I ever check in with the likes of ya. Step aside and get the fuck out of my face," I growl.

He scoffs and turns his attention to Brooklyn and Logan. "What the fuck happened to you two?" he says with a frown as he looks their faces over.

"We happened to each other. Imagine what happens to those we don't give a shit about," Brooklyn bites out.

Danny's laugh grabs my attention. I turn to find her walking out with a smile on her face as she looks up at the captain. I love that crazy laugh. It brings a smile to my face.

"I'm so sorry about all of this. I'll be happy to pay for the repairs," she says as she bats her lashes.

"Nonsense. We should be paying for your repairs, for putting you through this. Things like this happen all the time.

"My wife just did the same thing about a month ago. The spider actually bit her. I don't see why you were brought in for driving your husband's vehicle."

"Oh no. I hope she's all right now. Not many women who look like me have husbands with the last name McGowan. In their defense, I still haven't changed my ID.

"I was also a little nervous about how my husband would react when he found out what I did to his new truck. I believe your detectives took that as nervousness because the vehicle wasn't supposed to be in my possession."

"Bullshit, excuse my language. I want to apologize on their behalf. You have my number if you ever need anything."

Danny comes to my side, and I tuck her under my arm. Strong narrows his eyes at her as he works his jaw. He nods to himself and pulls a hand down his face.

"We'll meet again," he says.

"Ya should hope not. It's time ya start to listen to yer superiors."

"Fuck off."

I shrug and turn with my wife to leave. This eejit has never understood when to back off. I give Danny a squeeze.

"Is she okay?" she whispers.

"Aye."

"The brother?"

"I like him. He did right by his sister. They're both fine."

CHAPTER FORTY-TWO

Love of My Life

Ciara

Present …

"What are you thinking about?" Dylan asks as I stand in the mirror staring at my reflection.

I smile to myself as I lift my gaze to his. Dylan is still as handsome as the day I walked into his gym and triggered my memories of him. I sink back into him as he moves to wrap his arms around me.

"I was thinking that your family knows how to throw a wedding. That was so much fun. After everything we've all been through, everyone seemed to be so happy.

"I know it's not all over and we still have a few loose ends to tie up, but today felt like a win. Like, we're all that much closer to finding and plugging the holes. You know?"

"I know what you mean, and I believe you're right. We can all begin to move on with our lives. Ryan did a good thing.

"I think we all needed this—to be together as a family. We're all bringing in the New Year with a fresh start. New beginnings," he replies. "Yeah, we're still waiting to find them and be done for good, but to be honest, will it ever be over?"

I turn in his arms and look up into his eyes. He searches my face as he looks back at me. The last four years have been trying, but I've fallen so much deeper in love with this man.

"No, you're right. I don't think it will be. Ciarán is turning eighteen and he wants to come here to spend time with the uncles. I didn't want him to, but you're right. This will always be a part of our lives and he should know what that means firsthand.

"I can't hold on to him forever. Maybe it's time I let go and move forward with starting my own family. That is, if you still want that."

I hardly get to finish my words before he crushes my lips in a hard kiss. I hear more than see my dress being torn down the back. I snicker because he's looked like he wanted to tear it from my body since this morning, when I first got ready for the wedding.

I had a feeling the sheer panels would get me this kind of reaction. The dress was tasteful but sexy. Taegan and Dahila thought it was perfect. I wasn't sure until I saw Dylan's eyes light up the first time he saw me.

"I've wanted to start a family with you since the day you walked into my gym and back into my life. You have no idea how long I've been waiting to make you mine forever," he breathes into my mouth.

"Then show me. Let's make a baby," I whimper.

He steps back with a sexy smile on his lips and begins to peel off his tux. I'm a little sad to see it go. All the men cleaned up nice for today.

The people were just as gorgeous as the wedding. I hope to have a wedding as perfect as theirs someday. This all has been like falling into a wonderland.

I bite my lip as my man stands before me completely naked. My chest swells with pride as my gaze lands on the 3D tat of my name that runs up his torso on the right side. I love that piece.

I was so nervous but Dyl remained patient with me. I've been so entranced by him stripping, I didn't even think to remove my ruined dress. Instead, I've been standing here drooling the entire time.

I snap out of it as he comes closer and unzips the destroyed dress. The fabric floats down to the floor and he lifts me onto his waist. My bare breasts smash against his chest as he captures my lips for another kiss.

I hold on to his powerful shoulders as he carries me into the bedroom. The rooms here are so nice. There's a fireplace warming the large space that's bringing its own charm with it.

Dylan places me on the bed and climbs over me. The heat from the fireplace already has a shine of sweat on our skin. I run my hands down his smooth back to his ass and dig my nails in as he devours my mouth.

He breaks the kiss and looks me deeply in the eyes. "No matter where life takes us, remember how much I love you and that I'll do anything for you," he says.

I nod and bring his lips back to mine. He reaches for my panties and pulls them down my legs as we drink each other in. I push at his chest for him to fall onto his back.

I'm already slick between the legs, but there's something I need to do first. Dylan and I have spent a lot of time training my throat for him to fit without me gagging. It has turned into one of my guilty pleasures.

"Oh shit, baby," he groans as I begin to bob on his length.

I smile around him as I'm just getting started. I get him nice and sloppy wet. He fists the sheets as I take him deep for the first time. I go to do it a second time, and he bucks off the bed.

"That's my girl. Your head is fire. So fucking good. Play with your pussy for me. I want you nice and wet when I slide inside you."

"I've got you, baby," I purr as I tilt my head then lick the underside of his shaft. "I'm going to suck you so good, you won't have a choice but to fuck me hard."

"Is that what my girl wants? You want me to fuck you nice and hard?"

I don't answer with words. At least not words that make any sense. I take him deep a few times before he grabs the back of my head and holds me in place, causing me to gag.

"Fuck, come here," he says tightly as I lift my head.

He climbs from the bed and grabs me by the ankle to drag me to him. I'm surprised when he pulls me to my feet as he stands on the side of the bed. Turning me around, he drops to his knees and buries his face in my ass, then spreads my cheeks to give him better access.

I cry out and fall face-first onto the bed, grabbing fistfuls of the sheets as I moan and cry into the mattress. I love the way his tongue and fingers feel inside me. Dylan has made my body feel amazing every time he has touched me.

He usually knows just what I need before I can think of it. Like now, he stands, grabs one of my legs and holds it up and out as he thrusts into me. My eyes cross and I gush all over him. He angles his hips and keeps thrusting.

"Oh my God, Dyl. Shit, babe. Fuck," I scream into the mattress.

"Is this how you want it? Is this hard enough for you? Are you ready for me to put my baby in you?"

"Yes, yes, yes. I already stopped my birth control. I'm ready when you are."

He stills. "What did you just say?"

"I stopped my birth control. Like I said, my brother is turning eighteen. I'm a little sad. I want a baby."

"Fuck, Ciara," he grunts.

He reaches to pull me to stand then turns me to face him. He lifts me into his arms, hooking my thighs over his forearms. I drop my head back as he enters me again. The way he's bouncing me on his dick has me so wet I can feel my pussy rippling around him.

I bury my face in his neck and inhale him. It's like a hit of my own personal drug. I begin to convulse against him as my walls suck him in deep and grip around him.

"I love you," I whimper as I feel him begin to release inside me.

"You're the love of my life. Thank you for proving I'm doing the right thing," he says in my ear.

CHAPTER FORTY-THREE

Promises Kept

Dylan

I finally have an answer. This wouldn't be right if I didn't find a way to complete my promise. Lucky for me, Ciarán is a little genius.

"Are you nervous?" Ciarán booms beside me.

His voice is almost as deep as mine these days. Ciarán now stands at about six one and counting. I don't think he's finished growing.

He's one of my best boxers at the gym. However, he's amazing with technology. He and Felix can spend hours on the phone. I've been talking with them to make this all happen.

Am I nervous? Yeah, but not about the end goal. I'm more worried about whether we'll pull this off and if it will have the desired effect for Ciara.

"I'm good. You're the one who has to wear that weird-ass-looking outfit," I scoff.

He chuckles. "This is what's going to bring him to life for her. By the way, this is so dope. I've always known you loved my sister, but this really says how much. Bro, if I've never said it. Thanks. Thanks for everything you've ever done for us.

"Thanks for taking me in like your own little brother and thanks for covering my ass back when I—"

I tug him into me by the back of his head, cutting his words off. He wraps his arms around me and holds me tight. I love this kid. He doesn't have to thank me for shit. I'd do it all again.

"What you did and what you were willing to do earned my respect. I'd cover your ass a million times over without you having to ask once. I don't just love your sister. I love you too, man.

"You are my little brother, Ciarán. Long before we met, you were my family. Your Gaelic still sucks ass, but you're the best little brother I could ever ask for," I choke out.

"Yeah, well. I'm hoping to get better while I'm here with the uncles," he laughs and pulls away.

"You're really thinking about staying?"

"Yeah, Ciara has done nothing but take care of me. I've been thinking since you asked me to help you out. Maybe I'll just stay for a year. Don't worry, I'll still train. Taegan wants to keep booking fights for me.

"Maybe I'll be like my dad and train over here while fighting in the States. Ciara said I could have the farm in Ireland if I don't want to stay here, but dude, come on. This castle is as fire as you guys' place. Besides, the uncles treat me like royalty."

I pat his cheek. "Whatever you decide, we're always a call away. I'm going to miss you."

"Enough of the mush. Ciara will be here soon. We should get into our places."

I nod and punch my gloves together as I stand. Here goes nothing. Time to prove I always keep my promises.

Ciara

I'm ready to wrap my hands around Taegan, Dahila, and Lily's necks. I had planned to stay in and sleep the day away. I'm wiped from the wedding and making love all night. Okay, who am I kidding?

Dylan spent the night fucking me and I happily took every bit of it. I didn't even feel him get up and leave this morning. Instead, I woke to Taegan scratching at the door like a little cat. When I finally got up and answered the door, she rushed me to get in the shower and get dressed.

I still don't know what all of this is about. My curiosity goes through the roof as we pull up to the McDougal castle. I hadn't planned to come here on this visit.

My uncles turned out to be cool, but they are so stern and grumpy. Ciarán seems to bond with them a lot more than I do. It's not that they treat me bad. They're just … I can't explain it.

To be honest, I think they like me. Deja has a relationship with them, but she did live here for a while before moving to the little village with our great-grandmother.

However, from the looks of it, they're having a party or something today. There are a bunch of cars parked around the courtyard. Taegan rushes from the car and grabs me to pull me out with her.

"What's going on? What are we doing here?"

"You'll see soon enough," Lily says with a big, goofy smile.

She really did want a little sister. She spends more time in New York now, with both her father and brother gone. Once Theo woke that night, Dylan put him to sleep for good and Theo was buried with the others in the cement poured out back for the new edition.

Lily didn't have any hard feelings. She already knew the two were heading in that direction. It was only a matter of time. Besides, she met her boyfriend while working reception at my shop.

Our relationship has become stranger. She has proved her loyalty more than once since that night. I think she regrets not being able to save Sean, but she doesn't lose sleep over it.

"You guys are starting to weird me out," I mumble.

And then we step out into the backyard of the castle, and I freeze. The place has been transformed. There is a boxing ring in the center of the grounds and bleachers on either side.

The seats are already packed with our family and friends. Logan and Cole are in the front row, where these three are now dragging me.

"What's going on?"

"Ugh, she told ya. Ya'll find out soon enough. The sooner ya get to yer seat, the faster ya can find out."

I shake my head and follow them. I sit between Logan and Cole. Deja reaches across Cole to squeeze my hand as she gives me a huge smile. Taegan, Daliah, and Lily are sitting behind me.

I can feel the excitement coming off everyone around us. I look around, trying to understand what's happening. That's when Dylan is announced and comes into the ring. I watch on, wondering what he's up to.

I look over and see Ciarán step behind a curtain, wearing one of those suits they wear to create video games. Then the next fighter is announced and I can't stop sobbing. If I didn't know I loved this man before, I've fallen all over again in this very moment.

"In the right corner, in the blue robe and black trunks, weighing in as an ethereal presence, we have Donny 'Killer' Walsh."

I break down and begin to cry even harder. It's my dad. They have a surreal image of my dad stepping into the ring like he's truly alive. Laki is even in the ring to remove his robe.

I know Ciarán helped to make this happen, which only makes this that much more special to me. Cole and Logan each rub my back as I continue to cry.

I wipe at my eyes so I can see what's going on. Dylan and the image have an actual bout. In this moment, I believe in every promise Dylan has ever made to me.

This was the one promise I wasn't expecting him to keep because it was impossible. I should have known better. This is Dylan.

The boy who waited nearly thirteen years for me. As the round ends, everyone cheers. I glance around to see there isn't a dry eye here.

"Ciara, I made you a promise when you were eight years old. I didn't know then how hard it would be to keep that promise, but I knew I would.

"I've asked your uncles and Ciarán for your hand, but I needed to fight your da just like I said I would. I hope you can accept this version of a fight. Ciarán did say he would come out here and fight me in the flesh if this wasn't enough for you." He laughs and winks at me. "Come here, baby."

I stand up on shaky legs and head to the ring. Logan and Cole open the ropes and Jamie helps me inside. Dylan pulls me into his arms and dips his head to place his forehead to mine.

"I love you more than anything in this world. I want to spend the rest of my life with you. I'll be here to protect you, love you, and take care of you. Will you marry me, Ciara?"

"Yes, I promised you I would. Yes."

Another Promise

Brooklyn

We're sitting on one of the cliffs around the Black castle. I have DJ sitting between my legs as my chin rests on the top of her head while we look out over the water.

I'm proud of my little brother. He promised he would do something, and he held to it. No matter how impossible it was.

I've done things all out of order, but I love this woman just as much, if not more. Am I happy? I guess you could say that, but I want it all. For once, my role in the Alliance isn't breathing down my neck.

We can all take steps toward things in our personal lives. After all we've been through, we deserve more. It's our time.

"What are ya thinking about, Cole? It sounds like yer trying to start an engine with all that thinking," DJ says, breaking into the silence.

"I'm thinking about when ya took yer bat to my car."

She pulls away to turn and look back at me. Pursing my lips, I try not to laugh. She narrows her eyes at me.

"Are ya thinking about making me have to again?"

"Ach, no, love. I'm thinking about how I knew that night that I loved ya."

"Um."

I peck her lips and tighten my arms around her. She turns back to look out at the water. I inhale deeply. The plan is for me to be next.

This is going to be good. I promise it will.

Blue Collection Character Tree
Legally Bound 1
Bobby Mairettie and Paige Kemble-Mairettie.
   Father and mother of:
      Peyton and James Mairettie (*twin boys*)
      Sydney Mairettie and Maria Lynn Mairettie (*twin girls*)

Legally Bound 2
Marcus Mairettie and Rita Briggs-Mairettie.
   Father and mother of:
      Daniel Mairettie
      Hannah Mairettie

Legally Bound 3
Nathaniel (Nate) Briggs and Pamela (Pam) Kemble-Briggs.
   Father and mother of:
      Tiffany and Tracey Briggs (*twin girls*)
      Nathaniel Briggs Jr.

Legally Bound 4
Jasper Briggs and Marie Mairettie-Briggs.
   Father and mother of:
      Clay Briggs

Legally Bound 5
Sam Mairettie, a.k.a. LaSalle Samuel Locatelli and Monique Natasha Gabriel, a.k.a. Tasha Locatelli.
   Father and mother/stepmother of:
      Jessica Mairettie Locatelli (mother, Ellen, *deceased*)
      Megan Mairettie Locatelli (mother, Ellen, *deceased*)
      Sammy Mairettie Locatelli (mother, Ellen, *deceased*)
      Elijah Locatelli
      Paulie Locatelli
      Karen Locatelli
      Sunny Locatelli

The Mairettie Family
Grandpa Marcello Mairettie and Grandma Marie Ann.

Father and mother of:
  Marcello Mairettie Jr.
  Andrew Mairettie
  James Mairettie
  Jessie Mairettie
  Lynn Mairettie
  Gianna Mairettie
James Mairettie and Minnie Mairettie.
  Father and mother of:
    Bobby Mairettie
    Sam Mairettie (Ellen Kensington-Mairettie, *wife*)
    Marcus Mairettie
    Marie Mairettie

The Briggs Family

Thomas Briggs and Raquel Marinos-Briggs (*deceased*).
  Father and mother of:
    Nathaniel Briggs
    Rita Briggs
Earl Briggs (younger brother of Thomas) and Caitronia Marinos-Briggs (twin sister of Raquel).
  Father and mother of:
    Kelly Briggs-Fecteau (Alexie Fecteau, *husband*)
    Jasper Briggs

The Kemble Family

Peyton Kemble and Davina Kemble.
  Father and mother of:
    Pamela Kemble
    Paige Kemble

Other Important Legally Bound Characters

Camille (Cam) McWien-Carter (Seth Carter, *soon-to-be ex-husband*).

Father and mother of:
Seth Carter Jr.
Eddie Carter
Aiden Carter
Austin Mc Wien (*Camille's father*)
Baroness Olivia Kontos (Baron Kontos' widow, *ex-lover of Jasper/ Thomas Briggs's new love interest*)
Vanessa (Julissa) Smith-Mims (***deceased***) (Patrick Mims, *husband,* ***deceased***)
Czar Gabriel (Tasha's brother)
Brenda Gabriel (Tasha's sister)
Kurtrina Gregory (Tasha's sister)
Keisha Gregory (Tasha's sister)
Senator Roland Gabriel (Tasha's father)
Yolanda Gabriel (Tasha's mother)
Misha Krupin and Keisha Gregory (***deceased***).
>   *Father and mother of:*
>   Milanie Krupin
>   Faina Krupin
>   Pavel Krupin (***deceased***).
Logan O'Brien and Raven Johnson (***deceased*** *girlfriend of Logan*).
>   *Father and mother of:*
>   Shauna O'Brien
DJ, a.k.a. Desha
Phoebe Romaine (Ellen's grandmother, **deceased**)
Fifika Romaine (***deceased***)
Salvador Romaine (Ellen's uncle)
Uncle Alfanzo Locatelli
Marco Locatelli
D'Angelo Locatelli
Uncle Carlo Locatelli
Shura
Afanasy

Hush 1
Uri Donati and Valentina Caprisi-Donati.
>   *Father and mother of:*
>   Vita Khayla Donati

Nori Donati
Inzo Donati
Eva Donati

Hush 2
Luca Donati and Shannon Caprisi-Donati.
Father and mother of:
Carlo Donati (introduced in Ballers 2)

Hush 3
Michael Angelo Donati and Symphony Isabella Mansilla-Trovati-Donati.
Father and mother of:
Artemis Donati
Baby on the way

The Donati Family
Angelo Uri Donati (*deceased*) and Donatella Manzo-Donati~~Zuko~~.
Father and mother of:
Uri Donati
Nico Donati ~~Zuko~~
Annabella Donati ~~Zuko~~ (*Nico's twin sister*).
Michael Donati ~~Zuko~~

Uncle Nicholas Donati (brother of Angelo Donati) and Ava Donati.
Father and mother of:
Luca Donati

The Caprisi Family
Vincent Caprisi and Khayla Grant-Caprisi (*deceased*).
Father and mother of:
Valentina Caprisi
Lissette Caprisi (*deceased*)
**Shannon Caprisi (*Vincent's daughter*)

Other Important Hush Characters
Uncle Valentine Caprisi (*Vincent's Brother, head hitter*)
Iman Grant (*Khayla Sister, **Shannon's mother, **deceased***)
Roberto Donati–Zuko (*Donatella's husband, **deceased***)
    **Posed as Dale, the accountant from Legally Bound 3

Cole "Brooklyn" O'Brien
DJ, a.k.a. Deja

Ballers 1
Bradley Monroe and Tamara Hathaway-Monroe.
   Father and mother of:
      Brielle Monroe
      Ashley Monroe and Ashton Monroe (twins)
      Corey Monroe (*baby Tam is pregnant with at end of Ballers 1*)

The Monroe Family
Vernon Monroe and Gloria Monroe.
   Father and mother of:
      Trevor Monroe (Donna, *soon-to-be ex-wife*)
      Bradley Monroe
      Ann Monroe (Bradley's twin sister) (Tom, husband)
Trevor Monroe and Donna Monroe.
   Father and mother of:
      Jessica Monroe
      Toby Monroe and Paige Monroe (*twins*)
      Jonathan Monroe
Tom Rivers and Ann Monroe-Rivers.
   Father and mother of:
      George Rivers and Melissa Rivers (*twins*)
      Amy Rivers

The Hathaway Family
Byron Hathaway and Fiona Hathaway.
   Father and mother of:
      Ellerie Hathaway
      Tamara Hathaway

Other Important Ballers Characters

Stacey (Tam's best friend)
Reese (Tam's best friend, Nico's girlfriend in Ballers 1)
Alee (Tam's best friend)
Cyrus Pierson (Tam's boss).
    Father of:
        Tommy Pierson
        Carey Pierson
        Stephanie Pierson

Ballers 2

Nico Donati and Reese Bridges-Donati.
    Father and mother of:
        Nico Jr. Donati
        Lanya Donati
        Orso Donati
        Santo Donati
        Stefano Donati

Ballers 3

Cameron Perry and Maribel Amina Jones, a.k.a. Amina.
    Father and mother of:
        Cade Perry
        Chance Perry
        Cecilia Perry

Pieces of Trevor's Heart

Trevor Monroe and Lynn "Cakes" Galveston.
    Father and mother/stepmother of:
        Jessica Monroe (mother, Donna, *deceased*)
        Toby Monroe a.k.a Scoot and Paige Monroe a.k.a Snacks
(*twins*) (mother, Donna, *deceased*)
        Jonathan Monroe a.k.a Bam (mother, Donna, *deceased*)
        Brooklyn Valentina Monique Monroe, a.k.a Twinkle
        Brandon Moses Monroe, a.k.a Bird
        Clifton Travis Vernon Monroe, a.k.a Doc

Other Important Ballers Characters
Tiberius Roman (Reese's ex-husband)
Symphony (Michael's right hand)

Brothers Black 1

Wyatt Black and Lanelle (Nellie) Bryant-Black, *father and mother of:*

*Nora Black

*Evan Black

The Black Family

Joseph Black and Cassidy Black, *father and mother of:*

*Wyatt Black

*Noah Black

*Johnathan Black

*Felix Black

*Toby Black

*Braxton Black

*Ryan Black

The Lockhart Family

Rob Lockhart and Faith Lockhart, *father and stepmother of:*

*Heather Lockhart

Steve Lockhart and Nora Bryant-Lockhart (*deceased*), *stepfather and mother of:*

*Lanelle (Nellie) Bryant-Black

Chase Lockhart and Jennifer Lockhart, *father and mother of:*

*Rebecca (Bean) Lockhart (Noah's best friend and love interest)

Other Important *Brothers Black 1* Characters

Missy (Johnathan's ex-girlfriend, *deceased*)

Lucy (*Heather's girlfriend*)

Barry Coleman (*deceased*)

Brothers Black 2

Noah Black and Rebecca (Bean) Lockhart-Black, *father and mother of:*

*Brodie Black

*Connor Black

Baby on the way

Other Important *Brothers Black 2* Characters

Joshua (*deceased*)

Carmen (Nene) Nash (*reporter; niece of Mariah Briggs from Yours Series; Ryan's new crush*)

Logan O'Brien

Brothers Black 3

King Toby Black and Queen Ogeima Feechi (Kamara) Abioye-Black, *father and mother of:*

*Lulu Black

*TJ Black

Baby on the way

Other Important *Brothers Black 3* Characters

Missy (Johnathan's ex-girlfriend, *deceased*)

Lucy (*Heather's girlfriend*)

Barry Coleman (*deceased*)

King Elijah Abioye, a.k.a. Mr. Naidoo

Queen Ada Catherine Naidoo-Abioye

King Kwäzē Naidoo-Abioye

Celeste (Kwäzē's ex-girlfriend)

King Afafa (*deceased*)

Missy (Johnathan's ex-girlfriend, *deceased*)

Lucy (*Heather's girlfriend*)

Barry Coleman (*deceased*)

Joshua (*deceased*)

Carmen Nash, a.k.a. Nene (*Reporter, Mariah Briggs, from Yours Series, Niece, Ryan's new crush*)

Logan O'Brien

Dylan O'Brien

Jamie O'Brien

Cole 'Brooklyn' O'Brien

Uncle Jonah McGowan

Uncle Jack McGowan

Uncle Raymond McGowan

Uncle Ronan McGowan

Carrick McGowan

Malcolm McGowan

Graham McGowan

Jeremiah McGowan

Reilly McGowan

Brothers Black 4

Braxton Black and Heather Lockhart-Black, *father and mother of:*

*Riley Black

*Rowen Black

Other Important *Brothers Black 4* Characters

Debbie Lockhart-Kline (Rob's ex-wife, Heather's mother)

Lucy (*Heather's pretend girlfriend*)

Amanda Kline (Heather's half sister)

Ernest Kline (Heather's Stepfather, *deceased*)

Eugene, a.k.a. Crooked Nose

Logan O'Brien

Dylan O'Brien

Jamie O'Brien

Cole 'Brooklyn' O'Brien

Uncle Jonah McGowan

Uncle Jack McGowan

Uncle Raymond McGowan

Uncle Ronan McGowan

Carrick McGowan

Malcolm McGowan

Graham McGowan

Jeremiah McGowan

Reilly McGowan

Nicholas Lincoln

Sephora Lincoln

Thomas Briggs

Brothers Black 5

Felix Black and Kaye Porter-Black, a.k.a. Kaye Blaze, *father and mother of:*

*Dashawn Black

*Second child unannounced

Other Important *Brothers Black 5* Characters

Lakia Redding (*Kaye's writer friend*)

Dean (*Kaye's writer friend*)

Hayidah (*Doll for Club Desire*)

Pastor Wayne Porter (*Kaye's father*)

Danesha Porter (*Kaye's mother*)

Danny Porter (*Deceased, Kaye's brother and Felix's best friend*)

Grandma Reid (*Kaye's grandmother*)

Grandpa Reid (*Kaye's grandfather*)

Alberto Pérez (*Felix's best friend*)

Jacob McTavish (*lead actor in Kaye's movie*)

Mona Richards (*deceased, a fan*)

Logan O'Brien

Dylan O'Brien

Jamie O'Brien

Cole "Brooklyn" O'Brien

Connie O'Brien

Kate O'Brien

Ronan McGowan

Carrick McGowan

Brothers Black 6

Ryan Black and Carmen Nash, *father and mother of:*

*Jordan Black

*Second child unannounced

Other Important *Brothers Black 6* Characters

Kiyoshi Matsumara-Nash (*Carmen's father*)

Paloma Matsumara-Nash (*Carmen's mother*)

Nelson "Ne" Matsumara-Nash (*Carmen's Brother*)

Yui (*Nelson assistant*)

Bekia

Calu

Mariah Briggs (*Carmen's Aunt*)

Gigi (*Carmen's roommate*)

Torque

Alexander (*oldest triplet*)

Maximilian, a.k.a. Mil (*middle triplet*)

Tobias (*youngest triplet*)

Austin Mc Wien (*deceased*)

Logan O'Brien

Misha Krupin

Dr. Omid V-Shah

Connie O'Brien

Kate O'Brien

Don LaSalle Locatelli

Tasha Locatelli

Valentine Donati

Uri Donati

Brothers Black 7

Johnathan Black and Cherone "Roni" Pérez -Black, *father and mother of:*

*Mena Black

Other Important *Brothers Black 7* Characters

Natasha "Indigo"

Grissel Pérez (deceased)

Eliam Pérez (deceased)

Irina Krupin (deceased)

Yours Series
Nicholas Lincoln and Sephora (Sophi, a.k.a. Soph, a.k.a. Lilla du) Emilsson.
Father and mother of:
　　Nicole Lincoln
　　Nadia Lincoln
　　Nicholas Lincoln Jr.

The Lincoln Family
Dean Lincoln and Shelly Lincoln (***both deceased***).
Father and mother of:
　　Nicholas Lincoln
　　Rick ~~Carbon~~ Lincoln
　　Gavin ~~Carbon~~ Lincoln

The Emilsson Family
Liam Emilsson *(was thought to be deceased)* and Faraz Emilsson.
Father and mother of:
　　Lucian Emilsson
　　Ettie Emilsson
　　Sephora Emilsson

Lucian Emilsson and Kimberly Ann Clove.
Father and mother of:
　　Lilla Emilsson

Other Important Yours Characters
Mark Fienberg (Sephora's best friend)
Ivana Graves (Nick's ex-girlfriend, deceased)

Bianca (Liam's mistress, missing)
Winton (Nick's driver and security)
Jillian Carver (Nick's ex-temporary PA, *deceased*)
Harvey Carver (Jillian's father and Nick's family friend, *deceased*)
Bailey Wilder (waitress, Mark's girlfriend)
Dylan O'Brien

Nick's crew
　　Wyatt Black
　　Kevin Briggs (*wife* Mariah Briggs, *Nick's PA*)
　　Craig Hilton
　　George Ligal
　　Lucian Emilsson
　　Andrew Connor (*Ettie's husband*)

Ronan Book 1: Kings of New York
Ronan McGowan and Dean Foxx, a.k.a. Danika "Danny" Peoples-McGowan.
　　Fur Dad and Mom of:
　　Bullet McGowan
　　Blitz McGowan
　　KD "Killer Doll" McGowan

The McGowan Family
Cianán McGowan and Laoise McGowan
　　Father and Mother of:
Jonah McGowan
Jack McGowan
Raymond McGowan
Cassidy McGowan-Black
Ronan McGowan

Carrick McGowan
Graham McGowan
Malcolm McGowan
Jeremiah McGowan
Reilly McGowan

Aunt Róisín McGowan (Jack's wife)

The O'Brien Family

Logan O'Brien
Connie O'Brien
Cole "Brooklyn" O'Brien
Kate O'Brien
Jamie O'Brien
Dylan O'Brien

Other Important Kings of New York Book 1 Characters
Lyric Hughes
Byron Hughes (*Twin killed in accident,* **deceased**)
Myron Hughes (**deceased**)
Dayton Hughes
Marlow Givens
Percy Stratton
Den'Nisha Peoples
Uncle Freddie Philips
Rory
Lochlann
Bujar (*The Albanian boss,* **deceased**)
Dalmat (*Bujar's brother,* **deceased**)
Erjon (Bujar's cousin)
Oisín
Tadhg

Dylan Book 2: Kings of New York
Dylan O'Brien and Ciara Walsh, a.k.a. Cee-Cee Young

The McDougal Family
Grandpa Lennox McDougal and Grandma Orla Murphy-McDougal.
   Father and mother of:

Archie McDougal
Ewan McDougal
Kenneth McDougal
Duncan McDougal
Adline McDougal-Walsh, *formerly* Adline Murphy-O'Brien

The Walsh Family

Bram Walsh and Adline McDougal-Walsh.
  Father and mother of:
      O'Shea Walsh (Adopted son)
      Angus Walsh
      Donald Walsh
Donald Walsh and Iesha Rogers-Walsh.
  Father and mother of:
  Ciara Walsh
  Ciarán Walsh

Other Important Kings of New York Book 2 Characters

Daliah Gibson
Vega Stratton
Taegan Quinn
Simon Byrne
Cadla Sullivan
Theo Young
Sean Young
Lily Young
Laki Kalani
Amy Kalani
Iesha Roger-Walsh (*wife of Donald Walsh,* **deceased**)
Helen Walsh (*wife of Angus Walsh*)
Queeny Walsh (*wife of Q'Shea Walsh*)
Eoghan Quinn
Dimitri
Nashawn
Ross

Aidan
Booker
Kary

ABOUT THE AUTHOR

Blue Saffire, award-winning, bestselling author of over eighty contemporary romance novels and novellas, writes with the intention to touch the heart and the mind. Blue hooks, weaves, and loops multiple series, keeping you engaged in her worlds. Blue writes for her own publishing company, Perceptive Illusions as Blue Saffire, as well as Royal Blue.

Blue and her husband live in a house filled with laughter and creativity in Long Island, NY. Both working hard to build the Blue brand and cultivate their love for the arts. Creative is their family affair.

Blue holds an MBA in Marketing and Project Management, as well as an MED in Instructional Technology and Curriculum Design. She is also an NLP Master Practitioner.

ACKNOWLEDGMENTS

Oh my God. Listen, the perfectionist in me came out strong. I read the entire universe back and still went back and reread books to make sure I got it right. Then these characters were acting up. I did not mean to take months to figure this out, but here we are.

I love them and that's always my first goal. To fall in love with the story I'm writing. If I don't love it, it's not leaving this laptop. LOL. This one hit it all for me.

As always, my dear reader friends, thank you so much for your continued support and patience. The next time I make a goal for the year, it can't all be in a preexisting universe. Phew child.

Thank you for the encouraging emails, videos, posts, shares, comments, and DMs. Y'all are the absolute best. Remember, sharing is caring. If you have a friend who reads, let them know about me, please.

So much love to my husband. I didn't just talk his ear off this time. I kept giving him chapters to read to make sure I was doing what I thought. Ha ha ha ha. We both need a nap and a vacation.

Always on my mind and so glad to have your presence. All love and respect to my source. God placed me in a position to dig deeper during this journey. Not so much for the book and characters, but for myself.

I've never been more grateful to receive a spiritual download such as this. I am so grateful and thankful to God. I give Him all the glory. I love you with all my heart and thank you for continuing to bless me, this pen, and this journey.

Thank you for allowing me to grow, heal, and be able to pour my heart into my work. This peace is something new. Thank you. As always, unapologetically blessed and highly favored.

Next bae-be! *Brooklyn: Kings of New York. Another step closer to the Alliance.*

Wait, there is more to come! You can stay updated with my latest releases, learn more about me, the author, and be a part of contests by subscribing to my newsletter at

www.BlueSaffire.com

If you enjoyed *Dylan Book 2*, I'd love to hear

your thoughts and please feel free to leave a

review on my website. And when you do, please let me

know by emailing me TheBlueSaffire@gmail.com

or leave a comment on Facebook https://www.facebook.com/BlueSaffireDiaries or Twitter @TheBlueSaffire

Other books by Blue Saffire

Placed in Best Reading Order

Also available …

Legally Bound

Legally Bound 2: Against the Law

Legally Bound 3: His Law

Perfect for Me

Hush 1: Family Secrets

Ballers: His Game

Brothers Black 1: Wyatt the Heartbreaker

Legally Bound 4: Allegations of Love

Hush 2: Slow Burn

Coming Soon...
King of Gods Book 4: Immortal Iron Brothers Series
King of Past Book 5: Immortal Iron Brothers Series
Brooklyn Book 3: Kings of New York Series

Other Blue Saffire Series

Hold On To Me Series
My Funny Valentine
Be My Valentine

Hitter Squad Series
Remember Me

Work Husband Series
Unexpected Lovers
My Best Friend's Wish
The Ones Left Behind
The Last Ones Standing

The Lost Souls MC Series
Forever
Never
Always

The Moran Brothers Series
Love Notes
Stay With Me

The A**hole Club Series
Pit Book 1: The A**hole Club
Ox Book 5: The A**hole Club
Kelex Book 6: The A**hole Club

Immortal Iron Brothers Series
King of Knights Book 1
King of Inferno Book 2
King of Tides Book 3

Check out Blue Saffire exclusives on the
BlueSaffire.com website
The Fixer
His Miracle Baby

Razor
Dane
Trip
Professor Jones
Room 112

Other books from Evei Lattimore Collection Books by Blue Saffire
Black Bella 1

Destiny 1: Life Decisions
Destiny 2: Decisions of the Next Generation
Destiny 3 coming soon…

Star

Other books from Royal Blue Gay Romance Collection written by Blue Saffire
Kyle's Reveal
Beau's Redemption